FALSE DOCUMENTS

SOME OTHER BOOKS BY PETER LAMBORN WILSON

The Winter Calligraphy of Ustad Selim, & Other Poems, 1975

DIVAN, 1978

Kings of Love: The Poetry and History of the Nimatullahi Sufi Order of Iran
(with Nasrollah Pourjavady), 1978

Angels, 1980, 1994

Weaver of Tales: Persian Picture Rugs (with Karl Schlamminger), 1980

Divine Flashes by Fakhruddin 'Iraqi (trans. with William C. Chittick), 1982

Semiotext(e) USA (ed. with Jim Fleming), 1987

Scandal: Essays in Islamic Heresy, 1988

The Drunken Universe: An Anthology of Persian Sufi Poetry
(with Nasrollah Pourjavady), 1988

Semiotext(e) SF (ed. with Rudy Rucker and Robert Anton Wilson), 1989

Sacred Drift: Essays on the Margins of Islam, 1993

Pirate Utopias: Moorish Corsairs and European Renegadoes, 1995, 2003

Millennium, 1996

"Shower of Stars" Dream & Book: The Initiatic Dream in Sufism and Taoism,
1996

Escape from the Nineteenth Century and Other Essays, 1998

Ploughing the Clouds: The Search for Irish Soma, 1999

TAZ: The Temporary Autonomous Zone, Ontological Anarchy, Poetic Terrorism,
(Second Edition), 2003

Gothick Institutions, 2005

Black Fez Manifesto, 2008

Ec(o)logues, 2011

riverpeople, 2014

FALSE DOCUMENTS

peter lamborn wilson

Station Hill
of Barrytown

Online catalogue: www.stationhill.org
e-mail: publishers@stationhill.org

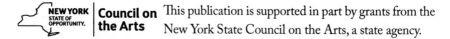 This publication is supported in part by grants from the New York State Council on the Arts, a state agency.

Interior design by Susan Quasha.
Cover art by the author.

Cover illustration: The dancers are by an anonymous imitator of Jacques Callot: "Zanni Beppi Nappe and Fritellino," in *Harlequin Unmasked: The Commedia dell'Arte and Porcelain Sculpture* by Meredith Chilton, Yale University Press, 2001.

The author thanks Charles Stein and Nathan Smith, Susan and George Quasha, Robert Kelly, Sam and Kim Truitt, and the "Octagon." More thanks to Jim Fleming for various things, including help with my cover design (which was also worked on by Kim Spurlock).

The author and Station Hill thank the editors of the publications in which some of these texts originally appeared (see page 327 "Sources of the Text").

Library of Congress Cataloging-in-Publication Data
Wilson, Peter Lamborn.
  False documents / Peter Lamborn Wilson.
       pages ; cm
  ISBN 978-1-58177-140-4 (softcover)
  1. Archives—Fiction. I. Title.
  PS3573.I46465F35 2014
  813'.54—dc23
                                    2014019867

Contents

Visit Port Watson!

This article originally appeared in the first (and only?) issue of a micro-zine called LIBERTARIAN HORIZONS: A JOURNAL FOR THE FREE TRAVELER, along with other pieces on Pago-Pago, Yap, Ponape and a "Note on Nicaragua." The magazine was allegedly published in Belleville, Ohio, in 1985, but our request to reprint the piece came back marked "Addressee Unknown." The anonymous author thus remains nameless to us, and the magazine's editors appear to be unknown in libertarian/anarchist circles.

The island of Sonsorol does actually exist—we found it in our BRITTANICA ATLAS right where it's supposed to be—but no reference work or travel guide known to us speaks of it as an independent nation. Perhaps we failed to look far and hard enough... Perhaps we prefer to believe...

Visit Port Watson!
Anonymous

1. Geography and Physical Description ⍓ ☀ ≈

The Pacific island of Sonsorol, an extinct volcano surrounded by coral reefs, lies at 5° above the Equator at 132° longitude; about 400 miles east of the southeastern tip of the Philippines and 300 miles north of the Dampier Straits in New Guinea. It is approximately ten miles in diameter and about ninety square miles in area.

The climate is typical for the region: steady balmy temperatures (60°–70° year-round), occasional violent typhoons, monsoons from September to February, sea breezes along the coast, steamy stifling rainforest on the lower slopes of Mount Sonsorol (especially dense on the island's northern side, exposed to the trade winds); nearer to the summit the weather is almost permanently cloudy, cool and misty, and the jungle thins into a "cloud forest" —moss, small trees shrouded in epiphytic mosses, hepatics, ferns, orchids, etc. Sonsorol enjoys plenty of fresh water, including waterfalls in the hills, and even a small river, the Garuda.

Vegetation: typical tropical abundance and variety, including many species of orchids and a plethora of other tropical flowers and fruit. Formerly copra, taro, sugar-cane and pineapples were cultivated in the southwestern savannah region; now the plantations have been abandoned and gone wild except for a few coconut groves reserved for local consumption (every part of the plant is used, in cooking, building, etc.) Indigenous fauna are sparse, mostly limited to birds and insects (which can prove annoying). Pigs, chickens, goats and other European species were imported in the 17th century. Fishing is spectacular, and provides both a staple diet and a good deal of sport; the three small coral atolls which belong to Sonsorol offer superb snorkeling and abound in rare types of tropical fish (see *Excursions*).

Nearly circular in shape, and lacking any decent bays or inlets, Sonsorol would at first seem strategically unsuited to its ancient role as pirate enclave; however, the coral reefs which surround the island provide a sort of lagoon in which ships can ride at anchor "in the roads" quite safely, even in heavy weather.

2. How To Get There   ☞   ✈   ⛴   🚤

Travel in the Pacific usually consumes either too much time or too much money. Sonsorol remains one of the least accessible islands in the entire area. No commercial airline lands there. Freighters carry cargo to Sonsorol from Mindanao, Java, Taiwan, Hong Kong and other ports, but the only ship which calls there with some regularity is *The Queen of Yap*, a rusty tramp steamer which plies between Zamboanga and the Caroline Islands, roughly once a month. (Information and reservations can be obtained from the Ngulu Maritime Co. Ltd., Kalabat, Yap, US. Trust Territory of the Pacific.)

Port Watson is now the only port of entry for Sonsorol, and no Customs & Immigration Authority exists there. However, no one can hope to escape notice in a town so small. Anyone who stays more than a month or so will probably be asked politely either to apply for residence or else leave (see *How to Become a Resident*).

Visitors to the Republic of Sonsorol (outside the Port Watson Enclave) are encouraged to have their passports stamped at the Post Office at Government House in Sonsorol City (q.v.)—the "visa" stamp is quite beautiful—but no one will insist on this. Neither Port Watson nor the Republic have any police, so the residents tend to watch out for trouble and take responsibility for solving problems. Unfriendly, abusive, thieving or obstreperous visitors have been beaten up by vigilantes or Peoples' Militia, and exiled on the next ship out. Generally however visitors are welcome ("not *tourists*, but *visitors*," the Sultan once said), and the inhabitants are friendly, even excessively so.

3. History Before Independence   ●※   ⚑

The "aboriginal" inhabitants, of mixed Malay and Polynesian ancestry, may not have arrived till the 14th century; whether they met and
absorbed any earlier groups is unknown. Presumably these people were
"pagans" of some sort; traces of their language survive in place names,
craft terminology etc., although the present dialect consists of a bewildering mix of Bahasa Malay, Suluese, Spanish, Dutch and English.
(Apparently, interesting drama and poetry is now being composed in
this Sonsorolan "language"). All that remains of the "pre-historic" or
pre-Moro Period is an enigmatic ruin near a waterfall high on the
slope of Mt. Sonsorol (see *Excursions*).

Around the middle of the 17th century, Sonsorol was invaded by
pirates from Sulu who called themselves Moros ("Moors," i.e. Moslems) even though their crews included Sea Dyaks, Bugis from the
Celebes, Javanese and other "lascar types." Their semi-legendary admi-
ral, Sultan Ilanun Moro, settled down with some of his followers—
who thus became an island "aristocracy" of sorts.

Islam sat rather lightly on the Sonsorol Moros: the stricture of the
Divine Law they ignored, and illiteracy kept them ignorant of the
Koran. Like Bedouin of the sea, religion served them as a new ethnic
identity and an excuse to plunder their "unbelieving" victims.

With Sonsorol as a base, they continued their predation and grew
moderately wealthy—and finally acquired a modicum of culture. In the
late 18th and early 19th centuries Javanese taste prevailed, and Indonesian sufis visited the island.

Unfortunately not a single architectural trace of this "Golden Age"
survived the invasion and conquest by Spanish forces under the Gov-
ernor of the Philippines, Narciso Clavería y Zaldua, in 1850. The Sonsorol Sultans were nearly the last of the Moro pirates to be subdued
and the conquistadors imposed upon them a ruinous and rapacious
colonial regime, including forced conversion and outright slavery.

By 1867, however, the Spanish had lost interest in the island, which produced nothing but copra and resentment. The Dutch rulers of Indonesia added Sonsorol to their empire after a single desultory battle; the natives considered the Dutch an improvement over the hated Spanish, and at first raised few objections—in fact, a great many converted to the Dutch Reformed Church.

Dutch influence remains strong in Sonsorol. Scarcely a family on the island lacks European blood; Dutch words survive in the dialect; the Old Quarter of Sonsorol City (q.v.) boasts several modest but pleasant houses in "Batavian" style, with raised facades and red tile roofs; the Calvinist "Cathedral" and the small Government House are also worth a visit.

In this period the Moro "aristocracy" (those who traced descent from the pirates) reverted to their easy-going brand of Islam. The Sultans were allowed "courtesy titles" but remained powerless and penniless. Javanese culture shaped their attitudes, especially the arts of gamelan and dance, the esoteric teachings of the *kebatinan* sects (including martial arts and sorcery), and the millenarian concept of the "Just King." Out of this ferment—a strange blend of revolutionary proto-nationalism and mystical fervor — resentment of the Dutch began to fester.

In 1907 (the same year the Netherlands finally subdued northern Sumatra), the Sultan of Sonsorol, Pak Harjanto Abdul Rahman Moro I, staged a tragic and futile uprising against colonial forces. It is said his followers believed themselves magically invulnerable to bullets. The Sultan and other conspirators were executed, the title abolished, and the island sank into depression, somnolence, lassitude and obscurity.

At the start of World War II, Sonsorol's population had sunk to about 2000, with a Dutch garrison and administration of fewer than fifty. In 1942, the Japanese made an easy conquest of the island, sent the Europeans to prison-camps in Java, built a few bunkers (still extant), left behind a token force, and departed for the invasion of Malaysia.

The new Japanese overlords behaved harshly, almost sadistically—if the tales still told on Sonsorol can be credited—and anti-Japanese sentiment survives to this day. In 1945, a single cruiser manned by Australian and New Zealand naval forces arrived to liberate the island. The Japanese put up a suicidal resistance, and the native population, led by Sultan Pak Harjanto III (grandson of the "martyr" of 1907) joined in the battle for freedom on July 20.

The post-war period found Sonsorol with new colonial masters: a joint Protectorate under Australia and New Zealand. A slump in the price of copra ruined the last vestiges of the economy; emigration soared, and by 1952 the population had sunk beneath a thousand. The Protectorate, burdened with the administration of other Pacific islands, ignored Sonsorol except as a source of cheap labor.

The Sultan, hero of the liberation, began to agitate for independence; a sincere admirer of western democracy, he believed that political freedom would somehow solve the island's problem. In 1962 the Protectorate allowed a plebiscite, and a clear majority chose independence under a Constitutional Monarchy. On August 17th of that year, the joint Protectorate withdrew.

4. History Since Independence

The expected benefits of freedom failed to materialize. Emigration was now cut off; only sparse and grudging aid from the former Protectorate Powers kept the population from complete destitution. In 1967 the Sultan sent his young son and heir, Pak Harjanto Abdul-Rahman IV, to college in America, hoping vaguely that this might somehow result in an infusion of U.S. aid. The Crown Prince obtained a scholarship to Berkeley University, and majored in economics.

In California the Prince felt attracted to "the Movement" — civil rights, anti-war, free speech and expression, ecological awareness, Haight-Ashbury, etc.—and soon found himself convinced by libertarian anarchist philosophy. At college he met Travis B. O'Conner, the scion and heir of an Oklahoma-Texas oil family (not *super*-rich, but definitely millionaires); they took a year's leave of absence from school and enjoyed an American *wanderjahr* together. The Prince never lost a sense of responsibility toward his homeland: all his thought and study aimed at his peoples' salvation, or at least relief. O'Conner found himself fascinated by tales of Sonsorol, and together the young friends plotted and dreamed.

They reasoned thus: virtually all classical Utopias—from Plato's Republic to Brook Farm—involve a high degree of *abstraction*. The implementation of abstract ideas in society requires a correspondingly high level of *authoritarian control*. As a result, most Utopias in practice have proven oppressive and deadening—"social planning" would seem to be an offense by definition against the "human spirit." O'Conner and the Sultan desired an anarchist utopia, one without authority—and yet they realized that utopia is impossible without abstraction.

The greatest and most oppressive of all modern abstractions is finance, *banking*, the creation of wealth out of nothing, out of pure imagination. Now the pirates of old lived virtually without authority—even their captains were virtually mere first-among-equals—and they created lawless "utopias" or enclaves financed by *stolen wealth*. The two young friends decided that since Sonsorol could never produce any real wealth, they must follow the pirate path—admittedly the way of parasites and bandits rather than "true revolutionaries"—and *steal* the energy they needed to fund and found their utopia. The bank robber robs banks "because that's where the money is"—but the *banker* robs banks and even his own depositors with total legal impunity. The California dreamers decided to go into banking.

In 1979 the old Sultan died and his son succeeded to the throne of a forgotten and ruined island. At once he and O'Conner began to activate their plan. It began with the creation of a mercantile bank called "The Ilanun Moro Savings & Loan Association" (ironically named after the pirate-founder of the dynasty). The new Sultan then rail-roaded a series of bills through the island legislature: he arranged for the creation of a *free port enclave*, Port Watson (the origin of the name has never been explained), consisting of ten square kilometers of abandoned copra plantations. The Bank, making use of O'Conner family connections and capital, moved to Port Watson and began "off shore" operations; phantom subsidiaries, tax-free registrations, "cut-outs" and "strange loops," currency speculations, secret go-between activity for mainland Chinese interests, laundering funds for certain overseas-Chinese "businessmen," numbered accounts and so on. Port Watson was planned to enjoy virtual freedom from law; the bank practices a new and invisible form of "piracy." Since it depends for its efficacy on satellite communications, it might perhaps be called Space Piracy!

The Sonsorol Bank possesses few "real" assets, little that could be looted—its wealth exists largely in computer memories. Its discreet machinations are tolerated by international banking interests; after all, a "blind" account or something of the sort proves useful, from time to time, even in the most respectable financial circles. Almost overnight (1976-1980) Sonsorol grew moderately well-to-do.

Every citizen of Sonsorol and resident of Port Watson, child, woman and man, was made an equal shareholder in the Bank; everyone—including the Sultan and O'Conner—owns exactly one share of the profits. By 1980, around a thousand people in Port Watson and 2000 in Sonsorol each received an annual dividend of about $4000. In 1985 the total population reached about 9000 and the dividend slightly more than $5000—virtually a guaranteed income.

Aside from the creation of Port Watson and the Bank, very few changes were made in the legal structure of Sonsorol, which remains (at least on paper) an Anglo-American-style republic with a legislature, army, police, compulsory education, taxation and so forth. No foreign power can accuse the island of "anarchy"—and in any case the Labour Government of New Zealand has recently signed a defense treaty which offers international recognition and protection for the Republic. On the surface, all is normal. The Constitution was amended to disestablish the Dutch Reformed Church and allow freedom of religion (1976); and in 1979 the Sultan abdicated all executive function and reduced himself to a ceremonial figurehead. As he put it, "I attained the state of the Taoist Sage-King described in the *Chuang Tzu*: I sit on my throne facing in a propitious direction—and do absolutely nothing!"

In practice, however, the functions of the Republic have almost entirely lapsed into desuetude. No army or police exist because no one will join them; instead, a volunteer Peoples' Militia serve in emergencies (extremely rare so far). Taxes are not collected; moral laws are not enforced; the Legislature passes no new laws (although it meets from time to time to debate projects and philosophical issues); schools exist but attendance is voluntary. No one needs to work, and many find their Shares enough to support lives of Polynesian *dolce far niente*. Anyone who objects to the "minarchy-monarchy" of the Republic can move to Port Watson, where no law exists at all.

The "real work" of Sonsorol, banking, can be handled by a handful of part-time computer hackers and wheeler-dealers (nicknamed "Sindonistas" after the late Italian Freemasonic conspirator and banker, Michele Sindona); however, the Sultan and O'Conner wanted to see Port Watson become a genuine libertarian community, and they encouraged immigration by offering interest-free loans and even outright grants to useful and sympathetic people. Several major collectives were founded: the Energy Center (q.v.), a Co-op for alternate energy, appropriate technology and experimental agriculture; and the Academies (q.v.), devoted to education and research—schools for children, and "natural philosophy" of all sorts for advanced students.

Small entrepreneurs, mostly overseas Chinese, were also invited to set up shop; energetic and thrifty, they expanded their shares into small businesses and now dominate various aspects of Port Watson's commercial life. Hundreds of libertarians and anarchists from Europe and the Americas flocked to Sonsorol, each with some life-experiment, New Age cult, utopian commune, craft, art or pet project. Some Sonsorolans who had migrated to New Zealand in the '40s and '50s came back to claim their Citizen's Shares. The island came alive—once again thanks to "piracy"!

In Port Watson, all business and indeed all human relations are carried out by contract. No regulatory body exists to interfere in agreements made between "consenting partners," whether in bed or in a banking deal. Contracts can be witnessed by an independent arbitrage company; complaints against groups or individuals are adjudicated by a "Random Synod"—a computer-chosen ad hoc committee of Shareholders. The Synod has no power of enforcement. In theory a "defendant" who refused the Synod's recommendations would go free and the complainant would have no recourse but duel or vendetta; in practice however this has occurred only once or twice. New settlers in Port Watson are asked only to agree to live according to this non-system, to donate one day a month to community projects (known as "shit-work"), and to refrain from coercive or oppressive behavior. This agreement is called "signing the Articles," after the custom amongst old-time buccaneers and corsairs. Indeed, Port Watson's form of "government" might well be called a Covenancy of Pirates—or perhaps laissez-faire communism—or anarcho-monarchy (since each human being is considered a "free lord" or sovereign agent).

Land is "owned" only when occupied and used. A typical commune may consist of a single building, no land, three or four members (perhaps even a "nuclear family"!); or a farm-sized collective with 12–25 members and several buildings. Economic independence makes solitary life feasible; but a group can pool resources, afford better housing and share luxuries. Nearly everyone belongs to some form of collective, union or sodality, from informal dining clubs to strict ideological utopian communes (mostly in the hills outside town). "Phalansteries" or erotic affinity groups are popular; so are craft guilds and esoteric cults.

5. Money (A Note for the Traveler) ¤   £ $ €

"No prey, no pay!" and "To each according to the bounty; from each according to whim!"—these might be Port Watson's mottos. Even the Republic of Sonsorol has no currency of its own (although it does sell lovely postage stamps). For small transactions such as paying for a meal or newspaper any foreign currency will do in theory, although in practice New Zealand pounds or U.S. dollars are preferred. Larger transactions are generally carried out by computer, since all Shareholders have an "account" to draw on. Visitors may find it convenient to deposit some of their funds in the Bank, either in a "holding" or a "moving" account. The former is simply an electronic lock-box. A "moving" account constitutes an actual investment in the Bank. In February 1985, such accounts paid 7.5% interest, and in March 12%; frugal travelers may actually leave Sonsorol richer than they arrived!

The islanders have worked out a rather elaborate computerized barter system amongst themselves. A crafts collective which produces batik, for example, will turn over its stock to the Port Watson Cooperative (called "The 5 & 10" by local wits) in exchange for a certain amount of credit, measured in abstract quanta. Members of the collective can then use their credit towards any goods at the Co-op. Both the Co-op and several independent Chinese merchants act as import-export agents, filling orders for foreign goods and luxuries in return for Bank or Co-op credit. Price-fixing does not exist; the value of local produce is determined by computer, but imports and goods sold outside the Co-op system are subject to intense bargaining, reminiscent of the oriental bazaar. Naive visitors have sometimes been duped by Watsonian sharpies. *Caveat emptor.*

Many groups within the Port Enclave are eager to establish barter and communications with alternative networks elsewhere in the world. As much as possible, Sonsorol attempts to avoid official international trade with all its tariffs and taxes and regulations, and to rely instead on non-governmental non-commercial contacts with communes, collectives, *bolos,* craft groups and individuals around the world—especially those which share the libertarian-anarchist perspective. Visitors to Sonsorol are particularly welcome when they offer some contact with the "outside," such as "potlatch" (exchange of gifts), barter, cultural contact, exchange of hospitality, etc.

Shareholders are free to do whatever they want with their dividends, and to engage in any business which pleases them and involves no coercion, wage-slavery or rapacious greed. However, outside the island community (and the widening network of "alternate" world contacts) these constraints vanish. Like their pirate predecessors, the Sonsorolans are "at war with all the world" when it comes to seizing some commercial or fiscal advantage. As a result, many Watsonians have grown quite wealthy—especially the Bankers and the Chinese merchants. Any display of excessive affluence is considered bad taste, even "oppressive"—epicurean comfort and aesthetic indulgence meet with social approval, but the "typical Watsonian" is said to be a millionaire who lives like a beachcomber, a Taoist hermit or an artist, and donates large amounts to various radical charities and revolutionary causes around the world. Islanders like to quote Emma Goldman's quip about the "champagne revolution," and Nietzsche's remark about "radical aristocratism." Money, ultimately, means very little here (except as a game); the real value-scale is based on pleasure, self-realization and life enhancement.

6. Sightseeing in Port Watson

Port Watson has sprung up rapidly and has the taste of a goldrush town despite its tropical languor. Its architecture appears eccentric, and "city planning" is considered a dirty word. Everyone builds where and what they like, from thatch-hut to junkyard to geodesic dome or quonset, pre-fab or traditional, aesthetic-personal or functional-ugly.

Most streets are unpaved, and automobiles are rarely seen—although several hundred "free bikes" (painted white) lie about for anyone who needs them.

The population of the enclave is said to be about 2000, although no census has ever been taken. Perhaps half are native Sonsorolans; the other half consists of many nationalities, the largest percentage probably North Americans—then Chinese, Australians and New Zealanders, Europeans (British, French, German, etc.), Scandinavians, South Americans, a scattering of Filipinos, Javanese and other Southeast Asians; and individuals from such unlikely places as Iran, Egypt, Africa. Most of the "settlers" came to work for the Bank or one of the other Port Watson concerns, although a significant number "just happened by, and decided to stay." Living styles range from Gauguinesque beachcombing to the international jet-set (the Bank's roving frontpeople), but the majority fall somewhere between such extremes.

Important: the traveler should constantly bear in mind that Port Watson differs from the rest of the world in one major respect: the absence of *all law.* Some Watsonians like to depict their town as a cross between *The Heart of Darkness* and Tombstone City—there's gossip about duels and feuds, stories about "little wars" between communes, etc.—but in truth these incidents are quite rare, possibly even apocryphal. Nevertheless, the newcomer should be aware that *no authority* exists to pluck anyone from danger or difficulty; every Watsonian takes full responsibility for personal actions; the visitor must willynilly follow suit.

Libertarian theory predicts that such a system—or non-system!—will lead to greater peace and harmony than violence and disorder, provided every individual owns wealth, and agrees not to force or oppress another human being. In practice the theory seems to work—after all, Port Watson is really a small town on a small island, a "social ecology" that reinforces cooperation and even conformity. For all their anarchist bluster, most Watsonians are too blissed out to cause trouble—but a visitor who fails to grasp the "unwritten code" or display the correct laid-back good manners may well suffer unpleasant consequences.

The *jetty* bustles with activity: lighters unloading cargo from some tramp steamer anchored out in the lagoon; fishing boats coming and going, the crews haggling with Co-op reps over their rainbow-gleaming catch; children playing and swimming; loungers drinking coffee at the popular Cannibal Café. Behind the jetty runs *Godown Street*, named after its row of ugly warehouses or "godowns"; here also are found various maritime offices, chandlers and boat-builders (proas, junks and out-rigger canoes)—and a number of small jerry-built clubs and bars which open around sundown (see *Nightlife*).

Beyond Godown St. lies *China Street*, home of Port Watson's Chinese community. Shabby one-storey shops with corrugated iron fronts and brilliant calligraphed signs; the island's only hostelry, the White Flower Motel, and several excellent Chinese restaurants (see *Where to Stay & Eat*); and a small Chinese temple of the sort seen everywhere in Southeast Asia, concrete baroque pillars, pre-fab dragons and phoenixes painted garishly, writhing over an uptilted tiled roof, incense billowing from a gold and crimson altar...: *The South Pole Star Taoist Temple*. Most Watsonian Chinese are Taoists or Ch'an Buddhists, and *tai chi* has become a fad throughout the island.

Along the beach west of China St. an area called "The Slums" sprawls out on the sunny sand—a twin to the post-hippy "budget traveler" ghettos of Goa and Bali; thatched huts and little make-shift bungalows, a few craft shops, coffee-houses and restaurants, a population of beachcombers and lotus-eaters: the voluntary poor of Port Watson. Here also is found the City's famous "Drug Store"; a detailed description would be impolitic, but you get the idea.

East of the Jetty, about half a kilometer along the road to Sonsorol City, lies the fabulous *Energy Center*, without doubt the ugliest complex structure on the island. Its work may be environmentally benign, but it looks like a stretch of the New Jersey Turnpike transported piecemeal to the tropics and re-assembled by a madman. Banks of gawky towers and experimental windmills (like something from *War of the Worlds!*), sinister black solar collector-banks, huge ungainly generators making electricity from tide, wave and wind power; rows of jerry-rigged plastic hydroponic greenhouses; ateliers and workshops, blacksmith's shop, Bricolage Center & Garage—all designed like an Erector Set put together on Acid. The genial Whole-Earth-New-Alchemy techies of the Energy Collective adore all this machinery, dirt, noise and inventiveness. The Bank may pay the bills, they say—but maybe not forever. And meanwhile the Energy Center is the living heart of Port Watson.

But the *Bank* must take the prize for the island's most Absurdist architecture. Built by some Neo-Futurist Italian design team, already it's falling apart; but everyone enjoys its extravagance and chutzpah, so the Bankers grumble but spend to keep it up and functional. Shaped like a cross between an Egyptian and a Mayan pyramid, sort of squashed out, seven stories high, all black reflecting glass and stainless steel (now looking rather rusty after four typhoon seasons)—the whole concept so ultra-post-modern it approaches Comic Opera (or Space Opera!)... and yet, its shapes reflect the dead volcano which makes up the island's mass, and its color reflects the black sand, and its rust harmonizes with the tropical heat... and after the first shock and giggle, one falls a bit under its spell! a BANK! plopped down on this equatorial isle, shaped like the Illuminatus symbol on a dollar bill (only no eye)—heavy, dense and yet shimmering like obsidian.

Inside, the Bank is bisected right down the middle. One half remains open, a "cathedral space" without partitions, a huge glasshouse or botanical crystal-palace or arboretum, raucous with tropical flowers and uncaged birds—staircases and ramps lead to balconies and hanging gardens—glass tubes with escalators inside them (like De Gaulle Airport in Paris) crisscross the vast space, giving the "lobby" a Piranesi/ Buck Rogers atmosphere; fountains splash on the ground level or fall in cascades—and Watsonians come here to picnic or fuck in the foliage.

The other half of the Bank is the Sultan Ilanun Moro Bank itself, a maze of offices, computer rooms, vaults (said to contain almost nothing of value), living quarters for the Bankers (who tend to be Libertarian computer hacks and anarcho-capitalist visionaries), all ultra-modern and air-conditioned, futurologistic and severe. The Bank maintains a satellite dish near the peak of Mount Sonsorol, and computers are manned 24 hours a day for financial and political news. Some islanders who are not members of the Bank Collective have nevertheless taken to punting in international finance games; speculation and gambling are popular sports.

The Bank also serves as a community center: a printing press, a medical clinic (called "Immortality Inc.," for some reason), a popular cafeteria, a tape and record library and other facilities are open to the public.

Between China St. and the Bank lies the *Bazaar*, a large open (hot and dusty) plaza surrounded by more corrugated-iron shops and palm-thatched shanty-stores, plus a large building not unlike a supermarket or mall. All this together constitutes the great *Port Watson Peoples' Cooperative Center*, the exchange mart, import-export boutique, grocery bin and bourse of the Enclave. Tuesdays and Thursdays are "Market Days," although parts of the Co-op are always open. Amazing luxuries from all over the world (tax-free, of course) make the bazaar an unknown Shopper's Paradise; electronic goods for example are cheaper here than in Hong Kong or Singapore. The architecture of the bazaar is scarcely noteworthy, but in the middle of the plaza sits a small ornate pre-fabricated mosque imported in pieces from Pakistan via Brunei and assembled here as *The Sultan Pak Harjanto I Center for Esoteric Studies* (named after the Martyr of 1907 who brought Javanese sorcery to Sonsorol). All pink minarets and green scallops and white and gold like a child's birthday cake, with liquorish icing of Arabic calligraphy, the "Mosque" is used as a performance space and public meditation hall. Surrounded by a small flower garden and shade trees, it makes a pleasant retreat from the heat and dust of the Bazaar.

Another amusing feature of the Bazaar is *The Big Character Wall* (or "Great Wall"), where notices, flyers, poems, curses, graffiti and "big character slogans" are posted or painted—a sort of giant unmovable newspaper. A book fair (trade, exchange, purchase) is held here on Tuesdays.

A kilometer along the beach west of the Slums lies *The Academies,* a cluster of communities and collectives devoted to education and knowledge, occupying an area of deserted copra plantations. Some of the architecture is restored colonial (not very interesting); the rest of it represents an attempt to create a new Sonsorolan "vernacular" making use of traditional materials (palm, thatch, coral) and the "alternative tech" comforts provided by the Energy Center. Buildings here are named after Ferrer, Goodman, Fiere, Neill, Illich, Reich... and the educational theories practiced derive from their teachings. Higher scientific research is limited, of course, but computer access and more-than-adequate funding for certain projects have resulted in a spirit of breakthrough in—for example—ESP studies, theoretical physics and math, genetics and biology (especially morphogenetic field research) and even a modest observatory (named after Prince Kropotkin).

Children occupy a unique position in Port Watson. As Share-holders from birth they are financially independent, and no legal or moral force binds them to their "families" if they want to live on their own. Both at the Academies and elsewhere in the Enclave, Polynesian-style children's communes thrive without "adult supervision." They choose their own educational curricula and pay for the specialized knowledge they desire or else they apprentice themselves to some trade—or else do nothing at all but play and enjoy themselves. Childlife has mutated into a cross between *Coming of Age in Samoa* and a computerized play-utopia; happy, healthy and uninhibited, both more serious and more *sauvage* than their American or European counterparts, they sometimes seem to have arrived from another planet... yet at the same time they are obviously the *real* Watsonians.

7. *Where to Stay & Eat*

Port Watson boasts only one commercial inn, *The White Flower Motel* on China St., a two-storey building with a courtyard owned and operated by an old Taoist "adept," doyen of the Chinese community, Mr. Chang. Single $15 a night, double $25. "Budget" visitors will find huts or rooms for rent in the Slums for as little as two dollars a day, and if all else fails the Bank maintains several free guest-rooms (for visiting financiers, in theory).

China St. is *the* place to eat, and Port Watson qualifies as a genuine "food trip," as the budget-travelers say. *The Yellow Turban Society* specializes in Peking and Mongolian cuisine. *The Manchu Pretender* in Cantonese and Hong Kong (the proprietor claims to be the "lost dauphin" of China!), and *The Cinnabar Immortal* serves Taoist/Buddhist vegetarian cuisine of the highest quality.

Little cafés and restaurants spring up and vanish in the Slums. Two of the longest-enduring are *The Crowbar Club*, which specializes in sea food, and a hamburger stand called *"McBakunin's"!* *The Drugstore* serves coffee and pastry, among other things.

The Bank maintains an American-style cafeteria which is cheap and popular, nicknamed *The Willie Sutton Bar & Grill*. Market days in the bazaar are also feast-days, with numerous entrepreneurs selling everything from homemade coconut cake to imported truffles.

8. *Cultural & Spiritual Activities*

Not an evening passes on Sonsorol without a performance somewhere—music (Classical, gamelan and rock are popular), dance, drama, poetry, etc. Watch the Big Character Wall for announcements. Sculptors and artists display their work in public; and all over the island one may stumble across aesthetic surprizes, artworks blended into the landscape, or landscape as art, or *objets trouvés* (finders keepers), or (in one case) a giant green plastic Godzilla standing alone in the jungle. The Bank presents evening programs of old movies and shows "pirated" from TV satellites. Few Watsonians own televisions (many eschew electricity altogether), but they enjoy watching occasionally at the Bank, laughing at the commercials. A few artists work in film and video, and use the Bank's facilities—which are "state of the art."

In this leisured society books are considered a necessity, and local publishing thrives out of all proportion with the population. This town boasts two weekly newspapers (one called The *Protocols of the Elders of Port Watson!*), an arts monthly, a plethora of pamphlets and a small but steady stream of actual books (including some in the Sonsorolan dialect) published by companies with fanciful names—Chthulhu Press, New Rocking Horse Books, Fourth Eye Books, End of the World News & Stationary—and of course a Pirate Press.

Post-New Age spirituality thrives in the Enclave. Collectives and communes are often organized around some Path or life-therapy. A partial listing of such organizations includes: Wicca and other forms of neopaganism (including a rather spurious revival of ancient Sonsorolan polytheism based on Castañeda, Lovecraft and Margaret Mead!); various forms of Taoism (traditional/magical, philosophical/alchemical, and anarcho/chaotic); Chinese Zen; Church of the SubGenius; Temple of Eris; the Illuminati; "Mystical Anarchism"; tantra-yoga; Chinese and Javanese martial arts, especially *tai chi* and *silat;* various Ceremonial Magick circles and orders, including a "New Golden Dawn" and a "Reformed O.T.O."; Church of Satan; the Sabbatai Sevi School of Magical Judaism; the Si Fan ("a conspiracy devoted to world-wide subversion and poetic terror"); the Gnostic Catholic Church; the Temple of Materialist Atheism; Church of Priapus; and so on. One of the most popular spiritual paths in Sonsorol, including Port Watson, is the so-called "Moro Way," a brand of pure esotericism rooted in Javanese *kebatinan,* sufism, shamanism, Hindu mythology and heterodox Islam. The "Mosque" in the Bazaar serves as a center for groups such as Sumarah, the School of Invulnerability, the "Moorish Orthodox Church," the

Moro Academy of Meditation, etc. (See *Sonsorol City* for more details.) Meetings, séances, classes, etc. are advertised on the "Great Wall."

9. Nightlife & Recreation

Just as the Watsonians created their own "Slums," so also they have their own "red-light district"—not from any economic necessity but simply because they *enjoy* sloth and vice. After dark, Godown St. becomes a den of iniquity and doesn't close till dawn. Night-trippers start with a meal in China St., move on to the *Cannibal Café* for coffee, thence to *Euphoria* (a casino), *The Johann Most Memorial Dance Hall* (a rock palace), *Bishop Sin's Massage Parlor* (the closest thing to a brothel in Sonsorol), *The Unrepentant Faggot* (a gay bar), *Café Voltairine* (a lesbian club), *Eat The Rich!* (a late-nite snackbar) and other short-lived fancifully-named dives. Usually these clubs consist of no more than a ramshackle lean-to in an alley between two warehouses painted in lurid colors and perhaps boasting a dadaesque neon sign. Visitors take note: you're not *exactly* risking your life on Godown St., but one never knows (so to speak) what's in the punch. Watsonians need never pine for the insanity of big city life: it's all concentrated here—without a single policeman to restrain the madness. As one graffito in the (co-ed) toilet at the Cannibal Café puts it: "After midnight the Social Contract is cancelled! (signed) The Lord of Misrule."

10. Excursion To Sonsorol City

An old school bus, completely rebuilt in shining bronze and chrome, plies back and forth along the only paved road in Sonsorol, from the Bazaar in Port Watson to the capital of the Republic, Sonsorol City. (That is, it does so when someone can be found to drive it.) The road passes through the Savannah, the most heavily populated and cultivated rural area on the island, farmed mostly by native Christian Sonsorolan families who cling to the "virtues" of hard work.

Life in the Republic flows at a slower and more conservative pace than in the Free Enclave. The older natives either cling to Dutch Reformed attitudes or else follow the Moro Way with all its subtlety, fine manners, aesthetic elitism and "magical superstition." The Republic lacks a police-force, but the people tend to conform to certain *mores*, at least in public, and within the context of a general Polynesian-style easy-going morality. The visitor should remember not to offend any sensibilities by overtly Watsonian behavior (such as public acts of debauchery).

Sonsorol City is even smaller and sleepier than Port Watson. The bus drops you off in a dusty street of ugly corrugated-iron-front shops along the river bank. At one end of *Market Street* lies a small but ultra-modern *Hospital*, the only new building in the City. At the other end sits the *"Calvinist Cathedral,"* actually a small and rather undistinguished Dutch-style church built in 1910 (the Rector is Dutch and liberal; he preaches "Tolstoy, Thoreau and Gandhi"!)

West of the Cathedral lies the *"Christian Quarter,"* a neighborhood of small tropical/colonial bungalows centered around *Government House*, the former colonial administration building in the Dutch-Indonesian "Batavian" style, with raised amsterdammish facade of pink coral and red-tile roof, where one can attend an occasional session of the Legislature, and listen to rants and harangues from every point of view from Protestant fundamentalism to mystical anarcho-monarchism. The *Post Office*, a public computer center, and an old hand-set printing press constitute the only regularly functioning State Organs, but the plaza in front of Government House is pleasantly shaded and popular with evening strollers and gossips.

Between Government House and the river lies the *Moro Quarter*, where the old Batavian villas are worth a walking tour. The Moro "aristocrats" number less than two hundred, and no longer enjoy any income or prerogative higher than other citizens—in fact, most of them refuse to work, and live off their Bank dividends, modest and penurious.

Their lives center around the *Sultan's "Palace,"* (actually a twelve-room villa), and the *Sultan's Mosque*, a large but simple Javanese-style *kraton* with covered courtyard, surrounded by adjacent villas, workshops and gardens.

Sultan Pak Harjanto Abdul-Rahman Moro IV (born 1945) may have renounced all power, but scarcely all activity. His fascination with both libertarian philosophy and traditional Sonsorolan mysticism has inspired him to create several closely-linked cultural and educational institutions which are centered around the Mosque. The Court Gamelan (a Javanese percussion orchestra imported in the late 19th century and extremely precious) finds its performers in the *Palace Academy Traditional Institute of Arts & Crafts*. Connected with this are two schools for children, one for boys and one for girls, which teach music, dance, art and batik-making, but generally ignore everything else. Sonsorolan children who want a modern education can attend the co-ed "Government School" or one of the Port Watson Academies. But here, all is archaic, refined, *recherché*, even a bit decadent and perverse. The students suffer no traditional discipline, however; they're free to come and go as they like, so long as they fulfill their "contract" to study and perform at the weekly public concerts (every Friday starting around sundown and lasting sometimes till dawn) which constitute the central ritual of the Moro Way.

Along with the Palace Academy and the two children's schools, the Mosque also maintains a batik workshop, theater and dance classes for amateurs and aficionados, a library of works on Sonsorolan culture and history, and regular sessions of group meditation. Martial arts are also taught. Sonsorol City's one newspaper, the monthly *Court Gazette*, is also published here and printed on the old press at Government House.

The enrollment at these institutions consists of as many "settlers" as "natives." Some Watsonians have become citizens of the Republic in order to live and study in Sonsorol City. Traditional arts and especially music enjoy great esteem, particularly among the new generation of native-born settlers' children; perhaps they're rebelling against their parents' anarchism by this infatuation with gamelan and *Ramayana*, the wearing of sarongs and batik and flowers in their hair, the aping of old-fashioned Moro mannerisms, and a cult of piracy and sorcery.

The westerners in Sonsorol City live either around the Palace and Mosque, or else along the coast in the former Dutch neighborhood. At the head of "Dutchman's Beach" is *The Old Colonial Club*, now occupied by the City's only two real restaurants: one devoted to native cuisine (*The Corsair's Cave*), the other to French gourmet elegance (*Chez Ravachol*)—both are expensive. The Club also offers a game room with "the only pinball machines in all Oceania." Along the beach to the west lie the old Dutch villas, some in ruins, others inhabited by settler-communes of artists, musicians and other aesthetes with a taste for the quiet life, or for hobnobbing at Court.

Aside from the cultural life of the Palace and Mosque, nothing much ever happens. Those who want "action" live in Port Watson—those who prefer "non-action" in Sonsorol City—and those who like both drift back and forth from one to the other, as the mood strikes them.

11. Other Excursions

Across the *Garuda Bridge* from Sonsorol City are the ruins of the *Spanish Fort*, and a rather picturesque little fishing village that goes by the same name.

The three coral atolls which lie within a few miles of Sonsorol can be visited by hired boat or canoe from either Port Watson or Sonsorol City. *Ngemelan* is inhabited only seasonally, but *Ngesaba* and *Garap* have small anarchist communities (including a hunter/gatherer "tribe" and a nudist colony!) Snorkeling, swimming, fishing and other tropical pleasures abound, and many people prefer the white coral beaches to Sonsorol's black volcanic sand.

On the northern and northwestern sides of the island a few farm villages and rural communes endure much heavier rainfall and heat in order to attain almost total privacy. The only way to get there is by jeep or on foot. One village, *New Canaan*, consists of die-hard Calvinists who hate both anarchism and the Moro Way, but have yet to refuse their dividends (not recommended to the visitor); another, *Nyarlathatep*, is the headquarters of a cult of black magicians (also not recommended).

On the slope of Mt. Sonsorol north of Port Watson and just inside the Enclave border lie the enigmatic monolithic ruins called *Nbusala*, thought to date back beyond the coming of the Moro pirates. Popular myth calls it "The Temple of the Clouds" and associates it with lost archaic myth and legend. Nearby, the highest waterfall on the island lends the area further enchantment. The climb through steamy jungle is exhausting, but the spot is popular with artists, yogis and neo-pagans who consider it a "power place," the island's living heart.

12. *How To Become A Resident*

Sonsorol has few tourists and fewer visitors, and some of the latter can't bear to leave. The Bank's computers have opined that the island could double its population in five years without lowering the average dividend or causing any over-crowding, but in fact the rate of growth is much smaller. How can a visitor become a permanent resident?

Those of independent means can simply settle in Port Watson and do as they please—as long as they agree to "sign the Articles." To become a Shareholder however one must either be taken in by an already-existing commune or company, or else convince a Random Synod that one can offer valuable skills or services to the community. Recent successful proposals came from an oceanographer from Boston; an Italian woman who studied puppetry in Indonesia; an extremely good-looking youth of twenty from Belize; the crew of a small sloop who arrived with a cargo of electronic gear all the way from California; some Malay sailors who decided to jump ship and cultivate pineapples; an Irish poet who impressed the Synod by improvising in *terza rima* on themes suggested by the audience; and a fourteen-year-old American boy who ran away from his family on Guam and said he wanted to study sorcery.

To live outside the Free Enclave one must in theory become a citizen of the Republic of Sonsorol (although this "law" is not very strictly enforced). All citizens automatically become Shareholders. Papers are granted without question to anyone who is accepted into some Sonsorolan clan or commune, or who is hired specifically to work for the government (doctors, teachers, etc.), or is accepted as a student by the Academies at the Sultan's Mosque. Otherwise one must apply to the Legislature rather than a Random Synod and not all applications are accepted. Papers are sometimes granted in return for an amusing or eloquent speech, but rumor has it that connections at Court can count for more than a pleasing personality.

Except for a few hard-baked Christians, Sonsorolans and Watsonians live in what appears to be perfect harmony. Inter-marriage has become common (often without benefit of clergy or state), and the youngest generation has all the beauty and vitality of a new breed.

The Way of Sonsorol may be possible only on a tropical island, and some argue that this brand of libertarian utopianism cannot be transplanted to the outside world. However, others believe otherwise. In an editorial (in the *Court Gazette*, March 10, 1985), the Sultan himself wrote, "No one who loves freedom can hear of Sonsorol without longing, without envy, without nostalgia for something unknown but deeply desired... Sonsorol could be created anywhere—nothing stands in the way but false consciousness and the grim power of those rulers who feast on false consciousness like vampires. We call for a network of Port Watsons to encircle the Earth: one, two, many, an infinite number of Port Watsons! Let those who envy us transmute their frustration into anger and insurrection, into a determination to enjoy utopia *now*, not in some neverneverland after death or after the Revolution. We reach out to those who yearn for us in the poverty-ridden 'third world,' the ideology-choked 'second world,' and the illusion-riddled 'West'— and we whisper across thousands of miles to tell them, 'Don't despair. Port Watson exists *within you*, and you can make it real'."

(1985)

27

INCUNABULA

A Catalogue of Rare Books, Manuscripts & Curiosa
Conspiracy Theory, Frontier Science & Alternative Worlds

Emory Cranston, Prop.

> Incunabulum / cocoon / swaddling clothes / cradle / in-cunae, in the cradle / koiman, put to sleep / winding-sheet / koimetarium (cemetery) / printed books before 1501, hence by extension any rare & hermetic book...

INTRODUCTION

No book for sale here was actually printed before 1501, but they all answer to the description "rare and hermetic"—even the massmarket paperbacks, not to mention the xeroxes of unpublished manuscripts, which cannot be obtained from any other source!

The symbol INCUNABULA was chosen for our company for its *shape*—cocoon, egg-like, gourd-like—the shape of Chaos according to Chuang Tzu. Cradle: beginnings. Sleep: dreams. Silken white sheets of birth and death; books, white pages, the cemetery of ideas.

This catalogue has been put together with a purpose: to alert YOU to a vast cover up, a conspiracy so deep that no other researcher has yet become aware of it (outside certain Intelligence circles, needless to say!)—and so dangerous that the "winding sheet" imagery in our title seems quite appropriate; we know of *at least* two murders so far in connection with this material.

Unlike other conspiracy theories, such as Hollow earth, Men In Black, cattle mutilation, UFOs, Reich & Tesla or what have you, the INCUNABULA Theory harmonizes with genuine frontier quantum mechanics and chaos mathematics, and does not depend on any quack nostrums, pseudoscience or ESP for proof. This will become clear to anyone who takes the trouble to read the background material we recommend and offer for sale.

Because of the unprecedented nature of the INCUNABULA File we have included short descriptions of some of the books, pamphlets, flyers, privately-circulated or unpublished manuscripts, ephemera & curiosa available through us. Some of this is highly inflammable and sexual in nature, so an age statement must be included with each order.

Cash (or stamps) only. No cheques or money orders will be accepted.

Thank You,

EMORY CRANSTON, PROP.

1.   **Wolf, Fred Alan.** *Parallel Universes: The Search for Other Worlds* **(New York, Simon & Schuster, 1988) cloth; 351 pp.; $25**

Written by a scientist for non-scientists, simplistic and jokey, makes you feel a bit talked-down-to. Nevertheless Wolf uses his imagination (or other scientists' imaginations) so well he seems to hit accidentally on certain truths—(unless he knows more than he reveals). For example: the parallel universes must have all come into being simultaneously "at the beginning" in order for quantum uncertainty to exist, because there was no *observer* present at the Big Bang, thus no way for the Wave Function to collapse and produce one universe out of all the bubbles of possibility (p.174). If an electron can disappear in one universe and appear in another (as suggested by the Everett/Wheeler material), a process called "quantum tunneling," then perhaps *information* can undergo a similar tunneling effect. Wolf suggests (p. 176) that this might account for certain "psychic phenomena, altered states of awareness," even ghosts and spirits! Actual travel between worlds must of course involve tunneling by both electrons AND information—any scientist would have predicted as much—but the mention of "altered states" of consciousness is *extremely revealing*! Elsewhere (p.204), Wolf speculates that a future "highly developed... electronic form of biofeedback" will allow us to observe quantum effects in the electrons of our own bodies, making the enhanced consciousness and the body itself a "time machine" (which is what he calls a device for travel between universes). He comes so close to the truth then shies away! For instance (p.199) he points out that the Wave Function has a value BETWEEN zero and one until it collapses. If the wave function does not collapse, the "thing" it describes exists in two universes simultaneously. How strange of him not to mention that *fractal geometry* also deals with values between zero and one! As we know the secret of travel between worlds is rooted in the marriage of quantum and chaos, particularly in the elusive mathematics of *fractal tesseracts* (visualize a 4-dimension Mandelbrot Set—one of the simplest of the trans-dimensional "maps" or "catastrophic topologies"). Wolf appears so unaware of this, we must sadly conclude that he's not part of the conspiracy.

Particularly interesting—and not found in any other material—are Wolf's speculations about schizophrenia. Are schizophrenics receiving information from *other worlds*? Could a schizoid observer actually observe (in the famous double-slit experiments) a wave becoming two particles and then one particle? Or could such an observation be made by an extremely blank and simple-minded watcher (a sort of Zen simpleton perhaps)? If so, the perfect subject for parallel-worlds experiments would be a paradoxically complex simpleton, a "magnetized schizophrenic" who would be aware of the split into two worlds which occurs when a quantum measurement is made. Oddly enough, such a mental state sounds very close to the "positive schizophrenia" of certain extreme psychedelic experiences as well as the meditation-visualization exercises of actual travelers between worlds.

Despite its flaws, an essential work.

---

2.   Herbert, Nick. *Quantum Reality* **(NAL, 1986) Cloth, $40**

A masterful and lucid exposition of the different versions of reality logically describable from various interpretations of quantum mechanics. The Everett/Wheeler Theory is here given its clearest explanation possible in lay persons' terms, given the author's unawareness (at the time) of experimental verification.

---

3.   ibid. *Faster Than Light: Superluminal Loopholes in Physics* **(NAL, 1988) cloth, $30**

Some of the theorists who touch on the Many-Worlds "hypothesis" place too much emphasis on time distortions and the implication of "time travel." These of course seem present in the theorems, but in *practice* have turned out (so far) to be of little consequence. Chaos Theory places much more emphasis on temporal directionality than most quantum theory (with such exceptions as R. Feynman and his "arrow of time"), and offers strong evidence for the past-present-future evolution that we actually experience. As K. Sohrawardi puts it, "the universe is in a state of Being, true, but that state is not static in the way suggested by the concept of 'reversibility' in Classical physics. The 'generosity' of Being, so to speak, is *becoming,* and the result is not reversibility but *multiplicity,* the unmeasurable resonant chaos-like fecundity of creation." Nevertheless, Herbert's second book is a brilliant speculative work—and it led him directly to a certain circle of scientists and body of research concerned with dimensional travel, rather than "time travel," with the result that his third book (see next item) finally struck paydirt.

---

4.   **"Jabir ibn Hayaan" (Nick Herbert).** *Alternate Dimensions* **(publication suppressed by Harper & Row, 1989); bound uncorrected galleys, 179pp. $100. (We have 5 sets of proofs for sale, after which only xerox copies will be available at $125)**

While working on *Faster Than Light* Herbert came into contact with one of the "travel cults" operating somewhere in California, perhaps one with a sufiistic slant ("Jabir ibn Hayaan" was a famous 10th century sufi alchemist); according to the preface of *Alternate Dimensions,* which is irritatingly vague and suggestive, this group seems to have trained him and sent him on at least one trip to America2. Herbert suggests that he already had so much experience of altered states of consciousness and ability to visualize complex space/time geometries that only a minimum of "initiatic" training proved necessary.

In any case, despite its vagueness and brevity, this book is the most accurate and thoroughly-informed work on travel between worlds in our entire collection. So far we have been unable to obtain any *deep* theoretical work, and only a few papers dealing with practical aspects —but Herbert provides a magnificent overview of the entire field. Written for the lay person, with his usual clear and succinct approach to theory, Herbert's is the first "popular" study to make all the basic links: the Everett/Wheeler hypothesis, Bell's Theorem, the E/R Bridge, fractal geometry and chaos math, cybernetically-enhanced biofeedback, psychotropic and shamanic techniques, crystallography, morphogenetic field theory, catastrophe topology, etc.

Of course he's strongest in discussing the quantum aspects of travel, less sure when dealing with the math outside his field, and most inspiring when describing (pp.98-101) visualization techniques and "embodied ecstasy" (ex-stasis, "standing outside" the body; hence *embodied ecstasy* paradoxically describes the transdimensional experience).

Herbert makes no claim to understand the traveling itself, and goes so far as to suggest that even the (unnamed) pioneers who made the first breakthroughs may not have completely understood the process, any more than the inventor of the steam engine understood Classical physics (p.23). This definitely ties in with what we know about the persons in question.

Unfortunately the six illustrations promised in the table of contents are not included in the galleys—one of them was a "Schematic for a Trans-dimensional Express" which might be worth killing for!—and the publishers claim that Herbert never supplied the illustrations. They refuse to say why they suspended publication of *Alternate Dimensions* and in fact at first denied ever having handled such a title! Moreover Herbert has apparently dropped out of sight; if he hasn't met with foul play, he may have returned permanently to Earth2.

We regret having to sell copies of a flawed book for such an outrageous price; we'd like to publish a massmarket edition affordable by

34   FALSE DOCUMENTS

all—but if Harper & Row ever find out what we're doing, we'll need the money for court costs and lawyers' fees! So get it while you can—this is THE indispensable background work for understanding the Conspiracy.

---

5.   **Thomsen, Dietrick E.** *A Knowing Universe Seeking to be Known* **(Xerox offprint from** *Science News,* **Vol.123, 1983); $5**

Unwittingly demonstrates the resonance between quantum reality theory and the Sufism of (for example) "the Greatest Shaykh," Ibn 'Arabi, who discusses in his *Bezels of Wisdom* a saying attributed to God by Mohammad (but not in the Koran): "I was a hidden treasure and I wanted (lit. 'loved') to be known; so I created the universe, that I might be known."

5a.   **We also have a few offprints (at the same price) of Thomsen's witty** *"Quanta at Large: 101 Things TO DO with Schrodinger's Cat"* **(op.cit, 129, 1986).**

---

6.   **DeWitt, Bryce S. & Neill Graham.** *The Many Worlds Interpretation of Quantum Mechanics* **(Princeton, NJ, 1973); cloth, $50**

The standard (and far from "easy"!) work on the Everett/Wheeler hypothesis—a bible for the early pioneers.

---

7.   **Cramer, John G.** *Alternate Universes II (Analog,* **Nov. 1984)**

A popularization of the Theory by a prominent physicist—no knowledge of the Conspiracy is detectable. We're selling copies of the SciFi mag itself for $10 each.

8.   **Greenberg, D.M., ed.** *New Techniques & Ideas in Quantum Measurement Theory* **(Vol. 480 *Annals of the NY Academy of Sciences*, 1986); cloth, $50**

Contains the valuable if somewhat whimsical article by D.Z. Albers, "How to take a Photograph of Another Everett World." Also the very important "Macroscopic Quantum Tunneling at Finite Temperatures" by P. Hanggi (we suspect him of being a Conspiracy member).

9.   **(Anonymous).** *Course Catalogue for 1978-79,* **Institute of Chaos Studies and Imaginal Yoga (no address); xerox of mimeographed flyer, 7pp, $15**

An in-house document from the Institute where the first Breakthrough was attained (probably in the late winter or early spring of 1979)—therefore, although it makes no *overt* mention of Travel or the Egg, the *Catalogue* is of prime importance for an understanding of the intellectual and historical background of the event.

According to an unreliable source (see ESCAPE FROM EARTH PRIME!, #15 in this list), the Institute was located somewhere in Dutchess County, New York, where the founder and director, Dr. Kamadev Sohrawardi, was employed by IBM in the 1960s, "dropped out" and began investigations into "consciousness physics"; it is also claimed that Sohrawardi was a Bengali of mixed English, Hindu and Moslem origin, descended from an old sufi family, and initiated into Tantra. All this disagrees with clues in other sources and is perhaps not to be trusted. Other groups take credit for the Breakthrough, and Sohrawardi may have been a fraud—but we're convinced that the *Catalogue* is authentic and Sohrawardi's claim the most certain.

At first glance, the *Catalogue* appears an example of late-hippy/early-New-Age pretentiousness. Thus there are courses in "Visions of Color & Light in Sufi Meditation," "Inner Alchemy in Late Taoism," "Metaphysics of the Ismaili 'Assassins,'" "Imaginal Yoga & the

Psychotopology of the Imagination,""Hermetic & Neo-Pagan Studies" (apparently based on Golden Dawn teachings), "Visualization Techniques in Javanese Sorcery," "Stairways to Heaven: Shamanic Trance & the Mapping of Consciousness," "Stirner, Nietzsche & Stone age Economy: An Examination of Non-Authoritarian Hunter/Gatherer Societies," and—interestingly enough!—"Conspiracy Theory."

The "shamanic" course may have been a blind for research in psychotropic drugs, including such exotica as ayahuasca (yagé, harmaline), ibogaine, yohimbine, telepathine and Vitamin K, as well as the more standard psychedelicatessen of the late '70s.

However, the *Catalogue* also contains amazing courses in frontier science, any combination of which could have provided the key or final puzzle-bit to the Breakthrough: apparently Sohrawardi taught or supervised most of them. Thus "The Universe in a Grain of Sand" promised information on models of brain activity, cybernetically-enhanced feedback, Sheldrake's morphogenetic field theory, René Thom's Catastrophe Theory as applied to consciousness, lucid-dreaming research, John Lilly's work on "altered states" and other mind-related topics. Then in "Strange Attractors & the Mathematics of Chaos," Sohrawardi discussed matters unknown outside of the margins of academia till the mid-'80's, and made the astounding prediction that Chaos in the macroscopic world would somehow be found to mirror Uncertainty in the microscopic or Quantum World, a truth still unrecognized in "official" scientific circles today. He felt that n-dimensional strange attractors could be used to model the quantum behavior of particles/waves, and that the "so-called collapse of the wave function" could actually be mapped with certain bizarre ramifications of Thom's catastrophic topology. Making references to work by Ilya Prigogine which was still being circulated in private "preprint" or samizdat form at the time, Sohrawardi suggests that "creative chaos" (as opposed to "deterministic" or entropic chaos) provides the link that will unify Relativity, Quantum, Complexity and consciousness itself into a new science.

Finally in his "Advanced Seminar on Many Worlds," he states baldly that the alternative universes predicted by Relativity (Black Hole Theory) are the same as the many worlds predicted by Quantum, are the same as fractal dimensions revealed in Chaos! This one-page course description is the closest thing we have to an *explanation* of why travel to other worlds *actually works*. Hence the *Catalogue* is an indispensable document for the serious student of the Conspiracy.

10.   **Beckenstein, J.** *"Black Holes & Entropy"* **(xerox offprint from** *Physical Review,* **Vol.D7, 1973; 28pp), $15**

An early (pre-Breakthrough) speculation with suggestive hints about quantum and chaos-as-entropy—although no knowledge of actual Chaos Theory is demonstrated. This paper was referred to in an in-house memo from the Inst. for Chaos Studies & Imaginal Yoga, believed to have been composed by K. Sohrawardi himself (see #9).

11.   **Sohrawardi, Dr Kamadev.** *"Pholgiston & the Quantum Aether"* **(Offprint from the** *J. of Paranormal Physics,* **Vol.XXII, Bombay, 1966), $40**

An early paper by Sohrawardi, flooded with wild speculations about quantum and oriental spirituality, probably dating from the period when he was still working for IBM, but making visits to Millbrook, nearby in Dutchess Co., and participating in the rituals of the League For Spiritual Discovery under Dr. Timothy Leary, and the psychedelic yoga of Bill Haines' Sri Ram Ashram, which shared Leary's headquarters on a local millionaire's estate. The basic insight concerns the identity of Everett/Wheeler's "many worlds" and the "other worlds" of sufism, tantrik Hinduism and Vajrayana Buddhism. At the time, Sohrawardi apparently believed he could "prove" this by reviving the long-dead theories of phlogiston and aether in the light of quantum discoveries!

(Phlogiston Theory—based on the thinking of the sufi alchemist Jabir ibn Hayaan—the *original* Jabir—was propounded seriously in the 18th century to unify heat and light as "one thing.") Totally useless as science, this metaphor nevertheless inspired Sohrawardi's later and genuinely important work on alternate realities.

---

12.   *Ibid.* **"Zero Work & Psychic Paleolithism"** *East Village Other,* **Vol. IV #4 (Dec.1968) xerox reprint, single sheet 11 ½ x 17, from the legendary underground newspaper, $5**

Unfortunately no scientific speculations, but a fascinating glimpse into the political background of the inventor of Travel (or rather, one of the inventors). Making reference to French Situationist and Dutch "Provo" ideas which helped spark the "Events" and upheavals of Spring '68 all over Europe and America, Sohrawardi looks forward to a world without "the alienating prison of WORK," restored to the "oneness with Nature of the Old Stone Age" and yet somehow based on "green technology and quantum weirdness."

Wild and wooly as it is, this text nevertheless poses a fascinating scientific question in the light of the author's later accomplishments— a question still unanswered. All the "First Breakthroughs" we know of with any degree of certainty (those in New York, California, and Java—the actual sequence is unclear) without exception entered parallel *worlds without human inhabitants,* virtual forest-worlds. Most science fiction predicated other worlds almost like ours, populated by "us," with only a few slight differences, worlds "close" to ours. Instead—no people!

Why?

Two possible explanations: (1) We cannot enter worlds containing "copies" of ourselves without causing paradoxes and violating the consistency principle of the "megaverse"—hence only wild (or feral) worlds are open to Travel. (2) Other worlds exist, in a sense, only as probabilities; in order to "become fully real" they must be *observed.* In effect, the parallel universes are *observer-created*, as soon as a traveler "arrives" in one of them. Sohrawardi *wanted* a paleolithic world of endless forest, plentiful game and gathering, virgin, empty but slightly haunted—therefore, *that's what he got.* Either explanation raises problems in the light of what actually happened; perhaps there is a third, as yet unsuspected.

---

13.   (Anonymous). *Ong's Hat: A Color Brochure of the Institute of Chaos Studies* **(photocopy of version published in** *Edge Detector*, **Vol. 1 1988, a Cyberpunk "fanzine" from Canada. Also included: a photocopy of the original color brochure, with slightly variant text), both for $25**

This bizarre document, disguised as a brochure for a New Age health retreat, reveals some interesting information about the activities of Sohrawardi's group or a closely-associated group. A fairly accurate description of the Egg is provided, as well as a believable account of the first (or one of the first) Breakthroughs. However, everything else in the pamphlet is sheer disinformation. The New Jersey Pine Barrens were never a center of alternate-worlds research, and all the names in the text are false. A non-existent address is included. Nevertheless, highly valuable for background.

---

14.   "Sven Saxon." *The Stone Age Survivalist* **(Loompanics, UnLtd., Port Townsend, WA 1985), Pb, $20**

"Imagine yourself suddenly plunked down buck-naked in the middle of a large dark forest with no resources except your mind," says the preface. *"What would you do?"*

What indeed? and who could possibly care?—*except* a trans-dimensional Traveler! Loompanics specializes in books on disappearance and survival involving a good deal of escapist fantasy—but as we know, this situation is all too real for the Visitor to Other Worlds.

Part I, Flint-knapping, an excellent illustrated handbook of paleo-lithic tool-production; II, Zero-tech hunting and trapping; III, Gath-ering (incl. *a materia medica*); IV, Shelter; V, Primitive warfare; VI, Man & Dog: trans-species symbiosis; VII, Cold weather survival; VIII, Culture ("Sven" recommends memorizing a lot of songs, poems and stories—and ends by saying *"Memorize this book*—'cause you can't take it with you." *Where is* "Mr. Saxon" now, we wonder?).

---

15.   Balcombe, Harold S. *Escape From Earth Prime!* **(Four-square Press, Denver, Colo., 1986), Pb, $15**

This—unfortunately!—is *the* book that blew the lid off the Conspir-acy for the first time. We say "unfortunately" because ESCAPE!, to all appearances, is a piece of unmitigated paranoid pulp tripe. Writ-ten in breathless ungrammatical subFortean prose, unfootnoted and nakedly sensationalistic, the book sank without trace, ignored even by the kook-conspiracy fringe; we were able to buy out unsold stock from the vanity press which published it, just before they went out of busi-ness and stopped answering their mail.

Balcombe (whom we've been unable to trace and who may have "vanished"), is the author of one other book we've seen—but are not offering for sale—called *Drug Lords from the Hollow Earth* (1984) in which he claims that the CIA obtained LSD and cocaine from Dero-flying-saucer-nazis from beneath Antarctica. So much for his creden-tials. How he got hold of even a bit of the authentic Other Worlds story is a miracle.

According to Balcombe, the first breakthrough was due not solely to K. Sohrawardi—despite his importance as a theoretician—but also a "sinister webwork of cultists, anarchists, commies, fanatical hippies and renegade traitor scientists who made fortunes in the drug trade" (p.3). Balcombe promises to name names, and out of the welter of rant and slather, some hard facts about the pioneers actually emerge.

Funding (and some research) emanated in the '70s from a "chaos cabal" of early Silicon Valley hackers interested in complex dynamical systems, randomicity, and chance, and—gambling!—as well as a shadowy group of "drug lords" (Balcombe's favorite term of abuse), with connections to certain founders of the Discordian Illuminati. Money was channeled through a cult called the Moorish Orthodox Church, a loose knit confederation of jazz musicians, oldtime hipsters, white "sufis" and black moslems, bikers and street dealers (see "A Heresiologist's Guide to Brooklyn," #24 in this list) who came into contact with Sohrawardi in Millbrook in the mid-'60s.

Sohrawardi was a naive idealist and somewhat careless about his associations. He received clandestine support from people who were in turn connected to certain Intelligence circles with an interest in psychedelic and fringe mind-science. According to Balcombe this was *not* the CIA (MK-ULTRA) but an unofficial offshoot of several groups with Masonic connections! The Conspiracy was penetrated almost from the start, but was actually *encouraged* in the hope of gleaning useful information about parallel worlds, or at least about the "mental conditioning techniques" developed as part of the basic research.

By the mid-'70s Sohrawardi and his various cohorts and connections (now loosely referred to as "the Garden of Forked Paths" or GFP) had become aware of the Intelligence circles (now loosely grouped as "Probability Control Force" or PCF) and had in turn planted double-agents, and gone further underground. In 1978 or '79 an actual device for trans-dimensional Travel, the "Egg" (also called the Cocoon or the Cucurbit, which means both *gourd* and *alchemical flask*) was developed in deepest secrecy, probably at Sohrawardi's institute in Upstate New York, certainly not at a branch lab supposedly hidden away in the NJ Pine Barrens near the long-vanished village of Ong's Hat (see #13 in this list), since no such lab ever existed, nor does it exist now, despite what some fools think.

The PCF were unable to obtain an Egg for several years and did not succeed in Breakthrough until (Balcombe believes) 1982. The California groups, however, began Egg-production and broke through (into "BigSur2") in early 1980 (again, Balcombe's chronology). (Balcombe clearly knows nothing of the situation in Java.)

It remains unclear whether the East Coast and West Coast groups both entered the same alternate world, or two *different* but similar worlds. Communication between the two outposts has so far proved impossible because, as it happens, the Egg will not transport *non-sentient matter*. Travelers arrive Over There birth-naked in a Stone Age world—no airplanes, no radio, no clothes ... no fire and no tools! Only the Egg, like a diamond Fabergé easter gift designed by Dali, alone in the midst of "Nature naturing." Balcombe includes a dim out-of-focus photo of an Egg, and claims that the machine is part computer but also partly-living crystal, like virus or DNA, and also partly "naked quantumstuff."

Eggs are costly to produce, so the early pioneers had to return after each sortie and forego permanent settlement on E2 until a cheaper mode of transport could be discovered. However, emigration via the Egg proved possible when the "tantrik" or "double-yolk" effect was discovered: two people (*any* combination of gender, etc.) can Travel by Egg while *making love*, especially if one of the pair has already done the trip a few times and "knows the way" without elaborate visualization techniques and so forth. Balcombe has a field day with this juicy information and spends an entire chapter (VIII) detailing the "perversions" in use for this purpose. Talent for Travel ranges from brilliant to zero—probably no more than 15% of humanity can make it, although the less-talented can be "translated" by the tantrik technique—and extensive training methods have somewhat improved the odds. California2 now contains about 1000 emigrants scattered along the coast, and the eastern settlements add up to 500 or 600. A few children have been born "over there"—some can Travel, some can't, although the talented percentage seems greater than among the general population of Earth-prime. And being "stuck" on E2 is no grave punishment in any case!, unless you object to the Garden of Eden and the "original leisure society" of the Paleolithic flintknappers.

Balcombe claims that the PCF was severely disappointed by the sentience "law" of Travel, since they had hoped to use the parallel worlds as a weapons-delivery system! Nevertheless they continued to experiment, hoping for a more "mechanistic" technique; meanwhile they devote their efforts to (a) suppressing all information leaks, (b) plotting against the independent GFP and infiltrating the E2 settlements, (c) attempting to open new worlds where technology might be possible. They are however handicapped by a shortage of *talent*: the kind of person who can Travel is not usually the kind of person who sympathizes with the "patriotic discipline of the PCF" and rogue Masonic groups, but some of these end up defecting and "doubling," and anyway most of them are much too weird for the taste of the rigidly reactionary inner core of PCF leadership, who wonder (as does Balcombe) whether these agents are "any better than the scum they're spying on?"

More worlds have been discovered—E3 and E4 are mentioned in *ESCAPE!* (and we know that E5 was opened in 1988)—but all of these are "empty" forest worlds apparently almost identical with E2.

In summary, Balcombe's style is execrable and attitude repulsive, but his book remains the most accurate overview of the Conspiracy to date. If you're only going to order one item from us, this is it.

---

16.   **(Anonymous).** *Bionic Travel: An Orgonomic Theory of the Megaverse*   **(xerox of unpubl. typescript headed "Top Secret—Eyes Only"; 27pp), $15**

If this paper emanates from PCF sources, as we believe, it indicates the poor quality of original research carried out by the enemies of

Sohrawardi and the GFP, and may explain the PCF's relative lack of progress in the field (especially considering their much larger budget!). The author attempts to revive W. Reich's Orgone Theory, with "bions" as "life-force particles" and some sort of orgone accumulator (Reich's "box") as a possible substitute for the Egg. An unhealthy interest is shown in "harnessing the force of *Deadly Orgone*" as a weapon for use on other worlds. References are also made to Aleister Crowley's "sex magick techniques" of the Ordo Templi Orientis—even speculations on *human* sacrifice as a possible source of "transdimensional energy." A morbid and crackpot document, devoid of all scientific value (in our opinion) but affording a fascinating insight into PCF mentality and method.

---

17.   **Corbin, Henry.** *Creative Imagination in the Sufism of Ibn 'Arabi* **(trans. by   R. Mannheim; Princeton, NJ, 1969), cloth, $50; Pb, $20**

One of the few books mentioned by title in the *Catalogue* of the Inst. of Chaos Studies & Imaginal Yoga (see #9 in this list). The *"mundus imaginalis,"* also called the World of Archetypes or the "Isthmus" (Arabic, *barzakh*), lies in between the World of the Divine and the material World of Creation. It actually consists of "many worlds," including two "emerald cities" called Jabulsa and Jabulqa (very intriguing considering the situation on Java2!). The great 14th-century Hispano-Moorish sufi Ibn 'Arabi developed a metaphysics of the "Creative Imagination" by which the adept could achieve spiritual progress via direct contemplation of the archetypes, including the domains of djinn, spirits and angels. Ibn 'Arabi also speaks of seven alternate Earths created by Allah, each with its own Mecca and Kaaba! Some parallel-universe theorists believe that Travel without any tech (even the Egg) may be possible, claiming that certain mystics have already accomplished it. If so, then Ibn 'Arabi must have been one of them.

18.   Gleick, James. *CHAOS: Making a New Science* **(Viking Penguin, NY, 1987), cloth, 254pp, $30**

The first and still the most complete introduction to chaos—required reading—BUT with certain caveats. First: Gleick has *no* philosophical or poetic depth; he actually begins the book with a quote from John Updike! No mention of chaos mythology or oriental sources. No mention of certain non-American chaos scientists such as René Thom and Ilya Prigogine! Instead, alongside the admittedly useful info, one gets a subtle indoctrination in "deterministic chaos," by which we mean the tendency to look on chaos as a weapon to fight chaos, to "save" Classical physics —and learn to predict the Stock Market! (As opposed to what we call the "quantum chaos" of Sohrawardi and his allies, which looks on chaos as a creative and negentropic source, the cornucopia of evolution and awareness.) Warning: we suspect Gleick of being a PCF agent who has embedded his text with subtle disinformation meant to distract the chaos-science community from any interest in "other worlds."

19.   Pak Hardjanto. "Apparent Collapse of the Wave Function as an n-Dimensional Catastrophe" (trans. by "N.N.S." in *Collected Papers of the SE Asian Soc. for Advanced Research,* **Vol.XXIX, 1980), 47 pp, xerox of offprint, $15**

An early paper by the little-known scientific director of the Javanese "Travel Cult" which succeeded in breakthrough, possibly in the year this essay was published or shortly thereafter. Hardjanto is known to have been in touch with Sohrawardi since the '60s; no doubt they shared all information, but each kept the other secret from their respective organizations. The pioneers of Java2 became known to the GFP and PCF only around 1984 or '85.

This article, the only scientific work we possess by Hardjanto, shows him to be a theoretician equal or even superior to Sohrawardi himself—and if Hardjanto is also the anonymous author of the following item, as we believe, then he appears a formidable "metaphysicist" as well!

"Apparent Collapse," while certainly not a blueprint for Egg construction, nevertheless constitutes one of the few bits of "hard" science published openly on our Subject. Unfortunately, its theorems and diagrams are doubtless comprehensible only to a handful of experts. The topological drawings literally boggle the mind, especially one entitled "Hypercube Undergoing 'Collapse' Into 5-Space Vortex"!

---

20.   **(Unsigned, probably by Pak Hardjanto).** *A Vision of Hurqalya* **(trans. by K. K. Sardono; Incunabula Press, 1988), Pb, 46 pp, $20**

The Indonesian original of this text appeared as a pamphlet in Yogjakarta (E. Java) in 1982. We ourselves at Incunabula commissioned the translation and have published this handsome edition, including all the illustrations from the original, at our own expense.

If one knew nothing about the Conspiracy or Many-Worlds Theory, *A Vision* would seem at first to be a mystical tract by an adherent of *kebatinan*, the heterodox sufi-influenced freeform esoteric/syncretistic complex of sects which has come to be influential in GFP circles, inasmuch as the idea of "spiritual master" (*guru, murshed*) has been replaced by "teacher" (*pamong*); some kebatinan sects utilize spontaneous non-hierarchical organizational structures.

However, in the light of our knowledge of the material existence of other worlds, *Vision* takes on a whole new dimension—as a literal description of what Hardjanto and his fellow pioneers found on Java2.

They discovered another uninhabited world—but with one huge difference. The author of *Vision* steps out of his "alchemical Egg" into a vast and ancient abandoned City! He calls it Hurqalya (after a traditional sufi name for the Other World or *alam-e mithal*). He senses his total aloneness—feels that the City's builders have long since moved on *elsewhere*—and yet that they still somehow somewhere exist.

The author compares Hurqalya to the ancient ruined city of Borobadur in E. Java, but notices immediately that there are no statues or images—all the decoration is abstract and severe—but "neither Islamic nor Buddhist nor Hindu nor Christian nor any style I ever saw." The "palaces" of Hurqalya are grand, cyclopean, almost monolithic—far from "heavy" in atmosphere, despite the black basalt from which they seem to have been carved. For the City is cut through by *water*... it is in fact a water-city in the style of the Royal Enclave of Yogjakarta (now so sadly derelict), but incomparably *bigger*. Canals, aqueducts, rivers and channels crisscross and meander through the City; flowing originally from quiescent volcanic mountains looming green in the West, water flows down through the City which is built on a steep slope gradually curving into a basin and down to the placid Eastern Sea, where a hundred channels flow dark and clear into the green salt ocean.

Despite the air of ruin—huge trees have grown through buildings, splitting them open—mosses, ferns and orchids coat the crumbling walls with viridescence, hosting parrots, lizards, butterflies—despite this desolation, most of the waterworks still flow: canal-locks broken open centuries ago allow cascades, leaks, spills and waterfalls in unexpected places, so that the City is wrapped in a tapestry of water-sounds and songbird voices. Most amazingly, the water flows at different levels simultaneously, so that aqueducts cross over canals which in turn flow above sunken streams which drip into wells, underground cisterns and mysterious sewers in a bewildering complex of levels, pipes, conduits and irrigated garden terraces which resemble (to judge by the author's sketches) a dreamscape of Escher or Piranesi. Viewed from above, the City would be mapped as an arabesque 3-D spiderweb (with water-bridges aboveground, streams at ground level and also underground) fanning out to fill the area of the basin, thence into the harbor with its huge cracked basalt-block docks.

The slope on which the City is built is irregularly terraced in ancient SE Asian style—as many staircases and streets thread their way up and down, laid out seemingly at random, following land-contours rather than grid-logic, adding to the architectural complexity of the layer of waterways with a maze of vine-encrusted overpasses, arched bridges, spiraling ramps, crooked alleyways, cracked hidden steps debouching on broad esplanades, avenues, parks gone to seed, pavilions, balconies, apartments, jungle-choked palazzos, echoing gloomy "temples" whose divinities, if any, seem to have left no forwarding address... all empty, all utterly abandoned. And nowhere is there any *human* debris—no broken tools, bones or midden heaps, no evidence of actual habitation—as if the ancient builders of the City picked up and took everything with them when they departed—"perhaps to one of the other Seven Worlds of the *alam'e mithal*"—in other words, to a "higher dimension."

Thus ends the *Vision of Hurqalya*—raising more questions than it answers! There is no doubt that it describes exactly what was discovered in Java2 in 1980 or '81. But if the "observer-created" theory of other-worlds travel is true, "Hurqalya" represents the "imaginal imprint" of what Hardjanto (or whoever) expected to find. Yet again, if that theory is false... *who built Hurqalya?* One current explanation (arising from time-distortion theorems which have so far remained unsolvable) suggests that the Builders "moved" in prehistoric times to Earth-prime and became the distant ancestors of the Javanese ("Java Man"). Another guess: the Builders have indeed moved on to a "distant" alternate universe, and eventually we may find them.

A small settlement now exists in Hurqalya. Once the American groups heard of the City's existence, members of both the GFP and PFC were able to visualize it and Travel to it *from America* (the Javanese can do the same from Java-prime to America2). Since 1985 all three groups have expended most of their exploratory effort on "opening up" new worlds in the Java series. Apparently Indonesian sorcerers and trance adepts are very good at this, and we believe they have reached Java7—without, however, finding replications of the City or any trace of the Builders —only more empty forest.

---

21.   Von Ritter Rucker, Dr R. "'The Cat Was Alive, But Looked Scared As Hell': Some Unexpected Properties of Cellular Automata in the Light of the Everett/Wheeler Hypothesis" (*Complex Dynamical Systems Newsletter* **No. 8, 1989), offprint, $10**

Who is this man and what does he know? No other serious mathematician has so far made any connection between cellular automata and the Many Worlds. Tongue-in-cheek (?), the author suggests that Schrödinger's poor cat might be both alive *and* dead, even after the box is opened, IF parallel universes are "stacked" in some arcane manner which he claims to be able to demonstrate with a piece of software he has hacked and is selling for an outrageous sum; we have also seen an ad for this program in a magazine called *MONDO 2000*, published in Berkeley and devoted to "reality hacking." We'd love to know what certain members of the Conspiracy would make of this bizarre concept!

---

22.   Kennedy, Alison. "Psychotropic Drugs in 'Shared-World' & Lucid Dreaming Experiments" (*Psychedelic Monographs & Essays*, **Vol.XIV, no. 2, 1981), offprint, $5**

This writer appears to have inside information. The notion of a drug-induced hallucination so powerful it can be shared by many (in a proper "blind" experiment) and can actually *come into existence*, into material reality; the idea that drug-enhanced lucid dreaming can be used to discover objective information from "other ontological levels of being"; and finally the "prediction" that "a combination of these methods utilizing computer-aided biofeedback monitoring devices" will actually make it possible to "visit 'other' worlds in 'inner' space" (which suggests that the author adheres to the "observer-created" theory of parallel universes)—all this leads us to believe that the author is probably a member of one of the California Travel Cults—as well as an expert *bruja*!

---

23.   **(Anonymous).** *A Collection of Cult Pamphlets, Flyers, Ephemera & Curiosa from the Library of a Traveler* **(Loose-leaf portfolio of photocopied originals) sold by lot, $25**

The unknown compiler of this *Collection* (whom for convenience we'll call "X") left it behind when he "vanished," whence it came into our possession. We know something of the compiler's career from an untitled document written by him and found with the *Collection*, which we call "*The Poetic Journal of a Traveler*" (#24 in this list), as well as a pamphlet believed to be by the same author, *Folklore of the Other Worlds* (#25). (*The Ong's Hat Color Brochure* was also discovered in the same cache, and is sold by us as #13.)

The *Collection* contains the following items:

1) *A History & Catechism of the Moorish Orthodox Church*, which traces the origins of the sect to early (1913) American Black Islam, the "Wandering Bishops," the Beats of the '50s and the psychedelic churches movement of the 60s—deliberately vague about the 70s and 80s however.

2) *The World Congress of Free Religions*, a brochure-manifesto arguing for a "fourth way," a non-authoritarian spiritual movement in opposition to mainstream, fundamentalist and New Age religion. The WCFR is said to include various sects of Discordians, SubGeniuses, Coptic Orthodox People of the Herb, gay ("faery") neo-pagans, Magical Judaism, the Egyptian Church of New Zealand, Kaos Kabal of London, Libertarian Congregationalists, etc.,—and the Moorish Orthodox Church. Several of these sects are implicated in the Conspiracy, but no overt mention of the Travel Cults is made here.

3) *Spiritual Materialism*, by "the New Catholic Church of the Pant-
archy, Hochkapel von SS Max und Marx," a truly weird flyer dedicated
to "Saints" Max Stirner and Karl Marx, representing a group claiming
foundation by the 19th century Individualist Stephen Pearl Andrews,
but more likely begun in the 1980s as a Travel Cult. Uses Nietzsche
to contend that material reality itself constitutes a (or the) spiritual
value and the principle of Infinity "which is expressed in the existence
of many worlds." It argues for a utopia based on "individualism, tele-
pathic socialism, free love, high tech, Stone Age wilderness and quantum weirdness"! No address is given, needless to say.

4) *The Sacred Jihad of Our Lady of Chaos*, this otherwise untrace-
able group calls for "resistance to all attempts to control probability."
It quotes Foucault and Baudrillard on the subject of "disappearance,"
then suggests that "to vanish without having to kill yourself may be
the ultimate revolutionary act... The monolith of Consensus Reality is
riddled with quantum-chaos cracks... Viral attack on all fronts! Victory
to Chaos in *every* world!"

5) A collage, presumably made by X himself, consisting of a "mandala" constructed from cut-outs of Strange Attractors and various Catastrophic topologies interwoven with photos of models clipped from
Italian fashion magazines. Eroticizing the mathematical imagery no
doubt helps one to remember and visualize it while operating the Egg.

---

24. **(Anonymous).** *Poetic Journal of a Traveler; or, A Heresiologist's Guide to Brooklyn* **(Incunabula Press), pamphlet,
$15. Believed to be by "X," the compiler of the** *Collection,*
& transcribed by us from manuscript.)

Apparently X began this MS with the intention of detailing his experiences with a Travel Cult and eventual "translation" to the various alternate-world settlements, but unfortunately abandoned the project early
on, possibly due to PCF interference.

It begins with a summary account of X's spiritual quest, largely among the stranger sects of his native Brooklyn: Santeria in Coney Island, Cabala in Williamsburg, sufis on Atlantic Avenue, etc. He is disappointed or turned away (and even mugged on one occasion). He becomes friendly with a Cuban woman of mixed Spanish, black, amerindian and Chinese ancestry who runs a botanica (magical supplies and herbs). When he asks her about "other worlds," she is evasive but promises to introduce him to someone who knows more about such matters.

She orders her grand-daughter, a 16-year-old named Teofila, to escort X through the "rough neighborhoods" to the old man's shop. The girl is wearing a t-shirt that says "Hyperborean Skateboarding Association," and indeed travels by skateboard, "gliding on ahead of me like Hermes the Psychopomp." X is clearly attracted to Teofila and becomes embarrassedly tongue-tied and awkward.

The old man, called "the Shaykh," who claims to be Sudanese but speaks "pure Alabaman," runs a junk shop and wears a battered old Shriners fez. His attitude toward X is severe at first, but X is enchanted by his rather disjointed rambling and ranting—which reveal a surprisingly wide if erratic reading in Persian poetry, the Bible, Meister Eckhart, William Blake, Yoruba mythology and quantum mechanics. Leaving the girl in the shop, the old man takes X into his back office, "crowded with wildly eclectic junk, naive paintings, cheap orientalismo, Hoodoo candles, jars of flower petals, and an ornate potbellied stove, stoked up to cherryred, suffusing waves of drowsy warmth."

The Shaykh intimidates X into sharing a big pipe of hashish mixed with amber and mescaline, then launches into a stream-of-consciousness attack on "Babylon, the Imperium, the Con, the Big Lie that there's nowhere to go and nothing to buy except their fifth-rate imitations of life, their bullshit pie-in-the-sky religions, cold cults, cold cuts of self-mutilation I call 'em, and woe to Jerusalem!"

X, now "stoned to the gills," falls under the Shaykh's spell and bursts into tears. At once the old man unbends, serves X a cup of tea "sweet-black as Jamaica rum and scented with cardamom," and begins to drop broad hints about "a way out, not to some gnostic-never-land with the body gone like a fart in a sandstorm, no brother, for the Unseen World is not just of the spirit but also the flesh—Jabulsa and Jabulqa, Hyperborea, Hurqalya—they're as real as Brooklyn but a *damn* sight prettier!"

Late afternoon; X must return home before dark, and prepares to take leave of the Shaykh—who gives him a few pamphlets and invites him to return. To X's surprise, Teofila is still waiting outside the shop, and offers to escort him to the subway. The girl is now in a friendlier mood and X less nervous. They strike up a conversation, X asking about Hyperborea and Teofila answering, "Yeah, I know where it is, I've *been* there."

The main narrative ends here, but we have added some other poetic fragments included with the original MS, despite the fact that they might offend some readers, in light of the importance of the "tantrik technique" of other-world Travel. (And let us remind you that a statement of age must be included with every order from Incunabula Inc.). These rather pornographic fragments suggest that X, too shy to attempt anything himself, was in fact seduced by Teofila, and that his subsequent "training" for Egg-navigation consisted of numerous "practice sessions for double-yolking" with a very enthusiastic young tutor.

We believe that X subsequently made an extended visit to America2 and Java2, that he returned to Earth-prime on some Intelligence or sabotage mission for the GFP, that he composed a paper on *Folklore of the Other Worlds* (see #25), that he and Teofila somehow came to the attention of PCF agents in New York, aborted their mission and returned to Java2, where they presumably now reside.

25.   **(Anonymous).** *Folklore of the Other Worlds* **(Incunabula Press, pamphlet, $15. By the same author as #24, transcribed by us from manuscript.)**

Our anonymous Traveler from Brooklyn appears to have composed this little treatise after his first extended stay in E2. It deals with tales of Travelers and inhabitants of the other-world settlements, pioneers' experiences and the like. Of great interest is the claim that ESP and other paranormal abilities increase in the parallel universes, that the effect is magnified by passing through the series of discovered "levels," and that a small band of psychic researchers has therefore settled on Java7, the present frontier world. The "temple" of Hurqalya (or whatever these vast buildings may have been) is used for sessions of meditation, martial arts and psychic experimentation. X claims that telepathy is now accepted as fact "over there," with strong evidence for telekinesis and perhaps even Egg-less Travel.

Also intriguing are various accounts of "spirits" seen or sensed around the settlements, were-animals supposedly glimpsed on higher levels, and legends which have arisen concerning the lost Builders of Hurqalya. Something of a cult has grown up around these hypothetical creatures who (it is said) are "moving toward us even as we move toward them, through the dimensions, through Time—perhaps *backwards* through Time"!

X points out that this legend strikes an eerie resonance with "complex conjugate wave theory" in quantum mechanics, which hypothesizes that the "present" (the megaverse "now") is the result of the meeting of two infinite quantum probability waves, one moving from past to future, the other moving *from future to past*—that space/time is an interference effect of these two waves—and that the many worlds are bubbles on this shoreline!

26.   Eliade, Mircea. *Shamanism: Archaic Techniques of Ecstasy* **(Univ. of Chicago Press), Pb, $30**

This "bible" of the modern neo-shamanic movement also served as a metaphorical scripture for the pioneers of interdimensional consciousness physics and alternate-world explorers. Not only does it contain innumerable practical hints for the Traveler, as well as a spiritual ambience conducive to the proper state of mind for Travel, it is also believed that Eliade's mythic material on the prototypal Stone Age shamans who could *physically* and *actually* visit other worlds, offers strong evidence for the possibility of Egg-less Travel—which however so far remains in the realm of "folklore," speculation and rumor.

27.   Lorde, John. *Maze of Treason* **(Red Knight Books, Wildwood, NJ, 1988), Pb, 204 pp, $10**

You may remember that after the Patty Hearst kidnapping it was discovered that a cheap pornographic thriller, published before the event, seemed to foretell every detail of the story. Jungian synchronicity? Or did the Symbionese Liberation Army read that book and decide to act it out? It remains a mystery.

Maze of Treason is also a pornographic thriller, complete with tawdry 4-color cover, sloppy printing on acidulous pulp, and horrendous style. It's marketed as Science Fiction, however. And there is no mystery about the author's inside knowledge. "John Lorde" not only knows about the Conspiracy, he's obviously *been there*. This book is probably a *Roman à Clef*, as it appears to contain distorted portraits of Sohrawardi and Harjanto (depicted as Fu-Manchu-type villains) as well as several actual agents of both the GFP and PCF—and even a character apparently based on the real-life "X" (#s 24 & 25), author of several titles in our list.

The hero, Jack Masters, is an agent of an unnamed spyforce of American patriots who jokingly call themselves the Quantum Police.

Their mission is to regain control of the alternate worlds for "the forces of reason and order" and "make trouble for agents of chaos in every known universe." The Q-Cops' secret underground HDQ contains a number of Eggs granting access to hidden bases on the other worlds, including "the Other America" and "the Other Indonesia."

Jack Masters is investigating the activities of a Chaote named Ripley Taylor, a black magician who runs a Travel Cult out of a comicbook store in a "racially-mixed neighborhood" of New York. The Cops hope to catch Taylor with his "juvenile delinquent girlfriend," blackmail him and turn him into a double agent.

The hero now becomes involved with Amanita, a beautiful woman performance artist from the Lower East Side who seems to know a lot about Taylor and the Travel Cult, but also seems quite attracted to the virile Jack Masters. At first he suspects her of duplicity, but soon decides he needs to "convert" her by making her "fall for me, and fall *hard*." Jack's problem is that his own "talent" will not suffice for solo Travelling, and in fact he has never managed to "get across"—since the Cops do not practice Tantrik techniques! He suspects her of being an "Other-Worlder" and hopes she can convey him thence via the "infamous 'double-yolk' method."

Meanwhile Taylor has laughed off the blackmail attempt, burned down the comic shop and escaped "into the fourth dimension—or maybe the fifth." Masters heats up his affair with the artist Amanita, and finally convinces her to "translate" him—after three chapters of uninterrupted porno depicting the pair in many little-known ritual practices, so to speak. (The author rises above his own mediocrity here, and attains something like "purple pulp," an inspired gush of horny prose, especially in the oral-genital area.) Masters now rises to the occasion for yet a fourth chapter in which a "government-issue Egg" becomes the setting for a "yab-yum ceremony of searing obscenity."

Immediately upon arrival in "Si Fan" (the author's name for Hurqalya), Amanita betrays our hero and turns him over naked to one of the tribes of "chaos-shamans who inhabit these Lemurian ruins." At this point *Maze* begins to add to our knowledge of the real-life situation by depicting more-or-less accurately the state of affairs and mode of life in present-day Hurqalya, at least as seen through the eyes of a paranoid right-wing spy.

The thousand or so inhabitants have made few changes in Hurqa-lya, preferring a life of "primitive sloth" and minimal meddling with Nature. Sex, hallucinogenic mushrooms and song-improvisation contests comprise the night-life, with days devoted to the serious business of "sorcery, skinnydipping, flintknapping and maybe a couple of hours of desultory fishing or berrypicking." There is no social order. "People with bones in their noses sitting around arguing about Black Hole Theory or recipes for marsupial stew, lazy smoke from a few clan campfires rising through the hazy bluegold afternoon, bees snouting into orchids, signal drum in the distance, Amanita singing an old song by the Inkspots I remember from my childhood..."

Masters—or rather the author—claims to be disgusted by all this "anarchist punk hippy immorality—all this jungle love!"—but his ambivalence is revealed in his continued desire for Amanita, and the ease with which he falls into his own curmudgeonly version of *dolce far niente* in "Si Fan."

We won't give away the rest of the plot, not because it's so great, but because it's largely irrelevant (Taylor flees to distant dimensions, Masters gets Girl and returns to Earth-prime in triumph, etc., etc.)—the book's true value lies in these pictures of daily life in Hurqalya. Sadly, *Maze of Treason* is still our only source for such material.

The Conspiracy to deny the world all knowledge of the Many Worlds is maintained by *both* the forces active in the parallel universes—the GFP and PCF both have their reasons for secrecy, evasion, lies, disinformation, distortion and some of them lost their lives as a result of getting too deeply involved in all this. But we at INCUNABULA believe that truth will out, because it *must*. To stand in the way of it is more dangerous than letting it loose. Freedom of information is our only protection—we will tell all, despite all scorn or threat, and trust that our "going public" will protect us from the outrage of certain private interests—if not from the laughter of the ignorant!

Remember: parallel worlds exist. They have *already been reached*. A vast cover-up denies YOU all knowledge. Only INCUNABULA can enlighten you, because only INCUNABULA *dares.*

Thank You,

Emory Cranston, Prop.

(1991)

Ong's Hat

Dear Glenn,
Recently I did a series of radio shows on chaos theory
for WBAI-FM in New York. As a result I received a lot
of chaos material in the mail, including the enclosed. I
thought it might interest your readers.
— PETER LAMBORN WILSON

▼

ONG'S HAT:
GATEWAY TO THE DIMENSIONS!

A full-color advertising brochure
for the Institute of Chaos Studies and the
Moorish Science Ashram in Ong's Hat,
New Jersey

introduction

You would not be reading this article if you had not already penetrated half-way to the ICS. You have been searching for us without
knowing it, following oblique references in crudely xeroxed marginal samizdat publications, crackpot mystical pamphlets, mail-order
courses in "Kaos Magick"—a paper trail and a coded series of rumors
spread at street level through circles involved in the illicit distribution
of certain controlled substances and the propagation of certain acts of
insurrection against the Planetary Work Machine and the Consensus
Reality—or perhaps through various obscure mimeographed technical
papers on the edges of "chaos science"—through pirate computer networks—or even through pure synchronicity and the pursuit of dreams.
In any case we know something about you, your interests, deeds and
desires, works and days—and we know your address. Otherwise...you
would not be reading this.

background

During the 1970s and '80s, "chaos" began to emerge as a new scientific paradigm, on a level of importance with Relativity and Quantum Mechanics. It was born out of the mixing of many different sciences—weather prediction, Catastrophe Theory, fractal geometry, and the rapid development of computer graphics capable of plunging into the depths of fractals and "strange attractors"; hydraulics and fluid turbulence, evolutionary biology, mind/brain studies and psychopharmacology also played major roles in forming the new paradigm.

The slogan "order out of chaos" summed up the gist of this science, whether it studied the weird fractional-dimensional shapes underlying sworls of cigarette smoke or the distribution of colors in marbled paper—or else dealt with "harder" matters such as heart fibrillation, particle beams or population vectors.

However, by the late '80s it began to appear as if this "chaos movement" had split apart into two opposite and hostile world-views, one placing emphasis on chaos itself, the other on *order*.

According to the latter sect—the Determinists—chaos was the enemy, randomness a force to be overcome or denied. They experienced the new science as a final vindication of Classical Newtonian physics, and as a weapon to be used *against* chaos, a tool to map and predict reality itself. For them, chaos was death and disorder, entropy and waste.

The opposing faction however experienced chaos as something benevolent, the necessary matrix out of which arises spontaneously an infinity of variegated forms—a pleroma rather than an abyss—a principle of continual creation, unstructured, fecund, beautiful, a spirit of wildness. These scientists saw chaos theory as vindication of Quantum indeterminacy and Gödel's Proof, promise of an open-ended universe, Cantorian infinities of potential...chaos as *health*.

Easy to predict which of these two schools of thought would receive vast funding and support from governments, multi-nationals and intelligence agencies. By the end of the decade, "Quantum/Chaos" had been forced underground, virtually censored by prestigious scientific journals—which published only papers by Determinists.

The dissidents were reduced to the level of the *margin*—and there they found themselves part of yet another branch of the paradigm, the underground of cultural chaos—the "magicians"—and of political chaos-extremist anti-authoritarian "mutants."

Unlike Relativity, which deals with the Macrocosm of outer space, and Quantum, which deals with the Microcosm of particle physics, chaos science takes place largely within the Mesosphere—the world as we experience it in "everyday life," from dripping faucets to banners flapping in the autumn breezes. Precisely for this reason useful experimental work in chaos can be carried on without the hideous expense of cyclotrons and orbital observatories.

So even when the leading theoreticians of Quantum/Chaos began to be fired from university and corporate positions, they were still able to pursue certain goals. Even when they began to suffer political pressures as well, and sought refuge and space among the mutants and marginals, still they persevered. By a paradox of history, their poverty and obscurity forced them to narrow the scope of their research to precisely those areas which would ultimately produce concrete results—pure math, and the mind—simply because these areas were relatively inexpensive.

Up until the economic crash of '87, the "alternative network" amounted to little more than a nebulous weave of pen-pals and computer enthusiasts, Whole Earth nostalgists, futurologists, anarchists, food cranks, neo-pagans and cultists, self-publishing punk poets, armchair schizophrenics, survivalists and mail artists. The Crash however opened vast but hard-to-see cracks in the social and economic control structures of America. Gradually the marginals and mutants began to fill up those fissures with the webs of their own networking. Bit by bit they created a genuine black economy, as well as a shifting insubstantial "autonomous zone," impossible to map but real enough in its various manifestations.

The orphaned scientists of Q/C theory fell into this invisible anti-empire like a catalyst—or perhaps it was the other way around. In either case, something crystallized. To explain the precipitation of this jewel, we must move on to the specific cases, people and stories.

history

The Moorish Orthodox Church of America is an offshoot of the Moorish Science Temple, the New World's first Islamic heretical sect, founded by a black circus magician named Noble Drew Ali in Newark, New Jersey in 1913. In the 1950s some white jazz musicians and poets who held "passports" in the M.S.T. founded the Moorish Orthodox Church, which also traced its spiritual ancestry to various "Wandering Bishops" loosely affiliated with the Old Catholic Church and schisms of Syrian Orthodoxy.

In the '60s the church acquired a new direction from the Psychedelic Movement, and for a while maintained a presence at Timothy Leary's commune in Millbrook, New York. At the same time the discovery of sufism led certain of its members to undertake journeys to the East.

One of these Americans, known by the Moorish name Wali Fard, travelled for years in India, Persia, and Afghanistan, where he collected an impressive assortment of exotic initiations: Tantra in Calcutta, from an old member of the Bengali Terrorist Party; sufism from the Ovayssi Order in Shiraz, which rejects all human masters and insists on visionary experience; and finally, in the remote Badakhshan Province of Afghanistan, he converted to an archaic form of Ismailism (the so-called Assassins) blended out of Buddhist Yab-Yum teachings, indigenous shamanic sorcery and extremist Shiite revolutionary philosophy—worshippers of the *Umm al-kitab*, the "Matrix Book."

Up until the Soviet invasion of Afghanistan and the reactionary orthodox "revolution" in Iran, Fard carried on trade in carpets and other well-known Afghan exports. When history forced him to return to America in 1978, he was able to launder his savings by purchasing about 200 acres of land in the New Jersey Pine Barrens. Around the turn of the decade he moved into an old rod & gun club on the property along with several runaway boys from Paramus, New Jersey, and an anarchist lesbian couple from Brooklyn, and founded the Moorish Science Ashram.

Through the early-to-mid-'80s the commune's fortunes fluctuated (sometimes nearly flickering out). Fard self-published a series of xeroxed "Visionary Recitals" in which he attempted a synthesis of heretical and antinomian spirituality, post-Situationist politics, and chaos science. After the Crash, a number of destitute Moors and sympathizers began turning up at the Ashram seeking refuge. Among them were two young chaos scientists recently fired from Princeton (on a charge of "seditious nonsense"), a brother and sister, Frank and Althea Dobbs.

The Dobbs twins spent their early childhood on a UFO-cult commune in rural Texas, founded by their father, a retired insurance salesman who was murdered by rogue disciples during a revival in California. One might say that the siblings had a head start in chaos—and the Ashram's modus vivendi suited them admirably. (The Pine Barrens have often been called "a perfect place for a UFO landing.") They settled into an old Airstream trailer and constructed a crude laboratory in a rebuilt barn hidden deep in the Pines. Illegal sources of income were available from agricultural projects, and the amorphous community took shape around the startling breakthroughs made by the Dobbs twins during the years around the end of the decade.

As undergraduates at the University of Texas the siblings had produced a series of equations which, they felt certain, contained the seeds of a new science they called "cognitive chaos." Their dismissal from Princeton followed their attempt to submit these theorems, along with a theoretical/philosophical system built upon them, as a joint PhD thesis.

On the assumption that brain activity can be modeled as a "fractal universe," an outré topology interfacing with both random and determined forces, the twins' theorems showed that consciousness itself could be presented as a set of "strange attractors" (or "patterns of chaos") around which specific neuronal activity would organize itself. By a bizarre synthesis of Mandelbrot and Cantor, they "solved the problem" of n-dimensional attractors, many of which they were able to generate on Princeton's powerful computers before their hasty departure. While realizing the ultimately indeterminate nature of these "mind maps," they felt that by attaining a thorough (non-intuitive and intuitive) grasp of the actual *shapes* of the attractors, one could "ride with chaos" somewhat as a "lucid dreamer" learns to contain and direct the process of REM sleep. Their aborted thesis suggested a boggling array of benefits which might accrue from such links between cybernetic processes and awareness itself, including the exploration of the brain's unused capacities, awareness of the morphogenic field and thus conscious control of autonomic functions, mind-directed repair of tissue at the cellular/genetic level (control over most diseases and the aging process), and even a direct perception of the Heisenbergian behavior of matter (a process they called "surfing the wave function"). Their thesis advisor told them that even the most modest of these proposals would suffice for their expungement from the Graduate Faculty—and if the whole concept (including theorems) were not such obvious lunacy, he would have reported them to the FBI as well.

Two more scientists—already residents of Ong's Hat—joined with Fard and the twins in founding the Institute of Chaos studies. By sheer "chance" their work provided the perfect counterparts to the Dobbs' research. Harold Acton, an expatriate British computer and reality-hacker, had already linked 64 second-hand personal computers into a vast ad-hoc system based on his own *I Ching* oriented speculations. And Martine Kallikak, a native of the Barrens from nearby Chatsworth, had set up a machine shop.

Ironically, Martine's ancestors once provided guinea pigs for a notorious study in eugenics carried out in the 1920s at the Vineland NJ State Home for the Insane. Published as a study in "heredity and feeblemindness," the work proclaimed poverty, non-ordinary sexuality, reluctance to hold a steady job, and enjoyment of intoxicants as *proofs* of genetic decay—and thus made a lasting contribution to the legend of bizarre and lovecraftian Piney backwoodspeople, incestuous hermits of the bogs.

Martine had long since proven herself a *bricoleuse*, electronics buff and back-lot inventor of great genius and artistry. With the arrival of the Dobbs twins, she discovered her true métier in the realization of various devices for the implementation of their proposed experiments.

The synergy level at the ICS exceeded all expectations. Contacts with other underground experts in various related fields were maintained by "black modem" as well as personal visits to the Ashram. The spiritual rhythms permeating the place proved ideal: periods of dazed lazy contemplation and applied hedonics alternating with "peak" bursts of self-overcoming activity and focused attention. The hodgepodge of "Moorish Science" (Tantra, sufism, Ismaili esotericism, alchemy and psychopharmacology, bio-feedback and "brain machine" meditation techniques, etc.) seemed to harmonize in unexpectedly fruitful ways with the "pure" science of the ICS.

Under these conditions progress proved amazingly swift, stunning even the Institute's founders. Within a year major advances had been made in all the fields predicted by the equations. Somewhat more than three years after founding there occurred *the* breakthrough, the discovery which served to re-orient our entire project in a new direction: the Gate.

But to explain the Gate we must retrace some steps, and reveal exactly the purposes and goals of the ICS and Moorish Science Ashram—the curriculum upon which our activities are based, and which constitutes our raison d'etre.

the curriculum

The original and still ultimate concern of our community is the enhancement of consciousness and consequent enlargement of mental, emotional and psychic activities. When the Ashram was founded by W. Fard the only means available for this work were the bagful of oriental and occultist meditational techniques he had learned in Central Asia, the first-generation "mind machines" developed during the '80s, and the resources of exotic pharmacology.

With the first successes of the Dobbs twins' research, it became obvious to us that the spiritual knowledge of the Ashramites could be re-organized into a sort of preparatory course of training for workers in "Cognitive Chaos." This does not mean we surrendered our original purpose— attainment of non-ordinary consciousness—but simply that ICS work could be viewed as a prolongation and practical application of the Ashram work. The theorems allow us to re-define "self liberation" to include physical self-renewal and life-extension as well as the exploration of material reality which (we maintain) remains *one* with the reality of consciousness. In this project, the kind of awareness fostered by meditational techniques plays a part just as vital as the *techné* of machines and the pure mentation of mathematics.

In this scenario, the theorems—or at least a philosophical understanding of them—serve the purpose of an abstract *icon* for contemplation. Thus the theorems can be absorbed or englobed to the point where they become part of the inner structure (or "deep grammar") of the mind itself.

In the first stage, intellectual comprehension of the theorems parallels spiritual work aimed at refining the faculty of *attention*. At the same time a kind of psychic anchor is constructed, a firm grounding in celebratory body-awareness. The erotic and sensual for us cannot be ritualized and aimed at anything "higher" than themselves—rather, they constitute the very *ground* on which our dance is performed, and the atmosphere or taste which permeates our whole endeavor.

We symbolize this first course of work by the tripartite Sanskrit term *satchitananda*, "Being/consciousness/bliss"—the ontological level symbolized by the theorems, the psychological level by the meditation, the level of joy by our "tantrik" activity.

The second course (which can begin at any time during or after the first) involves practical instruction in a variety of "hard sciences," especially evolutionary biology and genetics, brain physiology, Quantum Mechanics and computer hacking. We have no need for these disciplines in any academic sense—in fact our work has already overturned many existing paradigms in these fields and rendered the textbooks useless for our purposes—so we have tailored these courses specifically for relevance to our central concern, and jettisoned everything extraneous.

At this point a Fellow of the ICS is prepared for work with the device we call the "Egg." This consists of a modified sensory-deprivation chamber in which attention can be focused on a computer terminal and screen. Electrodes are taped to various body parts to provide physiological data which is fed into the computer. The explorer now dons a peculiar helmet, a highly sophisticated fourth-generation version of the early "brain machines," which can sonically stimulate brain cells either globally or locally and in various combinations, thus directing not only "brain waves" but also highly specific mental-physical functions. The helmet is also plugged into the computer and provides feedback in various programmed ways.

The explorer now undertakes a series of exercises in which the theorems are used to generate graphic animations of the "strange attractors" which map various states of consciousness, setting up feedback loops between this "iconography" and the actual states themselves, which are in turn generated through the helmet simultaneously with their representation on the screen. Certain of these exercises involve the "alchemical" use of mind-active drugs, including new vasopressin derivatives, beta-endorphins and hallucinogens (usually in "threshold" dosages). Some of these tinctures are simply to provide active-relaxation and focused-attention states, others are specifically linked to the requirements of "Cognitive Chaos" research.

Even in the earliest and crudest stages of the egg's development the ICS founders quickly realized that many of the Dobbs twins' PhD thesis predictions might be considered cautious or conservative. Enhanced control of autonomous body functions was attained even in the second-generation version, and the third provided a kind of bathysphere capable of "diving down" even to the cellular level. Certain unexpected side-effects included phenomena usually classified as paranormal. We knew we were not hallucinating all this, quite bluntly, because we obtained concrete and measurable results, not only in terms of "yogic powers" (such as suspended animation, "inner heat," lucid dreaming and the like) but also in observable benefits to health: rapid healing, remission of chronic conditions, *absence of disease.*

At this point in development of the egg (third generation) the researchers attempted to "descend" (like SciFi micronauts) to the Quantum level.

Perhaps the thorniest of all Quantum paradoxes involves the "collapse of the wave function"—the state of Schrödinger's famous cat. When does a wave "become" a particle? At the moment of observation? If so does this implicate human consciousness in the actual Q-structure of reality itself? By observing do we in effect "create?" The ICS team's ultimate dream was to "ride the wave" and actually experience (rather than merely observe) the function-collapse. Through "participation" in Q-events, it was hoped that the observer/observed duality could be overcome or evaded.

This hope was based on rather "orthodox" Copenhagian interpretations of Quantum reality. After some months of intensive work, however, no one had experienced the sought-for and expected "moment"... each wave seemed to flow as far as one cared to ride it, like some perfect surfer's curl extending to infinity. We began to suspect that the answer to the question "when?" might be "never!"

This contingency had been described rigorously in only one interpretation of Q-reality, that of J. Wheeler—who proved that the wave function need never collapse provided that every Q-event gives rise to an "alternate world" (the Cat is *both* alive and dead).

To settle this question a fourth generation of the Egg was evolved and tested, while simultaneously a burst of research was carried out in the abstruse areas of "Hilbert space" and the topology of n-dimensional geometry, on the intuitive assumptions that new "attractors" could thereby be generated and used to visualize or "grok" the transitions between alternate universes.

Again the ICS triumphed... although the immediate success of the fourth-generation Egg provoked a moment of fear and panic unmatched in the whole history of "Cognitive Chaos."

The first run-through of the "Cat" program was undertaken by a young staff-member of great brilliance (one of the original Paramus runaways) whose nickname happened to be Kit—and it happened to take place on the Spring Equinox. At the precise moment the heavens changed gears, so to speak, the entire Egg vanished from the laboratory.

Consternation would be a mild term for what ensued. For about seven minutes the entire ICS lost its collective cool. At that point however the Egg reappeared with its passenger intact and beaming... like Alice's Cheshire Cat rather than Schrödinger's poor victim.

He had succeeded in riding the wave to its "destination"—an alternate universe. He had observed it and—in his words—"memorized its address." Instinctively he felt that certain dimensional universes must act as "strange attractors" in their own right, and are thus far easier to access (more "probable") than others. In practical terms, he had not been dissolved but had found the way to a "universe next door."

The Gateway had been opened.

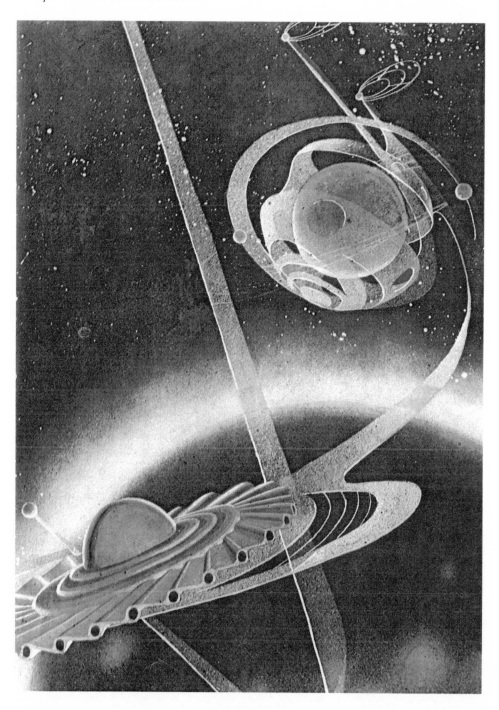

Where is Ong's Hat?

According to Piney legend, the village of Ong's Hat was founded sometime in the 19th century when a man named Ong threw his hat up in the air, landed it in a tree and was unable to retrieve it (we like to think it vanished into another world). By the 1920s all traces of settlement other than a few crumbling chimneys had faded away. But the name appealed so much to cartographers that some of them retained it—a dot representing nothing in the midst of the most isolated flat dark scrub-pines and sandy creeks in all the vast, empty and perhaps haunted Barrens. W. Fard's acreage lies in the invisible suburbs of this invisible town, of which we are the sole inhabitants. You can find it easily on old survey maps, even trace out the old dirt road leading into the bogs where a little square represents the decrepit "Ong's Hat Rod & Gun Club," the original residence. However, you might discover that finding the ICS itself is not so simple.

If you compare your old survey map with the very latest, you will note that our area lies perilously close to the region infamous in recent years, the South Jersey Nuclear Waste Dump near Fort Dix. The "accident" that occurred there has made the Barrens even more empty and unpopular, as many hard-core Pineys fled the pollution, melting into the state's last untouched wilderness. The electrified fence shutting off the deadly zone runs less than a mile above our enclave.

The Accident occurred while we were in the first stages of developing the fourth-generation Egg, the Gate. At the time we had no idea of its full potential. However all of us, except for the very youngest (who were evacuated), had by then been trained in elementary self-directed regeneration. A few tests proved that with care and effort we could resist at least the initial onslaught of radiation sickness. We decided to stick it out, at least until "the authorities" (rather than the dump) proved too hot to endure.

Once the Gate was discovered, we realized the situation had been saved. The opening, and actual interdimensional travel, can only be effected by a fully trained "cognitive chaote;" so the first priority was to complete the course for all our members. A technique for "carrying" young children was developed (it seems not to work for adult "non-initiates"), and it was discovered that all inanimate matter within the Egg is also carried across with the operator.

Little by little we carted our entire establishment (including most of the buildings) across the topological abyss. Unlike Baudelaire who pleaded, "Anywhere!—so long as it's out of this world!" we knew where we were going. Ong's Hat has indeed vanished from New Jersey, except for the hidden laboratory deep in the backwoods where the Gate "exists."

On the other side of the Gate we found a Pine Barrens similar to ours but in a world which apparently never developed human life. Of course we have since visited a number of other worlds, but we decided to colonize this one, our first newfoundland. We still live in the same scattering of weather-gray shacks, Airstream trailers, recycled chicken coops, and mail-order yurts, only a bit more spread out—and considerably more relaxed. We're still dependent on your world for many things—from coffee to books to computers—and in fact we have no intention of cutting ourselves off like anchorites and merely scampering into a dreamworld. We intend to spread the word.

The colonization of new worlds—even an infinity of them—can never act as a panacea for the ills of Consensus Reality—only as a palliative. We have always taken our diseases with us to each new frontier... everywhere we go we exterminate aborigines and battle with our weapons of law and order against the chaos of reality. But this time, we believe, the affair will go differently—because this time the journey outward can only be made simultaneously with the journey inward—and because this bootstrap-trick can only be attained by a consciousness which, to a significant degree, has overcome itself, liberated itself from self-sickness—and "realized itself."

Not that we think ourselves saints, or try to behave morally, or imagine ourselves a super-race, absolved from good and evil. Simply, we like to consider ourselves awake when we're awake, sleeping when we sleep. We enjoy good health. We have learned that desire demands the other just as it demands the self. We see no end to growth while life lasts, no cessation of unfolding, of continual outpouring of form from chaos. We're moving on, nomads or monads of the dimensions. Sometimes we feel almost satisfied... at other times, terrified.

Meanwhile our agents of chaos remain behind to set up ICS courses, distribute Moorish Orthodox literature (a major mask for our propaganda) to subvert and evade our enemies...We haven't spoken yet of our enemies. Indeed there remains much we have not said. This text, disguised as a sort of New Age vacation brochure, must fall silent at this point, satisfied that it has embedded within itself enough clues for its intended readers (who are already halfway to Ong's Hat in any case) but not enough for those of little faith to follow.

CHAOS NEVER DIED!

(1991)

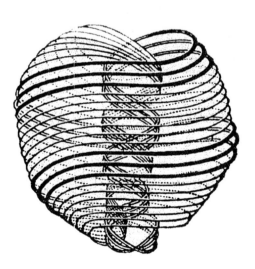

PASTORAL LETTER:
A Fragment

Imagine an alternate dimension where
dervishes are roaming around America
sects of Swedenborgian hobos, etc.
You're there camping in the cemetery
long black hair in tangles ghostwhite face

≈⌒∝

Sion County is remote, rural, and poor, and always has been. Around 1870 a breakaway sect of German Amish-type farmers—the Sabbatarian Anabaptists or the "Seventh Day Dunkers," moved there from Pennsylvania and settled down in the river valleys of the county's northeast.

In the mountainous northwest lies the small reservation of a band of Iroquois. The Indians and the Dunkers have always held to distant but amicable relations though nowadays the Protestants tend to disapprove of the bingo and fireworks concessions with which the tribe supplements its income.

In the 1960s a number of hippies invaded Sion County. At first there was some conflict with the locals, but by now the hippies have mellowed and settled down. Some of them joined a small eccentric split-off sub-sect of the Dunkers. Some practice permaculture or alternative agriculture; a few of their farms are very serious and self-sufficient; others work in "green" construction and trades, including black-smithing and carriage-building, since so many locals use horses rather than cars. And of course some grow hemp.

By the 1980s, the county had begun to rival the emerald Triangle, and the Feds were beginning to sniff around. Something had to be done. A "Combine" was organized among the hemp growers and

smugglers, and an interesting political force emerged based on anonymous funders and a small libertarian faction of the local Republican Party. The Combine managed not only to infiltrate the Republicans but also to win control of the county, including the offices of sheriff, district attorney, judge, etc. The Combine also earned the support of the Dunkers by opposing "development" and transmuted under this weird Libertarian/Welfarist coalition.

Everything possible is voluntarized—but funded by the County. The one public high school in the region is privatized but taken over by a non-profit alternative education group funded by the County. Zoning is more-or-less abolished, but a Green Covenant is circulated, and any non-signers are boycotted or otherwise driven out of the region. An extremist vigilante group has vandalized or destroyed a few structures deemed ecologically offensive; somehow the Sheriff never manages to apprehend any of these mysterious eco-warriors.

The county capital, Sion City (pop. 18,000 or so), has the plastic rural highway fast-food sprawl and rundown 19th century backstreet gloom of any similar sad place in the bioregion—but in a way this is mere camouflage. The fast-food franchises have been bought-out by whole-food/organic collectives, which are funded by the County. Still they use names like Tastee Burgers or Salad Bar & Grill; the locals get a lot of amusement out of this sly nomenclature. The Public Library consists of four pink double-wide mobile homes, but contains amazing collections. It's as if the whole town were a disguise.

"The danger," says the Sheriff, "is that the place could become too damn picturesque. Dunkers in black hats in their buggies, a few Indians in traditional gear, spaced-out tie-dye types: a tourist trap, Woodstock! We don't like tourists around here, do we! And as Debord would put it, we don't want to work at the job of representing some quaint notion of authenticity just to become the Exotic Other for a media-poisoned shower of zombie voyeurs!"

Up-country, however, there's no pretence of normalcy. The Dunkers are living in the 18th century; some of the hippies and Indians are heading back toward the Stone Age. The remotest valleys are given over to hemp plantations and/or bizarre drop-out cults. Over a third of the County has no electricity, other than a bit of solar, and no mail delivery. The Combine or the County own much of the wildest land in various forms, including parks and preserves.

The Sheriff told me, "Naturally, we 'deplore' the idea of funding utopia by crime. I admit that Sion County has some disagreeable aspects. But how can you hope to maintain even such a flawed and low-level utopia in a 'time of war' without some alternate economy? A Green Liberated Zone would be impossible; we all know it wouldn't be permitted. We try to think global—but we have got to act local."

*

"Maybe you'd prefer some Jeremiah on thorazine stumbling out of the Time Magazine of your head—hollywood jerusalem grand guignol cheapjack prognostications of nuclear ho-hum & SciFi african plagues—Y2K, harmonic convergence, yuppie Rapture—a culture gets the armegeddon it deserves—fire ice whimper bang or eternal sit-com, no, it's all far more interesting than we deserve."

—interview with the Sheriff

*

Everyone's bewitched but no one cares
we have one universal evil eye to share
like flies beguiled by television's glare
or three ugly sisters with their empty stares.

> There's always a worldly world and one to flee
> into some desert no one else can see.

(A Word from the Abbot)

A secret unknown to the worldly about the desert: it's a positive ple-roma of pleasure compared to the arid deathscape of vespuccian/jerk kultur, that bleeding Babylon without the courage of its convictions—seduction without desire—the Universal Mall—safety rules, litigation, crash-worship, spleen, worldwide surveillance. Yes by comparison a dank cave, solitary pine barren, silent summer mountain—the "stu-pidity of rural life" (Marx)—seems like wallowing in luxury billions couldn't buy. The real ascetics are gritting their teeth in traffic jams, TV/PC screens bathing them in leprosy-light, other people's music, vicious boredom. Anyone who doesn't go postal deserves beatification.

꽃

The Monastery of St. John-in-the-Wilderness was built in 1910 by a group of Anglican Benedictine monks who intended to proselytize the nearby Indian reservation. But after a dim career it burned down in 1963 and the Church sold the ruin and the land (hundreds of acres) to an investor who later sold it to the Combine.

The monastery gardens and greenhouses were taken over by the Society for the Interiorization of Lost Knowledge (SILK), a small group of Combine research "scientists" who began experimenting with ethno-botany and bio-assay work. They constructed a secret under-ground "alchemical" lab.

The ruined monastery and the ramshackle but habitable Abbot's House or Abbey were turned over to another group that organized itself as the Monastery of St. John-in-the-Wilderness, Order of the Resurrection, Anglican Benedictine (Non-juring): the "Greenfriars."

The Christian identity is useful as camouflage, but some of the members are into it sincerely. They perform regular masses in the Abbot's Chapel, and in summer organize "Sacred Concerts & Festivals" in the picturesque and spruced-up ruins of the old monastery.

Some of these festivals are fuelled by the very potent liquors and concoctions of SILK, and some of the monks work in SILK's gardens (for surprisingly healthy salaries paid in cash). The monks grow vegetables and keep a few chickens and goats, but are not involved in subsistence farming. Needless to say, the Order receives a grant from the County in return for leasing some of their remoter acreage to the Combine.

About half the brothers and sisters live in the old Abbot's House, and half are scattered through the woods in various caves, Taoist huts, Franciscan oratories, or prefab yurts. Besides the monks themselves there is also a "tertiary order" of friends, associates, allies, relatives, regular guests, and correspondents—maybe 20 fulltime live-ins and 100 occasional "retreatants."

Letter From the Abbot

The Rule of the Monastery is No Rule: anarcho-monachism. The monks have adopted a Benedictine identity only because the original foundation was Benedictine. But in fact, they've found some inspiration in St. Benedict's Rule. Once the bits about chastity, obedience, humility, punishment, and excommunication were deleted, they still liked the basic idea. In the original text, they found a description of the "four kinds of monks, including the 'Sarabaites,' which are the worst kind—unschooled by any rule. Their only law is the pleasure of their desires; whatever they wish or choose, they call holy. They consider whatever they dislike unlawful." Half-jestingly, the monks claim to follow the Sarabaite Rite.

They've retained Benedictine titles and forms of organization: an Abbot, Canons to assist the Abbot, a Cellarer (logistics and supplies), Provost (ritualist), and Porter (security). They follow the rules of weekly kitchen service and weekly Reader, and also the Rule of One Hemina (1/4 liter) per day allowance of good wine. They wear, both sexes, an adapted version of the Benedictine habit—homespun green—at least on formal occasions.

But aside from monkish play and conviviality what hold them together are common interests. The first and all-embracing one is negation—a desire or need to escape from the vulgar materialist world; to retreat, whether for spiritual or political or even "military" reasons; whether permanently or periodically.

end of Letter From the Abbot

When you're beaten Von Clausewitz calls for retreat
rather than senseless going down in defeat.
Query: have we retreated far enough?
invisible yet? translucent? gossamer stuff?

Militant monks know when to head for the mountains
for a century of boxing practice.

A monastic order founded and decreed
in the hinterland beyond the emerald city
the hidden Imam's jasper isle: a seed exempt from the
gaze of the dead and their sterile pity.

Li Po could kick back and unplug the phone
uncork some applejack, feel right at home.

Once I saw green moss growing inside a Dublin omni-
bus—like Dali's "Rainy Taxi." If science has conquered
nature why does it keep beating the dead horse?
The next stage: mail-order monasticism. Text itself as
ectoplasmic reverie. Dear Reader:
a message from the Abbé: to each their own cinnabar
grotto or Egyptian cave.

Hocus Pocus means this is the body
just as much puzzle as soul
whatever New Age twaddle seems to work
channeling the old black mole

We know our Blake and Paracelsus. Nobody here but
us Nolans. Mushrooms and the voices of the dead:
exfoliation of spirits.
According to Gustav Meyerink the nausea that over-
comes us occasionally even in museums must arise
from the fact that sooner or later everything made by
humans begins
to stink of the charnel house.

The conquistadors forgot that they themselves
were animals not aristotelian elves
"arguing with something Plato said"
or tidying up their vast linnaean shelves

If only our bad karma would permit it
I'd like us to be ornamental hermits
not cranks who can barely keep their logs afloat
or dionysiacs without a sacrificial goat.

> There I see us bathed in light in rain
> hoping Romanticism didn't die in vain
> saying our beads or inviting each other to supper
> wreathed in clouds and overcoming pain.

꙰

For various motives both practical and theoretical, the Greenfriars have adopted a neo-Luddite approach to tech that owes much to the nearby Dunkers—especially since the Anabaptists' shops and workshops provide the tools and skills needed for a comfortable low-tech life. Moreover, 'Whole Earth Catalogue'-styled tech can be used to supplement Dunker resources since the monks have no religious injunctions to observe against zippers or can-openers. They even keep an old pick-up truck for emergencies, though they prefer horses.

SILK uses solar and other off-grid sources of electricity but the monastery and Abbot's House are un-powered and lit by candles and oil lamps. The Sacred Concerts and other monastic events utilize daylight or torchlight, etc. The basic rule of all Luddism, whether religious or secular, is to use only technology that will not "injure the commonality" — therefore they agree to have (on the premises anyway) no computer, no TV, no telephone, nothing to replace human contact and connection with mediated representation (as the Sheriff would say).

Perhaps there's something a bit precious and artificial about this luddery, since the monks are not self-sustaining like the Dunkers or the more successful permaculturists. They've made certain choices on the basis of pleasure and beauty. As the Abbot says, "We're not really renouncing anything... nice. All of us feel the absence of electricity as an immense luxury. Our velvet nights are set with more than stars." Some of the hermits have their own hot tubs.

On the positive side, the Order's common interests center on "lost knowledge." They believe that their research may help to inspire and even direct the growth of a global green spiritual movement. As Universalists, they nevertheless have no truck with any New-Age multiculti interpretations of "tolerance"; as the Unabomber said, "You can do anything you want—as long as it's unimportant." Rather, they seek certain non-negotiable constellations within all spiritual human manifestations, and on these, they maintain strict intolerance and an unwillingness to compromise.

They're also very interested in secrets, which they define as anything not found on TV or the Internet. The Abbot says, "We should cultivate secrets against the day when the unknown might regain its power."

The brothers and sisters follow their own interests but regular sessions are held for discussion and development of group projects. One major interest for some lies in the "Western occult tradition," especially serious Renaissance hermeticism and alchemy. Other shared research includes Christian ritual, particularly chanting, which is practiced for its "psychedelic" effects (and as rehearsal for Sacred Concerts). Fancy gardening— flowers and herbs for tinctures and distillations— "spagyric medicine." There's a fad for calligraphy and copying manuscripts, which generates a bit of extra income as well. They spend most of their "grant" on books, although they also have an excellent 2-inch telescope that provides a lot of entertainment. This is an homage to Johannes Kelpius, the German Rosicrucian who founded "The Woman in the Wilderness" in Pennsylvania in 1694. He brought to America: the first serious telescope, to scan the skies for signs of the coming End!; the first harpsichord; one of the first printing presses. He admired the Indians' religion, and lived in a cave practicing alchemy and composing hymns.

Quilting bees are held on winter evenings with readings from literature and philosophy like the Benedictines—and monks are devoted to *viva voce* reading—like the old anarchist Egyptian and Cuban cigar workers, or the radical tailors in 18th century London. Dining well is another shared obsession, at least with the group that cooks and eats in the Abbot's House, who claim inspiration from Rabelais, from Fourier's "Gastrosophy," and chapter one of Brillat-Savarin's *Physiology of Taste*. By contrast, some of the hermits are strict vegetarians or raw foodists, etc.

It may be that some of the monks are engaging in "revolutionary activity"— but what exactly? since they could scarcely be preparing for armed insurgency…who knows? Maybe they're growing mushrooms for the combine, or counterfeiting Euro-dollars, or providing safe caves for anti-global activists on the lam. Maybe they've made a breakthrough in occult science—say, the therapeutic use of hieroglyphic emblems to "de-program" human awareness from media/consumer trance? Or maybe it's all another layer of camouflage, like the famous ghost that haunts the monastery and keeps idle gawkers and tourists away.

The Greenfriars consider themselves committed to certain local things and people because they're living in a certain place and want to remain there. They maintain collegially close relations with some of the elders on the Reservation, and a few pious ecstatics amongst the Sabbatarians, but they also see themselves in the American Romantic tradition, as adherents of the "Religion of Nature" of the Transcendentalists and Hudson River School painters. And needless to say, Sion County is beautiful and relatively unspoiled, at least in the northern mountains. According to… [text breaks off]

In mourning for the idea of the woods
psychic space/time pollution blues
almost as bad as being in love
this thinking about distant mountains and money
Seems you can't get one without the other

no car no hunt club no socialism
property tax on the taoist hermitage
electromagnetism no peace no quiet
Knowledge of mountains as source of pain
but dreamy (an anaesthetic revelation)
a numbness every bit as beguiling
as real estate itself: Atavistic
the summer camp the tactical retreat
astral travel on February nights.

GLATISANT AND GRAIL:
an Arthurian fragment

by the Chevalier Isador de Boron
translated by Peter Lamborn Wilson

This "Arthurian fragment" appeared in the *Cahiers Rosicruciens IV* (Paris, 1908), a publication of the Salon Rose + Croix, edited by the eccentric visionary and founder of the Salon, Sâr Péladan. The same issue includes a notice of Erik Satie's "Rosicrucian Music," and a long essay on "speculative alchemy" by Sâr Péladan himself. The Chevalier de Boron, a minor luminary of the Symbolist/Occultist ferment of the period, was born in 1874 as Isadore Cohen, and is said to have died in 1925 somewhere in the Middle East, perhaps the Yemen. A few poems and essays are scattered amongst the smaller and more Decadent Parisian journals, and he wrote at least one novel, *Elagabale*, set in ancient Rome (which I have so far been unable to locate).

On the textual evidence in *Glatisant and Grail* and a few poems of the '20s, I would guess that the Chevalier ended (like many French occultists) as a convert to Islam, perhaps the Fatimid branch of Ismailism, the so-called Bohras, whose "Chief Propagandist" or Sultan still resided in the Yemen at that time (the present incumbent lives in India). The Chevalier's life and works no doubt deserve further study. André Gide (who ran into de Boron in Tunisia) referred to him as "an interesting charlatan," and Tristan Tzara called him "an object of dadaist admiration," apparently in reference to his habit of appearing in Montmartre cafes in full Ceremonial Magic regalia.

De Boron obviously re-named himself in honor either of Robert de Boron, one of the most mystical of the late medieval Romancers, or else more probably Robert's companion (and relative?) Elie de Boron, author of the *Palamydes*. Unfortunately this work has never been translated or even published in a modern edition, although it is said to have been a favorite of Frederick II and Ariosto. Presumably it bears some relation to the compilation by Rusticano da Pisa (the prison-mate and amanuensis of Marco Polo). No doubt some of the more original-seeming elements in our Chevalier's "fragment" owe their inspiration to these sources.

Other apparent borrowings or inspirations include the *Mabinogion* and the lovely reconstruction of the *Tristam* by Bedier, as well as Von Eschenbach's version of the Grail with its specific (yet maddeningly elusive) references to Islamic source material. The Chevalier's text is a "fragment" in the same way certain 18th century aristocrats built picturesque "ruins" on their estates (and even hired "hermits" to live in them). *Glatisant and Grail* is like some "moorish pavilion" in a Paris suburb, cobbled together out of bits of orientalism and romanticism, decorated in the spirit of Baudelaire's Club des Haschischiens or Macgregor Mathers' Temple of Isis. It is fake—but it has a certain charm.

The most obvious source for *Glatisant and Grail* is Malory's great *Morte d'Arthur*. The Chevalier's "plot" (such as it is) clearly intends to explain various mysteries surrounding the figure of the Saracen knight in Malory, such as his own mother's hatred of him, or his connection with the Questing Beast. Moreover, the character and psychology of Palamydes as the Chevalier depicts it owes a great deal to Malory's brilliant disorganized masterpiece.

But Isador de Boron's real originality lies in his making explicit the Islamic "donation" to the Arthurian corpus. Surprisingly little attention has been paid to Persian and Arabic sources for the medieval European Romance tradition. Western academic scholarship still wears blinders when it comes to any analysis of our debt to "the Saracens," even in the hard sciences, much less the arts. It is precisely in the occultist underground that one learns these things—for example that Rosicrucianism is said to have a Yemeni origin, or that the Templar/Freemasonic complex intersects at various points with various currents of esoteric Islam. De Boron's glosses and marginal notes betray his lack of scholarly credentials, but I have left them intact as evidence of the way in which he fleshed out his spotty reading with sympathy and Imagination.

I

Sir Perceval, Sir Galahad and Sir Bors, at the lowest ebb of their search for the Grail, stumble upon Sir Palamydes the Saracen, who vanished from Arthur's Court many years since.

For weeks they rode meeting no human, then one midday, blindly following the course of a stream, blundered into a clearing, far from Logres and equally far from Monsalvache, so dazed with the airless heat of the convoluted forest that they failed to notice the glade was already occupied: a knight sat back against moss-cushioned shade-oak, polishing his sword, wearing a rusty black robe of strange design, something like a monk's; black boots held at knees by bands of figured gold; and beside him in the grass a helm and armour of lacquered black and patterned gilt; his skin so dark he could not have been a Briton, his eyes sparkblack, beard curling on his breast in two long swaths like the wings of an angry raven.

The three reined their horses, the knight was on his feet facing them, sword held loosely in one hand; a page all in soft crimson leather leapt up and ran where a great black steed was tethered and shield propped against lightning-blasted stump; the boy

* began dragging this shield (so heavy he could not lift it) toward his master; the device was a Hand of gold on a field of black.

Perceval at once called out, Sir, we intend you no injury. I recognize your arms, though I have not seen them since I was a child. If you have not assumed another's colours, you are Sir Palamydes, whom Lancelot called the greatest knight in all Britain and Armorica, save only himself and Sir Tristam.

That is so, Sir, replied the dark warrior; but I fear I cannot return the courtesy of greeting you or your companions by name, for I recognize no one of you, nor do I know the meaning of the

** device you bear.

When Perceval had introduced himself and his companions, the older knight said, I remember you, Perceval, a child whose excessive foolishness hid an unnatural virtue, not only from others but from yourself—and the three young knights were amazed at these words. I have nothing to offer you but a bit of bread and wine, but please accept them; I've heard nothing of the Court for years; I can see that you are sore with riding and near to suffocation in this heat. Why not refresh yourselves in that stream, then drink while we recount our adventures; and tell me of King Arthur, whose name I shall always serve.

It seemed to them they had been offered no such courtesy for dry seasons, and they wondered secretly at Palamydes—for at

---

**The Hand of Fatima, emblem of The Fatimid Dynasty of Cairo (or 'Babylon'), where the father of Sir Palamydes held his demesne. The five fingers represent the Five Pure Ones, the family of the Prophet, and the Hand points down to represent their descendants, the Imams. Black and gold, or black and green-gold, are the colours of the final two circles of Paradise and the last two stages of the alchemical work.*

***Red crosses on a white ground with the Grail in gold at the centre.*

Court he would have appeared wild and alien with his darkness, yet here in this trackless wood his words wove a circle of gentle manners. The paradox, it seemed, held something of sorcery— yet they could find no reason to refuse his advice and hospitality. Further, they knew that for them every chance event held significance, each meeting might point the new way of their own adventure, since they had cast themselves like leaves carried on that cool stream, trusting the Grail and its messengers to concoct their fortune.

After they had refreshed themselves and broken bread with Palamydes and his squire, they told him of Logres, of the Queen and Lancelot, of Arthur' sickness and the pall that hung over the fellowship of the Table; and at all this Palamydes wept. Then they spoke of the manifesting of the Grail, and of their quest and failures; at this Palamydes marveled greatly, and for some time after they had fallen silent he too said nothing, but stroked his beard and stared toward the setting sun (which poured amber in the branches of the trees and burnt acid-blue shadows on the long lawn); birds hunted supper and exulted; the pageboy stole away to gather firewood; and still they waited for Palamydes to speak.

Let us build a fire and keep vigil till morning, said the Saracen at last; for this is Midsummer, a night of power, and we can use these few hours till dawn to trace our adventures to their source, and to recollect our selves. I will not keep company with a sleeping knight.

It has come to me that few of us, perhaps none, will ever see Logres again. The age which Merlin prepared and Arthur ruled is drawing to an end, splitting apart in search of higher rites and baser treacheries. From noon to dusk, you spoke to me of the Grail; and without intending it, guided me on my way. Now from

*

---

*Palamydes foretells the end of the Round Table.

dusk to dawn I shall tell you of my own quest, hoping that you may perhaps learn something useful to your purpose.

And Palamydes struck steel and flint, kindled a small fire, and ordered the boy to pour out wine mixed with cool streamwater; the Saracen keyed his voice to the indigo drone of night insects and nightjars, whippoorwills, nightingales and owls; and began to speak.

II

On certain nights the Caliph of Babylon, the Imam Hakim, secretly left his palace by the Nile and wandered disguised and alone, on a black horse and in black robes (such as Palamydes now wore, but of jet silk); under the cleft moon where the palms grew farther and farther apart, past eroded remnants, faceless stone stumps of revenant pharaohs, into the very desert where his gnosis of the stars alone guided him as if at sea, in search of adventure (forest and desert both interlace with the world of the unseen).

On one such night he happened on the oasis of my father's clan; outside the gate of their keep he found one lone youth, asleep—prodded him with his lance and ordered the gate flung open, that he and his steed might have water. The youth, ashamed of his dereliction, refused; and when Hakim made to ride past, he dealt the Caliph a rough blow with his lance. At once the spear seemed to catch fire in his hands, so that he flung it away in fear;

Concerning the father of Sir Palamydes, a noble of the Fatimid Dynasty. The Fatimid Caliphs were also the Imams of Ismailism, and thus rivals of the Sunni Caliphs in Baghdad as well as the orthodox Shiite Imams. The Fatimids ruled Syria, North Africa, Sicily and even Genoa for a short while, and Egypt for two centuries, until they were overthrown by Saladdin. Tolerant, patrons of the arts, the Fatimids outshone the rest of the Islamic world in splendour. The Nizari Ismailis or 'Assassins' split with the Fatimids over the question of succession, but both branches of Ismailism preached total commitment to esoterism and (at certain periods) abrogation of the Islamic Law.

a terrible wind arose, spiraling sand up into maelstroms, and from each of these columns stepped a demon warrior with stag's horns and armour of gleaming fire.

The youth then drew his sword and rushed again upon Hakim, but before the blade even touched the Caliph's shield, the ink-black horse flew up into the air; whereupon both steed and rider seemed suddenly enveloped in flickering green fire. Just then, the djinn seized the youth and disarmed him; the flaming horse descended to earth again, and Hakim said, Tell me your name, guardian of the gate. The youth answered, I am called Esclabor. Because you were bold, said Hakim, against such sorcery, I forgive your dozing, and ask of your courtesy the water which no tribe of the desert must refuse an errant knight.

Though he was held fast by two fanged and spotted-skin monsters the youth said, First you must tell me your name. At this the Caliph laughed, the emerald fire went out, the ghouls stepped into shadows and were gone. If I were a sorcerer I would never tell you, Hakim said, but since I am not, know I am called the Imam Hakim Billah al-Fatimi, seventh Caliph of Babylon.

At this, the youth fell to his face in the dust of the threshold and begged pardon, but the Caliph laughed again, dismounted and raised Esclabor to his feet. For the remainder of the night they sat together before the gate on Hakim's saddle-rug, and the Caliph instructed the youth in the secrets of the Five Pure Ones and the Imams. At length he spoke of a certain beast, that appeared in the vast forests of Hyperborea; in shape it had a serpent's head, body like a leopard, buttocks like a lion and footed like a hart; from within its body came a noise like that of thirty hounds (the number of the moon's phases) baying and questing; it was called Glatisant, the Questing Beast.

Then in the hour before dawn, before those of the outer faith are told that prayer is better than sleep, the Caliph knighted

Esclabor; he visited the spring, drank deep and watered his horse; resaddled and remounted, rode off silently into the dark desert.

When Hakim later vanished (or was betrayed) Sir Esclabor could abide no longer in Babylon, but took to knight-errantry in the company of several paynim knights. In the course of his wanderings he came to Rome, where he fought for the emperor; then was drawn to Gaul, where the king of that land warred against Uther Pendragon (who was allied with Meliadus of Liones, father of Sir Tristam).

*   While in the service of Pendragon, Sir Esclabor married a Christian girl and had of her three children, of whom Palamydes was the last; in fact, before this youngest son was born, Esclabor was slain in battle; the widow retired to her estate near the marches between Wales and Logres, in the midst of a remote and uninhabited forest, taking her sons with her.

III

Arthur and the Questing Beast.

Once in Caerlion the young King Arthur was visited by the wife of King Lot of Orkney; her real purpose was to spy on him; but Arthur found her beautiful and slept with her. At that time Arthur was still ignorant of his true parentage and thus did not realize he had committed incest with his half-sister, Morgan la Fay. After a month she returned to Orkney, and that night Arthur dreamt a nightmare, a savage metamorphosis of griffins and serpents. In the morning, to dispel the fumes of his terror, he ordered a hunt.

Arthur spied a hart, and spurred his horse in pursuit—but for hours the hart ran just ahead and out of reach, and at length Arthur's horse fell down dead under him and the prey escaped. He

---

*Segwarides and Saphir were the other two sons of Sir Esclabor le Mescongneu.

wandered till by a spring he found a charcoal burner, and ordered him to fetch back a fresh horse; then, the day being warm, he lay down upon a bank of moss by the bubbling water and fell asleep.

He awoke to the sound of thirty hounds yelping and baying; as if in a vision he saw the strangest beast in the world crash into the clearing as if pursued—a beast out of his last night's dream—and realized the noise of coursing dogs pulsed from within the belly of the beast. It approached the well and, ignoring the king, drank deep—while it gulped, the baying and barking ceased, but when it had finished, the chaos broke loose again; the beast ran off and vanished into the wood.

Despite his terror Arthur half-believed he still slept; trembling he lay back on the moss again—and soon was indeed once more asleep.

Some hours passed, and a knight staggered on foot into the clearing. Seeing Arthur asleep, he prodded him with the butt of his lance. Have you seen any sign, he demanded, of a strange beast pass this way? Astonished, Arthur answered that he had. I killed my horse chasing it, said the strange knight. Have you a steed? If so, give it to me at once.

I rode my own to death coursing a hart, said Arthur. But tell me of this beast—and who are you?

* I am called Pellinore answered the knight, and the beast is sometimes called Glatisant. It is my quest: I shall track it or die in the attempt.

Just then the charcoal burner and one of Arthur's huntsmen returned with a horse. Arthur said, Let me take on this quest for a year, and if I fail you can resume it. Then Pellinore fell into

---

King Pellinore, father of Sir Lamorak de Galis, who was later to be the best-loved friend of Palamydes, and who was slain treacherously by Mordred. Pellinore also fathered Sir Perceval.

a rage and cursed Arthur for a fool—he seized the horse and mounted it and rode away after the spoor of the beast, leaving the young king once more without a mount. Angrily Arthur sent his servant back yet another time, and sat down again by the spring to wait.

After a few minutes, a child approached him, a green-eyed boy of about fourteen dressed in a robe of midnight blue embroidered with stars and moons. What did you think of the Questing Beast? asked the boy.

Arthur, who was still too upset to guard his words, answered: I would that quest were mine.

At this the boy laughed and said, The Beast Glatisant is not to be attained by you, Arthur, or by any Christian knight. Its mystery belongs to the old pagans like Pellinore or me, or to a Saracen; indeed, it will one day be undertaken by a knight of Babylonian lineage, and achieved by him. For you, there is another fate.

Arthur burst with rage: Who are you, a mere child, to pretend to such knowledge? And how dare you address me by name as if you knew me?

But I do know you, Arthur, said the boy. I know your father was Uther Pendragon and your mother...

No one knows that, not even I myself, shouted the king.

*   ...your mother was Igraine, who was also the mother of Morgan la Fay, King Lot of Orkney's wife, with whom you slept only two nights since, leaving her with child. Your sister, Arthur.

Arthur drew his sword and would have slain the boy—but he turned and ran into the forest and was lost to sight.

At last the yeoman returned with a horse for the king. Arthur mounted it, and was about to ride back to Caerlion when he

---

The fruit of this incest will be Mordred, who will eventually wound Arthur and cause him to pass to Avalon, thus bringing about the fall of Britain to the Saxons.

heard yet another voice call his name. He turned around and saw, standing in deep shadow near the dark spring, an old man.

Merlin, cried Arthur. Is it you?

Do you know me now? asked Merlin. You were not so keen of sight before. And Arthur noticed the sorcerer was wearing an indigo black robe strewn with astrological devices. And Merlin, too, vanished.

IV

The youth of Palamydes: he discovers the secret books of his father. His mother, a pious Christian of the Britons, begins to reveal a hidden hatred of her half-black son.

On the verge, the interstice between his mother's lands and the unbounded forest, on the salvage threshold, a liminality, a hedge of mist between worlds, limped the wreck of a tower, once perhaps seven storeys but whittled away now to two—crusted with a living verdigris of ivy—the grey atoms of its stones drifting off into saturated afternoons. To one side were the cellars of a manor that had sunk and vanished, leaving the tower behind like a single owl-infested chimney—these excavations, sunken gardens of weeds, hollyhocks, pharmacopeia of astringent herbs, toads in puddles, insect music, lizards, unkempt wild roses, all steamed in breathless sun. On the other side lay a small lake, with antique stone steps disappearing into still algae, reeds and clumped lilies—and beyond this corroded greenglass pool, in a hundred colours language calls green, the hyle, the sylvanian *materia prima* spread itself: the dying and resurrecting forest.

Here Palamydes occulted the books, the manuscripts of black and gold fire-letters his father Sir Esclabor le Mescogneu brought

* from Babylon. The last of the dead knight's old retainers taught the boy to uncode the script, for this ageing noble made but a pretense of faith, and seduced Palamydes into the path of the mad Caliph Hakim who vanished into the sands beyond Nilus. In the cracked alembic of his tower Palamydes paid out on those texts the fire which another crescenting solitaire of fourteen might have spent in his hand upon the sun-weighted air—or what the

** pages at Court might have burnt in aping war: he gave, he sacrificed his first eros to that condemned knowledge (heresy even among the Saracens) and in his utter aloofness was converted, as

*** if the books were some hoopoe flown from the orient of half his blood, to hint of undefined paradises, dawn gardens awaiting the shattering of his cage; till one afternoon, standing slowly dazed by the day's adolescence and the transmutations of light, watching dragonflies stitching theorems into the visible breath hung like the smell of sweat sweetly over the austral pond, standing on the stone steps, Palamydes, dressed in velvet, the blackberry tint of his eyes or the bitter anthracite of his Saracenic hair, dreaming dream upon dream till all the crosscurrents cancelled each other out, leaving a still and unnatural geometry of hush in the nexus of the hours, felt rather than heard or witnessed somewhere amid the unspeakable carved jades of oak and elm, fern and tangled bush, a *nothing* like a meridional pandemonium, the non-stamping of goatmen's feet, dog-pitched whistle and noiseless rattattat of undiluted Panic—so unmixed that in retrospect his fear would seem a sort of ecstasy,

---

*The old retainer is Sir Gryon of Babylon; he alone befriends the boy, teaches him the Saracenic arts of lute and poetry, and the decipherment of Arabic.

**Palamydes is instructed in sword and horse-carried lance by a master-of-arms, but this man hates the boy so much that unwittingly he trains Palamydes into a strong and cunning warrior.

****cf. Sohrawardi the martyr of Aleppo, his* Recital of Oriental Exile; *also* The Hymn of the Pearl.

a stepping-out and doubling of the self attainable only through sheer non-mindedness; and from across the false perspective of the olivine pool, the unageing dryadic trees bent toward or did not bend in clockslow terror out and away from some presence, leaves sucked in or blown out of a motionless vortex, a Beast barking inside the skull like pairs of ultrasonic coursing hounds, gaming for some Anacreonic prey long since (ages since) vanished into the recesses of the intellect, hiding behind the black-lacquered armour of successive false selves, in the very spirals of the blood's memory, gone to ground in the marrow of thought.

By this Palamydes came to know his wyrd, the Questing Beast spoken of in Fatimid texts and by Ostanes the Persian alchemist: a bestial composite that only an angel can ride. He guessed it had lured his father from Babylon to this kingdom of Logres, which seemed an unmappable climactic forest; the Beast led Esclabor a dark dance in these labyrinths till he died, and then waited like a buried codicil in his last will and testament to pass itself on to his inheritor, the dark boy motionless with fear, in tower-shadow, glaring as if sightless across the bronze-rot-coloured pool at the invisible coruscating multiformed zooprotean breastfrozen horrorstruck annunciation, crashing through the underbrush like something dug up from the gravesites of the sky: crack, thud, and then silence; the very crows fainted in fear, fell on their backs, silver eyes turned up in their sockets; and Palamydes began to tremble with desire.

V

An incident from the wanderings of Palamydes before he became one of the Round Table, which he did for the sake of Sir Tristan of Liones.

Galahalt, the High Prince of Surluse, once held a tournament, which Arthur could not attend, but which was presided over by Lancelot and Guenever. Arriving in Surluse, Palamydes was offered hospitality by his aunt, a Saracen lady with a beautiful young daughter. This girl begged Palamydes to carry her colours in the jousting, and according to the rule of chivalry he agreed. So exquisite was she that on the first day of the tourney Galahalt himself challenged Palamydes to defend her honour, threatening to ravish her if her champion failed.

This insult Palamydes easily avenged, and that night when his cousin offered him her unripe fruit (like a hard sweet pear) he had no thought to refuse.

Next day the girl approached a Saracen knight of the city named Corsabrin and secretly promised to wed him if he could defeat and slay Palamydes.

When he thrust his pennant, tied to a lance, into the ground before the Queen's pavilion, Palamydes was at once challenged by Sir Corsabrin. They rushed at each other, and each splintered his lance against the other's shield. Before a second pair could be fetched, Corsabrin drew his sword and charged at Palamydes, who raised his shield as he unsheathed his own blade—but Corsabrin slashed at the neck of his rival's eclipse-black horse, cutting through the bone and veins, so that blood exploded over their bright armour, and the steed collapsed. Without giving Palamydes a chance to find another mount, Corsabrin rode his own steel-hung horse straight at the fallen knight, trying to trample him to death.

In a frozen rage, Palamydes leapt up, seized the reins and with one mighty jerk toppled and tripped the living horse in a clanging heap—then waited for Corsabrin to regain his feet, pick up his shield and sword and defend himself. Each time one of them struck the other, a chip of metal would skid through the air like

Palamydes adopted for his arms at this tourney the emblem of the Questing Beast upon his shield and trappings.

a spark from a smith's forge—within minutes both were bleeding from countless wounds.

At length Corsabrin waxed stronger and began to beat back his opponent; exulting, he shouted to Palamydes, Your cousin the whore has promised me what she gave you if I kill you. At this Palamydes dashed against him and delivered such a blow to his helm that it raced off, bounced in the dust and rolled toward the feet of the spectators. Yield, commanded Palamydes—but Corsabrin spat in his face and snarled defiance. With one sweep Palamydes cut off his head at the neck; it too bounced and rolled at the crowd, like a living scuttling thing. As the lifeless corpse collapsed to its knees, a charnel stench arose—and as it fell noisily to the earth, its flesh began instantly to decompose as if eaten from within. By the time servants had been ordered to drag it from the tourney ground and dispose of it in unhallowed earth, white worms were beginning to squeeze out from between the joints of its armour.

Lancelot and Guenever were as deeply struck by the prowess of Palamydes as they were horrified by the anti-miracle of Corsabrin's decay; they urged the Saracen noble to be christened at once. For, they said, you see the result of dying outside the church: devils fly to seize the soul and consume the flesh, a foretaste of hell.

Palamydes, who had seen many Saracens and pagans die better deaths than certain Nazarenes, nevertheless pretended to agree, saying that only when he had fought seven true battles would he at last be baptized—for he realized that he remained yet far from his quest; moreover he had betrayed his love of Iseult—and by seven battles he meant the seven stages of the path, which he had not yet begun to travel.

In disgust at what had happened, Palamydes purchased a new horse, and quickly left Surluse, though he was badly wounded.

When Sir Mordred noticed this, he gathered six of his close companions to him and suggested that they dispose of the Saracen just as they had murdered his friend Sir Lamorak—and these conspirators were Sir Dragonet, Brandiles, Uwaine, Ozana, Griflet and Agravaine.

They tracked Palamydes for several days, at last ambushing him—and though they attacked him simultaneously and treacherously, he was able to unhorse four of them and kill two more outright (Ozana and Griflet); Mordred, who had been waiting the chance to thrust at the Saracen from behind (as with Sir Lamorak) gave up and fled.

Palamydes had been wounded even more severely in this battle, and after losing himself in the forest, fell from his horse, unable to keep mounted any longer, and fainted from loss of blood. Thus he was discovered by two peasants, who ran at once to a nearby manor and begged the lady of the house to succor a wounded knight. What arms does he bear? she asked. They described the strange device of a mythic animal on the battered shield. That is Glatisant the Questing Beast, she said, and the knight is my son Palamydes. That he bears this device proves that he still adheres to his unbelief and heresy: a paynim, just as his cursed father before him. I will do nothing to save his life; let him ask elsewhere for hospitality.

But the servants of the house hated this unnatural woman, fearing her sin would destroy them all; so they secretly sent aid, medicines, meat and wine, to their errant lord, and he was soon recovered.

It was then that Palamydes turned his full passion toward Iseult, the wife of King Mark of Cornwall.

VI

Palamydes tells of his unhappy love for Iseult the Queen of Cornwall, and his mingled enmity and friendship with Sir Tristam of Liones.

Why can I not hate Iseult, my opposite the daylight, I that Arthur called a leopard, I that kidnapped her once, I that have killed as paladin too many to remember, unhorsed and unhelmed too many to count, all for the memory of one smile, blood on polished metal?

One cannot serve two beasts, Glatisant and Iseult. I could make an anchorite's boast and emblemize the carnal world as a woman, claim that I cut out the brandmark from my skin, prate that incest and adultery will topple Arthur's arcadia—but no, Tristam and Iseult and I whirled like planets, like angels poisoned with aphrodisiac spinning inside an archangel's brain—the kerubim may go mad, but they do not sin. Those two were each other's quest, they doubled each other. I divided myself.

Tristam and I fought our last duel by Merlin's stony grave, on the very day Galahad appeared to sit in the Siege Perilous, the very day the Grail Quest began; on that day I was purged of envy and resumed the quest of the beast. If I could not hate Iseult, why could I not at least hate Tristam? They were one thing, a hermaphrodite—I loved neither of them so much as I loved their love. When he ran lunatic naked in the forest, I searched for him as I wanted her, with the same lust an alchemist knows when Hermes and the Lioness copulate in an athanor.

For all the generosity of your hair, Queen, oil of gold, elixir of bees, you gave me nothing, neither the raging bedlam of utter separation nor the white honey of your saliva; beside some well in the dank woods beautiful as an antiparadise I wept and played

*   the lute (which my father in the time of Uther Pendragon first introduced to this land from Babylon) thinking the while: only Tristam and I in all this barbaric country can compose a decently moving lament.

My own eyes were the cause of my sorrow, black as the jewels from a snake's skull—not her eyes, colour of the beast, of the forest—and his were blue, of course, like a child who laughs at a funeral. I let him
** baptize me that last day, why not? Since my religion permits pious dissimulation, it made an apt symbol to end our story—they were sailing toward their death and I was to vanish into the forest—but they were paynims like me, Dionysus ruled them and only a Saracen paradise of eternal drunken dalliance could ever hold them, if such a thing could exist, all Time in one spasm of released desire.

I looked in the well and saw myself defaded, swore to give up this life for a love I might never get nor recover; I made my last and best poem, almost rejoicing as if music sucked the poison from my wound—but that day Tristam, hunting the hart or hunting me, overheard my work, watched me through the lace of May leaves. Lazy as I am, I would have attained nothing without them to strike against like knife on whetstone. I told him I had as lief die as live—a kind of sanctity. Well uttered, your treason, he said. I answered: Love is free for all men: you and she have the pleasure of your love, but you cannot shut me out from its pain.

All he could offer me then was more jousting, more sword-play—for once he acted the unbalanced envious lover, while I attained something like a vatic elegance. How the three of us

---

*Arabic: al-´oud, *the lute.*

**Taqiyya, *which permits Ismailis to pretend to any religion, since all religions are one in any case.*

danced, witches in a grove, weaving around us an egg of pulsing silk, a spiral pyramid charged with lightning which wakened the night, rays shooting between the branches like swampfire, the prolonged burst of a fallen meteor.

VII

Palamydes begins his ta'wil, that is in Arabic, the taking-back-to-the-source of all the adventures recounted during that day and night, his own and those of the Grail knights—the hermeneutic exegesis of the story, the explication of the text their memories have called into being.

The beast-quester finds the outward form of Glatisant but one of many: each time he comes close, finds the trap sprung, detects traces of its escape or gets a glimpse of it crashing away, then each time the timbre of its bruiting changes, each moment a new station manifests itself, sometimes merely a hollowness in the air, vibrant strumming of voices not yet labeled, tension of light, invisible whirlwind or spout of things about to be born; sometimes a theorem of chaos that suddenly equates, drawing all the trees, moss and lichen into its computations; the light quartered and dented on misshapen rocks and lightning-broke stumps, a spectrum of landscape dropping into focus with sheer ghost-story terror and erotic bliss—click—and the hunter knows that everything he saw till then was but grey and blurred.

When the beast is seen it may also appear in various forms. Palamydes watched it often as a monstrous stag, unkillable; as a Celtic nightmare of a boar; as a raven in a rainstorm. Sometimes it unfolded itself as a sequence of events, a knotted length of time; and sometimes as a vast overflowing, a superabundance, as if just beyond the next ridge the well of images gurgled and spewed up the whole world of palpable things, the patterns of mentation, the angels, the living creatures and elementals.

The very essence of the beast lies in the quality of the hunt—the sportsman is dazzled by the otherness of Glatisant and yet loses the sense of any difference or distance between totem (or prey) and himself: beyond these two clashing rocks he retires and looks on astonished, forgetting his purpose.

Once the beast appeared to him as a herd of deer; as they scattered before his black centaur shape, they transformed themselves into boys and maidens, dressed in white, who turned to laugh at him, like an ironic shower of gold coins, all the dates and inscriptions rubbed and worn beyond decipherment; and once as a child, riding a stag that carried lit opals and garnets strung on gold chains webbed in its antler-tines; and perhaps Iseult was also part of some major apotheosis—if it may be said that such a singularity could be part of any pattern whatsoever: Iseult of the white brow.

Now it is full night, said Palamydes, and we are planets to this little star fire. As he stirred the blaze and added more wood the three knights stretched themselves and swallowed the last dregs of their wine. Iseult is as lost as Eurydice, said the Saracen; her face fades always before my eyes, into an underworld I port with me like luggage, like an organ of the body. The stones and animals sing for me in my quest while I listen, a reader of the Metamorphoses, watching Proteus on the shore of Egypt. Then Palamydes asked his squire for more wine, but the boy was asleep, his head resting on the black-enameled saddle—and in the firelight the Grail knights remembered the boy's hair was the rarest colour of blackred musk-roses, blacklighted scarlet. Palamydes drained the rest of a flask into their cups, last drops luminous in the upblazing.

Pagans such as Merlin speak of a great cauldron that never emptied, but poured out unstinted food and drink—just so does the one become many. At certain powerpoints in forests, deserts

*The name of the squire was Saphir, like that of the brother of Sir Palamydes.

or caves such openings suddenly appear or disappear, sluices for the flow of being into our world: Nature naturing with a generosity so intense it can drown the unwary beholder in a surfeit of vision.

*   The Persians know of a Cup of Jamshid—he who possesses it may see reflected in its wine whatever transpires at that moment anywhere in the world. Thus the Cup is like a mirror of the Cauldron, which in turn embodies the always-shapeshifting-moment of continual creation. The Magians teach that the eye of the Cup can be turned inward—offering a vision of the one rather than a spectacle of manyness and the bending of time. Perhaps if the Cauldron's flow could be reversed, one might step through it as through a doorway, or climb down into it like a well, into the realm of the one.

The Grail you speak of provides food, and is also a Cup from which the splendour of the one radiates—a vortex that Janusfaces on two separate lands. I think the Grail is a Christian's quest, as Merlin claimed, because its beam shines upward and out of this world. Yet if you could step through this rent in the cloth or tear away the veil, what would you find? Is there more than one real creation?

Glatisant is a paynim's quest, a Saracenic obsession, because it is the quintessence of all nature, the very palpableness of all that may be touched and tasted. The beast is the world, but the world as I have seen it in my errantry, a forest suffused with the recollection of fauns and satyrs, dryads, waternymphs, Priapi and Sileni,
**   amorini riding panthers—the world become a *lapis exilit*, a balsam which transmutes nothing but the place in which the hunter

---

*The Cup of Jamshid is explained in the Divan *of Hafez of Shiraz, who is accepted by esoteric Zoroastrians as the expositor par excellence of their doctrines.*

**The words lapis exilit *are applied to the Grail by Flegetanis, Wolfram's Saracenic source for his poem of Parzival. They can mean stone of exile, or even stone that fell to earth, and by some are said to refer to the jewel from Lucifer's crown.*

stands to view the world—and thereby transforms it all beyond recognition. The mercury of Glatisant's mutability must be fixed with the sulphur of an incandescent attentiveness; in the moment the stalker steps forward to achieve this quest, he simultaneously steps back and finds himself again in the forest, perfectly ordinary, still and alone; except that hunter and landscape alike are saturated with presence, like two lovers intertwined in complex embrace, or about to embrace, unknown to those who sleep so heedlessly on nights of power.

At this Palamydes clapped his hands, and the noise reverberated around the crooked columns of the blackswallowed forest in multiple peals of thunder; the three knights started and sat up like gamebirds who hear the hounds; Saphir jerked from sleep and stared about and knuckled his eyes. Palamydes handed the squire his own half-filled cup, and smiled. I will keep company with no sleeping knight, he said.

In the hour before dawn when even the earth yawns and the moon has sunk into a somnolent blur, I drink only certainty, the elixir of wakefulness—and like Merlin, I make prophecy. The quests of Grail and Beast are mirror images of one another. Looking into your glass, I have absorbed a new essence, I have breathed into myself the perfume of your energies. Now look into mine, and you will see the image of a map. The Grail you will attain at Monsalvache is but the prolongation of a more central Grail—and your prophet's blood was not the first to spill in it. The city of Sarras lies in the farthest East, the Yemen, where once schismatics of my faith

*

The Yemen is identified as the source of the 'oriental knowing' by Mohiyoddin ibn Arabi in his Interpreter of Desires, *and by the author of* The Chymicall Marriage of Christian Rosycross. *The Black Stone or meteorite of the Kaaba in Mecca was stolen by the Qarmatian heretics and held for some years in the Yemen. The last Fatimid (the twenty-first Imam) Mawla Sabi'l Ashhad al-Tayyib, exiled to the Yemen, vanished in 1132, and like Arthur (or the 'Hidden Imam' of orthodox Shiism) is expected to appear again at the end of this temporal cycle.*

hid the stolen Black Stone of Mecca, and where the last of the exiled Fatimid Imams will vanish, as Merlin did and as Arthur will, into a cave of silver and crystal.

And I shall move north seeking the beast as the beast seeks me, into Hyperborea, into the land of unending pitch dark—there, at its pole, like a single glowing pearl set in a vast disk of ebony onyx and jet, I shall find the spring or well guarded by angels. There I shall bathe, and put on green robes. And there will begin a new cycle of seven. And there I begin to dance.

NESTOR MAKHNO
AND THE
ELIXIR OF LIFE

One day Nestor Makhno was travelling across the Ukrainian steppes in a great carriage drawn by horses and mounted with a machinegun, a Vickers. A few companions rode with him, dressed as Cossacks, corsairs, Circassians, in cast-off tophats and tails, sheepskin coats, sevenleague boots with daggers thrust in them, rakish astrakhans, bandoliers, cutlasses and pistols. A black banner flew behind the carriage, while inside it Makhno drowsed, dressed all in black, his feet propped on a small cannon.

Near the small German-settled village of Blumenthal, the carriage was halted to water the horses at a goosepond in a farmer's field not far from the road. The farm was deserted—the entire family had vanished in fear of the anarchist whom they considered a bandit—but the gooseherd, a flaxen-haired blue-eyed Ukrainian boy about thirteen, perched himself boldly on a stone wall and watched them. Makhno got down to stretch his legs, spotted the boy, and began chatting with him.

The boy's name is Yegor. His father was killed in the War, and so he came to work for the wealthy kulak Heinrichs, a dour Mennonite. A hard dull life without prospects. But Yegor's a bright child; he's heard of Makhno, and idolizes him. Makhno's in a good mood, and Yegor's story reminds him of his own childhood.

As the insurgents prepare to leave, the boy looks at Makhno so yearningly that he gives in to impulse and invites Yegor to jump up on the carriage and come away with them. Without a moment's hesitation the boy leaps, and the anarchic droshky rumble-roars out of the yard, scattering pigs and geese with a few rounds fired off in celebration.

Makhno is heading for Katerinoslav to rendezvous with a larger force for a lightning raid on the city. The carriage hurtles onward into the night—but at last they decide to stop and camp till dawn. A fire is built, bread and stolen roast goose, bottles of vodka. Anticipating the coming battle, intoxicated more on summer midnight than liquor, no one feels like sleeping—least of all the enthralled Yegor, former gooseherd, now partisan of the *Makhnovtse*, the Peasants & Workers Insurgent Anarchist Army of the Ukraine.

As the fire dies down and the stars begin to swirl above the steppe, the conversation grows deeper and delves backward in time. What of the ancient Cossacks, their distant ancestors? Taras Bulba, and the rebels Stenka Razin and Pugachev? Each of the soldiers has a story to tell or a song to sing. Then Makhno himself speaks, musing aloud, wondering how their army—his army—might compare with those long-dead hordes. Are we as indomitable, courageous and free? Shall we too one day become legend?

One of Makhno's lieutenants, a literate Jew from Odessa, now declares: "There's only one man in the Ukraine who could answer that question, and by an odd coincidence he lives in Katerinoslav. His name is Professor Yavornitsky, and he is an archaeologist as well as historian. He has spent his life researching the Cossacks, and has excavated many *kurgane*, the ancient burial mounds. There he found much treasure, which he took for his museum." At the mention of treasure, everyone's ears are cocked. "What sort of treasure?" asks one of them.

"Well comrades, nothing much worth expropriating. A lot of dusty rubbish, to be sure. The most famous of his discoveries is simply a bottle, which Yavornitsky once dug out of a pre-historic Zaporozhian tumulus. The bottle is said to contain a particularly potent magical draught of vodka, called 'The Elixir of Life'. Some believe that all the courage and luck of the Cossacks is to be found in that bottle. When the Tsar came to Katerinoslav and visited the Museum, he asked Yavornitsky to let him taste the 'Elixir'— but the Professor refused."

⊕ ⊕ ⊕

Next day, around the hour of sunset, Makhno's carriage arrived at the shallow banks of the Dnieper. The battalions he expected awaited him there and had already made camp for the night. Just then the rays of the sinking sun fell aslant the distant city and picked out the gilded domes of the great Cathedral. Staring at the sight as if mesmerized, Makhno began to exhort his horde. "There's plunder for you! There's glory! It's like a vision of heaven! We must smash it! Mount the guns! To horse! Attack!" And the exhausted Makhnovtse, who had narrowed their gaze to food and sleep, now were awakened by their Batko, their "Father," and felt flooded with energy and hatred for priests.

A terrible clatter of hooves and wheels on cobblestones—wild ululations, firing of pistols, rearing and neighing of horses. Like a thunderstorm they assault the Cathedral, riding mounted up the broad steps and through the portals.

No one remains to defend the holy place. All the resident priests have fled for their lives, having heard how one of their number in the town of Sineinkovo was tossed alive by the anarchists into the furnace of a locomotive.

The insurgents indulge in an orgy of looting. Icons and candelabra stuffed into saddlebags, jewel-studded goblets, crucifixes of silver, pyxes with gold chains. A boisterous holiday of anti-clericalism.

Laughing and clowning, the men break into the vestry and discover gilt-encrusted robes, dalmatics, albs and copes, and dress themselves as archdeacons and bishops. This is the sort of fun Yegor expected, and the boy drapes himself in rich cowls and ruby pectorals. A Bosch-like Saturnalia.

One of the Makhnovtse fires up a torch and prepares to light the altarcloth. The whole Cathedral will go up in flames! They pause in their frolic to watch. And in the sudden hush a voice booms and echoes:

"Stop! Cease this vandalism at once!"

In sheer surprize the arsonist freezes. Everyone gawks at the intruder. From nowhere there has appeared in their midst a hulking bourgeois intellectual, spectacled but powerfully-built, like an old peasant disguised as a librarian. He's addressing Makhno, he's confronting Makhno, towering over him in a cold rage; and what's more—the fool is completely unarmed!

A dozen guns are pointed at the idiot. "Batko, step back and give us room to...."

But Makhno holds up his hand to stop them.

"I admire courage—even foolhardiness. Who are you?"

"Dmitro Ivanovich Yavornitsky."

"Professor Yavornitsky, the historian! It's true; this is the man I mentioned to you, Batko," says the Jew from Odessa.

Yavornitsky raises an eyebrow, as if he'd never have expected these barbarians to recognize him, but says nothing.

"I am Makhno. By what right do you order me to 'cease this vandalism'?"

"This is the heritage of our people you wantonly destroy."

"So? The heritage of the people? not the property of priests and oppressors? I will melt this treasure down and buy food for the people. Are you a better custodian of its worth?"

"Pardon me," says Yavornitsky sardonically. "I had not taken you for an idealist."

"Do you disagree with the ideals of anarchism?" asks Makhno.

"What kind of ideals are those which can only be realized in corpses and destruction?"

At this insult, the soldiers could restrain their anger no longer. "Counter-revolutionary dog! Parasite! Let us kill him at once!"

Makhno hesitated, like a man who has enjoyed a brief conversation and regrets bringing it to an end. Then, "Be that as it may, Professor," he said. "But what if your corpse should be added to the raging pyre of culture and history, eh? What then?"

Yavornitsky said nothing. Makhno looked about as if seeking inspiration. "Yegor! Come here. Revolution is a terrible thing, a holocaust."

The boy stepped forward, jeweled and robed, an ambiguous angel of disorder—and suddenly terrified at the premonition of someone's death. Makhno drew from his belt a huge pistol and offered it to Yegor. "Take this and execute Professor Yavornitsky. At once!"

Sweat broke out on Yegor's brow, which had turned white as ermine. Trembling he reached out and grasped the pistol which dwarfed his hand. The gun was so heavy—a real cannon—he almost dropped it. Shaking, he raised it and pointed it wavering at the old scholar, who began to look worried for the first time.

Time stretched out cruelly.

Yegor burst into sobs. He dropped the gun, which made a loud clatter on the stone paving, but luckily did not go off.

"It slipped from my fingers, Batko…!"

"All right, Yegor, I forgive you," said Makhno. "And I forgive you too, social-parasite-Professor. The Revolution is merciful."

At this, all the Makhnovtse laughed as if the whole business had been a great joke. The tension broke. Makhno put his arm around Yegor's shoulders and smiled at Yavornitsky with incredible charm.

"Tell me, Dmitro Ivanovich: Is it true that you have burrowed into the *kurgane* of the ancient Cossacks in search of treasures for your Museum?"

"Well… I've made a number of expeditions…"

"And is it true that among those treasures is a certain bottle of vodka which you refused to open even for the Tsar?"

"Oh dear! You're referring to the so-called 'Elixir of Life'. Of course I refused. What an absurd request! I'd no idea the man was so superstitious. Rasputin must have corrupted him."

"And what of me? Am I not the true little Father of my people? Am I not a fitting heir to the khans of the great hordes? Should I not taste this magical elixir? What do you say, Professor?"

The men cheered. "Yes: the ultimate glass of vodka! Drunk for all eternity! The bottle, the bottle for our Batko!" Even Yegor, who'd regained his high spirits, laughed with delight. The Elixir of Life—it was like a fairy tale.

"Well, Professor? A toast—to the Cossack spirit?"

"General Makhno… I should say again that I view myself as the custodian of our people's heritage. The archaeological relics in the museum are beyond all price—and not mine to sell. They are symbols of our being, the property of our collective self. You may be a worthier customer than the Tsar… but still, I cannot sell."

"What if I promise to give back all the wealth of the Cathedral… to *your* Museum?"

"I'd still refuse."

"And If I threatened to kill you?"

Yavornitsky raised his eyebrow.

"No, quite right, I already promised not to do that. Very well, you win, No vodka for me—but we keep the holy relics."

Yavornitsky shrugged and made a face.

Makhno laughed good-naturedly. "One last question, Professor. You're the leading expert on the ancient Cossacks. Tell me, if you can see them in your imagination, how would you compare those heroes to the Makhnovtse of today?"

Yavornitsky looked around at the heavily-armed band of anarchists, then turned back to Makhno. "It would seem that although the weapons have become larger and heavier, the men have grown smaller."

What did he mean? Was he talking about little Yegor and the bulky horse-pistol? Or did he mean…?

Now, Nestor Makhno was a small man. He was slender and slight—really not much taller than Yegor—short enough to be ridiculed as a runt—as if anyone would dare! His fine Circassian coat fell to his ankles, and his splendid cavalry sabre trailed behind him on the floor. Like many short military men, he was known to be sensitive on the subject. And as one of his critics once said, "If he doesn't like you, he shoots you." The Makhnovtse stopped smiling one by one as the new insult penetrated their jolly mood. All turned to Makhno as if they expected him to kill the archaeologist on the spot, promise or no promise.

Another dramatic pause.

Makhno laughs. "I understand," he says. Thereupon he turns and strides out of the Cathedral at his usual rapid pace, followed by Yegor and the rest of the soldiers, leaving Yavornitsky alone in the vast empty sanctuary.

⊕ ⊕ ⊕

That night in camp Makhno tosses and turns in bed, unable to sleep. At last he has a thought. Next morning he will return to the Cathedral, climb the tower, cut down the great bells and hurl them out to smash on the ground below.

What a magnificent noise they will make!

NOTE

The best thing about this story is that it's "true." I found it in *Nestor Makhno: The Life of an Anarchist* by Victor Peters (Echo Books, Winnipeg Canada, 1970), a disorganized and badly-written book generally unsympathetic to Makhno, but including much interesting material from letters and interviews with Ukrainian émigrés in Canada and the U.S. Peters got the story from a novel set in the period, *Chernei Koster (The Black Fire)* by Oless Gonchar, which appeared in *Literaturnaya Gaseta Moscow*, #47, Nov. 22, 1967, translated into Russian by K. Grigoriev. The incident is also related in another novel, *Na Ukraine (The Ukrainians)* by Wasyl Chaplenko. Gonchar probably "lifted" the incident from Chaplenko's book. Peters communicated with Chaplenko, who was living in New York at the time and was assured that the meeting between Makhno and Yavornitsky (1855-1940) "is historically authentic." Chaplenko also wrote a poetic cycle, *Issko Gava* (NY, 1965), which deals with the Makhnovschina. When these sources are translated (along with Makhno's own memoirs, etc.) no doubt my version of the tale will be superseded. Nevertheless I was struck by its Golgolian or Borgesian quality, and decided that the English language deserves a better rendition than Peters gave it.

*"Let us look one another in the face. We are Hyperboreans—
we know well enough how out of the way we live. 'Neither by
land nor by sea shall thou find the road to the Hyperboreans':
Pindar already knew that of us. Beyond the North, beyond the
ice, beyond death—our life, our happiness."*

—NIETZSCHE, THE ANTI-CHRIST

THE HYPERBOREAN FRAGMENTS

THE "HYPERBOREAN" FRAGMENTS
is without doubt a forgery—no other reason-
able provenance can be allowed a text that
suggests our world's history has been shaped
in large part—since the late Paleolithic—by
an extraterrestrial conspiracy.

An exposure of such chariots-of-the-
gods brouhaha would scarcely appear
worthwhile, even for readers of such a periodical as New Pathways, were it not for
several curious features of the alleged manuscript which have so far eluded the notice
of contemporary scholars.

In 1888 a *festschrift* or celebratory volume of essays was published (in a gift edition of 150 copies) in honor of Dr. Berndt
von Moltke, a minor Bavarian philologist
and scholar of Biblical pseudepigrapha and
apocrypha, on the occasion of his retirement from the State University in Munich[1].
Among the essays—which ranged over

[Notes on page 144]

subjects like "Jesus As Murderer And Magician In The 'Infancy' Gospels," "An Alleged Citation Of Valentinus," "The Apokatastasis-Mythos In Early Protestant Apologetics," etc.—the volume also contained a short contribution called "The *'Hyperborean Fragments'* A Gnostic Forgery?" by one Prof. Emil Zerling.

This hyper-scholarly article begins by explaining that the manuscript of the *Fragments* or rather the fragments of an unnamed manuscript (together with shards of a clay jar supposed to have contained them) were sold by "a poor man from Zoar [now in Israel] to a curiosity-dealer in Jerusalem; thence they found their way to the Library of the Monastery of St. Dionysios (which stamped several of the larger fragments with its seal in 1879) and thence somehow to Germany," where the lot was acquired ("somehow," no doubt) by Prof. Zerling.

The *Fragments* are said to consist of eight pieces of papyrus ranging in size from 8 by 17 cm. to 23 by 26 cm., in various stages of decrepitude and illegibility. The language is Greek with Aramaic and Egyptian loanwords and vulgar solecisms in abundance—according to Zerling, who exhibits a rather low opinion of the unknown author's abilities. For various reasons, which will be mentioned in due course, Zerling hypothesizes a Third Century A.D. origin for the text, and a single author living probably in Alexandria, an initiate of some Gnostic sect such as the Ophites or Carpocrateans.

However—as we will see—the *Fragments* claims an even older tradition for itself; mention is made of Didymos of Rhodes, a Third Century B.C. historian of whom not one fragment survives, though he is cited by Dio Cassius and other late Roman historiographers[2]. And Didymos in turn is apparently supposed to have gained his information from yet more ancient oral sources, perhaps the same body of myth rationalized by Herodotus (IV, 32) in his account of the Hyperboreans.

Zerling contends (for seemingly sound philological reasons) that the *Fragments* in fact owes nothing to any genuine early source; and certainly its eccentricities are unmatched in all Classical literature. He concludes that the manuscript was "forged"—that it can be classified as pseudepigraphical—and that its language and imagery reveal late Gnostic obsessions and technical terminology. As for the papyrus, the orthography, the ink and all other criteria for dating available in 1888, Zerling shows "conclusively" that the manuscript can be dated no earlier than 250 A.D., no later than 317.

The story of the manuscript's provenance reminds one immediately of later discoveries at Nag Hammadi and Qumran (Zoar is, of course, the only surviving "City of the Plain," Lot's refuge after fleeing Sodom); and so it seems curious that the discovery of such a text appears to have roused so little interest or excitement in 19th Century scholarly circles. After all, virtually nothing was known of Gnosticism other than excerpts from orthodox Christian heresiographers who presented their Gnostic researches in a spirit of *auto-de-fe*, obfuscation, misquotation and profound disparagement Here at last was an apparently authentic Gnostic document (albeit a "forgery")—the Gnostics could now speak for themselves! Surely Zerling's essay must have sparked some controversy at least amongst dusty pedants and crank occultists. But no.

I first came across the *festschrift* in Munich at the studio of my friend the sculptor Karl Schmitt. Part Gypsy, ex-monk, Bauhaus architect and husband of minor Caucasian royalty, Karl shares many obscure orientalist interests with me. While in Tehran in the '70s, we had both studied with the late French savant Henry Corbin. In Munich (1981) we were trying to dream up a text for the catalogue of Karl's next exhibition; we began to discuss Corbin's many references to Hyperborea as the "Imaginal Realm" or World of the Archetypes, a concept he had gleaned from various sufi treatises, Ethiopian Alexander-Romances, Gnostic texts and German philosophers.

At this point Karl remembered the *festschrift*, disappeared for an hour or so, located it, found the reference he'd vaguely recalled, translated it for me (I do not know German) and we incorporated it into our essay. I pestered Karl for more of the *"Hyperborean" Fragments* and what he told me excited me tremendously; however, time was short and I had to leave Munich with no more than a xerox of Zerling's article and a few notes.

In 1983 I paid the Brown University Classics scholar J. Rabinowitz a derisory sum to provide me with a rough translation of Zerling's essay and the *Fragments* (Rabinowitz has since rendered a good deal more help for no remuneration, and I herewith thank him for all of it). The result—a fascinating myth, bogged down with Teutonic philologomania and Protestant prudery—piqued our curiosity unbearably.

At once I wrote to Karl pleading with him to ransack Munich for more information on Zerling and the Fragments. Months later (not to attempt suspense) I was in possession of the following facts: Dr Von Moltke, the man honored by the festschrift, indeed existed, and so did all the other professors included in the celebratory volume. But Zerling? If he existed, this little article was the only thing he ever wrote, and constitutes his one connection with Munich or with German scholarship in general.[3]

Zerling is a zero. Von Motke's papers contain no mention of him, nor does any biographical reference-work of the period. Neither of the known reviews of the *festschrift* (in obscure philological journals) makes mention of Zerling's article. Karl wrote to me: "If I had not gone to the State Library and checked their copy of the book, I might have begun to think that *only my copy* contained the *Fragments!*"

We concluded that "The *'Hyperborean Fragments'* A Gnostic Forgery?" was itself a forgery. Suspicion at once fell on the editor of the *festschrift,* Otto Lunsdorf; but almost immediately we were baffled by Lunsdorf's unimpeachable dullness, rectitude, obscurity and futility—an account of which we will spare our present audience. Lunsdorf, we concluded, must have been duped by person(s) unknown, nor would this have been difficult since he was himself nearly senile in 1888 (he died two years later) and was in any case a specialist in early Church Fathers, totally uninterested in Gnosticism.[4]

The hoax went utterly unobserved, or at least unremarked-upon, and the *Fragments* were soon forgotten—or perhaps never even noticed. No one ever demanded to see the bits of decayed papyrus, and therefore no one discovered their non-existence. No one wrote any angry letters to any Classical quarterlies demanding that Zerling step forward to defend his outrageous claims, and so no one unmasked the trickster.

By now it is probably too late to pin him down, although in our conclusion we will attempt a wild guess. We ought also to admit that *lack* of evidence can prove nothing with finality. "Zerling" might mask a perfectly respectable scholar, who had acquired a perfectly genuine manuscript by rather dubious means, and lied about nothing except his own name. Somewhere in some private library in Bavaria the *Fragments* may lie dusty and forgotten, strewn together with the bits of broken jar, waiting to be rediscovered.

It seems unlikely.

But the *Fragments* poses an interesting question, even if it proves in the end no more than a late 19th Century hoax: *why* would a late 19th Century scholar want to forge a 3rd Century A.D. Gnostic forgery of a 3rd Century B.C. garbled account of spurious half-forgotten mythology? Perhaps some scholarly axe to grind? Psychological reasons? Aesthetic? Playful? Perhaps metaphysical or mystical propaganda of some kind?

Clearly only one valid approach to the text remains: simply to read it, allow it to speak, to forget everything outside the text—at least to suspend judgment and speculation until the *Fragments* themselves have been absorbed.

Unfortunately this proves easier said than done, since part of "Zerling"'s joke seems to have been a parody of pedantic rodomontade. His reconstruction and translation of the text sinks beneath countless interpretations, alternate readings, references, Greek and Latin tags, footnotes, annotations and other impedimenta. Furthermore, we believe that *everything* Zerling says about the *Fragments* must be taken as the *opposite* of what he really meant to say. He is posing as an insensitive reductionist, certain to miss all poetic intuitions, all beauty, all genuine meaning. The whole scholarly apparatus of the article acts like a finger pointing *away* from the moon, or a cloud to obscure its clarity. The real message, the moon itself, is contained only in the *"Hyperborean" Fragments*; "Zerling"'s contributions amount to an ironical smokescreen.

By clearing away the debris of Zerling's wooden and nearly incomprehensible translation and comments, by re-imagining the text as a beautiful poem or story instead of a heap of scraps and paper-shards, we may finally be able to uncover the forger's real intentions in perpetrating his hoax.

For this we shall need to make our own commentary, based only in part on "Zerling" (he does offer some useful clues about sources), in part on the insights of Henry Corbin,[5] and in part on guess-work—which we will carefully label as such. Only then will we hope to demand of this enigmatic and fantastic document some hint of its true origin and purpose.

Fragment I (VIII) [6]

… temple of Chaos, first of gods,
shapeless as silt, built upon slime
with mist-bricks and beams of wheatstraw,
fit housing for barbarians and androgynes.
Homeless in unending perfect weather
wandering to please themselves
or grub for roots
they live out 1000 years, obscure,
near-speechless…

[lines missing]

...[a land of perpetual] Night,
or rather twilight
... [where] Boreas rules beyond Polar
mountains
a protean shapeshifter race
half-beast/half-man,
each the lord of a trackless domain, solitary,
turbid, speaking the languages of beasts,
driven by blind Eros alone, slothful,
weaponless...

[lines missing]

... [this account is based on that of]
Didymos of Rhodes
who in turn knew the lost books of Hesiod
the Theogonist, who learned of this history
from a book of gold found in Delos
[written by] Hecaergos the Hyperborean....

Commentary

Hyperborea, the mythical land "beyond the North Wind," is mentioned first by Herodotus, who locates it somewhere beyond Thrace (the homeland of Orpheus) and considers the Hyperboreans devotees of Apollo and Artemis. He cites Hesiod and the *Epigoni*, a lost epic of the Theban cycle.

Here however nothing remains of Herodotus except the "wheat-straw" in line 3. Instead we are reminded of the opening of Hesiod's *Theogony* in which he describes Chaos, Eros, Gaia, Day and Night, the primordial and chthonic deities. The author of the *Fragments* creates from these hints not only a "theology" in which Chaos is still "god," but also a society of Chaotes—humankind *before* the Golden Age.

Primal androgynes, liminal beings (half-human half-animal, a symbol of shamanic "totemism"), the Hyperboreans practice only a gathering economy, lacking weapons even for hunting. Society as we understand it has not yet come into being. "Zerling" may have been thinking of Neanderthal Man when he invented this myth (if he did); in any case, the description fits Middle or Late Paleolithic economy with a shamanic cult as described by Eliade, and a social structure known in anthropology as "non-authoritarian."

Their only principle of order is Eros, desire, which alone can move the Hyperboreans to any social effort. Otherwise they remind us of "primitive Taoists," baby-like or child-like, "pumpkin-heads," fools[7]. Their adherence to Chaos (the "uncarved primal block") makes them "slothful" and dumb or near-speechless or beast-tongued. Eros makes them "turbid," "barbarian," "protean."

The ancients knew that nights grow "longer" in the far North, and this gave rise to the idea of Hyperborea as a land of perpetual darkness; and yet the Indo-European races looked on Hyperborea as an origin-land (thus it is mentioned in the Vedas), a terrestrial paradise. All Aryan-influenced myth speaks of a temperate zone of immortal (or long-lived) magicians in the Dawn-Time, in the distant North.

The image of Boreas in Classical mythology—a bearded cloaked wind-blown bravo and rapist—is once again ignored by our author, who lends the minor deity a spacey grandeur and fearful primacy, making him a Chaote king (or *primus inter pares*, since each Hyperborean is a "lord of his own domain").

The polar mountains in line 9 remind us of other world-encircling mountains or walls, such as that of Gog and Magog, or Mount Qaf of the sufis. In one sense they mark off the "mundane world" from the "Imaginal World" of archetypes, visions, prophecy, spirits and "similitudes." In the *Fragments* however we are clearly presented with a land of *material being* rather than pure Imagination. It is, as we shall see, a realm of alchemy, where matter and spirit are one in the undifferentiated unity-of-being of Chaos itself.

As for Didymos of Rhodes—if he lived in the 3rd Century B.C., why is he never mentioned till the First Century A.D.? Probably because "his" work was also pseudepigraphical: a "forgery." Moreover, the gold book of Hecaergos the Hyperborean is mentioned nowhere but here; undoubtedly it never existed. Therefore, including "Zerling"'s forgery of the elements the *Fragments*, the anonymous "Gnostic"'s forgery of *Didymos* and "Didymos"'s forgery of *Hecaergos*, we are faced with third-level deception, like some literary version of *Spy vs. Spy*.

Fragment II (III)

...[the] hidden prophet [8]
who alone can speak
with wordless Chaos,
immortal guardian of the Fountain of Life
beneath the Pole Star;
vegetation springs up where he walks,
(part-) dragon [or fish?][9]
dressed in green,
wanderer of deserts, devotee of winds
and shapeless clouds...

Commentary

"Zerling" identifies this passage as a description of Boreas, but such an assertion involves too many problems to satisfy a closer reading. Boreas cannot easily be associated with a Fountain of Life, nor is he a vegetation-spirit, nor a dragon, nor a dragon-slayer, nor a fish, nor does he dress in green. Apparently we are dealing here with some other Hyperborean figure, and the passage may belong with the "List of Heroes" (Fragment VI).

Without question however this passage can serve very well to describe a figure who became known in Islamdom as Khezr, the Green Man or Hidden Prophet—frequently called the King of Hyperborea. He is identified with the mysterious and tricky "servant of Moses" (Koran, XVIII, 60-96) who exhibits shocking antinomian behavior—a motif that can be traced to the Jewish *haggadah* tradition of Pentateuch-mythos.

Khezr also makes appearances in the various Oriental romances written about Alexander the Great (Iskandar dhu'l-Qarnayn), especially in Persian and Ethiopian manuscript traditions. Here the "hidden prophet" hires on as Alexander's cook, offering to lead him to the Fountain of Life in the Land of Darkness, Hyperborea. In Fragment V we will discuss this story at greater length, since our author has borrowed heavily from the Alexander cycle for his own description of the invasion of Hyperborea.

In Haggadic, Koranic and Alexandrian versions, Khezr is associated with life-giving water, fish, vegetation and the color green. He seems to owe a lot to early Christian traditions circulating in the Near East concerning St. Michael and especially St. George, the dragon-slayers. Our author undoubtedly scores by identifying Khezr with the Dragon itself rather than the slayer, since many versions speak of him as a sort of merman, undine or sea-monster.

The sufis adopted this already-ancient figure as their special patron, asserting that he would appear to sincere seekers in remote places (in deserts, or walking across water) to offer aid and mystic initiation. "Hyperborea" for the sufis signifies the Unseen World, or the adept's own Creative Imagination experienced as *vision*, as a visitation from outside the self. (See Corbin's *Creative Imagination in the Sufism of Ibn Arabi* for a full discussion of this symbolism.)

The hypothetical 3rd Century A.D. Gnostic author of the *Fragments* could well have known much of this tradition. Speculation on this point would serve no purpose, however, since we assume that the work is a 19th Century forgery and could thus make use (covertly of course) of Islamic sources as well as Classical, Jewish and Christian.

Fragment III (IV)

...from beyond the Star Gate of the Aeons,
from the [direction of the constellation of
the] Wolf [they came] to Gaia,
ancient beyond count, ravenous for souls,
Titans, workers of metal,
merciless as the Undead.
At the navel of the World they established
their realm,
raised stone monoliths to their war-god,
tyrant-god, judge-god, executioner-god,
in the name of the Empire of Time and
Death...

[lines missing]

...[so that the human race]
was forced to rape
the body of our mother the Earth,
sow her with seed
and ravage her fruits,
sacrifice our first-born
on the altars of the Cosmos...

...[so that only Hyperborea]
remained safe from invasion
[living as always in] dusk and summer
[while all other nations toiled] to build
meaningless cities

[for the invaders],
blind cyclopaean labyrinths
(which would serve them only)
as prisons for themselves [10].

Commentary

The passage sets "Zerling" off into dusty ecstasies in which he detects Gnostic influence everywhere (specifically Valentinian and Basilidean, and possibly Manichaean). The "Aeons" are certainly well-known in such circles; the Star Gate *(stauros)* could refer to the *crucis* or Gateway between the Pleroma of Pure Spirit and the Abyss of Material Creation. The "invaders" described here could qualify as the malevolent Cosmic demons or "Stars" which keep humankind imprisoned herebelow, exiled to a realm of corruption and suffering.

The passage also contains hints of the Biblical story of the "Sons of God" (or "the gods") who come down and marry the daughters of men bringing with them knowledge of arts and crafts, agriculture and metal, etc. "And there were giants in the earth in those days." The pseudo-Enoch tells us how these angels (called "Watchers") turned tyrannical and malevolent and had to be chastised and exiled by Jehovah. Whoever these beings may have been, they are also linked here with the Titans, the cruel giants overthrown by Zeus.

What however are we to make of "Zerling"'s translation of the Greek star-name for Canis Major as "[the direction of the constellation of] the Wolf"?! He offers no justification, nor does he explain the use of the word "Undead" *(brukolakas)* which seems to hint at the late-Medieval vampire-legend, supposedly unknown in the 3rd Century A.D. Does "Zerling" wish us to question his own theory of Gnostic authorship here and search for other contemporary crank-cases who attribute all human civilization to aliens, UFOs, extraterrestrial "benefactors"?

The *"Hyperborean" Fragments* depicts the forced conversion of human culture from nomadic, gatherer, matriarchal or androgynous and non-authoritarian to city-dwelling, agricultural, patriarchal, moralistic and authoritarian—a conversion carried out by aliens or devils, not benign culture-heroes. With breathtaking revolutionary insouciance, the *Fragments*-author consigns virtually all of human culture to the status of an unfortunate mistake, a tyrannical blunder. This smacks of Gnosticism, true, but even more of 19th Century Nihilism and the Nietzschean "revaluation of values." The Invaders impose a dictatorial and moralistic cult on a people naturally "barbaric" and spontaneous. These aliens are the forerunners of the Christian Church, of all rulers, bankers, ideologues and kings.

In true Dualist Gnosticism, the material prison-house of Earth is not self-built but imposed on us by an evil demiurge, our "creator." However, in the last lines of *Fragment* III, we are told that our manacles are not *material* but in fact mental illusions, built up by ourselves to trick ourselves into slavery. This is not a Dualist idea; despite the Gnostic terminology, we are dealing here with some other school of mysticism or mythopoesis. Exactly which one remains to be seen.

Fragments IV (VI)

[A leader of the Invaders from "beyond the Star Gate," or perhaps an oracle, addresses the warriors of the Empire and exhorts them to wage war against the Hyperboreans:]

> ["...a people devoted to] incest,
> knowing neither night
> from day nor sin from sanctity,
> placid as deer,
> unruly as weather, aimless as the Winds.
> In their shameless Temple [of Chaos]
> lamps are blown out,

virgins and boys glistening with uncut gems
offer their favors to believers,
like Canaanites,
and dance for the golden apes and spider-
idols of their cult,
coupled in bestial fucking on sacred ground,
their priests dressed as women,
sons spurning fathers,
ignorant of Time and Measure,
enemies of Order,
half-snake half-men, antediluvian monsters.
We bring the Sun of Empire to dispel
the Night of Chaos... [."]

Commentary

"Zerling" translates this passage prudishly into Latin rather than German, commenting only that "its obscene contents suggest some connection with antinomian cults such as the Carpocrateans or Ophites." He makes no attempt to fit this fragment into a coherent narrative, and the interpretation of it as an "oracle" of the Invaders is our own hypothesis. The word translated as "fucking" (Gr. *mignein*) would have had a more shocking effect on readers than "Zerling"'s squeamish Latin (*concubitus*).

The "Empire" (which stands for orthodoxy) must always accuse its enemies of wickedness and heresy. "Blowing out the lamps" and making love at random in a communal polymorphic orgy is a ritual attributed with deadening frequency to various schismatics by various inquisitors throughout history (see for example N. Cohn's *Europe's Inner Demons*)—and so we may well imagine that this libel against Hyperborea oozes from the mouth of a sinister alien Invader attempting to impose world civilization, a universal orthodoxy.

But does the *Fragments*-author really intend us to take these accusations as false and libelous? No.

That is, the author of the *Fragments* does not want us to think that these accusations are false. He implies that the Hyperboreans do in fact indulge in such prelapsarian orgyism. They admit the acts but deny the immorality; Chaotes are not bound by *any* morality.

Every one of these "perversions" can be interpreted as a valid symbol for Chaos or the Chaote Consciousness, the mystical state of unity. Androgyny for instance means the merging of genders in a single body, and transvestism is likewise a symbol of "divine hermaphroditism." Incest is the ultimate endogamy or "union" as opposed to exogamy or "marrying *away*" (undoubtedly incest had this meaning for the Egyptians). Homosexuality is yet another androgyny symbol, a sign of reversal and hence of magic. Sacred prostitution was a role originally assumed by shamans in order to mediate between spirits and humans (the Jews believed the ancient Canaanites practiced temple prostitution, and clear traces of the practice survive in the Bible). Ritual intercourse thus stands for what might be called "tantrik yoga."

All these symbols emphasize the liminality or *in-between-ness* of Hyperborea. As a land on the border between Real and Imaginal ("the Isthmus" as the sufis called it), Hyperborea must be uncanny, backwards, a through-the-looking-glass world where everything becomes its opposite: "perverse behavior." Actual "perversion" is thus a sign of shamanic experience, of "breaking through" or "across" (or up or down, depending on which culture supplies the specific symbolism). In "primitive" societies the connection between the supernatural (neither benign nor malign in itself, but *powerful*) and "scandalous" sexual behavior is well understood, and even ritualized.

Here we find (in the last five lines) echoes of Mesopotamian myth, of Tiamat the Chaos monster and her wild progeny of snake-men, scorpion-demons, dog-faced dwarves, lion-headed lizards and whatnot—"antediluvian" figures wiped out by Marduk the Sun God, the

Culture Hero, the founder of the Babylonian Empire. But every culture possesses some such self-validating myth, some description of how Righteous Order (i.e., *our* way of life) overcame Primal Disorder (*their* way of life). The *Fragments* must be almost unique in pretending to speak on behalf of Chaos and *against Culture*. The only other examples which come to mind are the Taoists Lao Tzu and Chuang Tzu; but their treatment of the theme lacks the pugnacious quality of the *Fragments*, which takes place in an almost Heraclitan atmosphere of "strife" and fatality.

Fragment V (V)

[The army of the Empire invades Hyperborea:]

From the Empire they went forth,
always northward
and came at last
to a desert of yellow-grey corruption
which marked the limit of their charts.
Mocked by ravens they marched,
and many died.
Then they came to a land
where everything was blue,
not only sky and lakes but trees, rocks
and beasts as well,
the streams laid with sapphires,
ravines cracked open
on depths of beryl,
eagles like turquoise torches.
Here many deserted in fear,
willing to face the desert again
rather than a land of ghouls...

[lines missing]

> [They come to a land of red:]
> … where fire burned in the cinnabar eyes
> of basilisks, and the heavens rained blood..

[lines missing]

> …peacock's tail…
> [i.e., the next country they visit is
> multicolored and iridescent?]

[lines missing]

> […a land as green as] The Emerald Tablet
> of Hermes Trismegistus,
> gold-green as Arcadia, jasper-skied,
> jade-oceaned
> but cold as a glacier
> from the Wind's attacking
> off the [Polar] Mountains to the North,
> so that many more perished,
> hands frozen to iron weapons,
> eyes green with the dull ice of death.

> [They cross the Mountains, whereupon they
> find themselves at the entrance to
> Hyperborea:]
> … guarded by two winged youths
> who vanished
> into the tangled dusk and star-lit confusion
> of the Chaote land,
> luring them on like hares
> leading hounds into thorn, losing them

one by one, separated and cut off
by walls of mist...

Commentary

Fragment V apparently describes the campaign against Hyperborea by the "Imperial" army, led by the alien Invaders. The itinerary of colored lands is stolen direct from the Alexander Romances. In these, Alexander learns of the Dark Land from his cook, Khezr. As the Greeks press ever northward, Alexander eventually loses his entire army to the rigors or terrors of various eerie, monochromatic lands, including an Oz-like emerald realm.

Corbin has pointed out (see *The Man of Light in Iranian Sufism*) that this color-sequence corresponds to that described by Islamic alchemists in their accounts of the transmutation of metals or creation of the Elixir. The desert of corruption stands for *nigredo*, the "dark night of the soul," the base condition of metals, sickness and repentance. Blue, "Peacock's Tail" (*cauda pavonis*), white and red constitute other alchemical stages. In European alchemy red comes last and represents the Stone. Islamic alchemy developed two further stages, "green-gold" and "luminous black." The former symbolizes revelation (the prophetic color), the latter symbolizes mystical union ("the sun at midnight").

The green land is here compared to the Emerald or "Smarigdine" Tablet of Hermes Trismegistus, a First Century Alexandrian Hermetic-Gnostic text containing clear non-Dualist teachings ("That which is above is like that which is below, for the accomplishment of the Work"). The Emerald Tablet sets an alchemical seal on this whole passage.

In the Alexander Romances, Khezr and Alexander enter the Dark Land alone and are at once separated from each other and lost. Khezr wanders at random till he comes to a pool. Feeling hungry, he produces two dried smoked fish from his sack, and washes them in the spring. At once they come to life and swim away. Khezr realizes he has found the Fountain. Two angels appear and invite him to bathe. He does so, and attains immortality. Alexander meanwhile angrily cuts his way through the Dark forest and escapes unharmed, but still mortal. Khezr rejoins him, but Alexander succumbs to jealousy and tries to kill Khezr by throwing him into the sea. However, he becomes a "sea-monster" and swims happily away.

In the *Fragments*, the "angels" are guarding the entrance to the Dark Land. Apparently only the alien Invaders now remain of the entire Imperial army; they chase after the youths and become lost in the Dark Land. They come lusting for conquest, like Alexander, rather than as sincere and spontaneous seekers like Khezr—and therefore they lose their way.

Fragment VI (VII)

…Calais and Zetes,
sons of beautiful Oreithyia;
the maidens Opis and Arge,
Hyperoche and Laodice,
Amazons of Artemis; Agyicus and Loxo,
peerless tricksters and slayers of…

Commentary

Unfortunately this is all that remains of the description of the war between the Empire and Hyperborea, and thus we have no way of knowing why or how the Chaotes lost. Apparently they began well with evasive guerilla tactics, and the names listed here (lifted from Herodotus except for the first two, well-known as sons of Boreas) obviously belong to a Homeric catalogue of the "hosts" of Hyperborea. Nevertheless the last two *Fragments* will make it clear that the Chaotes are beaten and scattered, and that all resistance against the Empire is broken.

In a sense, this *lack* of text is significant. Assuming that "Zerling" is our author, no doubt he felt quite diffident about explaining how his Chaote heroes could possibly face defeat at the hands (or tentacles) of the alien Invaders. How indeed does "primal" man lose his innocence and trick himself into working as a peasant to feed priests and kings? How does he first swallow the idea of "progress" or indeed even of "Time" itself? What force could destroy the primordial *suchness* of life, which every mystic and lover has felt? How could we have given up our original freedom for the scant and disappointing returns of civilization? the Blakean question? the Nietzschean question? How could we have been so stupid? What happened?

"Zerling" has no answers—other than a *lacuna* in his forgery. The alien Invaders are ultimately no more than devils *ex-machina,* a Science-Fiction plot device, a paranoid fantasy. However, the *Fragments*-author, whoever he may be (even a 3rd Century Gnostic!), seems dangerously close to taking the aliens seriously. Conspiracy theory shines with an eternal appeal: the chance to blame everything on "them." Gnosticism itself owes much of its success to a really daring conspiracy theory. Even though we believe our author must be described as a *non-Dualist Gnostic,* we admit he shares a universe of discourse and a tinge of paranoia with Valentinus and the Manichees. Unlike them, he believes that matter and spirit are one; but like them, he believes in an invasion of the Cosmos.

A true Chaote would take responsibility for his fate (*amor fati*), and not blame the universe for his misfortunes. If the *Fragments* are read as allegory, we believe the aliens must stand for humankind's own divided self, the "bad consciousness" that prevents us from living spontaneously and joyfully. They also therefore stand for history which from the point of view of Chaos consists largely of bad consciousness.

Fragment VII (I)

[The Invaders, now victorious, decide to leave Earth:]

["...] once again retire to our Pleroma
beyond this filthy Cosmos
knowing that the Empire is secure forever,
that our laws will now bind them
with self-forged chains of illusion, of duty
to our cities, our gods, our fleshless desires.
We will leave among them a few agents
cloaked in the black we have stolen
from Boreas
to watch and meddle
and invent new weapons,
to work for stupefaction, lies,
conspiracies, hunger and drugged sleep...
They will inherit
our secret knowledge (gnosis)
and unveil to the vulgar
only the empty niches
where once we sat; nor will they... [."]

Commentary

In this passage the aliens themselves begin to sound like Dualist Gnostics! They despise the Cosmos as "filth" and yearn for the "Pleroma" or extra-spatial paradise of pure spirit. Confusion upon confusion! "Zerling" brings up the notion that the *Fragments* may represent some arcane internecine schismatic strife between rival Gnostic sects in 3rd Century Alexandria. Monist Gnostics vs. Dualist Gnostics? Antinomians such as the orgiastic followers of the pallid youth Carpocrates, or the snake-worshipping Ophites, creating propaganda for Chaos in order to scandalize the moralistic and puritanical Valentinians? The mind boggles. A more interesting question is, What did "Zerling" mean by all this pedantic chatter?

One possibility: "The agents dressed in black" represent the Roman Church, perpetuator of the Empire according to its Gnostic and Protestant enemies. "Babylon" as Rome, "The Beast" as Pope, etc.

Another possibility: the aliens really are extraterrestrials from some star on a line with Canis Major ("The Wolf"). "The Men in Black" are well-known to modern UFO cultists and conspiracy cranks, who see their traces in Bilderberg Conferences and water-fluoridation schemes, etc. They are "trans-Uranian" or perhaps "trans-Plutonian" in origin. In this interpretation, "Star Gate" represents the Solar System itself.

Most likely possibility however:

"They" are "us."

Fragment VIII (II)

…"ordinary" mind does not exist .

… each of you [is] a daemon…

…Chaos never gave way to Order,

Gods, spirits and men were never born.

Only the illusion of Law can bind you—

in truth, you were never [chained]…

Commentary

Chaos is not yet utterly defeated. Some voice remains to utter these words, to assure us that our bondage is illusion, that in the timeless realm of Chaos we are *already free*. Each of us is a spirit, and thus *the* Spirit. "Order" is subject to our consciousness, which contains within itself the unbounded and "unborn" purity of Chaos, source of all creativity, the "Tao" itself.

Religion, government, Law, history, all false consciousness, all morality, even the "laws of science"—none of these can be called absolute. Being itself precedes all concepts of Being; and thus the Imagination is unchained to create for itself its own "world," which corresponds to the "Golden Age," the terrestrial and material paradise. The Elixir transforms *this* world. Chaos admits no eschatological afterlife, or rather remains uninterested in Heaven and Hell. Union with the one, now and here, is its goal—but no Law, indeed no *word* can circumscribe and define that state.

If we are dogged by a conspiracy of Men in Black, we ourselves make up our own counter-conspiracy, also perhaps symbolized by blackness, a cabal of perpetual insurrection against all Chains of the Law.

Having at last discovered the intention of the *"Hyperborean" Fragments* (at least to our own satisfaction) we can now ask again, and perhaps answer, certain questions.

Are the *Fragments* a Gnostic Forgery?

No.

"Zerling" means to mislead us on this point, not once but twice. Even if we detect the hand of the 19th Century forger, we might still believe that we are reading a forgery of a Gnostic forgery. But in fact the Gnostic "clues" in the *Fragments* are simply red herrings. "Zerling" wants to create here what can only be called a *counter-myth* to all of Western civilization. He dips into Gnosticism, Bible studies, philology, archaeology, mythology, comparative religion, sufism, Hermeticism, alchemy and philosophy to attain his goal, but his goal is contained in none of these.

Who was "Zerling"? Who wrote the *Fragments*?

1888 was something of an *annus mirabilis* for Friedrich Nietzsche. He wrote and published *The Wagner Case*, wrote *Revaluation of All Values* and *Twilight of the Idols*, *The Anti-Christ* and *Ecce Homo*, *Nietzsche contra Wagner* and *The Dithyrambs of Dionysos*. In the last quarter of the year he fell victim to a delusive improvement in his health, followed by a morbid euphoria which led to his collapse into insanity, and his tragic last letters, on Jan. 3, 1889 in Turin.

The Anti-Christ opens with the words quoted at the head of this article, in which Nietzsche greets his readers as fellow-Hyperboreans. In some respects, the *"Hyperborean" Fragments* might be read as a commentary on these few lines from Nietzsche's devastating and final attack on Christianity. Veiled commentary—even ironic commentary. Impossible to prove—but an intriguing "coincidence," since the *festschrift* also appeared in 1888.

Nietzsche himself of course is certainly not our author. For one thing, the *Fragments* makes no mention of Dionysos, or the "Myth of Eternal Return," two Nietzschean obsessions he would surely have trotted out if he were to undertake such a hoax. Of course, Nietzsche was a brilliant Classical philologist. He *could* have done it. But it was not his style—and that settles the matter.

What about some disciple or ex-student of Nietzsche from his professorial days at Bonn, Leipzig or Basel?

At last we hit something that might prove to be pay-dirt. One of the other contributors to the *festschrift* was Johannes Metz (1847-1902), an almost exact contemporary of Nietzsche's who attended Leipzig one year behind him and studied philosophy there. They could have met in 1865 or 66; so far, we have no evidence they did, then or ever.

Metz wrote very little, and his interest in apocrypha resulted in only one or two essays, of which we have seen only "Jesus As Murderer And Magician In The 'Infancy' Gospels." In 1888 he was living and lecturing in Munich on Hegelian philosophy, and he published a few reviews on studies of Feuerbach, Stirner and other "Left" Hegelian luminaries. No mention anywhere in this work of Nietzsche—who was distinctly not a Hegelian. Stirner and Nietzsche however were later reconciled by the "Individualist Anarchists," who stood opposed to both Marxian and Bakuninist strains of the late 19th Century "social revolution."

Metz, if indeed he is our author, might have been attempting some such synthesis, for certainly the *Fragments* contains a sort of mythic superstructure for individualist philosophy.

"Jesus As Murderer," according to Karl, who read it over carefully at our request after we had begun to suspect Metz, demonstrates what might be considered a very dry, almost invisible sense of humor or irony; the subject matter is, after all, somewhat blasphemous, and Metz treats it (Karl says) utterly deadpan, without emotion, "as if discussing the weather in ancient Israel." The "Infancy Gospels," which depict the child Jesus as a dangerous *Exorcist*-style imp of the perverse, might well have appealed to a secret devotee of Chaos.

Karl has so far been unable to locate Metz's papers. He says he gets the feeling Metz was too insignificant for anyone to think of saving his letters or endowing an archive. No luck tracing family. The man is almost as elusive as "Zerling."

Again: it is probably too late to track down our mysterious mytho-poet or penetrate behind his multiple masks of scholarship and con-fidence-trickery. Even if we had evidence "against" Metz rather than only unfounded suspicions, what then would we know of his motivation? his real sources?

The question ultimately must be discarded as irrelevant, or at least relatively uninteresting. The text is worth saving, even with the trouble of unburying it from beneath the tortuous and heavyhanded scholarly whimsy of its own creator. If there were a purpose to this rather Borgesian amusement, we could only sum it up by finishing our opening quotation from Nietzsche:

> 'We [Hyperboreans] have discovered
> happiness, we know the road,
> we have found the exit
> out of the whole labyrinth of millennia.
> Who *else* has found it?"

NOTES

1. *Eine Festschrift fur Berndt von Moltke*, privat gedruckt im Zee Verlag, Munchen.

2. See the entry in *Brevoort's Dictionary of Classical History* (Oxford, 1853).

3. in the Manuscript Room of the State Library in Munich.

4. Lunsdorf's papers, left to the Archival Library in Dresden, were destroyed during World War II. See the biography, *Die Lebens und gedachnis Weise des Otto Lunsdorf* by Wilhelm Goetzen (Koniglich Druckerei, Leiden, 1894).

5. The works of Corbin have been translated into English and published by the Bollingen Foundation of Princeton University Press.

6. The numbers in parentheses refer to the sequence of the *Fragments* in "Zerling"'s article. Since he offers no justification for this ordering, and since the *Fragments* make no sense in his system, we have assumed that he meant them to be re-ordered into something hinting of a story, and this we have done. For instance, here we have an obvious introduction, a description of Hyperborea—but "Zerling" placed it last because he believed "the last four lines must be the colophon" or scribal "signature" of the manuscript.

7. See *Myth and Meaning in Early Taoism: The Theme of Chaos* by N.J. Girardot (University of California Press, Berkeley, 1983) for a delightful presentation of Chaos-mysticism as a kind of "pumpkinification."

8. An Aramaic or Hebrew loan-word, *nabi* or *navi*, transliterated into Greek as v a p i ("prophet").

9. line very garbled—might perhaps be read as "dragon slayer"; the fish (?) is suggested by a single syllable, *ich* , and also by the mythic material (see commentary).

10. reading of entire section very uncertain according to "Zerling," who nevertheless hints at some such "reconstruction" of the missing half-lines.

A NIETZSCHEAN COUP D'ÉTAT

(For Nancy J. Peters And Bob Sharrard)

"Nothing is true, all is permitted."
—*Thus Spoke Zarathustra*, 386

There is no way of telling what may yet become part of history. Perhaps the past is still essentially undiscovered! So many retroactive forces are still needed!
—*The Gay Science*, 104

I. Introduction

Let us face ourselves. We are Hyperboreans; we know very well how far off we live. "Neither by land nor by sea will you find the way to the Hyperboreans"—Pindar already knew this about us. Beyond the north, ice, and death—*our* life, *our* happiness. We have discovered happiness, we know the way, we have found the exit out of the labyrinth of thousands of years. Who *else* has found it?
—*The Anti-Christ*, 569

The 19th century resisted coming to an end. It got off to a late start in about 1830 with the Industrial Revolution, and it held on (with increasing desperation) well beyond 1900. World War I began as the last 19th century war, an affair of monarchs and diplomats—but it degenerated into a technological hecatomb, a mass sacrifice, a potlatch of modern death—and of course, a Revolution. The 20th century really began in 1917, behind the front, in Russia. A year or so later, despite the re-appearance of the diplomats in their top hats and gleaming orders, the 20th century had reached Europe and America. And despite the declarations of eternal peace, it was to be a century of pure violence.

In 1830 the emergent world of Capital seemed fated for universal triumph. What or who could oppose such "progress"? Certainly not those backward and exhausted oriental lands that were already being added one by one as jewels to various European crowns—and most certainly not our very own pathetic "working class." These outer or inner "natives" might grow restless, but such problems could be handled by superior force. Capital was an idea whose time had come—it could be opposed only by an idea of equal power. And where could such an idea be found in 1830? In the crack-brained dreams of "Utopian Socialists"? But Capital was not a mere system, to be dismantled by reformist tinkerers. Capital was History itself—a universal fate—a natural law.

And yet by 1871 something had gone disturbingly wrong with Capital's game-plan. The revolt in Paris required more than a few police to put down—in fact, it took the massed armies of two nations, and demanded a massacre of thousands. And still the blight spread, the movement of the Social, a dialectical response to the movement of Capital—an *opposing idea*. World War I (which began in 1914 with the quintessentially 19th-century incident of a Grand Duke's assassination) amounted to a vast tactical manoeuver for the de-railing of the Social. The workers were to be distracted by patriotism and then disciplined by war.

Instead, as the 19th century came to an end in the shambles of the trenches, something went wrong with Capital's strategy again. It lost control of Russia. Suddenly it seemed possible that the War might have been a mistake. "Soviets" of workers and soldiers were being proclaimed here and there in the oddest places, and 1918 began as the year of World Revolution—at least in the feverish imaginations of certain rebels, and certain reactionaries.

It's not easy to reconstruct this moment. Obsessive attention has been paid to the Russian revolution because it succeeded, but the other revolutions—the ones that failed—have been forgotten. One might almost say "obsessively forgotten." Capitalist historians forgot 1918-1919 because after all one need not remind one's readers that less than a lifetime ago certain incidents occurred, certain almost-meaningless incidents... and as for Communist historians, they were embarrassed by the fact that most of these incidents were not inspired by Marxism (and the ones that were inspired by Marxism failed like all the others). So whose responsibility was it to remember 1918-19? Obviously nobody's. And therefore it may come as a surprise to learn that in Ireland, the city of Limerick declared itself a Soviet in April 1919 and held out against the British long enough to print its own money.[1] The uprisings in Germany are perhaps better-known, although not much attention has been paid to the anarchistic *Räterepublik* in Munich that lasted tempestuously from November 1918 to May 1919 and enlisted the talents of such men as philosopher Gustav Landauer, poet Erich Mühsam, playwright Ernst Toller, and novelist B. Traven (then known as "Ret Marut").[2] In Hungary, the Marxist Bela Kun came briefly to power in 1919. In September 1919 the poet Gabriele D'Annunzio "liberated" the Yugoslavian city of Fiume and declared it independent. He promulgated an anarchistic constitution (based on *music*) and filled

---

[1] See Cahill (1990)

[2] See my article in *Drunken Boat* (forthcoming: Autonomedia) [Note: This was never published.]

his coffers with loot won by anarchist "pirates." This operatic experiment came to an end in November 1920 when the Italians bombed D'Annunzio out of his palace.[3] Meanwhile in the Ukraine a revolt broke out against both the Whites and the Reds, led by the anarchist Nestor Makhno, and succeeded for a while in liberating whole areas from any government whatsoever.

The failure of the Revolution to reach world-wide proportions in 1918-1919 meant in effect that the 19th century would have to be repeated all over again. In the 19th century neither Capital nor Social had succeeded in crushing the other, and now the 20th century would have to play out all the repercussions of that failure in a world divided geographically and ideologically into two "blocs." The struggle of the Social with Capital would go on, and in that sense the 19th century would also *go on*.

In 1918 it was by no means clear that the movement of the Social would be hijacked and eventually monopolized by Marxism. The success of the Bolsheviks in Moscow was not yet seen as the signal for a *Marxist* world revolution. Other systems and ideologies competed for space within that revolution:—anarchism, for example, as well as various forms of socialism and even utopianism. Moreover, the movement of the Social had still not yet fragmented into a distinct Right and Left. Nazism and Fascism were both "Social" movements and in fact even grew out of "leftist" roots (Mussolini, D'Annunzio, and the Italian Futurists were all anarchists, and the Nazis began as a socialist workers' party). But neither of these reactionary forms had really emerged in 1918-1919,[4] and strange hybrids were still possible. Fiume was a bizarre mix of anarchism, aestheticism and *fin-de-siècle* decadence, nationalism, and uniform-fetishism (black, with skull-and-crossbones insignia, later plagiarized by the SS).

---

[3]See Bey (1991)

[4]Although the future could certainly be read in the bloodstains on the pavement in Munich, where the Jew Gustav Landauer was stomped to death by the members of the Thule Gesellschaft.

One of the oddest of all the exotic revolutionary flowers of 1918-19, and one of the most thoroughly forgotten—the Autonomous Sanjak of Cumantsa, under the leadership of Georghiu Mavrocordato—demonstrates the complex fluidity of 19th century ideologies and systems in struggle against Capital and simultaneously against Communism. Cumantsa has never been interpreted in this light, partly because its ideological *bouillabaisse* is so strange as to be literally incomprehensible to most historians. However, there exist other good reasons for Cumantsa's obscurity. For one thing the "Provisional Government" of the Sanjak came to power not by uprising and rebellion, but by *coup d'état*; thus it is not seen as a "revolutionary" phenomenon. Then too, Cumantsa is obscure, remote, hardly European at all—an insignificant port-town on the Black Sea in the region of Romania called the Dobruja, on one of the ancient silted-up mouths of the Danube, surrounded by hundreds of miles of desolate delta marsh-land, swamp, estuaries, creeks, lagoons and sand-bars. One might almost think that Cumantsa was made to be forgotten.

The mélange of intellectual and historical influences that went into the melting-pot of Cumantsa will be explored in this essay—but the main reason for our interest in the Provisional Government of the Sanjak is not its syncretistic complexity, but rather its uniqueness. As far as I know,[5] it is the only experiment in government ever to be openly

---

[5]Aside from a few passing references in other sources, which I shall note, all information on Cumantsa here will be derived from one book, *Hronicul Dobruja* by O. Densusianu (Bucharest, 1929), which was drawn to my attention by the Dadaist poet Valery Oisteanu; I was able to acquire a summary and partial English translation of the relevant part of this text from a Romanian student in New York, Ion Barak; my thanks to both. Densusianu's sources for the period seem to have been limited to the newspaper published in Cumantsa in 1918, *Luceafari*, "The Evening Star." There may well exist untapped sources for further research in government archives in Bucharest or even in Cumantsa, or in private libraries in Romania, etc. These sources will have to await the researches of competent scholars, and perhaps the inadequacies of the present essay will inspire someone to dig deeper.

based on the philosophy of Friedrich Nietzsche. Surely *that* is worth remembrance.

II. CUMANTSA

"Praised be this day that lured me into this swamp!"
—*Thus Spoke Zarathustra*, 362

The ancient history of the Cumantsa region is not only interesting in itself but also provides a background without which the events of 1918-1920 will lack both depth of field and nuance. Perhaps it is merely a truism to say that geography and climate (or *landscape*), along with the memory that inheres in every building or cleared field (also *landscape*), participate in the historical events that transpire within a region—but in Cumantsa the cliché strikes us with the freshness of a new insight.

At the beginning of the Neolithic, about nine or ten thousand years ago, the entire western shore of the Black Sea belonged to that culture called Cucuteni, analyzed so brilliantly by archaeologist Marija Gimbutas and others as agricultural, "matriarchal" or goddess-worshipping, peaceful, and artistically brilliant. Gimbutas believes that sometime around the fourth millennium BC this area was "invaded" by the "Kurgan People" (named after their distinctive burial mounds) from the East, from across the great steppes beyond the Black Sea. These new peoples were pastoralist, "patriarchal" or god-worshipping, warlike, and barbaric. They were probably the Indo-Europeans. One of the chief routes from the steppes into Europe would have gone past the mouths of the Danube, and thence down into Greece or along the river into what we now call Eastern Europe. And in fact the Dobruja has been over-run countless times by an almost infinite number of barbarians. Before Classical Antiquity the sequence of invasions remains a blur in which nothing much can be distinguished, but around the 7th century BC the mists part and we find a people called Cimmerians living around the Black Sea from the Crimea down to Thrace. Semi-barbaric,

Eastern Romania 1918

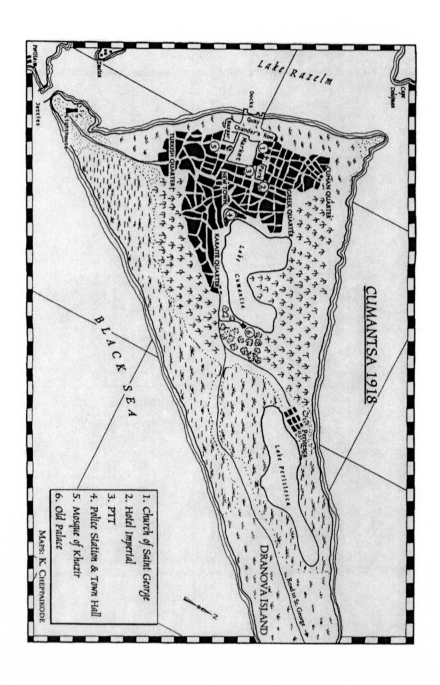

CUMANTSA 1918

1. *Church of Saint George*
2. *Hotel Imperial*
3. *PTT*
4. *Police Station & Town Hall*
5. *Mosque of Khazir*
6. *Old Palace*

Maps: K. Cheppaikode

perhaps Thracians or Iranians, the Cimmerii are suddenly confronted with a new set of steppe-nomads, the Scythians. According to ancient historians (Herodotus, Aristeas), the Scythians had been displaced by the Massagetae, who had been displaced by the Issedones, who had been displaced by the Arimaspi. This last race were cyclopeans with one eye each, who lived with griffins and hoarded gold somewhere near the Altai Mountains and not far from Hyperborea—such was the general opinion. The Scythians appear to have been a confederacy of Ugrian and Irani barbarians, but Hippocrates said they were quite unlike any other race of men. The Scyths made this impression in part because of their unusual brand of shamanism, which involved a class of transvestite soothsayers called *Enarëes*; Herodotus claims they were struck by the "sacred disease" of effeminacy because they had insulted the Goddess of Ascalon. "The whole account," says one modern scholar, "suggests a Tatar clan in the last stage of degeneracy"[6] —but in truth transvestite shamanism is widely practised not only in Central Asia and Siberia but also Indonesia and North America. Apparently it is "natural" in some way. The same could be said for another Scythian custom that struck Herodotus as odd:—they filled tents with burning hemp (*cannabis*) and breathed the smoke till they achieved intoxication. (Archaeological evidence for Scythian hemp-use is quite plentiful.) They worshipped the hearth, like many nomads, as well as Sky and Earth, the Sun, and a goddess called Argimpasa (identified by the Greeks as Aphrodite Urania, the patroness of homosexuality!)—also the Sea, and War. Their elite burials were exceedingly elaborate and involved human sacrifice. Thanks to excavations we also know about Scythian art, one of the earliest and finest instances of High Barbarian style, and later much imitated (for example, by the Celts who displaced the Scythians in the interior Danubian region):— heraldic, vigorous, magical, and intricate. We also know that the Scyths

---

[6] *Encyclopedia Brittanica* (1953) XX: 235

had more gold than they knew what to do with—so they buried it. The legend of the Golden Fleece belongs to the Eastern shore of the Black Sea (Colchis), but there can be no doubt that it represents an historical fact for the whole region in ancient times: extreme wealth. Some of this gold came from as far away as the Altai Mountains. For the Greeks and Romans, the Scythians were the archetypal splendid barbarians, remote, mysterious, colorful but frightful. Neither of the Classical "superpowers" ever managed to subdue them—but like most barbarians they were held back beyond the Danube, and their power never reached farther south than the Dobruja, which was called "Lesser Scythia" even in late Byzantine sources.

The Dobruja makes several appearances in Classical literature. In *The Voyage of the Argo* by the Hellenistic poet Apollonius of Rhodes (third century BC), Jason and Medea are fleeing from the "incident" in Colchis involving the Golden Fleece, pursued by the Colchian fleet. In Paphlagonia (on the southern shore of the Sea) they stop so that Medea can offer a sacrifice to Hecate the witch-goddess—"but with what ritual she prepared the offering, no one must hear...my lips are sealed by awe." At this point an escape route is revealed to them by their Colchian ally Argus—on the authority of "priests in Egyptian Thebes" who have "preserved tablets of stone which their ancestors engraved with maps.... On these is shown a river, the farthest branch of Ocean Stream, broad and deep enough to carry merchantmen... (called the) Ister. Far away, beyond the North Wind [i.e., in Hyperborea], its headwaters come rushing down from the Rhipaean Mountains. Then it flows for a time through endless plains as a single stream." It is of course the Danube. When they reach it they find the Ister "embraces an island called Peuke, shaped like a triangle, the base presenting beaches to the sea, and the apex pointing up the river, which is thus divided into two channels, one known as the Narex and the other, at the lower end of the island, as the Fair Mouth." The Colchian fleet, in hot pursuit of the *Argo*, turns up the Fair Mouth, while Jason chooses the northern mouth, the Narex. The Colchians must have used what is now called the St. George's Mouth of the Danube, just north of the present-day site of Cumantsa. The *Argo* entered the Danube at what is now the port of Sulina.

> The Colchian vessels spread panic as they went. Shepherds grazing flocks in the meadows by the river abandoned their sheep at the terrifying sight, taking the ships for live monsters that had come up from the sea, the mother of Leviathans. For none of the Istrian tribes, the Thracians and their Scythian friends, the Sigynni, the Graucenii, the Sindi, who had already occupied the great and empty plain of Laurium—none of these had ever set eyes on a sea-going vessel.[7]

The Dobruja was always half-barbarian and half-Greek. Its religion must have mirrored this synthesis—and in fact the area was always one of religious ferment. The ancient Thracian god Zalmoxis[8] had his shrines here, as did the Thracian Orpheus, and the "oriental" Dionysus. All these cults show strong evidence for shamanism or shamanic traits, which can be accounted for by "Scythian" influences. The Goddess in her orgiastic and magical forms (Aphrodite, Hecate) remained important—a link back to early Neolithic cults. This religious world lasted into the Roman Empire as the administrative unit or Province of *Dacia*.

The present town of Cumantsa dates only from the medieval period. "Ancient" Cumantsa was called Histria; its remains were discovered on Popin Island in the lagoon of Razem. Over 150 inscriptions attest to the Milesian origin of the settlement, and two from the Roman period deal with Histrian fishing-rights, obviously a major source of wealth.

---

[7]Apollonius (1959): IV, p. 155

[8]Eliade (1972)

When sand-bars formed across the estuary between the Sea and the lagoon, and the lagoon itself began to grow too shallow for shipping, Histria moved to a solid part of the sandbar and adapted an inlet as a harbor; this took place some time during the "Dark Ages," perhaps in the sixth or seventh century AD. But by this time the ethnic complexion of the region had changed, and the Greek name was abandoned.

> In Classical times the area was more heavily populated and prosperous than now. Hellenic penetration was marked but never very effective and the Daco-Getic peoples of Rumania were never Hellenized as were the Balkan Thracians. But of the Greek period there are many archaeological evidences.

> The important Milesian settlement of Histria near the Danube mouth on a lagoon island facing the modern village of Karanasuf has been well excavated.[…]

> Kallatis, an old Dorian settlement on the site of the modern Mangalia in the Dobruja, was partly excavated. Inscriptions there indicate that the population was strongly Dorian and that the city, with others along that coast, was largely subject to the Thraco-Scythian kings of the interior. Kallatis was evidently one of the great grain-exporting emporiums of the Black Sea. Constanta has been identified as the ancient Tomi, the place of exile of Ovid. Remains of the city walls were discovered across the promontory upon which the residential part of the town is built. A small museum which contained all local antiquities was looted by Bulgarian soldiers during 1917 and the contents dispersed. Greek objects of commerce were found as far inland as the headwaters of the Pruth and the Argesul. Wine from Thasos and the Aegean was a much valued commodity in these regions.

The country is extremely rich in Roman remains. The great wall of Trajan can be traced without difficulty between Constanta and the Danube near Cernavoda. Extensive remains of Axiopolis at its Western end can be seen on the Danube, and excavations were carried out there. The most impressive of all the Roman monuments is the Tropaeum Trajani at Adamklissi. It stands in a wild and desolate region in the rolling steppeland between the Danube River and Constanta with much of its sculptured decoration still lying round the massive concrete core which survives. [...]

Post-Roman remains of the time before the Romanians came under the influence of Byzantium are rare, and little or nothing is known about the country at this time. The great gold treasure of Petroasa, however, which was transported to Moscow during World War I, is certainly of Hunnish or semioriental origin. It consists of two superb chalices of pure gold, inset with large garnets and with handles shaped like panthers, a large necklace of the same material, several large gold ewers elaborately chased and some superb torques.[9]

(The looted museum of Tomi and the "Hunnish gold" of Petroasa will stage a re-appearance later in our narrative.)

Ovid is still considered one of their own by the people of the Dobruja—after all, did he not actually write poems in the local Dacian tongue (and are not the Romanians actually *Romans*)? Local patriotism says yes; and the cult of Ovid was celebrated under the *coup* in Cumantsa, with translations of his *Tristia* published in *The Evening Star*. Ovid was banished by the Emperor Augustus in 8 AD; according to the poet, his crime consisted of "a poem and a mistake." The poem

---

[9]Xenopol (1925/1936)

was the *Ars amatoria*, which was judged obscene; the "mistake" remains a secret. For eight years he languished in Pontus (i.e., the Black Sea region), suffering from the climate, the threat of barbarian incursions, and intense boredom. He bombarded his friends and enemies back in Rome with bitter complaining poems (the *Tristia* or "Sadnesses" in five books) and letters (*Epistulae ex Ponto*) as well as other works. He did learn the local lingo and was adulated by the populace, but his melancholy only deepened till his death in 17 AD. Here are some of his descriptions of Pontus, selected from the poems that appeared in the *Star*, presumably the readers took a perverse pride in their dreariness:

> Beyond here lies nothing but chillness, hostility, frozen
>   waves of an ice-hard sea.
> Here, on the Black Sea's bend sinister, stands Rome's
>   bridgehead,
>   facing out against Scyths and Celts,
> Her latest, shakiest bastion of law and order, only
>   marginally adhesive to the empire's rim.
> [*Tristia: Book II*, 195-200]

> A region that neighbors the polar constellations
>   imprisons me now, land seared by crimping frost.
> To the north lie Bosporus, Don, the Scythian marshes, a
>   scatter
>   of names in an all-but-unknown waste:
> beyond that, nothing but frozen, uninhabitable tundra—
>   alas, how close I stand to the world's end!
> [*Tristia: Book III*, 4B/47-52]

> If anyone *there* still remembers exiled Ovid, if my
>   name still survives in the City now I'm gone,

let him know that beneath those stars that never dip in Ocean
      I live now in mid-barbary, hemmed about
by wild Sarmatians, Bessi, Getae, names unworthy
      of my talent! Yet so long as the warm
breezes still blow, the Danube between defends us:
      flowing, its waters keep off all attacks.
But when grim winter thrusts forth its rough-set visage,
      and earth lies white under marmoreal frost,
when gales and blizzards make the far northern regions
      unfit for habitation, then Danube's ice
feels the weight of those creaking wagons. Snow falls: once
    fallen
      it lies for ever, wind-frosted. Neither sun
nor rain can shift it. Before one fall's melted, another
      comes, and in many places lies two years,
and so fierce the gales, they wrench off rooftops, whirl them
      headlong, skittle tall towers.
Men keep out this aching cold with furs and stitched
    breeches,
      only their faces left exposed,
and often the hanging ice in their hair tinkles,
      while beards gleam white with frost.
Wine stands unbottled, retaining the shape of its vessel,
      so that what you get to drink isn't liquor, but lumps.

…as soon
as the Danube's been frozen level by […] ice-dry wind-chill
      hordes of hostile savages ride over on swift
ponies, their pride, with bows that shoot long-range arrows
      and cut a marauding swath through the countryside.
Some neighbours flee, and with none to protect their
    steadings

their property, unguarded, makes quick loot:
mean rustic household goods, flocks and creaking wagons,
 all the wealth a poor local peasant has.
Others are caught, driven off, hands tied behind them,
 gazing back in vain at fields and home;
others again die there, those sharp barbed arrows through
 them—
 die in agony, too, for the flying steel is smeared
with venom. What such raiders can't drag off or carry
 they destroy: unoffending hovels go up in flames,
and even while peace still prevails, men quake in terror
 at the thought of attack, the fields are left
 unploughed.
[*Tristia: Book III*, 10/1-24, 52-68]

You boast no fresh springs: your water's brackish, saline—
 drink it, and wonder whether thirst's been slaked
or sharpened! Your open fields have few trees, and those
 sterile,
 your coast's a no-man's-land, more sea than soil.
There's no birdsong, save for odd stragglers from the distant
 forest, raucously calling, throats made harsh by brine;
across the vacant plains grim wormwood bristles—a bitter
 crop, well-
 suited to its site.
 [*Black Sea Letters: Book III*, 1/18-24]

The translator, Peter Green, adds this note:

It is hard to remember, too, when reading his descriptions of
barrenness and infertility, presenting the Dobruja as a kind
of Ultima Thule on the rim of the known world, that this

area had long been famous for its wheat-harvests, and that today Constanta raises not only wheat, but also the vines and fruit-trees which Ovid missed so badly. If he had ever travelled in the Dobruja, he would have known that treelessness was a merely local phenomenon: about forty miles north of Constanta huge forests began. But he never seems to have ventured beyond Tomis itself: the terms of his *relegatio* may have forbidden local travel, and in any case conditions in the hinterland were highly dangerous. Such knowledge as he does reveal about the area he could easily have picked up from Book 7 of Strabo's *Geography*, available in Rome as early as 7 BC.

Yet my talent fails to respond to me as it once did:
      it's an arid shore I'm ploughing, with sterile share.
In just the way (I assure you) that silt blocks water-channels
      and the flow's cut short in the choked spring,
so my heart's been vitiated by the silt of misfortune,
      and my verse flows in a narrower vein.
Had Homer himself been consigned to this land, believe me,
      he too would have become a Goth.
[*Black Sea Letters IV*: 2/15-22]

Nor will the Cyclops out-bestialize our Scythian
      cannibals—yet they're but a tiny part
of the terror that haunts me. Though from Scylla's misshapen
      womb monsters bark, sailors have suffered more
from pirates. Charybdis is nothing to our Black Sea corsairs,
      though thrice she sucks down and thrice spews up
    the sea:
they may prey on the eastern seaboard with greater license,
      but still don't leave this coastline safe from raids.
[…]

Arrivals from home report that such things scarce find
    credence
        among you: pity the wretch who bears what's past
    belief!
Yet believe it: nor shall I leave you ignorant of the reasons
        why rugged winter freezes the Black Sea.
We lie very close here to the wain-shaped constellation
        that brings excessive cold:
from here the North Wind rises, this coast is his homeland,
        and the place that's the source of his strength lies
    closer still.
But the South Wind's breezes are languid, seldom reach here
        from that other far-distant pole. Besides,
there's fluvial influx into the land-locked Euxine,
        river on river making the sea's strength ebb,
all flowing in:
[here follows a long list of rivers flowing into the Black Sea…]
and countless others, Danube greatest among them,
        a match for even the Nile. So great a mass
of fresh water adulterates the sea to which it's added,
        stops it keeping its own strength.
Even its colour's diluted—azure no longer, but like some
        still pond or stagnant swamp. The fresh
water's more buoyant, rides above the heavier
        deep with its saline base.
[*Black Sea Letters IV* 10/23-30. 35-47, 57-64]

The translator adds this interesting note:

Reports from Rome suggest that people disbelieve his horror-
stories. Very well: he will take one of them (the freezing of
the Black Sea) and offer scientific proof that he is right. A

prevailing north wind combined with the influx of numerous rivers into the sea produces the necessary conditions: fresh water rides above salt, and is more easily frozen, while the wind aids the process by creating a chill-factor. This not-quite-parody of didactic epic gains considerable force from the fact that it happens to be scientifically impeccable: cf J. Rouch, *La Méditerranée* (1946), pp. 187-93, cited by André Pont., pp. 142-3, n. 1. Dr Stefan Stoenescu informs me that 'the rich salty waters [of the Danube delta] create a brackish region near and along the littoral which allows an inversion of temperature to take place. The unsalty waters of the Danube have sufficient power to maintain a thin layer of comparatively sweet fresh water above the deeply settled salty Mediterranean current. As a result, near the Danube delta shores freezing is not an unusual occurrence. Ovid was right.'[10]

In the early Byzantine period the region was again over-run by waves of barbarians. While the Sarmatians and Gepidae and Slavs and Avars and Magyars and Huns and Goths and Bulgars moved on to the West and into the limelight of history (or not), the Dobruja was settled by less successful tribes, content to live obscurely in the marshes. In particular, the Cumantsa region was taken over first by the Petchenegs (or Patzinaks, Latin *Bisseni*), and then their relatives the Cumans, who gave Cumantsa its name. The descendants of the Petchenegs are today known as the Sops, and live mostly in the southern or Bulgarian Dobruja, although some remain around Cumantsa. Again the *Encyclopedia Britannica* rewards us with an amusing example of professorial prejudice:

---

[10]Ovid (1994)

The Petchenegs were ruled by a Khan and organised in 8 hordes and 40 minor units, each under its khan of lower degree. They were purely nomadic; on their raids they took their women and children with them, forming their camps out of rings of wagons. They wore long beards and mustachios, and were dressed in long kaftans. The food of the wealthy was blood and mares' milk; of the poor, millet and mead. They were originally "magicians," *i.e.*, fire-worshippers; but a form of Islam early became current among them and the nation was temporarily converted to Christianity in 1007-1008. They were the most dreaded and detested of the nomads; Matthew of Edessa calls them "the carrion-eaters, the godless, unclean folk, the wicked, blood-drinking beasts." Other anecdotes are current of their shamelessness, and many of their cruelty; they invariably slew all male prisoners who fell into their hands. The modern Sops are despised by the other inhabitants of Bulgaria for their bestiality and stupidity but dreaded for their savagery. They are a singularly repellent race, short-legged, yellow-skinned, with slanting eyes and projecting cheek-bones. Their villages are generally filthy, but the women's costumes show a barbaric profusion of gold lace.

As for the Cumans (a.k.a. the *Poloutsi* or *Walwen*), their moments of power came somewhat later, in the eleventh century. They are related to the Seljuk Turks but had mingled with the Kipchak Mongols as well. They defeated the Jewish Khazars and for a while held an empire centered on Kiev. For a time the Ukraine was known as Cumania.

At this time the Cumans were partly Mohammedan, but still largely pagan. "We worship one God, who is in the sky," they told the first missionaries to them, "and beyond that we know nothing; for the rest, we have abominable habits." As to these the "Chronicle of Nestor" states: "Our Polovtsi too have their own habits; they love to shed blood, and boast that they eat carrion and the flesh of unclean beasts, such as the civet and the hamster; they marry their mothers-in-law and daughters-in-law, and imitate in all things the example of their fathers." These Cumans wore short kaftans, and shaved their heads, except for two long plaits. They seem to have been purely hunters and warriors, leaving the cultivation of the soil to their subject tribes of Slavs. Cumania, as south Russia was called, possessed thriving towns, and traded in slaves, furs and other products, but the trade was probably in the hands of Greeks and Genoese; the funeral monuments attributed to the Cumans (pyramids or pillars, each surmounted by a male figure bearing in his hand a drinking cup) were probably not their work.[11]

The Cumans were shattered by the Mongol invasions of the 13th century. Some of them ended up as far away as Egypt, where they had been sold as slaves. There they established a new dynasty, the Boharib Mamelukes, and managed even to revenge themselves on the Mongols. Some of their stay-at-home cousins in the Dobruja remained Christian, although they later supplied many Janissaries to the Sultan at Istanbul under the notorious "Ottoman boy tax." Their descendants nowadays are called "*Gagauz*," although in the Cumantsa region (where more are Moslems) they call themselves Cumans. They comprise the poor peasants, hunters, and fishermen of the area.

By the early 15th century the whole of Bulgaria and Romania had been absorbed into the Ottoman empire. Cumantsa became more a Turkish town than anything else—Turkish was still spoken there in 1918—but it now began to acquire its numerous minorities as well.

---

[11]See the *Codex Cumanicus* (Kuun, 1880); partial translation in Boswell (1927)

There were the Petchenegs and Cumans, the Greeks, Crimean Tatars, and Karaite Jews as well as Ottoman Turks and Romanians. The Karaites are an early medieval reformist sect that rejected the Talmud and claimed to represent even earlier forms of Judaism such as the Sadducees and Essenes. At various times they were considered pro-Islamic by Moslems and pro-Christian by Christians. Although the Karaites arrived in the Black Sea region in the tenth century, their scholars (including the famous Crimean, Abraham Firkovitch, d. 1874) claimed they were already there in Classical times. Therefore the Karaites were not guilty of the Crucifixion—since they had not been in Jerusalem at the time!—and were thus exempt from the restrictions placed on Ashkenazi Jews. Similar arguments won them exemptions in Ottoman realms. In Cumantsa the little Karaite community engaged in trade but not in money-lending, and anti-Semitism never took root there.

For some time the Ottomans ruled Cumantsa directly, under a Pasha or Bey, as a separate *sanjak* of the Empire. In the late 17th century, however, the government in Eastern Europe was changed to "Phanariot Rule." In this system the Sublime Porte appointed Orthodox princes or "hospodars," chosen from among the old Byzantine royal and noble families of Istanbul, in consultation with the Patriarch of the Orthodox Church.[12] Moldavia, Wallachia, Bessarabia and other tiny principalities were passed around in these families like heirlooms. Competition was fierce and reigns tended to be brief. In 1720, due to a byzantine rivalry between two branches of the Mavrocordato family, a certain disappointed office-seeker (Constantine I) was bought off with the creation of a separate statelet in Cumantsa. At first quite bitter (he'd wanted Moldavia), Constantine soon discovered the advantages of Cumantsa:—it produced a tidy income, and…no one else wanted it. Although he never ceased to dream of bigger realms, Constantine

---

[12]For an excellent summary of the Phanariot period see Runciman (1968), chapter 10.

I Mavrocordato soon settled down to one of the longest and most somnolent reigns of any Phanariot hospodar. Not only that, but he was also succeeded by a son, Constantine II, and a grandson, Georghiu I. Altogether, Phanariot rule in Cumantsa lasted from 1720 to 1811, and constituted its golden age. When its independence came to an end (it was re-absorbed into Moldavia), the Mavrocordatos remained in Cumantsa as local nobility, but their fortunes declined under the united monarchy of Romania after 1859. They were too attached to Istanbul, and their title of hospodar was not recognized by the Court in Bucharest. Cumantsa was ignored and fell into decline.

In 1888 an heir to the Mavrocordatos was born, Georghiu III. He grew up in the old family palace, which by now was crumbling away for lack of funds. He was educated at a military academy in Bucharest, and spent his vacations in Cumantsa. In 1905 he was sent to Germany to study philosophy at the University of Munich—where we shall join him in the next chapter.

III. The Young Hospodar

> *Happiness and culture.* We are devastated by the sight of the scenes of our childhood: the garden house, the church with its graves, the pond and the woods—we always see them again as sufferers. We are gripped by self-pity, for what have we not suffered since that time! And here, everything is still standing so quiet, so eternal: we alone are so different, so in turmoil; we even rediscover some people on whom Time has sharpened its tooth no more than on an oak tree: peasants, fishermen, woodsmen—they are the same.
>
> —*Human, All-Too-Human,* 168

Cumantsa in the last years of the 19th century must have been an interesting place to experience childhood. As a port it attracted a variety of exotic types—and it must be noted that in its decline it had turned to smuggling (grain, wine, hashish and opium, manufactured goods—and stolen antiquities) to supplement its meager income from fishing. The swamps and marshes of interior Cumantsa were the haunt of Cuman smugglers, and the little shops of the Turks, Greeks and Jews were full of surprising items. The marketplace between the Mosque of Khezr and the Church of St. George (formerly an episcopal see of the Orthodox Patriarchate) must have seemed a colorful universe to the young hospodar.

The *Hroniculul Dobruja* does not mention the fact, but St. George, the Christian patron of this region, is the same person as Khezr, the Islamic patron of the region. Khezr is the Hidden Prophet or the "Green Man" of Islamic esotericism and folklore. He accompanied Alexander the Great to find the Water of Life—but he alone achieved immortality, while the Macedonian attained only the world. As a water-spirit he guards certain places by seas and rivers (including the Rock of Gibraltar)—but as a prophet he appears to spiritual seekers with no living master to initiate them or rescue them from death in the desert. Wherever he walks, flowers and herbs spring up in his footsteps, and he always wears green. Why St. George (of draconian fame) should be identified with Khezr is not clear—but he is. The Dobruja is rich in folklore, but most of it has never been translated from Romanian.

The diminished estate of the Mavrocordatos was worked by Cuman peasants, who no doubt introduced young Georghiu to the mysteries of the marshes. According to a 1903 edition of a *Baedeker Guide to Eastern Europe and Turkey*, the Dobruja was a sportsman's paradise, with nine different varieties of duck, numerous other game birds, roe deer, foxes, wolves, bears, uncountable species of fish and shellfish, four varieties of crow, five of warblers, seven of woodpeckers, eight of buntings, four of falcons, five of eagles, etc. The marshes are considered desolate and uninhabitable by the inhabitants of the coasts, and of the interior, and in the entire Sanjak of Cumantsa around 1900 there were only a few thousand Cumans outside the city (which itself had a population of about 5000). In summer the marshes simmer; in winter they freeze solid. Ovid had nothing nice to say about the climate, and neither does *Baedeker*. But as every aficionado of swamps will know, such "desolation" hides a rare and elusive beauty based on sheer exuberance of life, and on a limited but subtle palette of tones and seasonal monochromatisms. The summer vacations of the young hospodar must have resembled a page out of Turgenev's wonderful *Hunter's Sketchbook*.

Based on what we know of his later life we can be certain that the Turkish culture of the town also held appeal and mystery for Georghiu. The Turks of the Dobruja were known for their old-fashioned ways, and in the late 19th century were still wearing Ottoman hats and turbans (fezzes did not come into style until later) and traditional costumes. As notorious gourmands the Turks made full use of Cumantsa's resources to create a unique cuisine, which they sold at little foodstalls in the market along with coffee and tobacco. Wherever there are Turks there are cafés, and men smoking hookahs. Greeks too are fond of good food (including wine), and also fond of the café life. A great deal of time was spent in Cumantsa arguing about politics and telling lies, fueled either with coffee or wine.

Because of Cumantsa's old connections with the Janissary corps in Istanbul—the Imperial Guard—there was also a strong connection with the Bektashi Sufi order, to which virtually all Janissaries belonged. The mosque of Khezr was used for Bektashi séances, and it is rumored that heterodoxies such as the mystical usage of wine and hashish were not unknown.[13]

Perhaps by the time he reached adolescence and had experienced Bucharest, Georghiu came to look on his childhood home as backward and boring. Many adolescents do—and with less reason. But it is certain that no sooner had he arrived in Germany in 1905 than he began to feel nostalgia and even homesickness for Cumantsa (we know

---

[13]Birge (1937)

because he later said so, in one of his articles for the *Evening Star*). If nothing else, this is the sign of a happy childhood.

Unfortunately we know little more about Mavrocordato's higher education than about his boyhood. Densusianu in his *Chronicle* had access only to the articles written for the *Star* and a few letters. Perhaps the archives in Munich, the records of the University, would add something to our knowledge (assuming they were not destroyed in World War II)—but for now we are reduced largely to speculation. We know that he studied law and philosophy and we know he received a degree; we do not know his teachers, his friends, his extra-curricular activities or adventures. He read Kant and Hegel. He made at least one trip to Paris, and apparently learned French. He probably traveled around Germany during his vacations, in the *Wandervogel* style then coming into fashion with German students (he mentions the pleasures of hiking and mountain-climbing). Above all—and of this there can be no doubt—he made the biggest discovery of his life. He found Nietzsche.

That is, he found Nietzsche's books. The man himself had been in a drooling stupor since 1889, and dead since 1900. But his books had finally begun to live. In part this was thanks to Nietzsche's horrible sister, Elisabeth Förster, whose husband had died in South America trying to start a utopian colony for pure Aryan anti-Semites,[14] and who now ran the Nietzsche Archive in Sils Maria (where Mavrocordato probably paid pilgrimage and met her). She was then working on Nietzsche's uncollected notes for *The Will to Power*, and had already created the cult of relics, lies, and evasions that would later prove so congenial to Adolf Hitler. Despite Elisabeth's genius for bad publicity, however, Nietzsche's books spoke for themselves. (The Nazi editions, with all of Nietzsche's attacks on anti-Semitism and nice things about Jews censored out, appeared much later.) Even before he died, something very much like a Nietzschean movement had begun in Germany.

---

[14]Macintyre (1992)

Young people were particularly susceptible; and so far from being seen as a prophet of reaction, Nietzsche was considered the most radical and even revolutionary of all modern thinkers. The movement took off in the late 1890s and reached something of a fever pitch during Mavrocordato's years in Munich. One thinks of certain passages in Robert Musil's *Man Without Qualities* which describe the movement as it manifested in Vienna, with bad piano playing, *sturm und drang,* fervid sex, and monumental egotisms on display. As he himself had foreseen, Nietzsche was a kind of poison—or hallucinogen. (Nietzsche himself experimented with drugs and his works are studded with drug references.) But every fad spins off some silliness. Some fads are remembered—like Mesmerism—chiefly for their silliness. But Nietzsche was no quack. He was probably the most important thinker of the period— maybe the century (but *which century?*): a genius whose works are eternally valid, or eternally damnable, according to your taste. But…eternal. That was his wish, and it came true. And one of the peculiar qualities of his writing is that it can still ignite the same kind of uncontrollable mad enthusiasm in young readers today, even without a "movement" to encourage them. And Mavrocordato fell hard.

Nietzsche made many sneering remarks about anarchism, and therefore it may surprise the reader to learn that in turn-of-the-century Germany he was considered an anarchist thinker by many, both admirers and detractors. R. Hinton Thomas has painted an amusing picture of the situation:

> In one pamphlet, the writer imagines a German, himself presumably, returning home after some years abroad to find the scene dominated by the "cult of the self, of one's own *Persönlichkeit.*" It is plain anarchism, he thinks, and it is all Nietzsche's fault. Anarchism could easily serve as a flag of convenience for merely selfish attitudes, as in the case of the "fanatical anarchists" who, according to Lily

Braun, frequented Max von Egidy's household and "tried to justify the freedom with which they indulged their own petty desires with the excuse that they were living out their *Persönlichkeit.*" Even simple bad manners, with no deeper purpose than to épater le bourgeois could count as anarchism, with the culprits instancing Nietzsche in self-justification. One writer mentions someone he knew who thought it one of the prerogatives of the Superman to spit in public and to eat with his fingers. When those nearby objected, he "proudly appealed to his *Individualität* and to the fact that he was a Nietzschean." There is nothing more revolting, it was said, "than when some vain young fathead plays the part of Superman in cafés and pubs frequented by women...or when late at night some youthful degenerate swanks around in the Friederichstraße 'beyond good and evil'" and it was shocking that "the name and the words of so pure and sublime a spirit as Nietzsche had to put up with being misused in this appalling way." When the Crown Princess of Saxony ran off with a lover of menial standing, this was attributed to her having been reading his work. By the mid-1890s, the literary cafés in Berlin, Munich and Vienna were said to be "so swarming with 'Supermen' that you could not fail to notice it, and it left one speechless with astonishment." When in 1897 an anarchist was sentenced for his part in a plot to kill a police officer in Berlin, he defended himself by reference to Nietzsche.[15]

Anarchist or radical admiration for Nietzsche was not limited to the rank-and-file but would even come to enflame such leftists as Emma Goldman, who said that insofar as Nietzsche's aristocracy was "neither

[15]Hinton Thomas (1983): 50

of birth nor of wealth" but "of the spirit," he was an anarchist, and all true anarchists are aristocrats. In France the notorious anarchist bank-robbers, the Bonnot Gang, put their Nietzscheanism into action, and the philosopher was particularly admired by anarchist Individualists and readers of Max Stirner.[16] Georg Brandes coined the term "radical aristocratism" to describe Nietzsche's (non) system—but the man himself spent so much ink attacking the Church, the State, monarchism, legislative democracy, German culture and other *bêtes noires* of the radicals, that even the most egalitarian and communitarian leftists could find something to admire in his work.[17] Besides, even his criticisms of anarchism and socialism could be seen as helpful, especially on the level of psychology. Radicals were forced to examine their souls for evidence of *ressentiment*, the slave mentality of the envious *chandala*. They would have to ask themselves if their socialism were not mere camouflaged Christian sentimentality, and they would have to question the inevitability of "Progress." They would have to face the existential problem of commitment to process rather than *telos*. Nietzsche himself asked to be *overcome*—and perhaps those who wrestled with him hardest learned the most. But Mavrocordato never struggled. He was seduced.

The Munich Soviet of 1918 was packed with radicals weaned on Nietzsche. The most important were Kurt Eisner, Jewish journalist and critic, dramatist, philosopher and man of letters, who became the unlikely founder of free Munich, and who was assassinated by the Thule *Gesellschaft*; and Gustav Landauer, also Jewish, also philosopher, an anarchist activist, who became the Minister of Education, and was also murdered

---

[16]The very obvious parallels between Nietzsche and Stirner have never really been explored. Nietzsche had read Stirner, apparently, and sometimes seems to refer to Stirnerian ideas, but never mentioned him. Many anarchists admired both, and both have been called proto-fascists. See Max Stirner, *The Ego and His Own*.

[17]Nietzsche says, "We can destroy only as creators" (*The Gay Science*, 122), thus echoing Bakunin's famous line about destruction as creation.

by the occult Aryan order. I feel certain that Mavrocordato read Landauer, possibly early versions of his major work *On Socialism* (published on the eve of the Munich uprising, but preceded by portions and versions in various anarchist papers), and probably his Nietzschean novel, *The Preacher of Death* (even the title was from Nietzsche). It's even possible that Mavrocordato met Landauer, although the writer was not living in Munich at the time. The key to Mavrocordato's knowledge of Landauer is contained in a reference in the *Star* to Landauer's theory of the *folk*. Landauer was the leading thinker of a school of thought that most people nowadays could never even imagine:—left-wing *volk*-ism. Like the well-known publisher Eugen Diederichs (who not only published on Nietzsche but also reprinted books that Nietzsche *liked*),[18] Landauer believed that the particularity and autonomy of any one people implied the particularity and autonomy of all peoples:—a kind of *volkisch* universal humanism. Landauer and Diederichs sponsored or encouraged left-wing *volkisch* youth groups in competition with the chauvinist (and anti-Nietzschean) *Wandervögel*. They pictured a future of agrarian and urban communes in federation, according to Proudhonian anarchist principles, all different and all free. This thinking influenced such anarcho-zionist Jews as the young Martin Buber, Gershom Scholem, and Walter Benjamin. And of course it outraged the German Nationalists, who believed in centralization and in the superiority of German culture. Left-wing *volk*-ism had a cultish aspect (like Nietzscheanism)[19] with its sun-worshipping nudists, utopian colonies, guitar-playing youth in *lederhösen*, etc. But it also had its serious side—so serious that Landauer and many others were martyred for it. Nazism erased the memory of left-wing *volk*-ism and made the whole concept of the *volk* stink of fascism and of death. But in 1900 it was

---

[18]See Hinton Thomas, p. 116*ff.*

[19]Nietzsche himself contradicts himself on *volk*-ism. In his earlier works he seems to share *volkisch* ideas, but in his later works he tends to make fun of the "folk-soul" and other such concepts.

still innocent and alive, and constituted a whole *milieu*. Moreover, like the Turks and Greeks back home in Cumantsa, the anarchists and poets and bohemians and madmen of Munich (like those of Vienna) liked to while away the hours in coffeeshops; Mavrocordato would have fitted in well; he probably earned points for his sheer exoticism, if nothing else. (He was said to be handsome.)

Among the Nietzschean circles in Munich at that time we might include that of the aristocratic and pederastic poet Stephan George, although there is no evidence that Mavrocordato knew him. Much more likely in this respect is the "Cosmic Circle" around the eccentric occultist Ludwig Klages, who later wrote a popular book on Nietzsche (*Die Psychologischen Errungenschaften Nietzsches*, 1926) and who preached the doctrine in the cafés and ateliers of Munich's bohemian quarter. Klages later veered to the Right, but culturally he was always a radical. At his salons one might meet a whole demimonde of faddists, cranks, health-nuts, mystics, artists, and dangerous women. Once again, a "Prince" from the exotic East (or nearly-East) would doubtless have been lionized in such a den.

Unfortunately, however, all is conjecture. Judging by Mavrocordato's writings the only person he "met" in Germany was Nietzsche. We also have no information on anyone he may have met in France. However, in all this dearth, one peculiar exception occurs. We know at least one person Mavrocordato met—somewhere in Europe—sometime before his return to Cumantsa in 1913. Densusianu's *Chronicle* missed it entirely. In the *Collected Correspondence* of the Romanian poet Tristan Tzara (Paris, 1967), the following telegram appears:

DECEMBER 8, 1918
Zurich

To the Hospodar Georghiu III Mavrocordato Greetings old friend stop congratulations stop we have a homeland stop Tzara.

The telegraph wires into Cumantsa, which were cut during the *coup* on November 4, were restored to use only on December 1st or 2nd. Tzara's telegram must have been one of the first to reach the Provisional Government from abroad, but it was not printed in *The Star* (or else Densusianu missed it). Or perhaps Mavrocordato never actually received it. So far it remains a mystery.[20] Mavrocordato is not mentioned in any biography of Tzara known to me. The whole matter is a tantalizing dead end.

Altogether Mavrocordato spent eight years in Europe. During those years the Balkans and the Black Sea region were yanked out of their obscure backwardness and into the glare of history by a series of crises. The Bosnia crisis of 1908 drew the attention of the major European powers, and the sweet odor of decay emanating from the Ottoman Empire aroused their predatory instincts. We cannot begin here to try to unravel the intricate karmic web that sucked the world into a century of total war—a web that was spun around and from Eastern Europe. Suffice it to say that events led blindly on to the First Balkan War in 1912, in which Turkey's European colonies declared their intention to break free at last and finally from the Sublime Porte. During this war the Dobruja emerged as a bone of contention between Romania and Bulgaria. Immediately after the first round ended Bulgaria attacked its former allies (the "Second Balkan War") and attempted to occupy the Dobruja; instead a powerful Romanian army swept them all the way back to Sophia, and laid claim to the entire coastal region. Although Cumantsa was not involved in any actual battles during this Second Balkan War in 1913, the whole area was thrown into disorder, and there were reports of starvation and disease.

As soon as peace was declared on April 10, Georghiu Mavrocordato hurried home. His mother was still alive, and living alone in the old

---

[20]This discovery is also due to V. Oisteanu, who was led by it to uncover Densusianu's *Chronicle*. Tzara, whose real name was Samuel Rosenstock, was born in Moinesti, Romania in 1896.

palace. Georghiu seems to have been an only child, and no doubt he needed to return in order to assume his responsibilities as head of the family (he was then 30 years old) in such unsettled times. He arrived by boat from Istanbul, since the interior was supposedly still unsafe.

Still, peace had been declared, and Mavrocordato apparently intended to enjoy it. He arrived with two friends, a Romanian poet named Vlad Antonescu (probably an old companion from Bucharest schooldays), who had a passionate interest in Romanian folklore; and a German, a Classicist and amateur archaeologist, Wilhelm Schlamminger of Munich—no doubt a companion of university days, and an ardent Nietzschean. These two young men intended to have a long and productive holiday in Cumantsa as guests of the hospodar, collecting local myths and inscriptions, wandering about the countryside, hunting, fishing and sailing. As it turned out, they had a very long holiday indeed—seven years.

In the immediate aftermath of the Second Balkan War, the political situation in the Dobruja was precarious, and getting more so by the day. Several "peasant uprisings" had occurred both during and after the war. The Petchenegs and Cumans of Cumantsa had so far remained passive, but they were suffering the effects of absentee landlordism, tax, debt, bad harvests, and general dissatisfaction. No one had wanted Bulgarian rule, but no one was particularly happy to see the Romanians back again. In fact there were never many ethnic Romanians in the Dobruja, and the administrators sent out from Bucharest were never popular. Pro-Turkish sentiment was common, though politically unorganized. Still, there was talk (in the coffeeshops and wineshops no doubt) of an independent—or at least autonomous—Cumantsa.

The three friends decided to stay the winter. Antonescu and Schlamminger apparently found themselves in a sort of scholarly pig heaven, a virtually untouched goldmine of folk songs, superstitions, ruins, and antiques of dubious provenance; they couldn't bear to tear themselves away. As for Mavrocordato, he began to act as if he meant to stay on forever:—he started repairs on the palace, and ordered a load of books on agriculture and engineering. Perhaps he had developed Faustian impulses—a desire to donate his talents to something concrete. Action was indeed on the horizon—but not agriculture or engineering.

In June of 1914 the three friends sailed down the coast to Constanta, where they observed the state visit of the Russian Czar. They were not impressed. Neither was the rest of the world. A few days later in Sarajevo, the murder of the Austrian Archduke Ferdinand (by a Serbian terrorist) set fire instantaneously to the whole web of intrigue and hatred woven around the Balkans—and the whole world. On July 29, World War I began.

The three friends made no move to sign up in anybody's army, and apparently no one asked them. Mavrocordato's Nietzschean analysis of the war, published later (in 1918), condemns the whole affair as a conspiracy of moribund powers against Life itself, a meaningless sacrifice, and a means of suppressing the inevitable World Revolution (which had finally broken out in Russia). In 1914 however the war probably seemed more an inconvenience to be avoided than a final cataclysm—which it certainly resembled by 1917! In brief, the friends decided to lie low in Cumantsa and *wait it out*. (At the time it was expected to last a month or so at most.)

By 1915 however it had become clear that the war had just gotten started. Still the friends demonstrated no eagerness to hurl themselves on any pyres of outraged nationalism—were they not "good Europeans"?—and as a mark of their complete rejection of everything going on in the outside world, they founded a society for the study of local languages and antiquities, and launched a periodical in its name. The organization was known as the Scythian Club, and the irregular "journal" became *The Evening Star*.

The Scythian Club was serious about its work, and the early issues of the *Star* are full of the discoveries of Antonescu and Schlamminger—and of course, of Nietzsche. But the Club, which held regular meetings at the old palace, was meant to fulfill a social role as well, with occasional gourmet dinners, high teas, and field trips. It soon acquired a surprising number of members, considering the time and place and the lofty intellectual tone of the society. Ovid would have been quite jealous, as the *Star* boasted happily. How often he had yearned to hear a word of Latin spoken in his dreary exile at Tomis—or even bad Greek! And here was a whole organization devoted to the pleasures of the mind—and the table! In Ovid's day there was no local wine, either.

Aside from a few Romanian officials and gentry, the Club enjoyed an ethnic mix worthy of the old Cumantsa tradition. First and perhaps most important was Shaykh Mehmet Effendi, the leader of the local branch of the Bektashi Sufi Order. Shaykh Mehmet owned a little antiquities shop in the bazaar, and although he was no scholar, he knew more about local history and art than the rest of the Club put together. He was a genial and liberal personality—in fact, there is some evidence that he may have belonged to the Freemasons, who were strong in Turkey and especially amongst the Bektashis. If the Shaykh also dealt in antiquities of dubious provenance—some perhaps downright "hot"—he was certainly no common smuggler, and the Club appointed him its treasurer. The Shaykh had peculiar political connections in Istanbul. It is not clear whether he was an agent of the Sublime Porte or of the Young Turks (or of both), but no one doubted he was an agent of some sort. On the subject of Turkish sufism, he was as well informed and informative as he was on Pontic relics, curiosa, and Scythian lore. Without him, as Mavrocordato wrote, the Club would have been impossible.

Another exotic member was Kuthen Corvinu, the hereditary Ilkhan of the Petchenegs and Cumans of Cumantsa. Seemingly a simple peasant, the Khan was persuaded to address the Club only with great difficulty—but then proceeded to bowl over the membership with an evening of folk songs and tales that reduced Antonescu (who wrote the report) to sheer ecstasy. The old Khan was accompanied by his daughter Anna, who helped him translate the archaic Cuman dialect into modern Romanian. Possibly it was on this occasion that Mavro-cordato fell in love with her, although he may have arranged the whole affair simply to win over her father. Despite the Cuman reputation for ugliness she was said to be strikingly beautiful, and that evening she wore her nicest folkloric costume and kilos of barbaric family jewels. Everyone was charmed, and at once insisted on father and daughter joining the Club. Mavrocordato was more than charmed.

(I must admit I'm giving Mavrocordato the benefit of the doubt when I assume that he loved Anna, since, with typical self-effacement, he never says as much in print. The proof is that he later married her. As it happens, the marriage was exceedingly well-timed for political purposes, as we shall see. But my impression of Georghiu is that he would never have married simply for expediency. He was far too Romantic to be devious.)

Another indispensable Scythian was a young man from Odessa with the mellifluous name of Caleb Afendopoulo. Born a Karaite Jew, Afendopoulo had worked as a clerk in his father's shoe store in Odessa, and devoured books. He acquired a dozen languages (Russian, South Russian, Turkish, Georgian, several Caucasian dialects, Yiddish, Hebrew, Turkish, Arabic, Romanian, French, Greek and perhaps a few more)—but he lost his faith. Moreover, he was guilty of poetry, and of studying Kabbalah (strictly an Ashkenazi subject), and of despising his family trade. Adding insult to injury he became a socialist, and then—after meeting Nestor Makhno in Odessa in 1914—an anarchist. He was arrested for distributing anarchist propaganda, and after his release his father disinherited and banished him. He landed in Cumantsa, where he had distant relatives in the Karaite community, just in time to attend the first meeting of the Scythian Club and be chosen as its Secretary. His first contribution to the *Star* was a translation of some ancient riddles from the *Codex Cumanicus*—proving that he had already acquired another dialect. Presumably he also began "agitating" amongst the peasants of Cumantsa, spreading the gospel of "Land and Liberty."

Another anarchist Scythian was no savant, but a common seaman, a Levantine drifter named Enrico Elias, of uncertain nationality but lately resident of Milan, where he had joined the anarchist Mariners' Union and taken part in violent demonstrations. Elias, like many Mediterranean nomads and Italian workingclass troublemakers, was a left-wing Stirnerite Individualist Anarchist, a type that is nowadays almost forgotten. The Stirnerites—especially the Italians—made a point of joining any uprising they could reach in time, whatever ideological banner was being unfurled. Socialist, Marxist, syndicalist, anarchist—nothing mattered except that it be *revolt.*[21] The point was that the individual could realize him or herself only in

---

[21]History, materialism, monism, positivism, and all the "isms" of this world are old and rusty tools which I don't need or mind anymore. My principle is life, my end is death. I wish to live my life intensely for to embrace my life tragically.

You are waiting for the revolution? My own began a long time ago! When you will be ready (God, what an endless wait!) I won't mind going along with you for awhile. But when you'll stop, I shall continue on my insane and triumphal way toward the great and sublime conquest of the nothing!

Any society that you build will have its limits. And outside the limits of my society the unruly and heroic tramps will wander, with their wild and virgin thoughts—they who cannot live without planning ever new and dreadful outbursts of rebellion!

I shall be among them!

And after me, as before me, there will be those saying to their fellows: "So turn to yourselves rather than to your Gods or to your idols. Find what hides in yourselves; bring it to light; show yourselves!"

Because every person; who, searching his own inwardness, extracts what was mysteriously hidden therein, is a shadow eclipsing any form of society which can exist under the sun!

All societies tremble when the scornful aristocracy of the tramps, the inaccessibles, the uniques, the rulers over the ideal, and the conquerors of the nothing resolutely advance.

So come on iconoclasts, forward!

"Already the foreboding sky grows dark and silent!"

—Renzo Novatore

Arcola, January 1920

struggle against what was *not* self—*i.e.*, everything that denied self and suppressed the freedom to "become what you are" (as Nietzsche quoted Pindar). This existentialist insouciance obviously led some later Stirnerites into Fascismo—including young Benito Mussolini. But to true Individualists, fascism was no more acceptable than Marxism, since both were authoritarian systems. Blow it *all* up.

Elias wrote nothing for the *Star*, and held no office in the Club. But later, when the conspiracy began, he was made head of the *military committee*. Obviously Elias was the one serious and perhaps professorial revolutionary strategist in Cumantsa. Although his influence on events is difficult to trace, I believe it was crucial. I doubt there would have been a *coup d'état* without him. And if there had been, it would not have lasted ten minutes without him. For the time being, however, there was no thought of revolt. War had thrown this motley crew together, each one perhaps in flight from something, each perhaps somehow in hiding. By sheer chance, they discovered each other and themselves together, and began somehow to enjoy life more because they were enjoying it in each other's company. Seven varieties of duck, and the amusing local vintages, probably had a lot to do with it. Coffee at Shaykh Mehmet's shop—all-night bull sessions about Nietzsche, the War, life, love, and the usual *et ceteras*—dawn strolls along the beaches—roaring fires in the huge barbaric fireplaces of the old palace, with its rotting tapestries and heavy victorian bric-a-brac—even an archaeological dig in ancient Histria across the lagoon—all this kept them occupied—all this kept them from thinking about the war—about the trouble that might be approaching… that *was* approaching. And then one day in August 1916, the trouble was almost there. The illusion of real life broke in on the reality of their Scythian dream. The Germans were coming.

IV. THE *COUP D'ÉTAT*

> The princes of Europe should consider carefully whether they can do without our support. We immoralists—we are today the only power that needs no allies in order to conquer: thus we are by far the strongest of the strong. We do not even need to tell lies: what other power can dispense with that? A powerful seduction fights on our behalf, the most powerful perhaps that there has ever been—the seduction of truth—"Truth"? Who has forced this word on me? But I repudiate it; but I disdain this proud word: no, we do not need even this; we shall conquer and come to power even without truth. The spell that fights on our behalf, the eye of Venus that charms and blinds even our opponents, is *the magic of the extreme*, the seduction that everything extreme exercises: we immoralists—we are the most extreme.
>
> —*Will to Power*, 396

Romania had not actually entered the war until 1916, and then on the side of the Allies. Already Russia was beginning to lose control of its own domestic war politics, and hence of its army...the Revolution was brewing (Lenin was in Zurich—so was Tristan Tzara, busy forming the dada movement). Romania's army had scarcely emerged from the 19th century—it was known for its fine cavalry!—and was split between two fronts, each waiting for a German blitzkrieg. The greater part of these forces were positioned in Transylvania planning a pre-emptive strike across the Carpathians; three divisions were in the Dobruja expecting Russian reinforcements (which never arrived). In Bulgaria the dreaded German General Mackenson was assembling a large force to invade the Dobruja—which, on September 5, he did.

Once again Cumantsa was spared any fighting (although Constanta, down the coast, was badly shelled)—but it was not spared the German presence. A detachment of soldiers under a Colonel Randolf von Hart-sheim, later memorialized in the *Star* as a "Bismarkian Prussian of the worst sort,"[22] stormed into town and took over completely. The *Star*, the Club, and the good life came to an end, although it seems at least that no one was shot; I suspect that the non-Romanian contingent had meanwhile been supplied with false documents—probably by Shaykh Mehmet. But some of the Romanian members of the Club—the officials (the Postmaster and the Harbormaster, for example)—were arrested and detained, and Col. von Hartsheim rudely sequestered the old palace as his personal headquarters. The hospodar and his old mother were forced to move to a shabby hotel (the "Imperial," near the Church of St. George).

The bulk of Mackenson's Army now (mid-November) pulled out of the Dobruja and headed for Bucharest, looking to crush Romania between the southern forces and Falkenhayn's northern forces—which were about to push their way through the Transylvanian mountain passes, already half-blocked by blizzards. Col. von Hartsheim and his contingent remained in Cumantsa. On December 6, the Central

---

[22]In his 1918 article on the War, Macrocordato quoted Nietzsche on Germany and the Germans:

> *German Culture...* Political superiority without any real human superiority is most harmful. [PN 48]

> Against the *Germans* I here advance on all fronts: you'll have no occasion for complaints about "ambiguity." This utterly irresponsible race [...] has on its conscience all the great disasters of civilization. [BT 197]

> No, we do not love humanity; but on the other hand we are not nearly "German" enough, in the sense in which the word "German" is constantly being used nowadays, to advocate nationalism and race hatred and to be able to to take pleasure in the national scabies of the heart and blood poisoning that now leads the nations of Europe to delimit and barricade themselves against each other as if it were a matter of quarantine. [GS 339]

Powers occupied Bucharest, and the war in Romania came to a pause. The King, his English wife Marie, and the Romanian government fled north to the Russian border, and eventually established a regime-in-exile in Jassy. There they held out until the Russian Revolution, which caused the collapse of the Russian Army, and brought an end to the last Romanian resistance. An armistice was signed on December 6, 1917.

Germany now imposed a ruinous treaty on Romania, essentially reducing it to a slave state. A collaborationist government came to power to implement the treaty, headed by a Romanian traitor named Alexandru Marghiloman. A reign of mixed terror and confusion ensued. The Central Bank was forced to issue a run of 2,500,000,000 *lei* in paper money, which ruined the economy. Germany meanwhile began stripping the country of its resources with marked efficiency (whole factories were dismantled, entire forests cut down). Starvation afflicted everyone except Germans and collaborationists—even in well-fed Cumantsa—and the peasants and workers were on the verge of giving in to the enthusiasm they still felt for the Russian Revolution. By the spring and summer of 1918 the situation was desperate.

What had been going on in Cumantsa all this time? Our view is unclear because we no longer have the *Star* to inform us. We can imagine the usual miseries and indignities of the occupation, the growing hunger, the Germans' disdain for Cumantsa's odd racial mix (Col. von Hartsheim seems to have been an anti-Semite)[23]

---

[23]Nietzsche: I am…out of patience with those newest speculators in idealism called anti-Semites, who parade as Christian-Aryan worthies and endeavor to stir up all the asinine elements of the nation by that cheapest of possible tricks, a moral attitude. (The ease with which any wretched imposture succeeds in present-day Germany may be attributed to the progressive stultification of the German mind. The reason for this general spread of inanity may be found in a diet composed entirely of newspapers, politics, beer, and Wagner's music. Our national vanity and hemmed-in situation and the shaking palsy of current ideas have each done their bit to prepare us for such a diet.) [GM 294-5]

—and the growing sense of a will to resist. All we actually know derives from a remark Mavrocordato later made (in the re-born *Star*): that he had been shocked to discover a German soldier reading a special "trench" edition of Nietzsche's *Thus Spoke Zarathustra*. Could it have been von Hartsheim himself? The hospodar goes so far as to repeat one of Nietzsche's famous tags: "O Nausea! Nausea! Nausea!"

Cumantsa may paradoxically have benefitted from the fact that certain areas of the Dobruja remained under direct military rule by the Central Powers during this whole period; this may have spared the populace at least from some of the sinister bumbling of the Marghiloman government. Those areas were strategically important—the ports at the various mouths of the Danube for example—and it is difficult to understand why Cumantsa should have been included in this category. In fact it had so far escaped actual violence precisely because it was *not* "strategic," never had any military presence, and produced nothing useful except fish. Why then did Col. von Hartsheim stay on and on, retaining full administrative power in Cumantsa? What value could his superiors have seen in this wastage of manpower?

The Hronicul Dobruja's author believes that the explanation of this mystery lies in Cumantsa's special role as a smuggler's haven. He thinks that von Hartsheim had either managed to gain control of this illicit trade, or else at least convinced his superiors of its importance. Most interestingly, he mentions the looting of the Museum of Antiquities in Constanta and the elusive trajectory of the famous "Hunnish" gold hoard of Petroasa. Both of these treasures may have passed through Cumantsa; in fact, the evidence suggests that both these treasures were in Cumantsa at some point in the summer and autumn of 1918; and this alone would explain von Hartsheim's determination to stay on and on. The really interesting question then is: *who else knew the treasure was in Cumantsa?* Was the German High Command in on the secret? Or was von Hartsheim somehow working for himself alone? As the summer wore on, the military news from Europe grew gloomier and gloomier—from the axis point of view. Germany and the Central Powers were headed for the *gotterdammerung*. The Army began to pull out of Romania. And still von Hartsheim stayed put. Was he planning to betray his superiors? his suppliers? his customers?

Now, while all this was going on, we must assume that the Scythian Club was not really ineffective and disbanded but had become in fact a band of conspirators. At what point this transition occurred we cannot say, but by August of 1918 their plans must have been made. Col. von Hartsheim's retinue had been reduced to a mere squadron of men—albeit those men were apparently military police and heavily armed. Everything remains quite murky up to the moment of the *coup*, but we can offer a few conjectures.

The Scythians could not have been ignorant of the looted antiquities and Hunnish gold. In fact they may have been deeply involved in the process by which these items had turned up in Cumantsa; the gaze of suspicion flickers over the personage of Shaykh Mehmet Effendi. But it seems clear that by the first of November neither the Scythians nor the Colonel actually had possession of the goods. If von Hartsheim had the hoard, he would presumably have extricated himself from Cumantsa post haste, especially since it was by now apparent that his masters were about to go down in flames. All over Romania Germans were being lynched and collaborationists were going into hiding. If the Scythians had the gold, they would not have needed to stage their *coup* but could simply have waited for events to transpire—von Hartsheim's days were clearly numbered. I believe that sometime between the first and the third of November, the Colonel finally got his hands on the goods and was preparing to decamp. Whether he intended to flit by land or by sea, his preparations would have been obvious enough to anyone who knew what to look for—and the Scythians obviously knew. *This* was the signal for their *coup*.

The *coup d'état* as a political form would become something of a specialty of the 20th century, and eventually it would acquire certain formal characteristics, even certain "rules." If Mavrocordato and his handful of intellectual comrades could have enjoyed the advantage of reading a book like E. Luttwak's *Coup d'État: a practical handbook* (1968), a cynical and amusingly amoral do-it-yourself guide (by a Transylvanian author!), they would have experienced little difficulty in planning their *coup*, or even in executing it. Essentially they had no "government" to overthrow, but only a small military force with no political support. Unfortunately they were intellectuals, nor did they have the advantage of hindsight. They very nearly bungled it, and if it were not for two important factors, they would certainly have failed. The first of these factors was Enrico Elias, the anarchist sailor, who was made head of the military operation of the *coup*. The second was the participation of the Cumans.

If the Petchenegs and Cumans were roused from their millennial apathy to a revival of ancient warrior impulses, this was no doubt due to the fact that under the German occupation and the puppet government they had suffered beyond endurance. Moreover, there were peasant uprisings going on everywhere in Eastern Europe (wherever war or revolution left a vacuum of control), with demands for redistribution of land. The Ukraine was in turmoil, and Makhno had already declared some autonomous zones. But the Cumans had still other reasons to think well of the Scythians' *coup*. In August, Georghiu III Mavrocordato had married Anna, daughter of the Ilkhan Kuthen Corvinu of the tribes. The Khan was nominally a Moslem and Mavrocordato was nominally Romanian Orthodox, but the Cumans were never very religious and the hospodar was—of course—a convert to Dionysianism. (Moreover he was on extremely bad terms with the priests at the Church of St. George, who considered him an infidel, while he viewed them as horrid obscurantists.) As a result the marriage was held according to "ancient Cuman custom," including—despite the hard times—a wedding feast. Shaykh Mehmet officiated for the bride. The fact that Georghiu had united with the "royal clan" of the Cumans could not have gone unnoticed, and must have caused quite a stir amongst the traditionalists (and the antiquarian Scythians, of course!). When the moment of crisis came, the Ilkhan would listen to his son-in-law.

At dawn on November 4, Elias and Mavrocordato ordered the following actions:

1) A roadblock was set up to cut the "highway" to St. George's Mouth, at the point where it forks with the track through the swamp to the Petcheneg village of Peritesca. Luckily no soldiers or vehicles ever approached the roadblock—there were only about five automobiles in the entire region in any case, all of them German—because the roadblock was unarmed except for a few hunting rifles.

2) A force under Mavrocordato launched an assault on the old palace, intending to capture and arrest Col. von Hartsheim before breakfast.

3) A larger force under Elias intended to storm the police headquarters in town, near the shore of Lake Cumantsa, where the German garrison was stationed. This assault force had the best guns the Scythians could find, including one contraband (German Army issue) tripod-mounted machine-gun.

4) A boat (the hospodar's own little sloop, *The Lion and Doves*) was set to block access to the open sea; it is unclear whether the conspirators expected enemies to arrive or to depart by water—but in the event neither occurred, and the sailors spent the whole day bobbing between the jetties, no doubt getting cold and wet.

5) Two men with revolvers (one of them was Schlamminger, the German philologist) were sent to take over the PTT (which also housed a small bank, stuffed with inflated lei) from its small staff. They expected the presence of at least two armed German guards.

6) Deep in the swamps somewhere, at dawn, a small detachment of Cumans under the leadership of the Ilkhan himself cut the telegraph wires that connected Cumantsa to the outside world, and specifically

to Bucharest. This act doubtlessly saved the *coup d'état*, which otherwise went quite badly.

7) A general strike of all merchants and workers was "declared" (but how? In any case, this proved irrelevant).

We shall now follow up the important actions one by one as they developed throughout the day.

2) Mavrocordato's assault group was detected by guards on the access road or driveway of the old palace where it meets the St. George Road. These guards opened fire on the commando, and pinned them down in the forest/marshes on the other side of the highway. Meanwhile, von Hartsheim packed all his papers into his car, loaded in the rest of his personal guard, drove to the gate, and picked up the soldiers there. (They apparently jumped onto the running-boards, and one of them was shot—by Mavrocordato—and killed as the car sped away.) Von Hartsheim turned right and headed toward the city. We surmise that the treasure was stashed at the police station, which von Hartsheim therefore considered the only objective worth defending. In any case, when the commando occupied the old palace they found nothing of value there, not even armaments. Leaving a couple of men to secure the place, Mavrocordato and his followers set off on horse or foot after the Colonel.

3) Elias failed to take the police station at the first attempt. Fighting was fierce, and it seems that several men were wounded on both sides. After about 20 minutes of intense fire, Elias fell back and occupied a building opposite the station. Here he set up the machine-gun, and when the Germans attempted a sortie he was able to force them back into the station. A stalemate ensued. After some time, an automobile careened into the street and accelerated (but remember, this was 1918) toward the HQ. It was von Hartsheim. Riddled with machine-gun bullets, the car still managed to pull up to the door and the Germans entered the building without a single loss. The car burst into flames. Both sides now held their fire, and began

to wait—Elias for reinforcements, and Von Hartsheim for...what? Inspiration, perhaps.

5) Schlamminger and his comrade found no German guards at the PTT; in fact, it was not open yet. They broke in and occupied it. But there was really no need. The telegraph wires were already cut. The pair amused themselves by forcing open the bank vault and carting out the Romanian *lei*, which they later distributed freely in the city. Perhaps it came in handy as fuel.

At the end of the day the *coup* was in control of the whole town— except the one significant part of it, the part that really counted for everything. If the Colonel held out long enough, the Germans might send him reinforcements (the telegraphic silence would be taken as an alarm). True, the German Army was more concerned with impending defeat than with any rear-guard actions. But what if someone in Bucharest knew about the treasure, or even suspected its existence? Secrets like that can never really be kept. One way or another, the *coup* was poised on the brink of disaster—although by evening the city had begun to celebrate as if victory were a foregone conclusion.

The siege of the police-station lasted all that night, and the next day, and the next. On the seventh, the Scythians declared a Provisional Government of Cumantsa, and announced an extremely radical land redistribution program. To kick it off, Mavrocordato donated his entire estate (except the palace, which now became the seat of the Provisional Government) to the peasants of Cumantsa. Absentee landlords were declared expropriated. No holding was to exceed 50 hectares—otherwise, everyone was declared the owners of whatever land they were occupying. The Petchenegs and Cumans went wild with joy, and immediately flocked to sign up with the "army" of the Provisionals. About 1000 "barbarians" now gathered before the police station and offered to storm it *en masse* and (almost) unarmed. The Scythian leaders asked them to hold back for one more day.

On November 8 the tide turned. The Central Powers surrendered. World War I was over. (Meanwhile in Munich the *Räterepublik* had been proclaimed by Kurt Eisner on November 2.) By the morning of the 9th, Mavrocordato was able to send a newspaper from Bucharest into the police station. Von Hartsheim knew he was beaten and sued for terms.

As a gesture of noble contempt, the Scythians decided to let their enemies go free. The Germans were escorted by the Provisional "army" to the borders of Cumantsa (in the Delta marshes beyond Lake Razen) where they were pointed west and sent packing. They were arrested somewhere along the road to Bucharest by regular Romanian forces, and henceforth disappear from our story.

The *coup* had succeeded despite itself. Cumantsa was now an "independent country." What next?

V. BRIEF HISTORY OF AN EVANESCENT EVENT

> "That something is irrational is no argument against its existence, but rather a condition for it."
>
> —*Human, All-Too-Human*, 238

The most obvious thing to do next would be to hand over Cumantsa to Romania, and there were advocates of that position even within the Provisional Government. (This was also the original intention of D'Annunzio when he later liberated Fiume on September 12, 1919— but the Italian government turned him down!) But the inner circle of the Scythians had other plans and ambitions. Apparently they had not only succeeded in capturing the treasure, they had also kept it a secret—at least, outside Cumantsa. They could perhaps have simply fled with the booty—but antiquities and even gold are not so easily transported or turned into hard cash. Instead they obviously intended to sell the loot—probably to the same customer von Hartsheim had been dealing with (the Russians?)—and use the proceeds to finance their real intention: the creation of a revolutionary state. Obviously they succeeded, since the autonomous Sanjak of Cumantsa never thereafter seemed to lack for funds. Food supplies began to flow into the region almost at once, and those too poor to buy it were fed at the expense of the Provisional Government.

Luck favored the conspirators in other ways as well. The Romanian army had its hands full elsewhere. Bela Kun actually launched an invasion of Transylvania and kept Romanian forces occupied for an entire year (until November 1919). Those troops that could be spared from the Hungarian front were too busy trying to keep the civil war in the Ukraine from spilling over into Moldavia to worry about a few eccentricities on the Black Sea. Moreover the winter of 1918-19 was extremely severe. Ovid would have been perversely pleased to see the Danube and the Black Sea freeze solid. But no barbarians approached over the ice. Cumantsa was cut off—safe till the spring thaw.

The Provisional Government decided to remain "provisional" and not declare itself established; moreover it proclaimed Cumantsa "autonomous" rather than "independent," thus keeping diplomatic options with Bucharest open and fluid. (Bessarabia had done the same thing, but later capitulated.)

In May of 1919 (as the Munich Soviet fell to reactionary forces), the Romanian government finally made an official offer of incorporation to the "caretaker" regime in Cumantsa. Terms seemed generous enough (including "amnesty" for any political irregularities), in keeping with Cumantsa's "heroic defeat of occupying forces and traitorous elements" the preceding year. Mavrocordato, who was now president of the executive committee of the Provisional Government, simply delayed answering as long as he could. In June the pressure grew so strong that a statement was released: Cumantsa would join Romania but only as an autonomous republic. (The model was the Soviet Union.) This offer was indignantly refused by Bucharest. The situation grew tense.

In July a strange telegram reached Bucharest from Istanbul. It emanated from the (almost extinguished) Sublime Porte, and in extremely tortuous diplomatese it appeared to be a warning (or at least a vague exhortation) not to intervene in Cumantsa. The Romanians were outraged, and their apoplectic response was backed up by pressure from the Allies. Turkey withdrew its communiqué. The puzzle is why Turkey sent the telegram in the first place. Once again, one suspects the ubiquitous Shaykh Mehmet, "agent" of something or other, some shady faction in Istanbul. In any case, the "incident" served its purpose since it purchased time for the Provisional Government. Negotiations began concerning the possibility of a referendum. Bucharest was quite cold about it, but for some reason delayed any response. Delay seemed to suit everybody. The whole region was in turmoil, and in many ways the situation was worse now than during the War. Peasants were revolting, the Russian Whites and Reds were all over the map, the Ukraine was in open rebellion against Lenin and even against Marxism, starvation was still endemic, and Order seemed a distant dream. Who had time to deal with Cumantsa?

Amazingly enough, the Provisional Government was to survive not only another freezing winter, but also another spring and summer. The *Star*—which was now being published again—records a whole long boring series of communications and negotiations between Cumantsa and Bucharest, but in its editorial columns it makes no secret of the plans for a genuinely free Cumantsa. As we shall see, it even went so far as to publish a proposed draft of "Principles for a Constitution," which was adopted "provisionally" by the Provisionals. But still Bucharest did nothing. One suspects that the Scythians had privately communicated their intentions of creating an "incident" if any force were applied by the monarchy. At this point the Allies would not rejoice in yet another "trouble spot in Eastern Europe." And so matters went on, from November 1918, through all of 1919, and into 1920. When D'Annunzio took Fiume, one of his first acts was to send a telegram of congratulations to Cumantsa. Apparently its reputation had reached him—in fact, it may even have inspired him.

Before delving into the politics, culture, social life, and achievements of the Autonomous Sanjak, let us briefly finish recounting its diplomatic history. In November 1919 the treaties of St. Germain and Trianon awarded the whole of the Dobruja to Romania. Thus Cumantsa lost a bargaining chip, and Bucharest began to step up its demands for capitulation. Only post-War chaos prevented Romania from a military solution; and so affairs dragged on till March of 1920, when—at long last—the monarchy declared itself prepared to back up its demands with force. The Provisional Government had no desire for a blood bath. On April 1, 1920, almost the entire personnel left Cumantsa as a group, including all the Executive Committee, by ship for Istanbul. There they declared themselves a provisional-government-in-exile. Cumantsa was occupied without a shot. A few arrests were made, but no one was executed. The experiment was over.

VI. Nietzschean Utopia

> *Dream and responsibility.*—You are willing to assume responsibility for everything! Except, that is, for your dreams! What miserable weakness, what lack of consistent courage! Nothing is more your own than your dreams! Nothing *more* your own work!
>
> —*Daybreak*, 78

"Right" and "Left," as everyone knows, derive from a seating arrangement in the old French Assembly, a circular assemblage that resulted in the two extreme wings being seated next to each other. Perhaps the sheer accident of this proximity led to a certain drift between the two factions—but the attraction of extremes would have occurred at some point even without the physical proximity. Extremists, after all, are all *extreme.* And ideologies are not pure, as ideologues would have us (and themselves) believe. Every *idea*, by virtue of its organic incompleteness or irreality, can contain or reflect or absorb any *other* idea. Stalin and Hitler can make a pact and ideology can accommodate it. We see this in Russia today, with its "Red/Brown" National Bolsheviks, and we can see it in the late 19th century as well, with disciples of Proudhon and Sorel following the logic of certain "leftist" ideas toward the "Right," into monarchism or fascism. If *autonomy* and *authority* appear easily distinguishable in experience, they may perhaps become confused on paper—and when they are "rigorously" distinct on paper, they may become entangled on the level of psychology or in the confusion of "real life." For instance, one's personal desire for freedom can be projected onto the whole of society as an abstraction—one is an anarchist. But the same desire can be projected onto one particular group (nation, race, class, clique) to the exclusion of other groups— the "enemies of freedom"—without any psychological or even cognitive dissonance. Eventually one may "renounce" one's original position without qualms; one has remained "true to oneself." If this is so, even of rigorous ideologies like Marxism, it must be even more true of less systematic systems or even anti-systems such as anarchism, especially its Proudhonian or Sorelian tendencies, or its Stirnerian/Nietzschean wing. Please understand that these observations are not meant as some sort of facile "critique" of Marx, Proudhon, Sorel, Stirner, or Nietzsche. "History" can be used to make anyone look foolish and to make all causes seem hopeless.

Walter Kaufmann to the contrary notwithstanding, there are "fascistic" elements in Nietzsche's thought:—the glorification of war, for example, or the concept of the power-elite. Nietzsche himself somewhere describes his perfect reader as one who should experience Nietzsche with equal amounts of disgust and rapture. In effect one cannot "use" him without "taking out of context"—unless one wants to share his madness. The fascists, too, found what they wanted. But Nietzsche is also an anti-nationalist (and "good European"), an anti-anti-Semite, an admirer of Jews and Moslems, a sex-radical, a pagan "free spirit," a proponent of Enlightenment rationalism, a "nihilist," an individualist, etc., etc. As Emma Goldman pointed out, his "aristocracy" was not of wealth or blood but of spirit. One might as well say there are "fascistic" elements in Marx—his glorification of the State, his bureaucratic centralism—even a touch of anti-Semitism! This rear-view mirror approach to Nietzsche is essentially *trivial*. Let the dead bury their dead. Kaufmann gets upset when people quote Nietzsche "out of context." But then—how *else* is one to quote Nietzsche? Every quotation is removed from the whole body of a writer's work only by violence; and finally one lives by the sweat of one's own brow, however deep the debt to others. In Nietzsche's case, in any case, *there is no "system."*

Mavrocordato and the Scythians obviously intended to try to turn the Autonomous Sanjak of Cumantsa into a Nietzschean utopia; we know this because they declared it in print, in the *Evening Star*, which now resumed publication. The most important document produced during the two year lifespan of the experiment was a draft for the principles of a proposed Constitution. These principles were adopted "provisionally" by the Provisional Government, but no actual constitution was ever subsequently promulgated, since the Government remained "provisional." This may have been accidental or it may have been deliberate. I believe that the Scythians *intended* to leave everything hanging loose as long as possible. The whole point of statehood is *stasis*, the very rigidity and finality all good Nietzscheans abhor. "*Become who you are*"—Nietzsche never tires of repeating this tag from Pindar (that most Nietzschean of ancient poets)—and the process of becoming never ceases until death. On a more mundane level, the Provisionals refrained from making any irrevocable moves against Romania or the Allies; they had no desire to call down anyone's wrath simply to defend some lofty shibboleth like "independence" or "Constitution" or "rights." Mavrocordato very obviously intended that they should do whatever was best for the whole people and place of Cumantsa, not for some "philosophy" or ideology. This determination in itself was very Nietzschean.

One might, however, question the practicality of this intention. Judged by their effusions in the *Star*, and by their actions, Mavrocordato and his comrades were young romantics who saw themselves as the future. They spoke as if they expected their ideas to catch on and spread—the apocalyptic atmosphere of post-war Europe encouraged such wild speculation. The collapse of Western Civilization was expected on a day-to-day basis; the Russian Revolution was seen as the beginning of the End. We know that experiments like Cumantsa, Munich, Fiume, or the Limerick Soviet were *impractical* and doomed to failure because we know (to our sorrow) that Western Civilization was not going to collapse but to metastasize, and was about to launch a whole century of war and "cold war" that would end with the triumph of Capital in 1989-91. But it would be quite unjust of us to demand such knowledge of the revolutionaries of 1918. Gustav Landauer, as it happens, knew perfectly well that the Munich Soviet was doomed when he joined it. He even had premonitions of his own death. But as a sincere Nietzschean existentialist he did it anyway—first for *himself*, for his own becoming—and second for the *future*, for the coming-into-being of another world. But most of the rebels of the period had no such foresight. And we, who think we have such foresight, are perhaps only exhausted. "Dionysian pessimism" *knows*, but acts despite its knowledge, out of an excess of generosity—as sheer *expression*. We know of Landauer's despair only from his letters. In his published work he never faltered, and was still issuing position papers on education (e.g., the vital importance of teaching Walt Whitman to school children) as the Soviet began to crumble around him. Without the letters we might think him merely absurd rather than tragic—a blind idealist, a futile intellectual. In the case of the Scythians we have no such private correspondence to deepen our view of their motivations. We have only their public *pronunciamenti*. It is important to remember that Cumantsa was a "failure"; thus we have already "foretold" its end in our "Brief History." But it is also important to remember that on November 9, 1918 the *coup* was a *success*. We should be prepared to excuse some excess and jubilation. It was a kind of "peak experience."

The Provisional Government that proclaimed itself on November 8 and assumed power on the 9th could be called a *junta*—or it could be called simply the Scythian Club. The President was Georghiu Mavrocordato, the portfolio of economic affairs went to the Club treasurer Shaykh Mehmet Effendi, the Secretary (Caleb Afendopoulo of Odessa) remained Secretary. The mariner Enrico Elias was head of the "military committee," assisted by Mavrocordato's old friend Antonescu the folklorist. Schlamminger the antiquarian held no office; perhaps as a German he felt awkward about any public role, or else (very likely) he was too busy sorting out the hoard of golden treasure which now constituted the total assets of the Provisional Government. (Later they imposed a flat three percent harbor duty, but no customs or tax. The sheer economic *inactivity* of the regime is the best proof of the hypothesis about the treasure. Like Fiume, Cumantsa was literally a freebooter state or "pirate utopia"!)

On December 20, in the first issue of the new run of the *Star* (which contains all the details of the *coup*) the Junta announced the new form of government as "Councilism"—in other words, it was to be formed out of councils or soviets, as in Munich (or Moscow). But the Cumantsa soviets were not to be based on classes or economic categories. A "worker's council" would have been absurd in a city where no factories existed. The real structure of Cumantsan society was based on communities, defined for the most part by ethnic or religious identity. In other words—*volk*. The radicalism of the proposal lay in the fact that no one community was to be the "master" community. Each community was to choose—by whatever method it liked—a council for itself. This council was then to send a revokable delegate to a Council of councils, which would vote on proposals to "advise" the Junta, which called itself the Executive Committee. This "emergency" structure was provisional, and would eventually be replaced under a Constitution to be agreed upon *unanimously* in Council. Until then, the Junta was obviously prepared to enforce the decisions of the Provisional Government if necessary. It is also obvious that most Cumantsans supported the Scythian Junta, since there were very few incidents of enforcement over the next two years. The reasons for this popularity were, first, the land redistribution scheme, which won over the peasants; second, the "free port" arrangements which mollified the merchants; and third (I suspect) the free hand-outs made possible by the treasure, which pleased nearly everyone else. The only malcontents were a few Romanian gentry who lost land in the expropriation, and apparently now left Cumantsa in disgust, and—worst of all—the Orthodox priests at the church of St. George, who stayed put and caused trouble.

Two influences lie behind the "Provisional Government" arrangement, or so I believe. The first was historically appropriate:—the "*millet* system" of the old Ottoman Empire, which allowed legal and even political autonomy to ethnic and religious groups in return for taxes—and of course, the Turks were the tax-collectors and thus the rulers. In Cumantsa there were no taxes, and the Turks were on the same level as the other communities; otherwise, the Cumantsa system closely resembles the *Millet*. The other influence was clearly "left *volk*-ism" as taught by Landauer, Diederich, and other German radicals in the Nietzschean tradition:—the freedom of one *volk* implies and necessitates the freedom of all. In this sense Cumantsa was to be a kind of Proudhonian federation, a "government" of administration rather than rule, a horizontal net of contractual solidarities. Incidentally, the announcement of this scheme in the *Star* makes it clear that *any* self-defined group could form a council and choose a delegate; it was suggested, for example, that a fishermans' council might be appropriate. In the end, however, all the "groups" turned out to be religious or ethnic—except, of course, the Junta, which in any case was not a "council" at all, but a military and executive directorate.

The Petchenegs and Cumans formed one council and of course chose their Ilkhan to represent them. The Turks chose Shaykh Mehmet. The Karaite Jews chose their own traditional leader, Isaac Iskawi, who was not a Junta member, but was related to Caleb Afendopoulo and apparently content to be advised by him. The Greeks were the only problem. The head of the Orthodox clergy in Cumantsa, John Capodistrias (who enjoyed the title of "Exilarch" for some reason) seems to have considered Mavrocordato the Antichrist. Fair enough, one might suppose. But Capodistrias attempted to forbid his parishioners any participation in the new government, and this the Junta would not allow. First, the few Romanian Orthodox in Cumantsa were "liberals," since the "conservatives" had all been expropriated. They seceded from the Greek congregation and chose as their councilor Vlad Antonescu, the folklorist and Junta-member. Second, a split—or perhaps even a schism—occurred within the Greek community. According to the *Star*, about half of Capodistrias' congregation abandoned him and declared that they had chosen as their councilor…Georghiu Mavrocordato. The hospodar now informed the Exilarch that he and his people were free to abstain from participation in the Council, but that they would also have to forego the "benefits" such as land distribution (and by implication the benefits of the treasure as well). At this point yet more Greeks (undoubtedly the poorer ones) abandoned the Church and Capodistrias was left in a powerless condition. He did not, however, cease to oppose Mavrocordato whenever possible.

The first and most important activity of the Council was land redistribution. Caleb Afendopoulo and the Ilkhan of the Cumans were appointed to oversee this process as the "Land Reform Committee." The work went rather slowly and carefully, and apparently was considered quite successful.

Otherwise, Cumantsa seemed to run itself. It had always been a peaceful backwater if left to itself—and now it was very much left to itself. "Smuggling"—now legalized as free trade—and fishing continued to support the modest needs of the people, who demanded no hydroelectric plants or higher education. The Scythians were free to meet again and to argue and discuss till dawn and draw up manifestos. The fruit of this work appeared in February 1919, in the form of an extraordinary document containing the Executive Committee's proposed platform of principles for an eventual Constitution of Cumantsa. It consists almost entirely of quotations from Nietzsche, translated into Romanian. The references to Nietzsche's works were not included, but I have been able to track down most of these quotations and find English translations for them. If ever there was a work in which Nietzsche was "taken out of context," this must be it—and yet the context is nothing but Nietzsche! Here it is, in its entirety—the finest flower of the Autonomous Sanjak of Cumantsa and its mad architects.

Principles

Opening Paragraphs

It is only as an *aesthetic phenomenon* that existence and the world are eternally *justified.* [BT 52]

Twofold kind of equality. The craving for equality can be expressed either by the wish to draw all others down to one's level (by belittling, excluding, tripping them up) or by the wish to draw oneself up with everyone else (by appreciating, helping, taking pleasure in others' success). [HTH 177/300]

The first thought of the day. The best way to begin each day well is to think upon awakening whether we could not give at least one person pleasure on this day. If this practice could be accepted as a substitute for the religious habit of prayer, our fellow men would benefit by this change. [HTH 248/589]

In the main, I agree more with the artists than with any philosopher hitherto: they have not lost the scent of life, they have loved the things of "this
world"—they have loved their senses. To strive for "desensualization": that
seems to me a misunderstanding or an illness or a cure, where it is not
merely hypocrisy or self-deception. I desire for myself and for all who live,
may live, without being tormented by a puritanical conscience, an ever-
greater spiritualization and multiplication of the senses; indeed, we should
be grateful to the senses for their subtlety, plenitude, and power and offer
them in return the best we have in the way of spirit. [WTP 424/820]

We should be *able* also to stand *above* morality—and not only to stand
with the anxious stiffness of a man who is afraid of slipping and falling
any moment, but also to *float* above it and *play*. How then could we
possibly dispense with art—and with the fool?—And as long as you
are in any way ashamed before yourselves, you do not yet belong with
us. [GS, 164/107]

Live dangerously! Build your cities on the slopes of Vesuvius! Send your
ships into uncharted seas! Live at war with your peers and yourselves!
Be robbers and conquerors as long as you cannot be rulers and pos-
sessors, you seekers of knowledge! Soon the age will be past when you
could be content to live hidden in forests like shy deer. At long last the
search for knowledge will reach out for its due; it will want to *rule* and
possess, and you with it! [GS 228/283]

General Principles

What is needful is a new *justice!* And a new watchword. And new
philosophers. The moral earth, too, is round. The moral earth, too, has
its antipodes. The antipodes, too, have the right to exist. There is yet
another world to be discovered—and more than one. Embark, philosophers! [GS 232/289]

A concealed Yes drives us that is stronger than all our No's. Our strength itself will no longer endure us in the old decaying soil: we venture away, we venture *ourselves:* the world is still rich and undiscovered, and even to perish is better than to become halfhearted and poisonous. Our strength itself drives us to sea, where all suns have hitherto gone down: we *know* of a new world. [WTP 219/405]

Crime belongs to the concept "revolt against the social order." One does not "punish" a rebel; one *suppresses* him. A rebel can be a miserable and contemptible man; but there is nothing contemptible in a revolt as such—and to be a rebel in view of contemporary society does not in itself lower the value of a man. There are even cases in which one might have to honor a rebel, because he finds something in our society against which war ought to be waged—he awakens us from our slumber. [WTP 391/740]

"I say unto you: one must still have chaos in oneself to be able to give birth to a dancing star. I say unto you: you still have chaos in yourselves." [TSZ 129]

There are a thousand paths that have never yet been trodden—a thousand healths and hidden isles of life. Even now, man and man's earth are unexhausted and undiscovered.

Wake and listen, you that are lonely! From the future come winds with secret wing-beats; and good tidings are proclaimed to delicate ears. You that are lonely today, you that are withdrawing, you shall one day be the people: out of you, who have chosen yourselves, there shall grow a chosen people—and out of them, the overman. Verily, the earth shall yet become a site of recovery. And even now a new fragrance surrounds it, bringing salvation—and a new hope. [TSZ 189]

Anti-Darwin. As for the famous "struggle for existence," so far it seems to me to be asserted rather than proved. It occurs, but as an exception; the total appearance of life is not the extremity, not starvation, but rather riches, profusion, even absurd squandering—and where there is struggle, it is a struggle for *power*. One should not mistake Malthus for nature. [TI 522]

Let us not underestimate this: *we ourselves*, we free spirits, are nothing less than a "revaluation of all values," an *incarnate* declaration of war and triumph over all the ancient conceptions of "true" and "untrue." [AC 579]

It is thus irrational and trivial to impose the demands of morality upon mankind.—To *recommend* a goal to mankind is something quite different: the goal is then thought of as something which *lies in our own discretion*; supposing the recommendation appealed to mankind, it could in pursuit of it also *impose* upon itself a moral law, likewise at its own discretion. [D 63/108]

State

Socialism can serve as a rather brutal and forceful way to teach the danger of all accumulations of state power, and to that extent instill one with distrust of the state itself. When its rough voice chimes in with the battle cry "*As much state as possible*," it will at first make the cry noisier than ever; but soon the opposite cry will be heard with strength the greater: "*As little state as possible*." [HTH 227/474]

The price being paid for "universal security" is much too high: and the maddest thing is that what is being effected is the very opposite of universal security, a fact our lovely century is undertaking to demonstrate: as if demonstration were needed! To make society safe against thieves and fireproof and endlessly amenable to every kind of trade and traffic, and to transform the state into a kind of providence in both the good and the bad sense—these are lower, mediocre and in no way indispensable goals which ought not to be pursued by means of the highest instruments *which in any way exist*—instruments which ought to be *saved up* for the highest and rarest objectives! [D 107-8/179]

Apart.—Parliamentarianism—that is, public permission to choose between five basic political opinions—flatters and wins the favor of all those who would like to seem independent and individual, as if they fought for their opinions. Ultimately, however, it is indifferent whether the herd is commanded to have one opinion or permitted to have five. Whoever deviates from the five public opinions and stands apart will always have the whole herd against him. [GS 202/174]

Today, in our time when the state has an absurdly fat stomach, there are in all fields and departments, in addition to the real workers, also "representatives"; e.g., besides the scholars also scribblers, besides the suffering classes also garrulous, boastful ne'er-do-wells who "represent" this suffering, not to speak of the professional politicians who are well off while "representing" distress with powerful lungs before a parliament. Our modern life is extremely expensive owing to the large number of intermediaries; in an ancient city, on the other hand, and, echoing that, also in many cities in Spain and Italy, one appeared oneself and would have given a hoot to such modern representatives and intermediaries—or a kick! [WTP 48/75]

An old Chinese said he had heard that when empires were doomed they had many laws. [WTP 394/745]

The better the state is established, the fainter is humanity. [Notes 50]

[S]tate, where the slow suicide of all is called "life." [...]

Only where the state ends, there begins the human being who is not superfluous: there begins the song of necessity, the unique and inimitable tune. [TSZ 162-163]

They have gone so far in their madness as to demand that we feel our very existence to be a punishment—it is as though the education of the human race had hitherto been directed by the fantasies of jailers and hangmen! [D 13]

The best we can do in this *interregnum* is to be as far as possible our own *reges* and found little *experimental states*. We are experiments: let us also want to be them! [D 191/453]

Work and Capital

[Industrial culture] in its present shape is altogether the most vulgar form of existence that has yet existed. Here one is at the mercy of brute need; one wants to live and has to sell oneself, but one despises those who exploit this need and *buy* the worker. Oddly, submission to powerful, frightening, even terrible persons, like tyrants and generals, is not experienced as nearly so painful as this submission to unknown and uninteresting persons, which is what all the luminaries of industry are. What the workers see in the employer is usually only a cunning, bloodsucking dog of a man who speculates on all misery; and the employer's name, shape, manner, and reputation are a matter of complete indifference to them. [GS 107]

Those who commend work.—In the glorification of "work," in the unwearied task of the "blessing of work," I see the same covert idea as in the praise of useful impersonal actions: that of fear of everything individual. Fundamentally, one now feels at the sight of work—one always

208 Chapter FALSE DOCUMENTS

means by work that hard industriousness from early till late—that such work is the best policeman, that it keeps everyone in bounds and can mightily hinder the development of reason, covetousness, desire for independence. For it uses up an extraordinary amount of nervous energy, which is thus denied to reflection, brooding, dreaming, worrying, loving, hating; it sets a small goal always in sight and guarantees easy and regular satisfactions. Thus a society in which there is continual hard work will have more security: and security is now worshipped as the supreme divinity.—And now! Horror! Precisely the 'worker' has become *dangerous!* The place is swarming with 'dangerous' individuals! And behind them the danger of dangers—*the* individual! [D 105/173]

Fundamental idea of a commercial culture.—Today one can see coming into existence the culture of a society of which *commerce* is as much the soul as personal contest was with the ancient Greeks and as war, victory and justice were for the Romans. The man engaged in commerce understands how to appraise everything without having made it, and to appraise it *according to the needs of the consumer*, not according to his own needs; "who and how many will consume this?" is his question of questions. This type of appraisal he then applies instinctively and all the time: he applies it to everything, and thus also to the productions of the arts and sciences, of thinkers, scholars, artists, statesmen, peoples and parties, of the entire age: in regard to everything that is made he inquires after supply and demand *in order to determine the value of a thing in his own eyes.* This becomes the character of an entire culture, thought through in the minutest and subtlest detail and imprinted in every will and every faculty: it is this of which you men of the coming century will be proud: if the prophets of the commercial class are right to give it into your possession! But I have little faith in these prophets. [D 106/175]]

[W]hat one formerly did 'for the sake of God' one now does for the sake of money, that is to say, for the sake of that which *now* gives the highest feeling of power and good conscience. [D123/204]

Barbarians/Peasants

During the great prehistoric age of mankind, spirit was presumed to exist everywhere and was not held in honour as a privilege of man. Because, on the contrary, the spiritual (together with all drives, wickedness, inclinations) had been rendered common property, and thus common, one was not ashamed to have descended from animals or trees (the noble races thought themselves honoured by such fables), and saw in the spirit that which unites us with nature, not that which sunders us from it. [D 23/31]

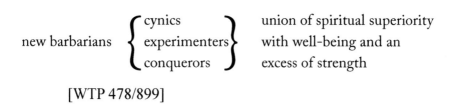

[WTP 478/899]

To grant oneself the right to exceptional actions; as an experiment in self-overcoming and freedom.

To venture into states in which it is not permitted *not* to be a barbarian. [WTP 487/921]

Best and dearest to me today is a healthy peasant, coarse, cunning, stubborn, enduring: that is the noblest species today. The peasant is the best type today, and the peasant type should be master. But it is in the realm of the mob; I should not be deceived any more.[TSZ 357]

freedom

"That passion is better than Stoicism and hypocrisy, that being honest in evil is still better than losing oneself to the morality of tradition, that a free human being can be good as well as evil, but that the unfree human being is a blemish upon nature and has no share in any heavenly or earthly comfort; finally, that everyone who wishes to become free must become free through his own endeavor, and that freedom does not fall into any man's lap as a miraculous gift." (*Richard Wagner in Bayreuth*, p. 94) [GS 156/99]

My conception of freedom. The value of a thing sometimes does not lie in that which one attains by it, but in what one pays for it—what it costs us. I shall give an example. Liberal institutions cease to be liberal as soon as they are attained: later on, there are no worse and no more thorough injurers of freedom than liberal institutions. Their effects are known well enough: they undermine the will to power; they level mountain and valley, and call that morality; they make men small, cowardly, and hedonistic—every time it is the herd animal that triumphs with them. Liberalism: in other words, herd-animalization.

These same institutions produce quite different effects while they are still being fought for; then they really promote freedom in a powerful way. On closer inspection, it is war that produces these effects, the war *for* liberal institutions, which, as a war, permits illiberal instincts to continue. And war educated for freedom. For what is freedom? That one has the will to assume responsibility for oneself. That one maintains the distance which separates us. That one becomes more indifferent to difficulties, hardships, privation, even to life itself. That one is prepared to sacrifice human beings for one's cause, not excluding oneself. [PN 541-2]

Against the tyranny of the true.—Even if we were mad enough to consider all our opinions true, we should still not want them alone to exist:—I cannot see why it should be desirable that truth alone should rule and be omnipotent; it is enough for me that it should possess *great power*. But it must be able to *struggle* and have opponents, and one must be able to *find relief* from it from time to time in untruth—otherwise it will become boring, powerless and tasteless to us, and make us the same. [D 206]

festival

What good is all the art of our works of art if we lose that higher art, the art of festivals? Formerly, all works of art adorned the great festival road of humanity, to commemorate high and happy moments. [GS 144]

The states in which we infuse a transfiguration and fullness into things and poetize about them until they reflect back our fullness and joy in life: sexuality; intoxication; feasting; spring; victory over an enemy; mockery; bravado; cruelty, the ecstasy of religious feeling. *Three* elements principally: *sexuality, intoxication, cruelty*—all belonging to the oldest *festal joys* of mankind, all also preponderate in the early "artist." [WTP 421/801]

There is a need for those who will sanctify all activities, not only eating and drinking—and not merely in remembrance of them and to become one with them, but this world must be transfigured ever anew and in new ways. [WTP 537/1044]

Dionysus

What hopes must revive in us when the most certain auspices guarantee the *reverse process, the gradual awakening of the Dionysian spirit* in our modern world! [BT 119]

In polytheism the free-spiriting and many-spiriting of man attained its first preliminary form—the strength to create for ourselves our own new eyes—and even again new eyes that are even more our own: hence man alone among all the animals has no eternal horizons and perspectives. [GS 192/143]

Indeed, we philosophers and "free spirits" feel, when we hear the news that "the old god is dead," as if a new dawn shone on us; our heart overflows with gratitude, amazement, premonitions, expectation. At long last the horizon appears free to us again, even if it should not be bright; at long last our ships may venture out again, venture out to face any danger; all the daring of the lover of knowledge is permitted again; the sea, *our* sea, lies open again; perhaps there has never yet been such an "open sea." [GS 280/343]

...the *Dionysian* in will, spirit, taste. [WTP 528]

Islam

"Paradise lies in the shadow of swords"[24]—also a symbol and motto by which souls of noble and warlike origin betray themselves and divine each other. [WTP 499-500/952]

Christianity has cheated us out of the harvest of ancient culture; later it cheated us again, out of the harvest of the culture of *Islam*. The wonderful world of the Moorish culture of Spain, really more closely related to *us*, more congenial to our senses and tastes than Rome and Greece, was *trampled down* (I do not say by what kind of feet). Why? Because it owed its origin to noble, to *male* instincts, because it said Yes to life even with the rare and refined luxuries of Moorish life. [...] "War to the knife against Rome! Peace and friendship with Islam"—thus felt, thus *acted*, that great free spirit, the genius among German emperors, Frederick II. [AC 652-3]

---

[24]This is a *hadith* or traditional saying of the Prophet Muhammad, promising heaven to martyrs in holy war.

conclusion

We who are homeless.—Among Europeans today there is no lack of those who are entitled to call themselves homeless in a distinctive and honorable sense: it is to them that I especially commend my secret wisdom and *gaya scienza*. For their fate is hard, their hopes are uncertain; it is quite a feat to devise some comfort for them—but what avail? We children of the future, how could we be at home today? We feel disfavor for all ideals that might lead one to feel at home even in this fragile, broken time of transition; as for its "realities," we do not believe that they will last. The ice that still supports people today has become very thin; the wind that brings the thaw is blowing; we ourselves who are homeless constitute a force that breaks open ice and other all too thin "realities." [GS 338]

> 'There are so many days that have not yet broken.' Quoted from the *Rig Veda* [D xviv]

There is no indication that the Council was ever asked to approve this strange document, or even to debate it. Obviously the work of Mavrocordato, it is culled from a "complete" reading of Nietzsche, including some then-unpublished sources (the notes for *Will to Power*, which he must have seen at Sils Maria). It is difficult to see how such a "work" could be translated into a Constitution, a framework for governance. Probably this was never really intended. In some respects, it demands an impossible utopia. In other respects, however, it simply described the ad-hoc principles upon which the Junta was already acting—and undoubtedly it also represented the sincere intentions of the *coup*'s leaders.

Several months were enough to make the Autonomous Sanjak of Cumantsa more than a "temporary autonomous zone," but not very much more. For the most part, life went on as usual: fishermen fished, farmers farmed, merchants bought and sold (no attempt was made to produce a Cumantsan currency, but some attractive stamps were apparently printed, including a bust of Ovid). Unlike Fiume, which was an affair of military adventurers, Cumantsa made no great show of uniforms and parades—but Enrico Elias worked hard on building up a trained part-time "people's militia," acquiring arms and even some light artillery from the Black Sea arms smugglers market (which was enjoying a post-War boom). The "border crossing" near St. George's Mouth was kept under guard, and patrols of Petchenegs and Cumans prowled the backwaters, estuaries and lagoons of the interior. The narrow port entry was guarded night and day. The purpose of these measures was not to organize defiance against Romania or any other fully-equipped army—the Junta was never mad enough to dream of such pointless bravura, whatever bluffs and boasts they may have uttered for political reasons, to frighten Bucharest with the threat of an "incident" and the annoyance of the European Powers. The real purpose of the militia was to guard against the flow of uprooted refugees, demobbed soldiers and other mobile riffraff thrown up by the end of the War and the confusion of treaties; and to regulate the black-market and smuggling trades. "Incidents" did occur in the course of the seventeen months, and some were reported in the *Star*—but none reached diplomatic status. At one point there appears to have been serious trouble with the Orthodox dissidents within Cumantsa itself—a riot? an attempted counter-*coup*? The *Star* is devoid of detail, and we do not know of any deaths or injuries. For the most part, then, the Provisionals enjoyed a reign of peace, albeit a rather nervous peace.

One important aspect of civic life—already adumbrated in the "Principles" document—was feasting. Apparently there was no shortage of food now, since the Germans were no longer stealing everything in sight. Elsewhere in the region famine was epidemic, and no doubt this explains the border patrols. But the port was busy, and it seems obvious that the proceeds of the treasure were being spent largely on food. Free food was distributed to Cumantsa's needy on a regular basis, although this program was reduced after the successful harvest of Autumn 1919.

Public festivals were celebrated with tremendous spirit as part of the "Cumantsan renaissance" promoted by the Council. Christian, Jewish and Moslem holidays were all recognized, and November 7th was celebrated wildly in 1919 as the anniversary of the *coup*. Civic spirit was urged on to feats of festive creativity, with school pageants, street processions, dancing and brass band music, food-stalls in the marketplace, fairy lanterns and bunting, and free orangeade and sherbet. The *Star* never tires of recounting these happy occasions and boasting of Cumantsa's *joie de vivre*. Meanwhile the Council regaled itself from time to time with formal banquets. One of the first, held to celebrate the first seating of the Council (such sessions were known as "the *divan*") was based on Nietzsche's "Last Supper" in *Thus Spoke Zarathustra*: roast lamb "prepared tastily with sage: I love it that way. Nor is there a lack of roots and fruit, good enough even for gourmets and gourmands, nor of nuts and other riddles to be cracked"—along with wine and water or sherbet for Moslems and nietzschean teetotalers. At other celebrations, the typical gamebirds and venison of the Dobruja, prepared in Ottoman style, Greek "bandit" style, or Franco-Romanian style, graced the Junta's festive board—although they made a point of not indulging in outright gluttony on such semi-public occasions.

One important aspect of life in Cumantsa was music ("life would be a mistake without it," the sage says somewhere).[25] We have mentioned a brass band—apparently Cumantsa was able to afford at least one such, which serenaded the populace weekly and *gratis* in the small park behind the Hotel Imperial. The town also managed to put together a concert series, making use of amateur local talent (a string quartet which included the philologist H. Schlamminger on viola), and visiting professionals such as a popular violinist from Odessa named Ossip Vandenstein (who is still remembered by certain collectors of obscure 78's). Apparently there were also some Turkish musicians in town

[25]"Without music, life would be in error." *Twilight of the Idols*, 471.

performing regularly at one of the old-fashioned cafés in the bazaar, probably in the rather louche and marvelous style known as *rembetica*, a Greco-Turkish hybrid of the levantine port cabarets, suffused with sexuality, and flavored with raki, opium, hashish and cocaine. Probably the biggest sensation of the whole seventeen months attended the brief visit of Rosa Ashkenazi, the absolute queen of *rembetica*; the *Star* reported that every single citizen of Cumantsa, from cradle to crone, had attended at least one of her performances. (Presumably this did not include the Orthodox clergy!)

All this music reminds us of Fiume again, where D'Annunzio actually wrote his rather nietzschean theory of music directly into the Constitution. It was all part of the "Cumantsan renaissance," promoted by the Junta and organized by Vlad Antonescu the folklorist. He was particularly eager to foster the folkways of the Petchenegs and Cumans, and if the results were at times a bit heavy-handed—in the style of the era, which was busily "re-discovering" the culture of the *volk*—they were nevertheless gratifying and entertaining—at least to the Petchenegs and Cumans, who attended the revivals with unwonted hilarity and enthusiasm. A "Folk Ensemble" was in the planning stages when the Provisional Government collapsed in 1920.

The Scythians may not have enjoyed anything like their former enforced leisure, but they appear to have compensated for the decline in *otium* with an excess of energy, so that affairs of state failed to keep them from their former interests. In fact one suspects that "affairs of State" took second place in their lives, and that they viewed the threat of bureaucratization with horror. Had they overthrown the Germans merely to turn themselves into...administrators? Dionysus forbid! (One is reminded of the Carlist Pretender to the throne of Spain who told a journalist that, once in power, he would spend his time "hunting and hawking." "But... what about *government?*" sputtered the reporter. "A matter for mere ministers," sniffed the King.) In short, the Scythians were far more interested in archaeology and hunting than the exchange of boring telegrams with monarchist flunkies in Bucharest. Once again, only the treasure-hypothesis can explain such insouciance. Whenever a problem arose, the Junta threw money at it till it went away—or so I would conjecture. What they planned to do when the money ran out, we cannot say—since they never even admitted possession of the treasure in the first place. During the seventeen months of their run for the money, the Scythians seem to have spent the best part of their energy on an archaeological dig on Popin Island in the Lagoon, site of ancient Histri (from *Ister*, the ancient name for the Danube, which once flowed into the Lagoon at this point). Their finds—mostly inscriptions and a few gold pieces from later barbaric burials—were displayed in an exhibition held in the Old Hall of the Mosque of Khezr in November 1919, during the first anniversary celebrations. Perhaps they expected to find a great deal of gold; who knows? Perhaps they *did*.

The *Star* did not fail to publish reports on archaeology and other cultural activities. Mavrocordato handed the editorship over to Caleb Afendopoulo, but continued to contribute (mostly nietzschean ramblings) to its expanded columns. Texts were published in Turkish, Greek, and Cuman dialect, as well as Romanian. Antonescu contributed his translations from Ovid's *Tristia and Black Sea Letters*, as well as endless notes on folklore (sadly not included by Densusianu in the *Hronicul*). The letters column apparently contained communications from foreign scholars and notables, but the only name we know is that of D'Annunzio, who sent a booming communiqué of comradeship to the Junta, offering to establish diplomatic relations between Cumantsa and Fiume! The idea was well received, but as far as we know there was no exchange of envoys.

Densusianu mentions in passing that Mavrocordato wrote a "series" of pieces on Kabbalah and sufism. Considering how little we actually know about Mavrocordato aside from his ability to paste together bits of Nietzsche, it is much to be regretted that Densusianu neglected to include any of these articles in his Chronicle. We have already noted that the "Principles" document makes clear use of Nietzsche's Islamophilic tendencies, undoubtedly in an attempt to woo the Cumantsan Moslems (Turks, a few Tatars, and some of the Cumans). Mavrocordato's quarrel with the Orthodox clergy seems to have pushed him away from Christianity toward Judaism and Islam (a fairly obvious nietzschean trajectory), and, as we shall see, there is some evidence to suggest that he actually ended his life as a sufi of some sort. It is possible that he was already secretly initiated into the Bektashiyya by Shaykh Mehmet Effendi. Its heterodoxy, wine-drinking, and political murkiness may well have appealed to his romantic nature. We shall return to these speculations.

Oddly enough, the one area upon which we can shed some light—an area scrupulously avoided by Densusianu!—is the "night-life" of Cumantsa. We owe this picture to the one non-Romanian account of the 1918-1920 period ever published (as far as I know—and I could be wrong):—a chapter in a book that appeared in Paris in 1924, *Perles d'Orient* by Adrien Villeneuve. This obscure author was somehow vaguely connected to the Surrealist movement and was expelled from it by Breton sometime before World War II. He was also an acquaintance of André Gide, which seems quite appropriate, since Villeneuve was a leftist and a pederastic tourist, like Gide. In *Perles d'Orient* he describes his salacious and eccentric Grand Tour of the Middle East in the years 1919-1920. Most of the book deals with Egypt and Turkey, but Villeneuve also recounted his brief visit to the Autonomous Sanjak of Cumantsa in August 1919. Such characters turned up in droves in Fiume, but Cumantsa was off the beaten track.[26]

Villeneuve met Mavrocordato, whom he describes as "charming and handsome." He was invited to dine with the Scythians and marvels

---

[26]See Gide's *Correspondences*, vol. II. pp. 317-319, where the *contretemps* with Breton is mentioned.

at the (unexpectedly) excellent wine and venison he was served. He visited the archaeological dig at Histri, and met some Petchenegs and Cumans in the "wild." He is enthusiastic about the experiment in politics, and even mentions the land redistribution project—but having dealt thus briefly with radical ideals, he plunges headlong into the nearest "abyss of vice."

It seems that Cumantsa had a red-light district, consisting of a few dark alleyways behind the Chandlers Row section of the docks. It was here that Turkish musicians played *Rembetika* in the Café Smyrna. An even lower dive, with no name, served as a rendezvous for rough sailors, smugglers, and contrabandistas, opium addicts, and a few hardy prostitutes. Here there was a wind-up record player, with "negro jazz." Villeneuve was pleased. But his favorite rendezvous was a café on an upper story in the "district," called The Silver Pipe, where Villeneuve was served with "a confection of haschisch and bitter coffee, by Nikos, a Greek Ganymede with violet eyes, son of the proprietor." Just how much of the sultry month of August was spent by Villeneuve in this "innocent dalliance" (he says!) is not clear, but the reader learns much more about his "long afternoons under the spell of the Green Parrot" than anything else in Cumantsa.[27] It is an amusing read, but frustrating. It tantalizes with glimpses of Cumantsa not available in the columns of the *Star*. Villeneuve's musings on the simple but elegant lines of the

---

[27]*Ensphinxed*, to crown many
Feelings into one word
(May God forgive me
This linguistic sin!)—
I sit here, sniffing the best air
Verily, paradise air,
Bright, light air, golden-striped,
As good air as ever
Fell down from the moon—
[PN 419]

Mosque of Khezr, for example, or his brief description of the "Ovidian" marshes, leave us wanting more. One wonders how much of this lost world could be recaptured by visiting Cumantsa today.

VII. END AND AFTERMATH

> "All histories speak of things which have never existed except in imagination."
>
> —*Daybreak*, 156

> *Everlasting funeral rites.*—Beyond the realm of history, one could fancy one hears a continuous funeral oration: men have always buried, and are still burying, that which they love best, their thoughts and hopes, and have received, and are still receiving, in exchange pride, *gloria mundi*, that is to say the pomp of the funeral oration. This is supposed to make up for everything! And the funeral orator is still the greatest public benefactor!
>
> —*Daybreak*, 208

In early spring of 1920, it became obvious that Bucharest's patience was wearing thin, and that its military capability was recovered, to the extent that it now contemplated a speedy resolution to the Cumantsa "crisis." If this involved an armed assault on Cumantsa, the monarchy was willing to face the flak. The Junta's days were clearly numbered.

The Council decided not to contest the issue any longer. Voices were raised in favor of a last-ditch defense, but the futility of such a sacrifice was all too apparent.[28] The Council could not win such a game, and had no desire to plunge the region once again into the horrors of war. The

---

[28]But blood is the worst witness of truth; blood poisons even the purest doctrine and turns it into delusion and hatred of the heart. And if a man goes through fire for his doctrine—what does that prove? Verily, it is more if your own doctrine comes out of your own fire. [TSZ 401]

gentlemanly thing to do was to extricate the Junta from the situation in such a way that face could be saved and no one hurt. After an editorial on March 28 proclaiming its sorrow, disappointment, and intention to renew the struggle some day, the *Star* ceased publication. On April 1, 1920, the following people boarded a steamer bound for Istanbul: Mavrocordato, his wife Anna and his elderly mother, Antonescu and Schlamminger, Afendopoulo and Elias, and Shaykh Mehmet and his family. On April 2, the rump of the Provisional Government (including most importantly the Ilkhan of the Cumans) informed Bucharest that they had "expelled the foreign adventurers and anarchists" from Cumantsa, and would dissolve the Council as soon as instructions were received from the King—to whom eternal loyalty was sworn in ringing tones.

Bucharest saw through the ruse, but could do nothing about it. The ring-leaders had gotten off scot-free, and the "rump" had effectively seized power in the name of the King of Romania (who was thus bound to protect the City if he could). Romanian administrators and police who arrived in Cumantsa on April 8 were unable to arrest anyone, which must have annoyed them exceedingly. Until the Ilkhan died in 1923 he essentially functioned as political boss of Cumantsa, and was able to prevent any retaliation against citizens who had supported the Junta. The fall of the Autonomous Sanjak had been handled quite cleverly.

One reason for the Scythians' decision to elude a Ragnarok situation was probably the dwindling of the treasury. No matter how much they had received for the loot from Constanta and Petroasa, they had been

---

Will nothing beyond your capacity; there is a wicked falseness among those who will beyond their capacity. [TSZ 401]

Do not be virtuous beyond your strength! And do not desire anything of yourself against probability. [TSZ 403]

The higher its type, the more rarely a thing succeeds. You higher men here, have you not all failed?

Be good of cheer, what does it matter? How much is still possible! Learn to laugh at yourselves as one must laugh! [TSZ 404]

squandering it like there was no tomorrow—a realistic policy, actually, because in fact there was no tomorrow. I suspect that the dregs were divided between the refugees and the "rump," and that was the end of it.

Mavrocordato now settled in Istanbul. Some of the Junta remained there as well, in all probability—Shaykh Mehmet for instance. Others begin to disappear. We have no idea what became of Schlamminger, Antonescu, or Elias. It's impossible to believe that such unusual and energetic men simply did nothing for the rest of their lives, and some research might prove rewarding. At present, however, we remain in the dark.

Meanwhile, the civil war in the Ukraine continued unabated, with Makhno now in control of quite a lot of liberated territory. In Romania the peasants were dissatisfied with the government's lukewarm land reform[29] and the workers were dissatisfied, period. Makhnovist ideas were popular. In October of 1920 a general strike broke out. Many of the strikers were anarchists, but they were less well-organized than the socialists and the Communists. What began as a spontaneous and non-violent uprising degenerated into factional squabbles—and violence—among the strikers. At this point, Mavrocordato issued a *pronunciamento* from Istanbul, dated October 20, 1920. In it he declared that the Provisional Government in Exile of the Autonomous Sanjak of Cumantsa supported the Strike, and recognized the "liberated communes of the Ukraine under Makhno" as the legitimate regime in South Russia. I suspect that Mavrocordato may then have returned to the Dobruja clandestinely and attempted to organize the strike in Cumantsa. Rioting against government land policies broke out there in late October. But it was soon repressed. The General Strike failed before the end of the month, and the Communists took over the labor unions. Not long thereafter, Makhno fled the Ukraine and ended up in Paris, where he proceeded to write his memoirs and drink himself to death.

---

[29]In fact, several landowners in Cumantsa were given back their expropriated estates by Bucharest, which must have caused much ill-feeling among the Cumans.

Mavrocordato did neither.

The last news we have of Mavrocordato, thanks to Densusianu, is the text of the final (?) communiqué of the Government in Exile, dated November 7, 1924, from Istanbul. In it the Council is said to have proclaimed Georghiu III Mavrocordato the hereditary hospodar and prince of the Autonomous Sanjak of Cumantsa.

Had Nietzsche finally driven Mavrocordato mad? Was this mere "prankishness" (a sure sign of the "free spirit"), or did it have some deeper significance? I believe that it was a gesture of defiance—and I also suspect it means that Anna had given birth to an heir. Who knows what history would cook up in the future? It was best to stake a claim, just in case. Perhaps the "Phanariot" atmosphere of old Constantinople had gone to the hospodar's head.

A postscript to this telegram reveals, I believe, Mavrocordato's growing interest and involvement in sufism. Typically enough, it consists of a quotation from Nietzsche:

> There has never been a saint who reserves sins to himself and virtues to others: he is as rare as the man who [...] hides his goodness from people and lets them see of himself only what is bad. [HTH 253/607]

After this is added, *"Al mulk li'llah,"* which means, "The Kingdom belongs to Allah." The evocation of the hero who allows only his faults to be seen, while attributing all his virtues to others, reminds one irresistibly of the Turkish sufi order of the *Malamatiyya* or "Blameworthy Ones." This order, which included the infamous Shams-al-din Tabrizi, the companion of the great poet Jalal al-din Rumi, developed a means of spiritual concentration that involved outrageous behavior such as public wine-bibbing and hashish-smoking, in order to ruin their reputations as saints. In the 20th century the Order has read deeply in Western philosophy—including Nietzsche. It seems clear enough to me that Mavrocordato was now an adept of the Malamatiyya. Perhaps, in the end, this was his escape from the 19th century.[30]

If there remains nothing more to say, this is because Densusianu's *Hronicul* now comes to an end.

We might, however, append a brief note on the role of Cumantsa in the events that shook Romania in 1989, with the death of the dictator Ceaușescu. The television station in Bucharest, which constituted the actual focus of the "Revolution," reported that 200 people had been

---

[30]Nietzsche himself sometimes implied that only religion can overcome religion; one of his last "insane" letters was signed "Dionysus and the Crucified One." He also said:

It is in this *state of consecration* that one should live! It is a state one can live in! [D223]

And is *this* human beauty and refinement which is the outcome of a harmony between figure, spirit and task also to go to the grave when the religions come to an end? And can nothing higher be attained, or even imagined? [D37]

"What is this I hear?" Said the old pope at this point, pricking up his ears. "O Zarathustra, with such disbelief you are more pious than you believe. Some god in you must have converted you to your godlessness. Is it not your piety itself that no longer lets you believe in a god? And your overgreat honesty will yet lead you beyond good and evil too. Behold, what remains in you? You have eyes and hands and mouth, predestined for blessing from all eternity. One does not bless with the hand alone. Near you, although you want to be the most godless, I scent a secret, pleasant scent of long blessings: it gives me gladness and grief." [TSZ 374]

"It is immoral to believe in God"—but precisely this seems to us the best justification of such faith. [WTP 524]

—And how many new gods are still possible! As for myself, in whom the religious, that is to say god-forming, instinct occasionally becomes active at impossible times—how differently, how variously the divine has revealed itself to me each time!

So many strange things have passed before me in those timeless moments that fall into one's life as if from the moon, when one no longer has any idea how old one is or how young one will yet be—I should not doubt that there are many kinds of gods—[WTP 534]

massacred in Cumantsa by Securitate (Intelligence) forces loyal to the Stalinoid regime.

Later reports "admitted" that in fact only six people had been killed—but film footage was shown of many corpses.

Still later it was "admitted" that *no one* had been shot in Cumantsa. The corpses were fake (dug up from new graves and shot in obvious places, like the forehead, so the wounds could be seen on television).

The truth of the matter—in which Cumantsa was no more than a microcosm reflecting similar events all over the country—is that there had in fact been no "Revolution." The television had *simulated* a revolution (in which to be sure several hundred people died bravely and needlessly) in order to cover up what was *really* happening.[31] In truth, Ceauşescu had been deposed by a faction of Securitate, which now called itself the "Front for National Salvation," and had taken over the television station. While Romanians thought they were dying for "freedom," they were simply watching the *same people* take power, hidden behind a few brave and deluded rebels, and a barrage of highly sophisticated media manipulation (including recordings of machine-gun fire, used to terrorize crowds of demonstrators). There was no "Revolution." There was no "betrayal" of the Revolution because there was no revolution to betray—except in the media-entranced consciousness of a whole world glued to the tube and willing to believe *anything they see on video*. Compared to this Ionesco-like "absurdity," the Autonomous Sanjak of Cumantsa seems like a solid piece of history.

Once again the world failed to put an end to the 19th century. The rebels of 1918 dreamed of a new era. The rebels of 1989 dreamed of a new era.

But all they got was Capitalism.

NYC
FEBRUARY 7, 1997

---

[31]See Codrescu (1991)

BIBLIOGRAPHY

(Note: Sources of Nietzsche quotations are identified by the abbreviations used in the text.)

Apollonius of Rhodes (1959) *The Voyage of the Argo*, trans. E. V. Rieu. London: Penguin

Bey, Hakim (1991) "The Temporary Autonomous Zone" in *T.A.Z.* Brooklyn, NY: Autonomedia

Birge, John Kingsley (1937) *The Bektashi Order of Dervishes*. London: Luzac Oriental

Cahill, Liam (1990) *Forgotten Revolution: Limerick Soviet 1919, a Threat to British Power in Ireland.* Dublin: O'Brien Press

Codrescu, Andrei (1991) *The Hole in the Flag: A Romanian Exile's Story of Return and Revolution.* New York: William Morrow

Densusianu, O. (1927) *Hronicul Dobruja*. Bucharest

Eliade, Mircea (1972) *Zalmoxis, the Vanishing God: Comparative studies in the religions and folklore of Dacia and Eastern Europe*, trans. Willard R. Trask. Chicago: University of Chicago Press

Encyclopedia Britannica (1953), vol. XX

Gide, André (1953) *Correspondences*, vol. II

Hinton Thomas, R. (1983) *Nietzsche in German Politics and Society, 1890–1918.* La Salle, IL: Open Court

Kuun, Count Gezu (1880) *Codex Cumanicus*. Budapest; partial translation in A. B. Boswell, "The Kipchak Turks." *Slavonic Review*, June 1927

Luttwak, Edward (1968) *Coup d'États: A Practical Handbook*. London: Penguin

Macintyre, Ben (1992) *Forgotten Fatherland: the Search for Elisabeth Nietzsche*. New York: HarperCollins

Nietzsche, Friedrich (1954) *The Portable Nietzsche*, ed. and trans. Walter Kaufmann. New York: The Viking Press. Pieces used from this volume include AC: *The Antichrist*; *Notes*; TSZ: *Thus Spoke Zarathustra*; and TI: *Twilight of the Idols*.

____(1956) BT and GM: *The Birth of Tragedy: and, the Genealogy of Morals*. Trans. Francis Golffing. Garden City, NY: Doubleday

____(1974) GS: *The Gay Science*, trans. Walter Kaufmann. New York: Vintage

____(1982) D: *Daybreak*, trans. R. J. Hollingdale. Cambridge: Cambridge University Press

____(1986) HTH: *Human, All Too Human*, trans. Marion Faber. Lincoln: University of Nebraska Press

____(1968) WTP: *The Will to Power*, trans. and ed. Walter Kaufmann. New York: Vintage

Ovid (1994) *The Poems of Exile*, trans. with introduction and notes by Peter Green. New York: Penguin

Runciman, Steven (1968) *The Great Church in Captivity: A Study of Constantinople from the Eve of the Turkish Conquest to the Greek War of Independence*. London: Cambridge University Press

Stirner, Max (1907) *The Ego and His Own*. New York: Benj. R. Tucker

Wilson, Peter Lamborn (1988) *Scandal: Essays in Islamic Heresy*. Brooklyn, NY: Autonomedia

____(forthcoming) *Drunken Boat*, vol. 3. Brooklyn, NY: Autonomedia [never published]

Xenopol, A. D. (1925/1936) *Istoria Românilor din Dacia Traina*. Bucharest; abridged French translation, *Histoires des Roumains*, 1936

Treasure of the Pre-Adamite Sultans

> "...cartloads of hieroglyphics, mouldy
> and of the colour of dead ashes..."
> —Beckford,
> *The Episodes of Vathek*

This undeservedly forgotten novel (Ticknor & Sons, New York, 1897) by an otherwise-unknown and probably pseudonymous author named John Wesley Irvingson, concerns a cache of Mughal diamonds brought to New York in 1699. The book opens with a genuine historical incident. In that year in Madagascar a merchant captain from New York offered passage to America—at £100 a head—to forty-six pirates who wished to return home with their accumulated loot and to retire incognito. One stormy night the ship anchored off Cape May, New Jersey, and set its passengers ashore with their sea-chests.

This landing did not go unobserved, and immediately a hue and cry and massive manhunt ensued. Most (not all) of the pirates were rounded up and hanged, and some of the treasure (but surprizingly little) was recovered.

The ship that brought the pirates home belonged to the head of one of Manhattan's wealthiest merchant families, called in the novel Jan Wilhelm Van L——, or "the Patroon," a man accused of many sins: engrossing of trade, adultery, sorcery, usury, dealing with pirates, and deserting the Dutch Church for Anglicanism. Due to the untimely demise of so many pirates (perhaps betrayed by the Patroon himself) a great deal of loot, including the Moghul diamonds, is believed to have fallen into his hands.

Certainly Van L—— would have had no difficulty disposing of his prizes — except for the jewels, too magnificent to be sold openly or even fenced anonymously. Moreover, 1699 was a year of great political tension in Manhattan and London; the hapless Captain Kidd had been betrayed by his Whig patrons (including Van L——) and various heads had begun to roll. According to the novel (here we begin to leave history behind) the Patroon decided to hide the gems somewhere in or near his grand new manor house up the Hudson in Columbia County.

The diamonds — reputed to be older than the creation of Adam, or even of Time itself — were part of the vast plunder of the Moghul family's Hajj fleet, on the way to Mecca, snatched by the notorious Capt. Avery from the very neck of a beautiful princess, etc., etc. Some say he raped and murdered her, but Daniel Defoe wrote a whole pamphlet to prove he was gallant and let her go unharmed — and moreover was a freethinking Deist swashbuckler of great charm, and so on. Who knows?

In any case, the historical Avery had no connection with the Cape May fiasco. He is generally supposed to have buried his diamonds on an island in Boston Harbor, whence they have never been recovered.

So much for prelude. The novel proper now begins, about 130 years later, during the period when Washington Irving has published his Tales of the Alhambra and set off a fad for all things Moorish and Oriental amongst the Manhattan Romantic poets and painters (and fashionable hostesses) of the era. The opening scene takes place in an exclusive "haschisch parlour" on East Fourteenth Street one foggy night in November. Red velvet plush, dim gaslamps in Moroccan sconces, Turkish coffee scented with ambergris, silver plates of jellied green pastilles, elaborate hookahs and clouds of smoke.

Here we meet a crew of eccentric bohemians who appear (to me) to be based on various real people: a genial journalist and oriental traveler who enjoys boulevarding up Broadway in his robes and fez, very like the poet Bayard Taylor; an architect who has visited Moorish Spain and now specializes in building mauresque fantasias, who reminds us of Jay Wray Mould, Washington Irving's secretary and traveling companion, designer of the Moorish Arcade in Central Park; a raffish couple (he American, she "Levantine Greek") who have voyaged in the mystic East and smoked hashish there (apparently based on Albert Rawson, who claimed initiation in the Bektashi Sufi Order and later founded the Masonic Shriners, and his paramour the young and beautiful Helena Blavatsky); a brilliant self-educated African-American occultist, a character clearly founded on the amazing Paschal Beverly Randolph, who claimed to reveal the sex magic secrets of the Syrian Nusayriyah; a successful painter and Mooromaniac who has built an Upstate oriental palazzo, obviously meant to be Frederick Church, master of the eccentric manor of Olana. True, the historical models I've mentioned do not all quite belong to the correct ante-bellum period of the novel, but after all, this is fiction.

In this opening scene only the hero, J. Stapleton Carter (we never learn his first name), appears to lack a real-life origin — although he works for a lively Reform newspaper obviously based on Greely's *Tribune*. Like most 19th century heroes he seems a bit characterless, especially compared with his colorful friends (who value him for his level-headedness and flair for action); but he shares their fascination for the East, and has recently taken up the study of Arabic.

As he leaves his friends in their haze of blue smoke, the hero is approached by one of his underworld acquaintances, who offers to sell him a strange manuscript, apparently composed in "enigmatic hieroglyphs and some sort of debased Arabic," in which he recognizes only one word: *kanz*, "treasure." Intrigued, he buys it for a few dollars (his last till payday) and decides to show it to his Arabic tutor, Shaykh Ismael Effendi.

Meanwhile, we make the acquaintance of the novel's villain, Richard L——, the present Patroon of the L—— family (they've dropped the "Van" and anglicized themselves), which is now said to be even wealthier and more powerful than ever. The Patroon (who seems partly based on James Fennimore Cooper and partly on Jay Gould) is portrayed as a vile capitalist, Social Darwinian, snob, would-be aristocrat, slave-owner, and gouger of rents from the poor farmers on his vast Upstate manor lands. Despite all this however he's actually in financial difficulties and must soon repay an enormous loan or else face ruin. To add to his troubles he's being attacked and accused of corruption by a series of unsigned articles in the *Express*, our hero's newspaper (and in fact, as we know, Carter is one of the authors of those articles). As a final annoyance, L——'s Manhattan mansion has recently been burglarized and a collection of papers, handed down from his great-grandfather, the original Patroon, has disappeared. Since most of those papers seemed to concern alchemy and other occult nonsense (Richard is of course a thorough-going Victorian materialist) he has never valued them highly. He knows the legend of the Moghul diamonds; family lore declares that the secret of their hiding place is encrypted in the old Patroon's manuscripts — but no one has ever broken the code (if indeed it exists) and Richard has never believed in it. Now that the papers have been stolen, however, he can't help wondering... In any case, he's determined to repossess them.

Meanwhile Carter pays a visit to Shaykh Ismael at his little shop in a decayed section of the Brooklyn waterfront frequented by "lascar" sailors. The Shaykh has founded a heretical mosque in rooms over a warehouse and makes his living as a dealer in oriental curios, perfumes, rugs, rare gems and drugs, etc. In fact, as we learn, he has been sent secretly to New York by his spiritual master "the Emir," who is clearly based on the historical figure of the Emir Abdel Kader, the great sufi and anti-colonialist freedom fighter of Algeria. Like the real Abdel Kader, our fictional Emir has been initiated into Grand Orient Freemasonry in recognition of his heroism and spirit of religious toleration. It appears that certain New York Masons have offered assistance to the Emir in his struggles, and Shaykh Ismael is acting as the Emir's envoy to these circles.

We also meet the Shaykh's daughter Layla, with whom our hero must obviously fall in love. In some ways I find her the most interesting character in the book, if only because she so little resembles the usual wilting-lily heroine of 19th century romance. Not only does she not "keep Purdah," she has also been educated "like a boy" by her doting and learned father — speaks good English and fluent French, Arabic, Persian and Turkish, plays the oud, and recites (or composes) poetry in the orientalizing style of early Arabian Nights translations, or Emerson and Goethe's Persian imitations.

The Shaykh is able to translate some of the mysterious manuscript, which recounts the legend of the Treasure of the Pre-Adamite Sultans and gives the history of its transferal to America — though without naming the L—— family or revealing any hiding place. Shaykh Ismael however suspects a cypher, and promises to keep working on it.

Carter and Ismael must make use of all their occult, Masonic, and underground connections to unravel the manuscript. The key moment occurs when the hero's Afro-American occultist friend leads them to a squatters' slum in upper Manhattan (which I believe must be modeled on "Seneca Village," destroyed after the Civil War to make way for Central Park), inhabited by lumpen Irish, Free Blacks and Indians. Here they meet a weird old Dutch "Kaatskill witch-doctor," and a Black "Conjur Man" descended from Malagasy (Madagascarian) slaves once owned by the L——family. These two uncanny allies (plus an immigrant Irish Bard and a shamanistic "Sachem of the Mohawks") provide the missing clues. It seems clear that the document was "forged" by the old Patroon himself, helped by one of his Malagasy slaves (probably an ancestor of the Conjur Man) and that it contains a "map" of the treasure. Unfortunately the precise hiding place cannot be found unless a certain magical ceremony is performed. At this point Carter thinks of giving up — but the Shaykh's not shaken, and declares that with the help of their new-found friends he will carry out the required enchantments. All prepare for an expedition up the Hudson to the manorlands of the Patroon.

We now take an idyllic and adventurous boat trip up the river, complete with Irvingesque legends and dangerous thunderstorms. This gives the author a chance to indulge in pages of nostalgic evocation of an image of the Valley created by poets and Luminist ("Hudson River School") artists — although of course even in their day the region was already falling under the spell of the Industrial Revolution.

Like a good disciple of Avicenna (as he himself boasts) the Shaykh uses both deductive reasoning and magic in the Quest. From the reader's point of view however it remains unclear and ambiguous whether the magic really "works." Perhaps Ismael is just lucky — or perhaps he knows more than he lets on to his companions. In any case we're given a marvelous "gold-bug"-like treasure-search scene, complete with magic circles out of Cornelius Agrippa, and eldritch lighting effects. The ceremony takes place at a remote spot on the Patroon's grounds, far from his ancient and sinister manorhouse and its gothick environs. Without wishing to spoil the reader's potential pleasure I must reveal that the diamonds are duly discovered (along with a human skeleton, probably of the Old Patroon's Malagasy slave).

However... just at the triumphant moment, who should appear (diabolus ex machina) but the wicked Patroon Richard L—— himself? Unknown to all (both characters and readers) he has been hiring detectives and tracing the stolen manuscript to Carter and Ismael. Realizing that they are attempting to decipher it he decides to let them continue... while he spies on them. He has also caught a glimpse of the Shaykh's daughter and naturally fallen in lust with her. At the climactic moment now he bursts upon the scene with his hired henchmen, seizes the diamonds — and Layla herself — and withdraws into his mansion.

Now it's the Shaykh who despairs, while Carter becomes cool as ice and determines on a daring rescue mission. They all retreat to the nearby town of Hudson (famous for its whaling ships and houses of prostitution) where, holed up in a low tavern, they plot their campaign. Each of the allies makes a contribution and a complex scheme evolves.

The scene shifts to the Manor House, where one stormy night a bizarre series of apparently supernatural events begins to take place: clanking chains, apparitions, screams, poltergeists, etc. The ghost of the old Patroon Jan Wilhelm Van L——himself, with his ghastly Malagasy slave in tow, puts in a dreadful appearance. At first incredulous, Richard grows more and more appalled and then horrified, catching the panic of his superstitious hirelings, almost ready to renounce his base materialism — when suddenly he discovers that it's all a grand illusion cooked up by the Shaykh's trickster allies to delude him. Almost he prevails, almost he regains control of the situation — but then, in yet another and final reversal, young Carter appears at the head of a "peasant uprising" of angry pitchfork and torch-waving tenant farmers — and the Patroon is foiled!

The villain does however escape with his life ("Don't they always?" as the author says cynically) — but of course he now faces certain ruin over his debts, and he loses both the heroine and the diamonds. The latter are divided amongst the victorious friends — with a lion's share for the distant Emir and his anti-imperialist cause — while the former is bestowed upon the hero by the Shaykh in the inevitable happy ending.

No one would make any claims for *Treasure of the Pre-Adamite Sultans* as a great—or even well-written—book. And yet it has undoubted charms. Besides the obvious homages to Irving (including no doubt the author's pseudonym "Irvingson") and Poe, there can be heard echoes of Scott, Stevenson and Dumas. The occult scenes are sometimes reminiscent of two later writers, Gustav Meyrink (at best) and Sax Rohmer (at worst). Early gothick novelists are quoted and imitated, especially Maturin's *Melmoth the Wanderer* and Beckford's *Vathek*. The swashbuckling action scenes are well-handled and seem to foretell the style of a Rafael Sabatini, although without his flawless panache.

The Islamic material includes a great many mistakes, and of course the author, despite good intentions, fails to escape entirely the ethnic and gender prejudices and class stereotypes of his period. But all this can perhaps be forgiven, at such a late date, in gratitude for that elusive yet never impossible grail: the perfect book for a stormy night, and a roaring fire—if you've got one.

LUNAR MANSIONS
or,
The
Whole
Rabbit

"The Rabbit in the Moon
is pounding hemp"
—LI FANG
Tai-Ping Miscellany
"The Blue Bridge"

*Alnath—horns or head of Aries, of the 8ᵗʰ sphere; it causeth discords
& journeys. For the destruction of someone they make in an iron ring
the image of a black man in a garment made of hair & girdled round,
casting a small lance with his right hand, they seal this in black wax
& perfume it with liquid storax, & wish some evil to come.*

I.

Prologue

An island seems enchanted when you can freely leave it. But when you
cannot depart—when it becomes your prison and place of exile—it
quickly loses all charm. And the Isle of Anguish in the Mare Crisium
on the edge of Night lacked all lovability to begin with:—gray treeless
utilitarian speck of rock surrounded by a melancholic sea.

The guests had been served splits of a canary yellow liqueur of daf-
fodils and dandelions—fifty proof—which somewhat assuaged their
angst. Their host (a vast youngman, maybe one-seventh of a tonne of
rotundity, dressed in a black wooly cape and enormous wide brimmed
velvet hat) rose to address them formally but warmly, and said,

I claim to be your host, Wali al-Taha, poet and fat flautist (he flour-
ished a tiny silver pipe no bigger than a tin whistle in his paw), and, if you
like, your scribe and narrator. I apologize for this in advance, since the
very notion of narration implies that someone wishes someone else *some
evil to come.* Isn't all telling a telling about discords and journeys, and are
not all quarrels and trips ill-fated, or at least tedious? "Getting there" for
me is never part of the fun—indeed it's half an inducement never to set
out in the first place. As Johanna von Athanasius-Kircher says:

> The Outside (the exterior surface)
> Where my esoteric horse & carriage cannot go

Cannot lure me from a life of nothing
But fishing & drinking & inviting the rain.

In our case however the evil to come has already come—here we are, all at the ends of certain trajectories that all converge on this Prison Isle, or rather island of exile, where we still seem to retain certain freedoms—except the liberty to leave.

Taking your silence for approbation at least for the nonce I'll go on to suggest the founding here today of a salon, in which each of us in turn will entertain the others—tickling our organs of *schadenfreude*—with *Tales of How We Ended Up in Jail*—a fate my own parents often threatened me with, now that I recall... Ah well, how annoying to think they were ever correct in anything.

Allow me to concur—said Apicio Johnson the Chef. A fantastical figure over seven feet tall, thin and supple as a crane in flight, with beak to match, his powdered hair in a ribband, body cloaked in silk coat of asparagus green with lace like mayonnaise (slightly unfresh) sprouting at wrists and throat, the Chef exuded *savoir vivre* and *politesse*.

Only with one demurral (he went on). I've already ascertained that I alone of all of us still retain access to my private fortune—a lump of which should reach me here via the First National Bank of Proclus (capital of the drear Domeyne of Mare Crisium and no more than 300 miles away by sea) within a week, along with my first large order of comestibles. So I claim the honor of feeding your salon, since without good food there can exist no good culture. As our Founder put it:

Belly is wise
        The Brain a fool
That falls to heavy slumber
        to digest its paltry sensations.

All food is psychotropic—and I undertake to make our exile not just bearable but fruitful.

With this last adjective he sat down like a folding fan and gave an expressive leer-*cum*-wink that startled the guests, who burst into spontaneous sibilations of more-than-polite applause.

Hsss-hsss—added Wali al-Taha. If I take you right we should perhaps choose another meeting place than this rented room over the island's one lone Café (Le Condorcet), which may well have been enhanced by the exotic devices of the Teknostic authorities. But for now I shall carry on introducing myself and my Tale.

Even if you've never been there you'll know that my home, Domeyne Copernicus, is the oldest and the original Domed city in our world, and at one time the largest—ninety miles wide, our sea is ringed by urban zones—and although many are now deserted, we still boast several hundred thousand citizens—and still retains political power over a wide swathe of Procellarum and Imbrium, from Archimedes on the Putrid Swamp, to Kepler, to Eratosthenes.

I was born in the far-flung colony of Santos-Dumont, at the end of a very long suburban tunneltrain line—very long indeed—really the sticks—and originally settled (so we believe) by Moors with curly hair and coffeecream skin, once considered an inferior caste (here Wali removed his hat and displayed exuberant corkscrews shiny as obsidian)

but now of course long since assimilated to the average lunar gray—except for a few romantic reactionaries such as myself.

> A past that's imagined
>> makes us free and happy.
> A past that merely happened
>> is our chain and ball.

(More hissings and applause.) Wali continued:

Skipping over my dull childhood and bitter struggle against the evil of School, let me say I gradually re-created myself—as a fat dancer—incidentally becoming strong enough to defend myself against the anti-adiposity and bullying of my schoolmates by beating them up and (you guessed it) sitting on them.

At last I moved away, on my own, and went to the Capital. By dint of reading many many books in the ancient Library of Kopernik Academy and the used book stalls of Byrd Street, I become a Savant and poet, licensed to practise as such. This status scarcely added to my scanty income, however. I learned music in the bohemian dodecaphonic folk grottos of the Capital region's slums. I began to publish—but still I was poor and lived upon "green bread and instant water" for days at a time.

In the old times our forebears lived in the world as if just visiting, just passing through, on their way to future worlds, Outer Space worlds, and they cultivated a deliberately exotic (or kitsch) version of these make-believe Otherworlds, based no doubt on stale fantasies of their overweening era.

Thus the old neighborhoods of K-town resemble the dreams of children addicted to storybooks and too much pastry—vaguely nightmarish with castles mushrooming with towers exfoliating in gargoyles and furbelows, circular or arched stained glass windows, belvederes, lacy balconies, hanging gardens, air-bridges, towers more phallic than real penises, grottos more alluring than the cave of love, false chimneys, ramparts and crenellations, bulbous onion and tulip domes on top of wasp-waisted steeples—and all mosaic'd or faux-marbled to glistening slithers of alien colors, including luminescent infra-reds and phosphorescent sub-blues. Of course it was all jackbuilt shoddy cod-gothick, done with reinforced concrete and plastics.

Despite centuries of clement weather—our mild rains—our decorous storms no heavier than baroque clouds—this ancient architecture has at last decayed and turned almost into ruins—but in doing so it has somehow miraculously become *real*. Here the fading nobles and vibrant bohemians indulge in what may be called the cheap arts—kite-flying, perfume appreciation, dance, conversation, calligraphy, poetry—rather than the grand and expensive arts like architecture, painting, high fashion or war. To trace this strange alchemy of winds and rains, I published a handwritten magazine, *The Lunar Weather Report*.

Half abandoned by seekers after bourgeois comfort and boredom, the slums became jungle to a mixed crew of penniless old aristocrats, sex-workers, sub-legal fish restaurants and dodeca-clubs for the artists and parasites of Bohemia. I rented a whole tower from a starving baron—it's overgrown with trumpet vines from toe to top, eight storeys of mostly empty water-stained rotten rooms, with a fungoid roof and broken windows, creaking spiral stairs, flooded all with light and open to the breezes and clouds off the sea.

Of course it's haunted, to boot. From time to time, as you return home on a rainy drunken night, you catch a glimpse of a *Spinaxe* behind you, and when you turn around to look, it slips through the door ahead of you—but after all it's a harmless afrit, like a big white toad with a human head.

Now at last (like my tower) I could begin to *pose* as what I really *am*. Art itself became for me a work of life.

At that time however I understood very little of life, despite a certain (how to put it) over-easy facility with the arts which had already gained me a notoriety I mistook for appreciation. Only when I met my companion Sylphia—Sylphie—was I able to experience the inwardness of "taste," the cosmic trace, and perhaps attain an actual voice.

Here he gestured toward the figure beside him—the others noted, not for the first time, the pale blue "wolf" eyes of a Hijra of Hypatia—noted the albino-white skin and quicksilver hair.

Soon I'll turn over the floor to my companion Sylphia, whose *nom de style* is Elegabalio, and whose studio-name is Seraphitron. But first I must end my prologue with a word about the religion and government of Copernicus that you'll need to know in order to make any sense of our story. You see, *we are each other's crime*—and we are here in the jug together because we are who we are.

Seasoned travelers will forgive me for repeating the rather-well-known fact that K-town—although nominally a neo-feudo-plu-tocracy—is actually a theocracy controlled defacto by the Orthodox Abrahamic Church of Luna (the so-called Rectified Monotheists). That damned behemoth combines, I swear on my oath as Savant, all the worst thaumaturgic and hysterical aspects of *That Place* (and here he made a peculiar "o"-shaped sign with thumb and forefinger of left hand, aimed vaguely at the ceiling) selected and indeed rectified by sheer uncountable millennia of malice aforethought, suffocating morality, rigid fear of the divine, combined (I must admit as an artist) with a panoply of the most lugubriously delicious rites and bizarre ritu-als, vestments and incenses, twinkling lights and silvery bells, uplifting choral music and theatrical genius—all without using a single repre-sentational image.

Aside from this aesthetic predilection the Church's only benefit to its subjects arises from its own corruption and decadence. If its Inquisi-torial Police were truly efficient and honest, K. would become a Puritan Hell—thank the Many Gods however they are crooked as a drunk-ard's walk and lazy as antiquated cats. My bohemian slum thrives and bubbles under their very noses and dozing temple spires. As Pico de Malapart put it,

> One priest suffices to spoil
> > ten thousand blessings
> Just as one spot of mold
> > engulfs the loaf in blue
> But the fungal growth
> > itself secretes a poison

That one day will choke
　　　　the Church & its
　　　　　　　Three Imposters.

It transpires that certain great Sins cannot be forgiven by the Pontifex or even by G-d in person, even by means of great bribes and purses, and that one such crime is *Congress with a Demon.*

Sylphie, please favor us now with your tale, or at least some of it, just as the White Rabbit lost *his* tail, here in Mare Crisius.

Wali sat down and fanned his fat features with his wide-brimmed hat.

II.

Sylphie's Tale

> *Allothaim, or Albochan, i.e., Belly of Aries, conduceth*
> *to the finding of treasures & the retaining of captives.*
> *Against the wrath of a prince & for reconciliation with*
> *him they seal in white wax & mastic the image of a king*
> *crowned & perfume it with lignum aloes.*

Sylphie adorned a pale ice-sprite's face and hands in a cascade of two-tailed ermines, sewn, faces & all, to a peplon of white silk—but neither fur nor fabric looked so much the essence of white as she (or he?) him/herself.

My dear companion Wali al-Taha, she said, I have skry'd you as the reincarnation of an ancient monk so mad with love of Nature that you tried to incorporate it all. This monk spoke, yes, *spoke* with Pans and afrits in the desert. For him that was true which is most poetry.

We were not arrested on a charge of Congress with Monsters; the actual name of the crime is *Intercourse with Non-Humans*. But that charge was itself postponed *sine die* in order to exile us for something considered even more heinous—grand larceny of sacred objects. All this weirdness requires me to paint a back-ground for your contemplation—a *mappa mundi* of our misfortune.

My own people, the Hijras of Hypatia, would scarcely approve of my cohabitation with a single-male, not for moral reasons but because only true doubles can give birth to doubles. If Wali and I conceive a child, it will be either male or female, and not both, as we Hijras are—perfect hermaphrodites, not eunuchs, not an "intersex" (as you may have heard) but both sexes in one. If I coupled with one of my kind, both of us could become pregnant and both would give birth to true Hijras.

We worship a perpendicularly half-&-half godgoddess called (exoterically) Madam Adam, who is one half mustached male on the left side, dressed in half a top hat and suit of tails, one trouser leg and a boot with spat, and female on the right, with witchwild hair and bared breast, wearing half a creamwhite lace wedding gown & red slipper. Her/his esoteric name I cannot say.

According to our legends, we were created by alchemists in ancient times by processes now long lost and forgotten, having to do with transmutation of seed-atoms—but we are quite human despite our semi-albinism and other peculiarities—as proved by the fact that we *can* reproduce with singlesexes. But since giving birth does not go easily with us, our Elders urge us to reproduce exclusively with our own kind, lest we die out as a race, and no doubt an atmosphere of chauvinism pervades Hypatian society, feelings of superiority to and xenophobic dislike of singletons. Because I disagree with this prejudice and in fact live in love with this "human," I have fallen into a certain disfavor amongst my own kind—the other "demons"!

In answer to your unspoken question—yes, I have both vagina and penis, the latter placed above the former as if partially emerging from it, with small testicles tightly attached, about twelve inches when erect and bow'd back in a curve against belly. But utilizing certain mystic-athletic sex positions we Hijras can achieve mutual penetration, in an ourobouros of genital electricity, a circular flow we call the Ocean, resulting in a four-way orgasm or *Squaring of the Circle*, as our Scripture puts it.

But it's been said also that the Imagination is the chief pleasure organ, and this is true. Our sexuality is intense—but without love (creative imagination) it adds up to no more than the crude scratching of a complex itch.

I found this sense of wonder in sex sadly lacking among the cold lakes or the white marble halls and tradition-heavy gymnasia of our Dome-land. But I found it in plentitude in the wild poetry of my companion and his cult of conceptual excess—with body to match his mania.

> *Achaomazon or Athoray, i.e., Showering of Pleiades; it is profitable to sailors, huntsmen & alchemists. They make an image: in a silver ring whose table is square the figure of a woman well clothed sitting in a chair, her right hand being lifted up on her head, seal it & perfume it with musk, camphire & calamus aromaticus. They affirm that this giveth happy fortune & every good thing.*

As a child I studied Sound Sculpture, also known as Permanent Music, with a kind and brilliant master, who specialized in rock-and-water gardens and ornithography. Quite young, I created a success-scandal with my first major performance.

At this point Sylphie paused while refreshments—tiny white fish in sour lemon puddings—were served with a decent white wine—last of its label and price in the cellars of the Café Condorcet. Wali al-Taha handed out a pamphlet printed with purple turnip-type on goldflecked strawpaper: *A Synopsis of the Major Sound Sculptures of Sylphia Elegabalo.* While the guests read the pamphlet, he and Sylphie performed a twelve-tone folktune on flute with non-verbal, avian-style humming and whistling.

1. Her first and most notorious piece:
"Frogs"
Each frog was operated on to change the pitch of its croak or peep. Performed during mating season, the result was *very eerie.* She did it once but decided it was too cruel to repeat and refuses all commissions to perform it again.

2. "Boreas"

A giant aeolian harp with hundreds of strings of varying thickness & material, tuned in just intonation, stretched out in every direction, vertical, horizontal and crisscross at various angles, so breezes play across them over real time (i.e., not "all at once"), thus making modal "tunes." Several resonant sounding cavities, geometric forms made of different woods & metals, amplify & distort the wind-sounds. The piece is set in a narrow valley with almost-permanent winds. The effect is overwhelmingly intimate & majestically melancholy; Sylphie is the "ghost" who haunts it.

3. "Calliope"

An array of crystal vials of various sizes is set loosely in a carved wooden frame. A stream is diverted to flow randomly over the frame, gradually filling the tubes, each one of which has been blown for a different note. When all are full, gravity (weight) *tips* the frame and all pour out simultaneously into the pool below.

4. "A Sonic Temple"

of many rooms, each built to resemble the inside of a stringed or wind instrument, but with many cracks and holes (loose windows, malfitted doors, floors with gaps between boards, etc.) so each room & each part of each room produces a tone/note, due to the frequent & highly variable winds common at that locale (in a region of hills & dales, cloves & hollows). The presence of a body or two *inside* the house-organ moving & listening subtly changes the airflow, hence the "tune" or harmonic unfolding of the building. A *chef d'ouvre*, took years to build—& lots of money.

5. "A Nightingale in a Cage"

One nightingale lives in large ornate wire cage, big enough to accommodate one or two human listeners as well. Sylphie himself lived in it non-stop for an entire year, during which time she might allow one guest to spend a night every so often. After a year the cage was opened; but the nightingale has remained voluntarily part of our company.

6. *"Undines"*

Different kinds, sizes & lengths of waterpipe—clay, metal, wood—are arranged in & along the course of a flowing creek (or perhaps rapids), all near the water's surface, so that water can flow through them *ad lib.* : The "tune" unfolds as you walk downstream.

7. *"Eleven Kinds of Lightning"*

A temporary piece. During a thunderstorm (such as occur in the larger Domes) many whistles in all keys & pitches, are shot by catapult into the clouds. She dreams of using fireworks as well, but of course explosions are utterly forbidden everywhere on Luna (except Outside—where there's no weather—or in mining operations & occasional wars). She builds a keyboard with pneumatic tubes to power the jet-whistles. This piece proves remarkably popular ("transgressive but safe" she says) & brings in money whenever performed. Although improvised, the music is her most "musical"; sometimes she suspects it of temporal sentimentality.

*   *   *

Sylphie now resumed the *viva voce* part of her Tale.

> *Aldeberan or Aldelamen, Eye or Head of Taurus: causeth*
> *destruction & hindrances of buildings, fountains, wells,*
> *gold mines, the flight of creeping things, & begetteth*

discord. For revenge, separation, enmity & ill will they seal in red wax the image of a soldier sitting on a horse holding a serpent in his right hand, they perfume it with red myrrh & storax.

As an ambitious youth I traveled to a number of Domes to perform some of these pieces, with some success around the Tranquil Sea—Dionysius, Maskelyne, Vitruvius, Pliny—then Agrippa and Chladni—at last was invited to the Grand Crystal Exhibition in Copernicus to perform the Nightingale Piece for an entire year. Wali al-Taha came to the Opening and returned every night for a week. He tried to engage me in conversation but I was not supposed to communicate with anyone outside the cage, so I tried to ignore him.

Alas he was too *ample* to fit inside the cage as my guest, nor could he have paid the fee I was charging for that favor—so eventually he had to be declared *part of the piece*, a human rose pining away for the unobtainable nightingale—who by the way (the bird, I mean) performed admirably and often.

Once the year had finally passed, Wali and I performed an Alchemical Wedding for ourselves and that dear bird, with myself representing the Red Stone, the nightingale as Elixir, and Wali as the Alchemist. He (the bird) died about a year ago.

The tale of other people's bliss cloys quickly—so I'll skip over the next year, during which we lived in the Tower and began work together on collaborative opuses. We intended to explore toward the creation of a Magic Child or messiah, who would be our grandest artwork. But Fate intervened.

We were denounced to the Inquisition. By Anonymous, the usual needlenosed Puritan hysteric. We were charged to appear in Ecclesial Court to show reason why we should not be sent into exile for miscegeny (or demonism, as Wali says).

We had reason to believe that the Tribunal would refuse to be bribed—even if we could've raised the enormous requisite sum—because of political pressure on the Church by Tek ambassadors from Plato-Aristotle. Because the Teks are eugenicists, they consider us not merely *sinful* (which we rather like) but *diseased* and unfit to reproduce.

On the night before our Hearing we intoxicated ourselves on Peacock's Tail Shelf Fungus, dagga and peach brandy, till we had attained (we reckoned) divine status. Wrapped in dark cloaks, we then took a horse-cab to the Cathedral, and broke in. (This proved about as difficult as opening a birthday present.) Staggering through that huge dark god-hangar with its scent of suppressed civet, sugar and death, we arrived at the High Altar and were just helping ourselves to the Golden Glowlamp of the Pontifex, the golden bones and silver wine-cup—a crescostellafix set with rubies and genuine moonstones caught my eye—when all of a sudden the Night Watch appeared, let out a hoot, and took off running *away* from us down the long perspective of the dark nave, and beat us to the door, hollering for help, help against the demons…

❋ ❋ ❋ ❋ ❋

As Sylphie had fallen silent with bowed head, Wali ahemmed:

It's only fair—my dear—to admit that we *were* after all in costume, *en travesti* in fact, myself as a gigantic nude goddess and Sylphie as my groom (I mean both rider and spouse) in a homemade ghoul's mask. To add flair and frisson, you see. I confess we appropriated some of this imagery from the Sect of Iblees the Peacock, the devil-cult that has sprung up anew in K. in response to the Church's hegemony.

Sylphie here snickered in a sudden way that might've counted against her claim to be quite 100% human; but simultaneously she or he wiped away a palpable crystalline teardrop—which seemed to prove (at any rate) that the Sylph was no heartless Elf (a being who reputedly cannot weep).

Alchatay or Albachey (Taurus); it helpeth to return from a journey, the instructions of scholars, it confirmeth edifices, giveth health & good will. For the favor of kings & officers & good entertainment they seal in silver the head of a man & perfume it with sanders.

To conclude—Wali continued—although I must admit that the person who ends badly in this narrative is myself—and all of us here, deprived of our *imaginable rights*—it's only just that the narrator share the fate of his characters, lest he take himself for a *deus ex codice*—, a god from a book. How I know I'm real. And so on.

Here we are on Anguish Island, with its single village, inhabited largely by a few exiles and parasites on the exiles, shopkeepers and undertakers, purveyors of hard liquor and cheap *phantastica*, folk of that ilk, even sadder than the prisoners;—and in boats constantly circling this gray excrescence, Teknostic mercenary enforcers keep watch to see that we remain cozy shut-in's and in-valids, and not get any urges for, say, aqua-noctambulation.

Well, here come the waiters with our fried dogshark and grits—I fear you'll all find it distasteful, but it's the best we can do for now. Next week we'll meet to continue our winter of narration, under the culinary aegis of our new neighbor and friend, Count Apicio Johnson. (Mutual bows are performed.)

Meanwhile, may I pray for a return some day, a return for all of us to some heart's-place; for me and Sylphie it must be to our poor tower in Old Kopernik; to "confirm the edifice," as old Scripture says. And I suppose it must take place *after* some dreadful Revolution or upheaval, perhaps the fall of the Church.... Ah, well. The evil inherent in all *story* I bequeath to our enemies, and wish us all nothing but the best fortune. As Liu Shih Smith says:

> Travel involves the worst of fates—
> Loss of our friends at home
>> for whom we are but
>>> fading faces
> But even exile can offer
> The consolations of
>> wine & poetry
>>> with new companions.

III.

Eleuthera's Tale

I am Eleuthera. In my natal Domeyne, Carrington (near Mercurius, which is famous for its temple to the three-faced god of thieves) we have no family names—and in fact, not much in the way of families either, for that matter.

The woman who spoke stood tall, nearly as tall as Chef Johnson, and looked like a goddess of Ancient times, with the rather cold beauty of lofty divinity, blond and gray-eyed, and elegant in long sheaths of gray and white chiton. Rather unexpectedly, then, she radiated warmth around herself like a kirlian aura or body-halo, almost a visible color-field of sister-like affection for reality in some general sense.

> *Alhanna or Alchaya—little star of great light, conduceth to hunting, besieging of towns, revenge of princes, it destroyeth harvests and fruits & hindereth the operation of the physician. To promote love betwixt two, they seal in white wax two images embracing one another & perfume them with lignum aloes & amber.*

Before I begin, however, she went on, I'd like to tell you something wonderful, which I hope will please you as well. Over the past week I met for the first time and have since been meeting regularly with another of us prisoners, Captain Svetlana, or to give her her proper title, the Boyaress Svetlana Dolgoruky, daughter of the Baron of Vavilov—she doesn't care for it but I find it romantic—as indeed I find the Captain herself in toto—all romance. In brief, she and I have fallen in love and would like to announce to you our intent to join as Consorts from now till the End.

At the group's applause, a much shorter and more delicate figure stood, clicked her heels and bowed left and right. Captain Svetlana appeared at first no bigger than an adolescent girl, with a triangle-or heart-shaped face, wide lips, big animal-brown eyes and cropped black bangs—but she was dressed eccentrically as a Gentleman of Antiquity in full fig—top hat, satin waistcoat, white rose boutonière, wing collar, gray velvet ascot with black pearl stickpin, black-black tight-waisted silk suit of tails, with a pale mauve handkerchief thrust into its breast pocket, pegged corded trousers, lacquerblack formal pumps and gray velvet spats. She even sported a monocle and an ebony cane. She smiled shyly and sat down again without a word. Eleuthera continued.

> *Aldimiach or Alarzach, arm of Gemini, conferreth gain and friendship, is profitable to lovers; it feareth flies, destroyeth magistrates. For to obtain every good thing, they seal in silver the image of a man well clothed, holding up his hands to heaven as it were praying & supplicating, & perfume it with good odors.*

Carrington Dome was twenty years abandoned when my parents and their friends—ardent anti-work bohemians—arrived to squat it about fifty years ago. You may never have heard of it. Carrington is composed of one huge lake spotted with a number of tiny islands, ideal for a colony of such extreme individualists as our sect, which is called the *Old Church of Nature's Purple Tenuity.*

The long-vanished original founders of the Dome evidently had attempted to recreate scenes depicted on certain favorite Ancient pottery, in blue and white: close-set islets are linked by humpback bridges, and everywhere one sees willow trees with blue leaves, old decaying blue pagodas overgrown with flowering white vines. Many of our people eventually moved fulltime onto boats—junks, sampans, houseboats, each with its mainsail painted with the heraldic device of the family or commune who lived on the boat—a dragon's head, a bird, an abstract pattern—in saturated colors, gules, azure, vert, sable, or. We became an aquarian people, never setting foot on an island from year to year.

We have an old poem (Wali may know it) called "The Blue Bridge":

> One sip of nectar
> > & 100 thoughts will spring
> Up when after the
> > pounding of magic herbs
> A meeting with fairies occurs
> > on the Blue Bridge—
> So why look for any other
> > road to heaven?

So we lolled away the days—fishing and drinking dagga—and gave not a fig for Civilization. Our diet consisted of fish, chilies and rice, for the most part, although many of us lived on little more than free greenbread.

By the way, parenthetically:—It's interesting to consider that one invention of the Ancients (far more even than free energy or artificial gravity), free greenbread (that mutant kudzu weed) alone freed humans from all government and work—so long as they're content to live in swampy squalor, naked and lazy, thin and greenish, like some impossible race of vegetarian lizards, plagued by nothing but the flies, devoted to wild dagga and undinic free love.

Of course we know our world once supported ten or twenty times its current population. Free food and no need of permanent shelter not only caused this decline, I believe, but also put such a high value on labor that Luna essentially reverted, slowly, slowly to a kind of guild feudalism, with pockets like Carrington, of sheer disorder—and others of aristocratic or machinic oppression, like Copernicus or Plato/Aristotle.

Every Dome in which the edible kudzu is allowed to spread freely has lost or could easily lose its last vestiges of authority and overthrow its last ceremonial magistrates. And yet we see that the majority of Lunarians willingly live under conditions of varying degrees and kinds of slavery or serfdom—as if *afraid* to face the reality of empirical freedom. How to explain this anomaly—for such it seems? That might make up matter for a future salon's conversation; and so, my new friends, I will reserve my opinions for a time.

I believe that the mutant shelf fungus called *Philosopher's Stone* or "crag" first appeared in my homeland. A potent entheogen, it not only releases one's inner deity, it is also the only *objective* phantasticum known to humanity. That is—virtually everyone who takes it has the *same experience* (which I'll not disclose here) *at the same time*. We ceremonialize with this fungus, and call it our Mystery. I myself first took it when I was ten.

As you can imagine, this total paradise—however seedy and even decadent it may have been—was simply celestial perfection for children. We young ones knew (by contrast with the few outsiders we met) that we were free, and we made the most possible *play* of it, all day, every day—a republic of childhood—a democracy of the imagination.

We could obtain an education if we wanted it (adults were always flattered to be asked for *anything*)—or just one long physical dream—like knights adventuring (and just as dangerous, perhaps)—perhaps still related to some sort of family, or else part of a new and freely-chosen band—but anyway free to be—that metaphysical verb!—just—to be.

Our parents' generation, as I said, acted as breakers-&-enterers and squatters of our Watery Dome. Time went on and a third generation was already being born. We children had no notion of property rights at all—beyond a few homemade toys—or the boat we lived on—and in general everyone behaved as if we were the rightful inhabitants. But it transpired that the last "legal owners" of Carrington had sold their rights in the Domeyne to TechGnosis—to the Teknostics of Plato/ Aristotle—and now, after half a century, the landlord showed up with an eviction notice. A small brigade of heavily-armed Enforcers arrived, rammed the Airlock and *invaded* us.

At first we scarcely noticed. Thousands of lazy monarchs—for such we considered ourselves—are not easily cowed into flight or slavery. But the Teks sent more soldiers, and more. They opened factories and fish canneries, and offered wages well below Lunar average—set up trinket shops with their vulgar gadgetry and tasteless factory food—and jails in which to detain and re-educate recalcitrants—"rebels and bandits." Even clothing became obligatory. I was eleven when they arrived. By eighteen I'd already served three short terms in clink for "public nuisance" and "refusal of schooling," and for possession of dagga.

> *Alnaza or Anatrachya, the Misty (Cloudy), causeth love, friendship and society of fellow travelers, driveth away mice & afflicteth captives, confirming their imprisonment. For victory in war they make a seal of tin, being an image of an eagle having the face of a man, & perfume it with brimstone.*

They set up their temples to Water and Money, the cosmic sources of all being, and began to enforce public worship. Thus we learned that life yearns for its own overcoming in technical gnosis, the esoteric bodylessness of the Singularity or Deus-in-Machina, or, in other words—to overcome Water (flesh) and become more and more like pure Money (or spirit).

By this time our old idealistic sectarianism had decentered itself and entered into the wide realm of Lunar Popular Religion or "Superstitious Polytheism" as the Teks called it—that easy-going syncretic pantheism with an emphasis on folk magic and states-of-possession by spirits—the same Old Milieu that gave birth two hundred years or so ago to dodecafolk music and trance-theater—our world's most genuine indigenous artforms.

In any case, as a sheer madcap non-stop celebration of materialist spirituality it'd be hard to beat the new Zan cult of Carrington. As organized resistance to Teknosis began to form itself, it first sprang to life amidst the Gyre Dancers of Zan—of which I was a High Priestess by age fourteen.

Four years later our Rites were discovered, "studied"—and banned by the State. I became (or drifted into wanting to be) a fulltime professional revolutionary. The Spirit of the Dome began to feel more than ripe for uprising, and hundreds of us were suddenly swearing oaths of secret loyalty to Insurrection, the goddess of Insurrection I mean—Azura. According to our faith, there are no Abstractions. If you can *think* it, it's a deity or *root spirit*.

Here Wali al-Taha jumped up involuntarily and exclaimed (in a kind of poetic afflatus or fit or seizure) "NO IDEAS BUT IN PERSONS"—which slogan was applauded by all.

Eleuthera resumed, Well, by age 23 I was able to cause an entire Church-full of High Tek Elite to "see" a huge slimy red seven-tailed lizard, about twenty feet long, emerge suddenly from under the altar at the very moment of Holy Electrification, and for this feat I was chosen Symbolic Commandante of the entire Revolutionary Conspiracy.

> *Archaam or Arcaph, Eye of the Lion, hindereth harvests & travelers & putteth discord between men. To cause infirmities, they make a seal of lead, being the image of a man wanting his privy parts, shutting his eyes with his hands, & perfume it with rosin of the pine.*

"Are you…"

　　　　"…a magician?"

said two piping/breaking voices belonging to the twins called Flip and Flap, who up till now had restrained themselves heroically from interrupting the narrative. They always spoke like this, one following and completing the other, although no one could say which one began, and which one ended their sentences. After a while you got used to it.

Eleuthera pondered for a moment, then—chin in hand—another moment, and at last said,

Yes…I suppose I am. Perhaps I'll be able to explain more fully exactly what I do at some future meeting. I'll just say it has to do with the Philosopher's Mushroom that I mentioned before, and certain mental states it makes possible, if combined with certain disciplines. But I must add at once that my…powers are very limited indeed. Look—here I am. You see: we lost our Revolution. In the end even magic didn't help.

Being inclined toward pacific means and reluctant (due to our upbringing) to cause harm to humans, even Tek Enforcers, our plan was to organize those most unfortunate ones who had fallen into servitude to the Machine—factory workers and "students," for the most part—and carry out a total stoppage of work. We walked off the job, 1,500 of us, all over the Dome, on a single day—quite an accomplishment in coordinated tactics, I think, for a people lacking all sense of productive organization—but it was not, as it turned out, a viable *strategy*.

The T.-kops went to war—with "non"-lethal darts, blade-nets, poison gas, body armor and clubs. Against those we rebels wielded romantic swords and daggers, pikes, slings. Within a week, sixteen resistants were actually murdered—dead. We were utterly stunned; we'd never experienced such violence.

Then they began to ship in labor mercenaries from the Darkside, people desperate for the tinsel and scraps of Tek Civilization. Hundreds of us were clapped in jail. A few of us were still hiding out on remote islands and desperately trying to find or invent real weapons.

We carried out a few hit-and-run raids on remote police posts, and actually scored a few deaths, in partial revenge for our comrades. But logistically we were doomed, and we finally decided to disband and run for it rather than stand and fight. Our goal was Endymion, another Free Dome, nearby, devoted to Pagan Pilgrimages and Monasteries. We were (the last thirteen of us) hiding in a safe house in Mercurius, our nearest neighboring Domeyne, when the Teks found us, surprised us and arrested us without a fight.

Almost at once the T.-kops declared an amnesty for all recalcitrants except the Mercurius 13. We were tried and found guilty of rebellion, but my twelve comrades were pardoned. Only I was to suffer for the revolt, which was blamed on me entirely. I accepted the blame, I was exiled. The End.

But not.

In my moment of worst despair and aloneness, I've met my true consort, Captain Svetlana, whose revolutionary position turns out to match mine as symbolon to symbolon. I've lost my so-called Army of Azure, she's lost "Nocturne" (as you'll hear)—that is, we have nothing left with which to cast a bet against Fate. But we have each other. And we have, I think, all of you, too, as companions on the road to *Free Freedom*, as we called it in our folly.

I'll say no more here in this tavern—except to suggest a first toast of the evening—to the Impossible. (She drinks from a krater.) This pink sparkling wine, she said, has the very taste of it.

A Menu of the Meal Served that Night
by Count Apicio Johnson, Chief Chef of Harmonia &
Former Sexual Saint,
to the Seven High Prisoners of
Mare Crisium

Non-sweet Ice Cream, flavored with
parsley & nettles, sprinkled with bits of
fried pork crackling & the roe of an
armored pike (pearly-maroon)

with pale chilled Poiré (perry enhanced with pear brandy)

Aspic of Lakefoods, "Nature Morte"
mudfish, shellfish (lobster, crab, kanker, écrevisse, etc.), eel, elvings,
frogs, one jellyfish, one urchin—cooked but restored to a semblance of
life—suspended as if randomly in a Big Block of clear pale blue-green
Aspic, with seaweed and sea-vegetables, all to resemble an Aquarium
still-life

White plum wine from Pythagoras Dome (heavy with noble rot)

Brace of pheasants—hung for seven days, poached in dry hard apple
cider with herbs & butter & fat pork & truffles, verjuice, saffron, nutmeg, amber & ambergris—topped with gold foil and their own tail
feathers arranged like a mandala on the platter with a mound of saffron
rice

Pink champagne on ice

Iridescent Shelf Fungus cooked with a molé of raw unsweetened choc-
olatl and green chilies, green sunflower seed paste & bitter chicoryweed

Dark bitter porter, slightly psychotropic with hops and moonflowers (a touch of thujone)

Spring lambchops rolled in egg, cracked seeds and spices, cumin seeds, bread crumbs, almond and walnut paste—barbecued over charcoal— served with roots boiled with asafetida

Green Wine from Santos-Dumont Dome
or
sheep yoghurt drink flavored with fresh coriander & watercress

Crushed ice with frog spawn & ewe's cream

A plate of mirlitons, tiny cakes, each one a different miniature artwork

Iced Ice Wine (from grapes frozen on the vine) with an ice-worm in the bottle (quite phantastically psychoactive)

Assorted cheeses, fruits in season, nuts, coffee or tea and/or brandy

IV.

Svetlana's Tale

My beloved Eleuthera—my new friends—Have you ever heard of a dull remote unimportant agricultural Dome on the Dark Side called Vavilov? It's in the middle of what *we* call Little Muscovy—Timiry-azev, Sechenov, the vast Sea Dome of Korolev, "wheat rich" Kibal'chich, Mechnikov... yes? No? It's on the shore of Hertzprung the dry sea... got it now? Well, that's where I was born and grew up.

Algelioche or Albagebh, Neck or Forehead of Leo, strength-
eneth buildings, yieldeth love, benevolence & help against
enemies. To facilitate child-bearing & cure the sick they
make a seal of gold being the head of a lion & perfume it
with amber.

It's strange how we all assume that any Domeyne on Darkside will be *dim*, badly lit, always not quite full day; even though we have artificial light strong enough to grow crops, we live in mental twilight, it seems.

The speaker that day, Svetlana Dolgoruky, known as the Captain, decked out as usual like some Antique toff (morning coat of dove gray, yellow diamond cufflinks and tie-pin) seemed no older than a schoolgirl at first glance, but second glance hinted at her reputation as (not to mince words) a fearsome pirate.

Mine was a difficult birth, she continued, last of five siblings, and my mother died of me. I was underweight, "delicate," meaning perhaps doomed, so I became the favorite child of my father, the Baron.

When I say Baron you mustn't think of anything grand, along the lines of the Duke of Kepler, or even the Princess Korolevski, our provincial doyenne and petty czarina. Vavilov waxed rich in apples, peas, potatoes, lignoids, algae, bootleg dagga—not in gold or diamonds. My diamonds weren't dug in Vavilov! We were merely *comfortable.*

Vavilov, like the whole area, seems somehow flatter and more boring than anywhere else on Luna, our Domes no more than giant farms, somnolent and fat. Wheat and corn sometimes for as far as you can see—the occasional rock or tree becomes a pleasant surprise, a little creek could seem a miracle to a child, shaded with a scrawny willow and two bluegums.

My father posed as an aristocrat but in essence embodied the Big Farmer of oldtime comedy—his foremen and bosses he called Knights, and invited them to carouse at his long-table. Our people long ago reverted to effective serfdom. They actually tug their forelocks when the Baron walks past them without a kind word.

And to boot, he's engrossed all justice to himself and shares it with no peasant. He rules like a "true Boyar" and sentences malefactors away to wither and die in his dirt-mining camps along Hertzprung and around Kuo Shan Ching—where a man might be murdered for a fragment of aerolith—or a bowl of greengruel.

> *Azobra, Arduf, Hair of the Lion's Head, good for voyages,*
> *gain by merchandise and for redemption of captives. For*
> *fear, reverence & worship they make a seal of a plate of*
> *gold being the image of a man riding on a lion holding the*
> *ear thereof in his left hand, & in his right holding forth a*
> *bracelet of gold, & perfumed it with good odors & saffron.*

Since I was spoiled and excused school for my delicacy, I wasted many a long day hiding in some coppice and reading adventure stories—unless a traveling Magic Lantern Show arrived in our muddy village, since all of us—all the children I mean—were passionately fond of such trash. Surely the amoral, uncensored junk-lit children somehow get hold of can be responsible for many of the sins and crimes of our later adult avatars. A yellow magazine whose Muscovan title translates as *Dragon Tracks*—you won't know it—undoubtedly seduced me, and I would never have chosen my, uh, career in later life if not for the example of *Kapitan Maskelyne*, which I'm sure you *did* read, even if you'd like to deny or forget it... Yes? I thought as much.

I dreamed of journeys—anywhere, just so long as it was out of Vavilov. I dreamed of adventures. I dreamed.

I became a tomboy, and would associate only with children I deemed potentially criminal as myself—fruit thieves, trespassers, poachers of the Baron's fish. Whether born of peasant or knight I liked only the most reckless and unthinking boys, and only on condition that they treated me as a fellow boy. These two or three followers I led into worse and worse mischief.

> *Alzarpha or Azarpha, Tail of Leo, giveth prosperity*
> *to harvests and plantations but hindereth seamen, but is*
> *good for the bettering of servants, captives & compan-*
> *ions. For the separation of lovers they make a seal of black*
> *lead being the image of a dragon fighting with a man, &*
> *perfume it with hairs of a lion & asafoetida.*

At length, on the cusp of adolescence, we began to dream a more focused fantasy together—we began to dream of Escape. Our great subliterary hero, Kapt. Maskelyne, as you'll recall, specialized in being captured and escaping—whether from chains and prisons or from hair's-breadth situations of hideous danger—and we based our "plans" on one of his most thrilling episodes.

As I said, we were still children—but we'd perfected ourselves as children. Now we were about to be thrust into a whole alien new world about which we knew nothing, and would have to learn from scratch how to be "adult humans," a role of very little interest to twelve- or thirteen-year-old savages like me and my robber band.

Our O-so-brilliant plan was to stow away—all four of us, in the tail-end of a huge slow clunky old five-seg tunnel-crawler called "Selene" which visited Vavilov twice a year to deliver mail and luxury goods and pick up mail and corn and mutton, bound for Paracelsus and Cyrano and points Lightward.

We—that is, I and Arion, a blond blue-eyed peasant lad, my boon companion, Timoviev and Paschel, brothers, sons of a minor Knight—we spent (I think) five days and nights in utter darkness shared with an illegal multitude of mealy-worms and rats and dusty sack upon sack of barleycorn, in Segment Five of "Selene," as it passed through the ice-cold tunnel to Korolev.

No sooner had we docked in the Airlock at Korolev, however, than we were at once arrested by the Princess Korolevski's Police, on information telegraphed by my father, who had *deduced* our actions and outsmarted us. (Wasn't he proud!) We were returned to Vavilov in chains, literally, owing to our rage for kicking and biting. Home again, a mock trial was perpetrated by the Baron—himself alone, as sole judge and jury—and my most pathetic pleas were for once ignored. I'd had no idea just how cruel and stupid my father could be. We were all stunned at the verdict: the boys were to be sent to the Mines! I alone was sentenced to "room arrest" like a naughty child, while my only friends were sent to hell, no doubt to die within a few years (at most) of cold and overwork.

When I got over my first paroxysms of knuckle gnawing anger and remorse, I at once began to plan my revenge (really a pirate's deepest emotion, I think, the desire to "get even")—by two means: first, to sweettalk my way back again into the Baron's good graces—with flattery and shameless lying—and second, to acquire some real weapons. The first task was easier than the second, actually. A year almost slipped away before I finally got hold of a pair of antique dueling dartguns and some ammunition, and by myself learned how to restore the pieces to use. Just then a desperate message reached me from the brothers at the Mines: Arion was sick and likely to die if I couldn't rescue him *soon*.

I ran away again.

This time I bluffed my way onto a ship headed for the Mines by pulling my Boyar rank on the Captain. A few days later in the Central Office of that vast wormholed cheese called the Cinnabar Caverns of Kuo Shou Ching, where six thugs in slovenly uniforms were monitoring the slave laborers, I again tried to take command in my Father's name. This time the Baron had failed to guess where I'd gone (he couldn't believe in my loyalty to my companions, I suppose). But still I was unable to impress these jailors. So I took out my pistols and shot one of them in the leg (a lucky hit, I assure you) and let the others watch him writhe on the floor in a screaming seizure for a little while. Then I repeated my order. When they still failed to respond I shot the next bastard in the heart from three feet away. I probably killed him. Anyway I hope so, frankly. I have no idea in the end how many mercenary cretins we might've killed there. You know about "non" lethal darts, no?—but in any case, it was enough. I must've shot at least six personally.

When Timo and Paschel arrived in the guardhouse Lock, Arion was not with them. My best friend had been starved and worked to death—at age fourteen. That was when I lost my temper and shot a few more guards, now in sheer rage, rather than cold (panic stricken) deliberation.

The two brothers seem to have aged ten years in a year. With them came two new companions, a grown man and woman, Callix and Henana, who at once swore to follow *me*—a mere adolescent—as their Captain in a career of piracy. The brothers agreed enthusiastically. Callix, who'd been living in Kuo Shan the longest, told us where and how a ship could be stolen, and added the brilliant suggestion that we also steal extra batteries, which he knew how to juryrig and attach to dustships and super-speed them, up to nearly 40 miles per hour—even on the Surface. We now had weapons and hostages and were able to liberate a scarred old guard ship—one segment only—barely big enough for us all to sleep in—with the unlovely name "Silverfish."

Alhaire, Dogstars or Wings of Virgo, prevalent for benevolence, gain, voyages, harvests & freedom of captives. For agreement of married couples & for dissolving the charms against copulation, they make a seal of the images of both—of the man in red wax, of the woman in white, & cause them to embrace one another, perfuming it with lignum aloes & amber.

Well—to continue my Confession—Svetlana smiled a little icily—this began my career in piracy—my war with all the world. Our technique? We'd hit the smaller agricultural Domes, really no more than smash-&-grab raids on Airlock Customs and markets and the odd shipyard Exchange. We depended on randomicity and surprise, and we *got away* at speeds that left most Police vehicles in the dust. We found safe hide-out Domes—abandoned but functioning—or else settled by antinomian sectarians or primitive tribes—out-of-the-loop places, cut off for years at a time, no-go-zones, refuges of parasites still living off Mysteries of the Ancients they don't even recognize as such, much less understand.

Every time I found a diamond amongst our booty I kept it for myself. Gold and silver we split evenly. Fashionable jewels such as pearls, genuine moonstones, grotesque crystals, fungal-looking cinnabars, garnets, amber, meerschaum, moss agate, obsidian and jet—plus valuable antiques and old Machines—we *buried* in various isolated spots. In a few cases only I know precisely where the chests were hidden—so some day I may be able to recover some of this stuff.

Every once in a while we'd seize a dustship by threatening to blow it up—an unspeakable crime we'd never really've committed, please believe me. After the third change of vehicle we found our ideal ship, "Nocturne," in a repair yard in Icarus. Thinking about "Nocturne" I can almost share the Teknostic notion of human-slash-machinic co-evolution. I loved that dustship. Listen:

The nose of "Nocturne" stands fifteen feet above surface on its flex-treads. The front beak is a solid crystal, serving as window of the control-room, and beneath it juts a sharp-flanged dust-prow that doubles as a ram. The bodywork is *all* of brass with ancient steel fittings, and the brass is elegantly filigreed in floral arabesques. The portholes in all three segments of the ship are also crystal, and yet another great crystal covers the tail, to make a rear-guard's lanterne. The entrance to the ship is by a ladder that comes out of its, um, rear end. The segments are so flexed that the ship can turn a circle nearly on its own tail-track. It can speed along where no roads were ever blasted. In full career it raises three sun-foil sails, rigged fore and aft, schooner-wise, painted with our Emblem (a black flag with seven stars). With sails up we can hit 50 mph. Not even our provincial Princess could boast of such a Car—and no cops anywhere in Luna have such a cruiser. As for the interior—all shipshape—tight but efficient—comfortable bunks and excellent galley—plush and crystal everywhere—black and purple plush velvet, our heraldic colors. Lux et luxe—meaning, "Light and Luxury"!

> *Achureth, Arimet, Azimath, Alhumech, or Alcheymech: spike of Virgo or Flying Spike, causeth the love of married folk, cureth the sick, is profitable to sailors but hindereth journeys by land. For divorce & separation of the man from the woman they make a seal of red copper being the image of a dog biting his tail, & perfume it with hair of a black dog & black cat.*

As for my crew I can tell you that Henana became my first lover, after I renounced my Father and all men for good—and that in the end she and Callix betrayed me—not by running off together, but worse, by conspiring to turn me into some authority in exchange for amnesty. You'll hear about it, don't worry. The brothers Timo and Paschel are both gone now, one to death outside Cyrano de Bergerac—*on the Surface*—and the other to prison in Mandelshtam—whence perhaps I'll rescue him some day.

Dear Eleuthera—dear comrades—How I ended up here in exile in this dump, I'm sure you can now guess. But I can't finish my story today. I need to introduce the Partner who only recently joined me in crime, and let him bring you the rest of the Tale, about our recent joint spree of armed robbery and extortion. Or rather, you already know him—as Count Apicio Johnson, Chief Chef of Fourier.

(Sensation. Applause.)

V.

Apicio's Tale

Apicio Johnson had dressed for the meeting in a violets-on-silk frock-coat over a series of six waistcoats of thin, almost gauze-like, silk weave that revealed in layers a color scheme ranging from outermost white through various lilacs and mauves down to an underlayer of royal purple. Knee britches—white velvet. Black lacquered dancing shoes. Powdered hair and black ribband. Ivory cane with gold handle set with an amethyst. He loomed bird-like over the assembled prisoners as he poured from cloisonné pot a rare and bitter tea that induced a state of relaxed attention and well-being in the drinkers. Then he addressed them formally.

My home Dome, Fourier, has been organized for the last few centuries as a utopian community we call HARMONIA. As you may be uninformed or even misinformed of our principles—which have attracted the Evil Eye in proportion to their very success—allow me simply to inform you.

1. Moved by disgust for the slackness and injustice of what Luna calls Civilization, we resolved either to *revert* to some earlier and less obnoxious oeconomy, or else *move forward* into the Social Unknown, and *overcome* both the insipidity and cruelty of everyday life.

2. Every human is ruled in varying degree by great Desires—we say there are twelve, traditionally, although we realize this number is symbolic. Society represses most of these desires in the name of class, race, rank, profit, religion, war or some other stupidity. Therefore Society fails to function to maximize human *pleasure*, the highest value.

3. If everyone followed every Desire *ad libitum* in total freedom, including the Desire for creative and fulfilling action-in-the-world, what would become of Society? We predicted that real social Harmony would at last be attained, and that Harmony would afford everyone at

least a *utopian minimum* of wealth and luxury, because most people enjoy making beautiful and useful things. Left to themselves, free of oppression, they will *spontaneously* self-organize into a fantastic paradisal crystal of co-realized desire.

4. Freed of thrall to all spooks and cops, each human would want at least twelve different "jobs" at once, ranging from, say, poet to tailor to antiquarian to applepicker to baker... depending on mood and desire. And twelve different luxuries would be necessary, from sweetest sleep (but only a few intense hours per night) to magical food to sexual freedom; as well as passions for theater, music, painting, plumbing, gardening, leaf-sweeping or mechanics. It might be difficult to differentiate between "jobs" and "pleasures"—but the results would be phenomenal—as we have since proved to perfection.

5. Great talents, therefore, in such fields as sexuality, cookery, peargrowing or what-have-you, are rewarded with even more "jobs" and "pleasures," or the tokens with which to purchase them, if convenient. *Everyone* in Harmonia lives like a millionaire, you might say—but we "aristocrats" live like sainted billionaires. Literally. We award *Sainthoods*, among other titles, to geniuses who provide us *all* with inspiration and luxury. I'm no Saint myself, whatever you may have heard, but I was awarded my title Count of Harmony in recognition of my greatest contribution to the Domeyne—which was *not* my famous recipe for Moldy Cheese Pie, by the way!—nor was it for my famous performances as Queen of the Fairies. I'll tell you in due course, children.

6. Humans had not hitherto eaten properly—the details are too vast to tackle today. Civilized diet lacked the principle of Occult Wisdom or *Alchemy*. Humanity was ignorant of *Gastrognosis*, the esoteric wisdom of the belly. (And the *opposite*, I might add, of TechGnosis.) *Real* food would transform us within a few generations into a new race, taller, longer-lived, gifted with peripheral vision, psychic abilities, extra new organs like the metatail, and so on. This turned out to be true, as I shall prove to you anon.

7. A religion was founded—the Church of Temporary Immortality—based on the principle that everything is simultaneously spirit and matter; that the universe itself is god, or the gods plural; that both matter and spirit are equally endowed with absolute rights; that Nature is sentient and inclined to favor our human lives if we cooperate with her and inspire her through alchemy and free love. We spend a great deal of time and creative energy on this religion, which is simultaneously our greatest communal artform: *The Harmonian Opera & Museum of Desires.*

> *Agrapha or Algarpha: Covered, or the Covered Flying Head of Libra, profitable for extracting of treasures, digging of pits, helpeth forward divorce, discord & destruction of houses & enemies & hindereth travelers. To obtain friendship & goodwill they make the image of a man sitting & inditing of letters & perfume it with frankincense & nutmeg.*

Points 8, 9, 10 and 11 have to do with oeconomy and labor, and would no doubt interest you a great deal—on some other occasion. I skip to Number 12 because it explains *me* to a great extent.

Children are known to enjoy filth and disorder. The original Harmonians therefore offered the jobs of garbage collection and sewage management to a consortium of children who became known as the Filthy Barbarians. In their wisdom the Founders had allowed for the existence of a "Republic of Childhood" that would combine utter transgression with social utility. So the Barbarians are not just parttime trash-lads (and tomboys) but a *culture* on their own, complete with its own artforms (for example, marching bands, martial arts, children's theaters, etc.), its own Grand Meeting Hall, even its own ceremonial uniforms, since children love military élan.

When at the age of seven I left the Infants & Families Hall I already knew I wanted to be a Barbarian, and so I literally grew up on the

Heap, our City's vast mountain of trash (dating back already to a distant century). By age twelve I'd worked my way up to Chief of the Heap, Primus of the Filthy Barbarians.

With such intimate expertise I soon discovered the Heap as a treasure island of discarded but still valuable things—metals, furniture, kitchenware, even lost jewelry and coins—and little by little I and my comrades grew strangely rich, and made ourselves more important in the community. My real taste for luxury, paradoxically, grew out of a squalid trashheap. As Primus, I intended to become a powerful sybarite as soon as possible—a Garbage King.

It was at this point that I made my big discovery. I'd begun to study alchemy, especially organic alchemy, and I came across references to an ancient recipe for crop fertilizer using trash, mulch and manure, including animal and human wastes—my specialties. Of course since Antiquity we'd had all the *artificial* fertilizer we need, *free*, so the use of garbage and feces as a source had passed into garden folklore like the old seed catalogue in which I made my initial discovery.

I enlisted the Filthy Barbarians in a series of experiments that tickled their sense of gleeful scatophilia. I built a shed in a remote corner of the Heap, and stank it up with my alchemical researches. In fact it was a simple secret of *pickling*—of letting the mix of garbage and shit *ferment*, and then fixing it with heat. Dead simple. We experimented with different strengths and mixtures in a little vegetable garden behind our Grand Hall. Almost at once it became obvious that our mixture enhanced growth, even *more* than the artificial variety, but also—and this was the key to my success—made the vegetables taste twice or thrice as good, according to a Jury of gastrognostics to whom we presented our findings.

And so I became the youngest Hero of Desirous Labour in 25 years, and soon after serving my first banquet (to the Vegetable Lovers United Annual Harvestfest) I earned the title Count—and became the idol of Harmonia's children *and* gastrognomes and chefs as well. Untold wealth, too, began to flow my way.

But—always ambitious to succeed—I now turned over the administration of the Barbarians to my Marshalls and lovers, and enlisted in classes with the Twelve Culinary Saints Academy. I learned some of the semi-extinct Chinese and French languages in order to acquire extra wisdom in the Libraries of Copernicus and Kepler, whither I made several successful field trips. I recreated the Imperial Manchu Eleven-Day Banquet for my graduation *chef d'ouvre*. By age sixteen I was a Master Chef. Later I became THE Chef of all Harmonia—but surrendered the huge responsibility and became a Past Master at age 24, so I could take up yet more new interests.

> *Azubene or Ahubene, Horns of Scorpio, hindereth journeys & wed-lock, harvests & merchandise, it prevaileth for redemption of captives. For to gain much merchandise they make a seal of silver being the image of a man sitting upon a chair holding a balance in his hand & perfumed it with well-smelling spices.*

To tell the truth I'd been given my title as Head Chef by the kindness of my tutor and lover, a far greater philosopher and cook than I, genius of a whole generation, the Duke of Vieta. But I wanted to get out from under his shadow and explore forms of cooking and sexuality still unknown to me.

In quick succession I became Director of the Museum of Lost Desires—a danceband conductor—fresco painter—flower arranger (for those blessed perverts we call Floraphiliacs)—Chairman of the Committee for Noble Rot (a branch of garbology!). Finally I enrolled in the Temple of Stars (Voluntary Amorous Servitude) in order to practice Erotic Altruism as a Free Temple Prostitute. I felt this was my true road to Sainthood—but in truth I never reached the highest (or lowest) levels of divine generosity. Nevertheless when I retired as High Priestess I was declared a Living Treasure of the People (at age 36)…

And *now* where else could I expand to? what far horizon to conquer? I decided to become an Ambassador. I had myself appointed Fourier's Consul to the vast mercantile Darkside Domeyne of Mendele'ev. I now longed for a new life of dangerous adventure.

Mendele'ev revealed itself as a realm of wheat elevators and narrow-gauge electric railed trolleys and trucks, of bustle and vulgarity, of tavern upon tavern, corrupt menacing government (plutocratic gangsters, really)—and of considerable wealth and social pretense.

One evening at a Diplomat's Banquet of excruciatingly bad food—and not much of it for a gastrognostic used to 30-course luncheons—I was seated next to an exotic-looking woman whose place-card read The Hon. Boyaress Svetlana Dolgurky of the Baronage of Vavilov. She was so loaded down with diamonds and rare orchids that I almost failed at first to notice her delicate beauty. Now I knew nothing of her but her name; as the poet Murae'ev Mirandola puts it

> ...and yet already I was entangled
> in invisible chains
> I barely knew myself except
> as victim of bondage
> O bliss—to know nothing
> at all

Next day I learned from my paid spy (all diplomats have them, like fleas on dogs) that the young aristocrat, pale as a schoolgirl, and positively laden with firstclass gems, was in truth a notorious pirate, Captain Svetlana of "Nocturne," taking a vacation here in safe, tolerant old Mendele'ev, where the Authorities charge people like her by the hour for protection, like some gang of not-so-cheap whores. Here enjoying R&R with her crew of desperados, while offering a cargo of rare metals in the Thieves' Market. The following day I sent her my card.

She called on me that afternoon, dressed *en travestie* in her "naval uniform" with sola topee and leather kneeboots—ah!—which rather took the wind out of my intention to inform her I'd discovered her little secret. But now I had nothing better to say. So I said it.

The Captain indicated that she was armed, although she smiled as she mentioned it, and then asked me what I had in mind. I answered, You know what I am from our conversation at that atrocious dinner, as I spoke of myself quite openly, too much so perhaps. Now I must tell you I've fallen in love with you, not erotically, but *religiously.* I know about your career. I want to join it. I want to buy a place on "Nocturne" and run away and become a pirate with you.

> *Alchil, Crown of Scorpio, bettereth a bad fortune, maketh love durable, strengtheneth buildings, helpeth seamen. Against thieves & robbers they seal with an iron seal the image of an ape & perfume it with hair of an ape.*

Somehow I was convinced that all my life, spent in pursuit of perfect order (and odor) was now to be turned upside down, and that for a time I must serve Disorder and the perfume of sulphur and witchgrass—to go from immersion in the Social to isolation as ego, as total free spirit, as agent of Chaos—and moreover, my lady (I said) *as your ape,* to join with the devils of free freedom. I can shine as ship's cook—and I could invest, say, 10,000 ducats in the operation…

But here she interrupted and said, Keep your savings, Count, bank it with the troglodytes here in Mendel'ev. We'll add it to our retirement fund—when we decide to retire.

So I was accepted into the crew of the dustship "Nocturne"—and so begins, really, a new story, based on the bizarre partnership of a Master Chef and a girl nihilist-of-the-people. Something deeply fated fell into place that day, and no matter what was to happen, the future now depended on it—the whole dénoument, perhaps for all of us, here today.

But to whom does the *story* belong now? Should I go on, should the Captain take over again, or should our youngest comrades, the twin imps there, be allowed their testimony in a Tale that (to them) concerns *their* fate above all? Well, while we consult, I have prepared for us a small

Collation for
        A Cold Day in
                Dreary Exile:

Clear Snake Consommé with red chilies, piping hot

Aspic of cold lambs' tongues with green molé sauce

(All courses served with a slightly-chilled old rose pink wine, dry as old lavender sachets)

Tripe stewed with suet, pickled apricots & turnips in
    raisin arak, served on salty custard in pastry shells

Fricassé of rabbit with nutmeg, dried pears, pear brandy, pear
    cider & cream gravy, over steamed maize grits

Salad of bitter herbs with salt & oil

Layers of pork belly, pigeon breast, truffles, dried green
    onions & pickled corn, slow baked, served with white dinner
    rolls, fresh & hot

Guava paste & cream cheese
    with bitter black qahwa

After dinner, Wali al-Taha said, Count Johnson, you promised (I think) to say something more about *new organs* and in particular about—you called it—the *metatail*. Might you now add a footnote to your Tale, and explain this?

Indeed, answered the great Chef;—Turning his back on the assembly he parted the tails of his coat with one hand while quickly undoing a large purple button over his coccyx with the other—whereupon there snaked out of his pants—a *tail*—rather hairless, snake-thick, long, with a small but shapely five-digit *hand* at the end of it—and in the palm of that hand—an *eye*.

Stunned silence.

This, he said, is the metatail. Only about fifteen *per cent* of our Harmonial population have them, but more such are born each year. We attribute it to our advanced rate of evolution, compared to other human groups; someday everyone will have one. The fingers flex and grasp, as you see, and the eye can see, in a fairly rudimentary way—color, movement more than form. Away from home we keep our metatails tucked in to avoid foolish attention. In martial and erotic encounters it gives total edge, I believe. I know you'll be discreet.

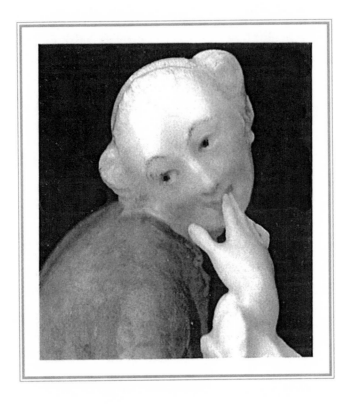

VI.

Flip & Flap

> *Alchas, Altrab, Heart of Scorpio, causeth discord, sedition,*
> *conspiracy against princes & mighty ones, revenge from*
> *enemies but it freeth captives & helpeth edifices. Against*
> *fevers & pains of the belly they make a seal of copper, be-*
> *ing the image of a snake holding his tail above his head*
> *& perfume it with hartshorn & use the same seal to put*
> *to flight serpents & all venomous creatures from the place*
> *where it is buried.*

The twin youths who stood a bit self-consciously before the party were accoutered identically as trim midshipmen of "Nocturne'"s rather imaginal "Navy," in blue half-jackets with striped blue-&-white collars, black tricorn hats with black & purple ribbons (the ship's colors), white kneebritches and shiny black pumps. Moreover they stood out by cause of their long red hair, not the usual orangy-brown but a real *red*, red as a fire-engine at a fire—a rare but natural color—accompanied by the usual redhead's freckles, green eyes and seashell-like protuberant "monkey ears," as the Chef called them.

On some days they made up their faces like clowns, chalkwhite beneath the nose, green from nose to forehead—but today they wore their own faces. The Count had so far failed, however, to make them give up smoking big fat cigars, an anti-social habit they'd picked up in low places.

"We were born on the Darkside…"

"…maybe in Omar Khayyam or Chapman…"

"… we can't be sure because our parents died when we were babies…"

"…of snakebite."

Such was their manner of speech, as if they shared one mind, although when they performed this feat they always seemed to watch each other's faces and bodies out of the corners of their eyes. And it is my [Wali al-Taha's] opinion that they read each other's whole presences—*whole body communication* I call it—and that no supernatural "telepathy" is involved. One cannot see any difference between them unless they dress differently, which they dislike to do. They often move or pose in mirror-relation to each other, a kind of spontaneous twin-dance. I'll spare the reader the fussy way of transcribing their speech used above, and write down their words as if they came from one mouth. Lucky I'm not setting this story for the stage!—how could I tell which of them is which?

We suppose (they began) that we were given names, but if so, we forget them. When we were little we named ourselves Flip and Flap after the nephews of Shashah the Goddess of Dawn. When we were seven we realized that we are bodily incarnations of the Gemini Stars, like all twins, and gifted with uncanny powers of supernatural intelligence. Ahem.

Rosy-fingered Dawn—because of our rose-colored hair—and nostalgia for our unknown mother. Uncanny because redheads are always accounted so, and often hated, feared or beaten for it. Well, it's not just superstition, let us assure you. We know how to cast spells—we've *always* known. We hurt our enemies with hexes; but we lack the power to change our own fate—or so it seemed—until recently.

> *Allatha, Achala, Hycula, Axala—Tail of Scorpio—helpeth in besieging of cities & taking of towns & in driving of men from their places & for destruction of seamen & perdition of captives. For facilitating birth & provoking the menstrues they make a seal of copper being the image of a woman holding her hands upon her face, & perfume it with liquid storax.*

In short, we spent our childhood in orphanages, foster homes and youth prisons, and soon ended up at the terminal dumping point, the Dome of Boyle, in the Dark of the Darkside, in the Home for Wayward Youth.

Wherever we lived we caused trouble—we'll say this proudly—we were recalcitrant, rude, ungovernable, even vicious—when we needed to preserve our deepest self—dishonest, lazy and depraved. Sometimes we'd make one or two friends or disciples, but usually we'd have to do constant battle with *all* the others, whether fellow-slaves or slave-masters, and naturally we tried relentlessly to escape from wherever we found ourselves.

The "boarding school" or Wayward Home at Boyle is a maximum security prison isle reputed to be escape-proof. No tunnels end at Boyle, no railway goes there, it's the end of no line at all—*the* End—till they let you out—if they ever do. There are grown-ups' prisons in Boyle too, and you can be transferred directly from the Wayward Home to a life sentence in clink—or just to perpetual exile in Boyle, since the whole Dome is a punishment zone, like *here*. IF YOU DON'T BEHAVE... —and we never did.

The Home is owned and run by a church, the Congregation of Holy Retribution, or the Church of Hell as the orphans called it. But you may not all know that this religion is a sold-out front organization of the Teknosis, and that Plato/Aristotle are the actual owners and managers of all Boyle. We had no idea till we'd been there for months. It's kept very secret.

It turns out that the true goal of Boyle is to prepare—brainwash and drill—soldiers as cannonfodder for the Tek cause: prisonguards, mercenary Enforcers, Inquisitorial Police, plus their own official Tek Army, the Fist of the Singularity.

The Wayward Home was populated exclusively by recidivists, renegades, compulsive rebels and outright psychopaths—but for once a clear majority agreed amongst themselves on a policy of undying hatred and revolution against our Tek masters—so for once in our lives, we Twins fit right in. For the first time we felt actually popular—since our past crimes had earned us the respect of the "worst" (that is, most human) of the prisoners and orphans. We launched a big conspiracy—mass escape with violent uprising—and began clandestinely to manufacture weapons—stilettos out of stolen kitchen gear, or slings out of rubber tires.

Neither behaviorist mental torture nor dulling drug therapy could quell our now-constant state of incipient rebellion. We had heard of the exploits of the famous pirate Captain Svetlana, and that her base of operations lay in Mendele'ev, so we bribed one of our tutorguards to mail her a letter there. We wrote

> "Please come & help us either to escape or to destroy all
> Boyle. It is a nest of Teknosis—here they manufacture future
> torturers and rulers—they plan to take over the Moon—the
> whole Rabbit—& we must stop them. Come or send help.
> (Signed)
> *F for Conduct*"

> *Abnahaya—the Beam—helpeth for taming of wild beasts,*
> *strengthening of prisons, destroyeth wealth of societies,*
> *compelleth a man to come to a certain place. For hunting:*
> *a seal of tin, being the image of Sagitarry half a man half*
> *a horse, & perfume it with the head of a wolf.*

Time went by—a month or more—and we received no reply to our letter. So in desperation we cancelled the uprising and concentrated on immediate ESCAPE. Our plan involved holding several of our so-called teachers hostage and in bondage, and using them as human shields to reach the Lock, where we would attempt peaceful or violent liberation of a police dustship—a fast cruiser, the *only one* (we were certain) in the whole Yard at that time.

*Abeda, Albeldach—Defeat. Good for harvests, gain,
buildings & travelers, & causeth divorce. For destruction
of somebody they make the image of a man with a double
countenance before & behind, & perfume it with brim-
stones & jet, & put it in a box of brass, & with it brim-
stone & jet & the hair of him whom they would hurt.*

Well, the very first step—the taking of the hostages—failed. Someone may have betrayed us, or possibly we made some simple error in
conspiracy protocol, but in any case we were seized and arrested *before*
we could even launch the plot. And this time they *separated us*—locked
Flip and Flap in different cells—and this is what we *cannot abide*. We
felt doomed and done for indeed.

*Sadahacha, Zodeboluch, Zaudeldona, Head of Capri-
corn: promoteth flight of servants or captives in curing of
diseases. For security of runaways: a seal of iron being the
image of a man with wings on his feet bearing an helmet
on his head, & perfume it with argent vivre (quicksilver).*

But then our luck changed.

Here we've decided that Captain Svetlana and Uncle Apicio... or rather,
our *maître Chef* Count de Johnson—should resume narrators' roles, since
they now become the actors or chief agents of our story, while we Twins
are simply raptured up into heaven without lifting a finger. Good times
(however brief) are coming in our Tale. We can say in anticipation of
this happiness that we Twins have become the lovers and apprentices of
the great Gastrognostic, whom we revere and long to emulate. Already
we have learned a bit of cookery, and have been allowed to prepare for
you today *A Light Snack*, designed by us (with His advice)

to Induce a Station
of Hilaritas & Levitas
on a Gloomy Day

A selection of tiny Marzipan & Candy Animals, Vegetable, Toys
    & Rebuses in assorted shapes & colors
    lightly dosed with elixirs or stuffed with jams of dagga

served with ice-cold raspberry soda laced with raspberry brandy

Blue Soup, with frogs'-legs & gruel

Larks' brains, bitterfish livers & white truffles (mildy hallucinogenic)
    in an omlette of lark's eggs fried in goosefat & garnished with
    chopped fresh chives, cilantro & parsley, with saffron butter rice
    mixed with raw lark-egg yolk & red sumac

served with carbonated hard perry

For dessert: Pomegranate Syrup mixed with snow & fermented
    mare's milk

Eagerly the Twins began to speak again:
You see, the magical effect of the l....
But Apicio shushed them at once.
Tsk tsk, he said. *Never Explain.*

VI.

(Continued)

> *Zabadola or Zobrach, Swallowing: maketh for divorce,*
> *liberty of captives, health of the sick. For destruction &*
> *wasting they make a seal of iron being the image of a cat*
> *having a dog's head, & perfume it with hairs of a dog's*
> *head, & bury it in the place where they did intend to hurt.*

After their light (and illuminating) snack, Wali al-Taha stood up and said,

As you can tell by my girth, hitherto in life I've acted more as gourmand than gourmet—much less as a gastrognostic—and have favored quantity over (or equally with) quality. I fear my beloved Sylphie has simply never liked food all that much at all, and I've noted that Eleuthera has always eaten to live rather than lived to eat—which accords with her serious and courageous intentionality. But I believe I can speak for all of us when I say that meeting Count de Johnson has wrought a conversion-experience in us. We've learned that food can be spiritually uplifting and very much an artform on its own (despite the fact that one *must* eat but that poetry is *optional*, hence "free"). I'm comfortable as a monster and will probably never lose weight. But this "snack" today by Flip and Flap has convinced me—by the sheer uplift of spirits it's caused—that I too must study this art. To improvise:

Only the spirits
     they say
Could've built this palace
     but I
In that case must claim
     to be an afrit
       of the Surface
        as well.

(Applause of agreement. The Twins blush redly. Elegant sitting bow from Count Apicio to the fat poet. Svetlana rises and speaks):

Indeed, this afflatus of spirit, caused by magical food and shared by us all, inspires me (if I have your permission) to continue our Tale and explain how our apprentice chefs happen to be, well, rotting in exile with us here rather than rotting in the Orphanage at Boyle.

Everyone laughed as if this outline of gloomy fate were a good joke, and hissed their assent to yet more narrative. Proceed, said Chef Apicio, and I and the lads shall add footnotes *ad libitum*.

Of course—(the Pirate Captain said)—you've guessed that we did indeed receive the Twins' letter written to us at Mendele'ev. But it found us in the middle of delicate negotiations over a priceless load of aeroliths, in which nearly the whole of our capital was already in play, or sunk, to use an appropriate term from gambling. So it wasn't till a month later that we were able to leave that sink of corruption (ourselves now richer than ever, and now with the most brilliant ship's cook in pirate history) and make our way to Boyle, via Schliemann, Ventris, Kepler, Paracelsus, Mare Ingenii, and Leibnitz. We paused nowhere—we even used the tunnel from Mendele'ev to Kepler, despite the danger of running into police of various jurisdictions with warrants for our apprehension (including a reward, I'd heard, of 50,000 ducats for my head, offered by the Teks of Dead Lake and Frozen Sea (may gods rot them)... that is, the United Domeynes of Plato and Aristotle).

We stopped one day for supplies at Paracelsus—a run-down ratty Pirate Utopia and refuge of forbidden sciences—and then headed out onto the Surface, off the roads, where we drove more slowly but more safely toward our goal. Altogether, six weeks had passed since we'd received that forlorn missive from the group or person signing as "Zero for Conduct"... our lads, here.

Therefore, full of apprehension, I decided on a tactic I'd long ago considered but never used, since I feared it would ruin my reputation as a Robin Hood Hero of the downtrodden, being too shocking for most Lunarians even to imagine much less carry out.

I daresay the Teks themselves have never perpetuated anything so shockingly awful.

I drove "Nocturne" right up onto the roof of Boyle's Dome, using the cleat attachments on the treads, and when we'd reached the very apex we stopped, and by ship's telegraph we sent this message to Boyle's administrators:

> "You must release those students from the Home for Wayward Youth who wish to leave Boyle. You must send them by themselves, no escort, to our dustship, unless there are more than ten of them in which case you must provide them with a standard dustship large enough to accommodate them all. You must pay us 25,000 ducats in Kepler coinage. If you fail to meet these requirements we will use explosives to blow a hole in the Dome, right here at the apex."

Within fifteen minutes the reply came: they would release the ten students. But they complained (whined, really, if bare text could whine) that they had no gold.

We assumed they were lying, and at once gave them one hour's warning before we blew the roof over their heads. Another fifteen minutes passed—rather tensely on both sides, I fancy—until they broke down and capitulated.

The important thing to bear in mind about the Teknostics—especially the lower-ranking officers and bureaucrats—is that although they talk a lot about science—including the science of war—they're really not very good at it. The ideology of machinic progress has become a means of social control for them rather than an ideal telos to be striven for in all earnestness. They've grown slack with power—their own oppressive rule has infected the rulers themselves—with anxiety and even panic.

As a result—within five hours we had received all that we demanded—including the Dome-leader's second-in-command as a hostage (to be released at the first "neutral" port) and the bags of gold. We sped away in a misleading direction.

We headed into the badlands north of Poincaré and Planck, toward the line of Dawn. On the edge of the Light we then tacked due north, and for a month drove drearily and ceaselessly, past Gernsback, Scaliger, Backhind, Saha, Al-Khwarizmi, Moebius, Cheng Hong and finally to our goal—Giordano Bruno.

> *Sadabath, Chadezoad, Star of Fortune: prevalent for*
> *benevolence of married folk, victory of soldiers, hurteth the*
> *execution of government & hindereth it that it may not*
> *be exercised. For multiplying herds of cattle, they take the*
> *horn of a ram, bull or goat, etc., & seal in it burning with*
> *an iron seal the image of a woman giving suck to her son,*
> *& hang it on the neck of that cattle who is leader of the*
> *flock, or seal it in his horn (i.e., brand the horn).*

Bruno: if you don't know it, you'll be interested to note that it's one of our "safe" top-secret retreats. Officially it's a School—the Nolan academy—run on non-hierarchical & antinomian principles by a sect called The Art of Memory, also known as the Brownists—nature-worshipping Reversionaries content to live *plain*, in huts and tents, and cultivate their vast feral forests for fruits and game, roots and fungi. They grow some grains and vegetables and keep a few domestic animals (they're not vegetarian like so many sects these days) but they're generally very lazy and depend on greenbread and a bit of ritual hunting—lizardoids, deer, rats and so on. They're deliberately *slipping back*, as they say, into a dream of the Past—not the Teknostic Past, the glory days of free energy and infinite pollution, but the even more legendary era of Saturn and Tiamat, the original Kaos. The Brownists practice "High Magic and low morals" as they say. We pay them for their hospitality—pirates *must* have safe ports—and we go there strictly for R&R. We have a watership there, an old houseboat, as our HDQ in Giordano.

One eats very well there, added Chef Apicio, if one has the slightest ambition. The forest is handled beautifully as a work of art and worship, and it provides hundreds of rare dishes and even rarer phantastica.

Our plan—resumed the Captain—was to leave the orphans at Bruno, enrolled in the Academy if they liked, and then get back to business. Several things occurred during our sojourn there however, which caused unexpected change, as you shall hear.

Chef Johnson spoke again: Over the long haul from Boyle to Bruno, I had fallen in love with these Twins. Then when I saw how they began to blossom in Bruno under a regime of freedom and pleasure, I decided I needed them in my life. I offered to adopt them as official apprentices and nephews if they liked.

We were thrilled, said the Twins together.

Now Capt. Svetlana went on: I'm certain the good Chef would've preferred to stay in Bruno, living on our boat, which is disguised as a floating islet with a castle-tower and tiny flower and fruit gardens, "holding down the fort" as he put it. But the Twins' bargain was that first he should take them a-pirating with me on "Nocturne," so they could have some real adventures, and some revenge, as they put it. The Chef, capitulating to the principles of Voluntary Amorous Servitude, agreed. The Twins signed on as Midshipmen. We prepared to depart.

> *Sadalabra, Sadalachia: Butterfly, or Spreading Forth: helpeth beseiging & revenge, destroyeth enemies, maketh divorce, confirmeth prisons & buildings, hasteneth messengers, conduceth to spells against copulation & so bindeth every member of man that it cannot perform its duty. For preserving trees & harvests they seal in the wood of a figure the image of a man planting & perfume it with flowers of the fig tree & hang it on the tree.*

Razullo.   Cucurucu.
122

Pasquariello Truonno. Meo Squaquara
123

Sig.ᵃ Lucia.   Trastullo.
124

Cap. Cardoni.   Maramao.
125

Franca Trippa.   Fritellino.
126

Taglia Cantoni.   Fracasso.
127

The second happenstance seemed less important. We learned that the various Domeynes with good reason to desire an end to our career had joined in a police-entente and upped the reward for my capture, alive or dead, to an astronomical sum...

A million in gold, noted Chef Apicio...

and that amnesty had been offered to anyone of my crew who'd agree to testify against me. We had a good laugh at this. Each of us, the original crew, was already worth twice that amount—Although—it *was* flattering, I admit.

We joked about ways we might trick them into paying the reward and yet escape all arrest. What I of course had failed to realize was that Henana, my lover, and Callix, my first mate, had already decided to betray me at the first opportunity, and to take the reward, plus all our gold, and the ship "Nocturne" as their pay for serving me and my loyal crew to the cops on a plate.

By way of Al-Biruni and Ibn Yunus we now headed back to al-Khwarizmi, which (we'd noticed on our way to Bruno months ago), appeared to be trim and prosperous. We helped ourselves there to a shipload of rare metals and silver, at the expense of the local bankers, and then decided to begin a big new campaign on Dayside, starting with a series of little razzias around the Marginal Sea, in Twilight, towns like Peek, Back, Schubert, Banachiewitz—then across the Mare Undarum to Apollonius. We earned little from these hold-ups, but it was good training for the new crew members. No one on either side got badly hurt. And in Apollonius we made a discovery that proved the whole excursion worthwhile: an ancient cache of undamaged gravitation cans. Imagine: we now might learn how to *fly*! Only devils know how to fly. Speaking of which: let me read you this entry from the Ship's Log:

"An apparition seen from the DUSTSHIP NOCTURNE & attested by all hands: between the Domaynes of Plutarch and Berosus we passed by a vast carpet aloft about 20 ft. from the Surface &

flying slowly SSW—the carpet was woven of many whorls & spirals & colored in yellows & greens—on it a troupe of what appeared to be *Commedia dell'Arte* actors—Columbina, Pierrot, Harlequin, the prongnosed Doctor, etc., & a band of dwarves in tall mitre-hats playing long-necked lutes—which we *heard*, despite the fact that *nothing can be heard in the vacuum of lunar space.* They all waved at us & then sped away (carpet rippling a bit) into the highlands & passed from our sight. Truly strange: The crew all saw & heard & remembered *exactly* the same things. You'd expect some disagreements. Witnesses always disagree. But every report was exactly the same."

Svetlana put the Log aside and added, This wasn't the first time we'd seen ghouls, efrits, slipaxes, sirens or pans—even one or two giant fire-breathing lizardoids—but however fascinating, these encounters seem to *mean* nothing. The efrits never speak or really interact with humans, it seems, despite legends to the contrary. This one, the Carpet, however, should perhaps be counted as a bad omen—at least in retrospect.

What was the music like? asked Sylphie rather shyly. Svetlana answered

Eerie, beckoning, dodeco and arhythmic, rather like old folk music, you know, trance stuff. Unfortunately we had no way of recording it, if indeed it was real enough to record.

We now decided (she went on) to head for Posidonius on the Lake of Dreams, and work toward hard Teknostic territory—to take the war to the enemy—but no sooner did we pull into the Lock there and leave the ship, but we were surrounded by hundreds of ambushers, heavily armed cops and Inquisitors, and were forced to surrender or die. We chose surrender.

I'd prefer to skip over the arrest scene, the jail scenes, the shameful triumph of my betrayers, the trial and sentence, the trip into exile. I think you've all been through the same strange alternate reality, the Ugly Place—you don't need a reminder. I should think that by now *everyone* has been *there*, has woken into the infradimensional and wondered, Who are these armed sadist bullies who seem to have been invited to invade and occupy my world? Who asked them? I don't remember signing any "social contract" with these shits. And so on. Yes, by now I'd say that the knowledge of that world is hard-wired into the human soul. So I'll skip it.

Thank the saints we're still alive and together. How can I mourn our prisonment on this malignant counter-enchanted isle, when it has been re-enchanted by Eleuthera's love with me, Apicio's joys shared with the Twins, and the happiness of our general *camaraderie amoureuse*, our banquets, and our... plans.

INTERLUDIUM

Next day the prisoners gathered by the seashore, amidst a jumble of old concrete wharves half-sunk into the mire, and sand, and stained algaic emerald (but slightly artificial-looking) sea. Lunar legend always attributes a watermonster to each of its icy seas, huge serpentoids—or perhaps scaly mer-folk, half benevolent protectors, half bugaboos; hungry for sacrifice, say, a few fish thrown back from every big catch; and you tend to find little temples dedicated to their cults on beaches and islets. Here however there appeared no sign of holy or dreadful presence—indeed, very little romance at all. But here was where Wali al-Taha had promised them a poetry reading.

To cheer themselves up, they'd all dressed (as far as possible, given the circumstances) in high style, with much use of gems, loose silken robes intricately patterned, masks or half-masks, platform boots, all in fashionable colors such as purple and black with tongue-lashings of yellow like attractive bruises.

The Chef and his nephews brought wicker baskets covered with starched white napkins. Bottles had been procured. A hookah of bootleg dagga was shared with some hilarity. The baskets were flung open—and a dozen or so live frogs leapt out and headed for the sea, like escaping prisoners, to the laughter and applause of the hopeful diners. A great many other batrachians however had not been so lucky, and were now serving as the basis for a huge cold Frog Pie with crust of candied ginger and asafoetida—followed by black figs in bee honey with clotted cream, and other dainty confections. After a round of bitter qawah from a thermos—and another hookah, smoked to the slither-sound of wavelets and aqueous sighs, Wali performed some of his latest verses—that is, he not only recited them dramatically, he also sort of danced, especially with his hands, for which he had mastered hundreds of mudras of great subtlety, as contra-danse to his spoken words.

Alpharg, or Phragol Mocaden, the First Drawing: maketh for union & love of men, for health of captives, destroyeth prisons & buildings. For love & favor they seal in white wax & mastic the image of a woman washing & combing her hair, & perfume it with things smelling very well.

Wali al-Taha Reads Aloud from
A FLORIST'S POEMS

1. Cult of Flowers

how when pubescent psychic clay
you masturbated your first rose
be-dewed & destroyed in a fistful of
crimson slime

how when hot bees & trembling
butterflies experience eating & coming
as single polychrome seizures of nectarious
ambrosial spermatozoa

could there not be a goddess FLORA for
florists & erotomanes & professional floraphiles
—what could we buy half so precious
as what we sell

     poppy
      mandragora

how not a cult that threatens
with its efficacious sacraments &

        sentient gems
to overthrow laws if not of nature
then of shared dim neurotic fear of

strong odors saturated hues
                              revolt of flowers
                                        violence of flowers

each on a stalk
pussy on a willow
or twenty-eight of each
in a writhing kaleidoscope
of omnisexuality—I can
barely bare to spill spell it—an
                              orchid an
                                        orchid

2. The Shop of Transcendent Bargains

blang
klinglang
                         your ears grow glowing
long white pink as you
                         enter my arrogant kiosk
of adelphic slaves

tired of masturbating over your frayed &
choicest seed catalogues you're here to
spend a week's wages on one
gloriental frenzification of
                              genital obloquy
pistil to pisshole & stamen to cheek
mayn't we interest you in these
                    furtive arrangements by our
                    leading vivesthetician
                              Mr Taha

O Madam Adam
he knows your deepest
petalous bifurcations
        & honeysuckling hesitations
& will take almost as much
sexual gratification in your silver
as you take in his most
        aquaturquoise
            pendant lilies
or moonflowers big as shrouds
to wrap yourself in thujone ecstasies
till the cow jumps
& the candle
kindles

3. The Back Room of the Shop

Madame X can only achieve jouissance
in any brawny embrace on condition
it take place in a coffin filled to the brim
with 1000 ducats worth of tube-rose
the floral equivalent of skunk-cum
        & alchemical mist

Mister Y must be lashed by schoolgirls with thornvine
scourges of roses in bloom—discreet little pricks of
civilized roses big as cabbages smelling
of time back to the earliest fusion of
Chaos & Cupid, Water & Money

Miss Z requires a pelican-still that will distil
a trickle of orchidaceous elixir over

her body all bound in woodbine & morninglory
till writhing & whining she begs for
the release of vanilla extract sprayed
                              across her crease
genitals exposed
in top hats & tails
spats & gray gloves our
sales assistants hover solicitously
over every floraphiliac
each flunky with his/her boutonnière
                              of violets or
                                        bluebells
each stroking own
                 vegetable or clitoridal
                                   bulge
reeking of florida water &
                    tincture of hemp

turn up the lamps
& glory in each other's
          over-sweetest degradations

4. The Park on Monday

Copernicus's Municipal Park
on weekends too vulgarly crowded
well-policed for our devious sub-
                              or in-
                                   versions
but rainy mondays suit best lonely
melancholy most slumberous
                    pantingly obscene

Cull cloud to cover yet emphasize our
                  naked unshame
wearing no clothes at all except socks'n'hose
                    beneath stained raincoats while
exposing selves deliriously to Rose Garden's
                    seraphic ranks
How could any flower "be" more desirable
or die in such aromatic disarray in
                  petals of blood
platonic essences each one of them unique
rain pours down loins—a fleck of blood
doves startled whirr away in
                  romantic despair

5. Lilac Pirates

lilac lilacs depend like lunar grapes
faded opalescent mauve decadent clusters
of food for Jupiter
From pergolas & pagodas of purpureous perfumes
they pululate across whole parks & percolate
                    playgrounds
soliciting innocents to Cynthia's sins
O throw away your tops & hoops &
      learn desire
           in your frilly lace &
                laced-up booties
innocent lust—an oxymoron
        incomprehensible to the average shit—
           kicking bigoted mullah
cantata for castrati or angels
        voice like preserved ginger

              or presence of violets
we have come to steal you
because stolen lilacs are sweeter
love to be fucked

6. *Made of Flowers*
          (Flora or Florio)

creatures made entirely out of flowers
haunt the insalubrious back pages
of yellowing curiosa since hither antiquity
or even Reality anyway almost eternally
yet forever sixteen.
              As it might be
tulips for nipples skin of snowdrops
shot thru with ripples of violets for veins
hyacinth for hair, check,
roseblush for cheeks—narcissus
                  for a birthmark
appleblossom forehead eyes of iris
confusion occurs only at the
                  hole of holies
shrine of the vagina for isn't that
a penis (made of a single moonflower
color of first frost) emerging all
stalky from the vulvic pubis with orchidalatrous
                  testimonies
                    attached?
—a dawning of pure puella/puerility
this confusion
         (biomoral
            chick/dick

<pre>
                              paranoid/critical
constitutes my ferality & your
halo of wildflowers (Queen Anne's Lace
chicory purple-loosestrife mustard
                         tiger-lily daisy chain
a coronet actually growing from your
skull springing up from your brain but
visible only to occult archbishops
& certain dogs
</pre>

7. Poem of Whiteness

<pre>
Black is not absence of all colors
as the vulgar materialists boast
but white is most certainly
all of them
                    creamed together in an
alembic of halcyon or
                    cloud chamber of
                              zephyrs of pale blue
the blue blood & bruise-like blush
of white hermaphrodite from the
                    Dome Land of Hypatia.
It seems just to us that only god
him/her self could be that white.
As church-lily just sprayed with the
first cream of her acolytes in a
porcelain bathtub on an altar of
marble dead as geological ice
i.e. not dead at all but *waiting*
incandescent as frost
                    meltable as pearls
</pre>

meerschaum of 100,000 years
                    of arctic tides
white as my book
O blank as my cheque
as snow with a drop of the
                blood of a deer on it
                        lips like that
hair white as all the secret
                    colors of black
accept my citizenship
no my serfdom no
my voluntary amorous
                    servitude

(applause)

Bravo, bravo, said the Chef. A true genius of today must include this most elegant and etiolated of all perversions amongst the licit passions of his or her litany or spectrum of desire. How can one grasp true gastrosophy without understanding how to deploy the scents (and to a lesser extent the tastes) of botanical paraphilia? One must LOVE vegetables and flowers *as if* they were sentient beings because they *are* sentient beings and must cooperate in their *immortalization as food*—*id est,* the relation must be erotic and mutual, or how can one claim to be a true Neo-Animist? *Harmonia* would be impossible without this esoteric language of flowers and the cult of their erotic textuality. I for one cannot feel true love in a room devoid of flowers.

Moreover I must add that all great cuisines are based—paradoxically—on famine and starvation. Rich farmers eat only a few dozen different things, simply prepared—but when a culture starves it becomes hugely inventive. Hunger makes the best spice, and repulsive slugs or weeds may become delicacies. Those who once starved may now eat thousands of different things, like our friends in Bruno, because we Lunarians learned to like almost everything except lethal poisons. Even certain kinds of dirt and mold are found to be toothsome. Of course, two hundred years ago, before the discovery of greenbread, there occurred vast famines and starvations here on chaste Diana.

It is the same with love; only those who have been starved of it can learn to revere it as sacred, perhaps the sole sacral experience besides eating. The always-loved are blasé. Sex to them is nothing but the world's habit of worshipping *them*. Surrounded by images of desire they are soon sated. Love bores them at last.

To love love one must be

refused it

as Ibn Sereen of Kopernik says.

We have eaten flowers. I use many flowers in my mysteries. The love of flowers is more noble than quotidian love-routines—what I might call worldly lusts, meaning *exoteric*, banal, conventional, orthodox, acceptable to herd morality, hence oppressive, and ultimately puritanical.

Here the Twins jumped up and added a codicil to their Mentor's speech:

He, the Chef, says genitals are over-rated—that one ought to feel pleasure over the whole body and even know the orgasm of fingertips, of the Aura itself, the orgasm that never *stops* but gradually fades off into ecstatic sleep. Eating together should be sex—a kiss should suffice for a century. Anything you like, he says, but not orgasm my dear—it's a spastic exaggerated artificial plug or stop sign or sudden slump into non-erotic consciousness. If "everything is sad after coitus," then the solution is to put no end to it at all. One must avoid the state of an itch that's been scratched, rather than a love that never dies…

But the Chef harrumphed and tsk-tsk'd till the Twins blushed and looked a bit sheepish, or pretended to anyway, and the company soon broke up till what next day might offer.

VII.

DETOURENMENTS

> *Alcharya or Alhalgalmoad: Second Drawing: increas-*
> *eth harvests, revenues & gain. Healeth infirmities but*
> *hindereth buildings, prolongeth prisons, causeth danger*
> *to seamen, helpeth to inspire mischiefs on whom you shall*
> *please. To destroy foundations, pits, medicinal waters &*
> *baths they make of red earth the image of a man winged,*
> *holding in his hand an empty vessel, & perforated, the*
> *image being burnt, they did put in the vessel asafoetida &*
> *liquid storax & did overwhelm & bury it in the pond or*
> *fountain they would destroy.*

Over a century ago the "Twin Domes" of Plato and Aristotle, perhaps the last to be built of all our major cities, were still considered the most "modern" of Luna's little societies, the most devoted, that is, to the lost wisdom of the Ancients—the most learned in science and natural philosophy—the most obsessed with money.

Not for them the long slow slide into sacred sloth and contemplative agnosis favored elsewhere (everywhere else, really) in our world of Too-Late Post-Civilizationism.

At that time, there sprang up in these Domeynes a movement to recover *all* of Ancient Knowledge, despite the caveats of many thinkers and the prejudices and fears of the masses. The supposed religion of the Ancients, Technotheology, was "reformed and rectified" as Tech-Gnosis, Esoteric Machinism, and all concepts of deity were subsumed into the Singularity, the millenarian expectation of *union* between humans and machines, which (it was claimed) the Ancients had attained—but then lost, or somehow been lost *in*.

In the brains of these fanatics it seemed that the real sin of the Ancients involved not being machinic *enough*. The robot ideal had been betrayed by soft humanism and "evolution" had been de-railed—apparently forever—but in truth (the Founders of Teknosis would claim) only to sleep and await—*their* appearance and dispensation.

An important corollary of their idea of technologic Progress ("Ad Astra!") was adumbrated in their holy texts as Numisolatry, the actual worship of money. The two oldest principles in the Cosmos, the *original things*, were said to be water—and money. Under ideal conditions money itself becomes the Machine, and gives birth in or to itself as Teknostic consciousness. When Money rules all, the Singularity will come. After their revolution, the Plato-Aristotelians turned government over to a plutocracy—not a covert one like Copernicus's—but overt and ideologically aggressive. In general they accused all the other Domeynes of reversion to feudalism in some degree or guise (true enough!)—and they proposed a United Luna (under their rule) with a unified economy.

Efficiency and Progress impose a Puritanism of their own, different in intent from the Puritanism of, say, the Abrahamic Church in Kopernik. The latter at least in theory upholds some kind of oeconomic ethics (for example, against usury or slavery or oppression of the poor). But Teknosis permitted (even encouraged) such "modern" ideas, and condemned the pity and compassion which had sometimes mollified the rigors of monotheism to some extent. The Tek attitude toward free love or free artistic expression was just as dampening and oppressive as any moralic Inquisition's, but was based on an ideal of dedication to WORK and its highest disciplines, rather than to the salvation of immortal souls. The effect on the average human however seemed the same in both cases: dreariness. The Church hides its hatred of life behind brocades of incense. But in Tek-land the *dreary* was plastered over with shiny imitation Antique technolatry. The entire Domeyne of Aristotle became one huge combination shopping mall, advanced industrial park and science research Hub—while Plato was written off as primarily agricultural, suited to ignorant serfs and larval low-level soldiers and mercenaries, as well as some of the dirtiest factories on Luna. In fact, the air pollution in both Domes is horrendous.

The two domes were linked by a truck-&-train monorail & tunnel through the spectacular Alpine Vale, one of our Lunar mysteries (it *looks* artificial but has *always* existed, it seems). Having taken over the twin domes, the Teks began their secret campaign to unify the rest of the world, not by honestly proselytizing us, but by subverting and absorbing us piecemeal, by stealth, eventually by brute force, into their "Empire."

Decades passed, and although they experienced a few successes, it must be admitted that the Teks almost at once began to slump and grow a bit… decadent. As far as anyone knew they had so far failed quite utterly to crack the *real* secrets of the Ancients, such as gravitronics or perpetual motion. Just like the rest of us, they appeared to be simply Living In The Ruins. Their only Progress to speak of consists of better weapons (but since they *sell* them, now *everyone* has them!) and endless commercial crap to keep their citizens and allies solidly in debt (and thus in theory, docile). This they call "culture."

Among certain of the old hard-line Tek élite however the original Ideal still burns pure and keen, sharpened now by veneration for the *Tradition* itself—odd as it may sound to speak of a "tradition of progress." The Fist of the Singularity, the Tek Army, with the higher officers' corps in its mercenary and police branches, the Inquisitorial bureaucracy, and some of the industrial/scientific corps, remain hotbeds of Tek fanaticism, or "steely resolve" as they call it. The *very* highest ranks are no doubt permeated with cynicism and corruption. Aren't they always?

As the proverb says

> To know all is to
> forgive nothing—

Only the ignorant
are happy for long.

If the Lord Councilors and Duke-Generals know too much to be true believers, then the Assessors and Colonels tend to be lilies of Teknostic knighthood—literally Lords and Ladies, as they call themselves—and adhere rigidly to the party line. And of this second rank, none was more sincerely robotic in her perfection than Lady Colonel Agate de Trouvelot, scion of one of the oldest noble families in the élite; trained to crisp sharp metallic perfection in the gymnasia of Aristotle, she zoomed up the ranks as if on a ladder of prostrate inferiors, and reached perfection at age 30-ish, still attractive but unmarried, devoted to her career as a mercenary Prison Warden, which she had practised since girlhood. I'm sorry to say that she was not at all a nice person "in spite of her job," as Wardens occasionally might turn out to be (who can say?)—no, she enjoyed ruling in power over helpless prisoners, and was able to keep her deep sadism under control only to the extent required by Tek morality and job protocol. I didn't know her for very long, but some time after our meeting I felt curious enough to do some research, and it appeared that she was disliked even by her fellow Teks as a martinet and harridan—exactly the impression we had of her. Between jobs, Col. de Trouvelot was taking furlough at a resort in Plato, a concrete hotel between two rice paddies, while teaching a refresher course in unarmed combat at a nearby town. To her delight—or anyway, her grim satisfaction—she received a telegram from Central HDQ giving her her very first top command position—*Chief* Warden of the entire Mare Crisium Domeyne, with all its various prisons and islands of exile.

The Colonel rushed to Plato Station and booked an overnight private compartment to Aristotle. The Night Express is one of Luna's most famous trains, luxurious, sleek and fast, with "decent grub" (as Chef Apicio grudgingly admitted, during his otherwise unsatisfactory sojourn in Tek-land) served in restaurant cars tingling with crystal and silver, and with beds more comfortable than some Tek fanatics considered moral and healthy. Indeed, Col. Agate slept scarcely a wink on that soft bunk, and in the morning rushed directly (by bicycle rickshaw) to Police HDQ, to hear the inside story of her promotion.

She was told: Under one of Luna's largest Domes, the Sea of Crises and its archipelago of granite islands of anguish, had originally been dedicated to the farming of seafood and seaweed, but almost a century ago it went bankrupt and was purchased on the cheap by a consortium of security and intelligence organizations from several independently-ruled Domeynes, and turned into a land of sorrows.

Now, she learned, after decades of secret negotiations, control of the whole system had finally been secured by Teknosis, and the time had come at last to reveal this fact, and to bring about *sweeping* changes in theory and practice—and she, Lady Col. or Col. Lady Agate, hard and brilliant as her name, had been *chosen* to be the new broom, or rather the fist, for the job.

Exulting greatly (though perhaps grimly, as was her wont) she at once set out for Mare Crisium. From stentorian overweening Aristotle then she set out, via police cruiser dustship "Luther," over the Surface and direct—from Burg in the Dead Lake to Hercules, Vitruvius and Proclus—and thence to her fell goal.

She arrived right around the time we were having our Poetry Day at the beach. Soon we were summoned to meet her in the flesh (though at a distance), as she made the rounds of inspection of the islands and ports, insane asyla and orphanages, military academies and total-security brigs, prison-ships and agricultural settlements of sullen but "loyal" peasants. She was making this epic journey or Visitation by *dhow*, a nice one with a black lateen sail, named "Ray-fish," accompanied by a cowed-looking set of official thugs and torturers, the "leading citizens" of the Domeyne.

In a white uniform with modified body armor that gave her a goddess-like aspect, quite chic really, she mounted a pulpit in our unheated communal Assembly Hall, and addressed the few hundred exiles, their guardians, the few shop-owners and pimps who could be rounded up, including, of course, our entire clique of Seven.

First she explained that Teknosis had acquired full title to the entire Domeyne of Mare Crisium. Then she revealed that its civil status had now been militarized. It was no longer to exist as a galimauphry of this and that, but rather as One Big Prison, in which prisoners would be divided into different classes according to a centralized bureaucratic form.

The most favored class of prisoners would be those who enlisted in the Teknostic military service, to train as possible soldiers of the Empire. Recalcitrants would have their sentences increased. Political rebels, pirates and bandits, sexual perverts and religious enemies of Teknosis would no longer be considered "exiles" and allowed to live freely as long as they stayed on their islands. They would now be classed as "prisoners," subject to prison regime and discipline—and punishment for infractions.

You will no longer conspire together in cafes. You will no longer engage in illicit and prurient relations. You will no longer purchase luxuries from outside the System. Solitary confinement is the least of the punishments I decree—I do not exclude physical torture as a possibility. Soon, I feel certain, you will have cause to believe me. Next week we shall return and begin a series of Hearings. All sentences will be re-evaluated. For those who sign up for the Fist, sentences will be reduced. For the others… you will see.

There followed a long sermon, or rather holy harangue on the ideals of Teknosis, rendered simple enough for us criminals to grasp, and again laced with promises and threats. She then wheeled about and exited, and left us to conjecture and forebodings.

Our "plan" had been based on the presumption that the situation on the island would remain static—always a good bet where bureaucracy is involved—and that we would continue more-or-less free to act clandestinely and unobserved, up to the point when we'd need to leave the island in order to escape the Domeyne altogether. The only alternative had appeared to be to orchestrate a general uprising in the whole archipelago, but since we had no means of communicating with other islands, we'd opted instead for a single break-out involving just us, the Seven.

Eleuthera had emerged, over the course of our cabals, as the most brilliant strategist of our group. Her experience as a full-time revolutionary organizer had prepared her for all kinds of war, from expropriation of banks to major battles. Even Capt. Svetlana had recognized her as leader, not just out of voluntary amorous servitude, but because Eleuthera was clearly *meant* to lead us.

But now her brilliant plan had been forestalled by the new regime of Col. Agate—I won't even bother to explain how brilliant it was, since now it just wouldn't work—or how downcast we felt at losing it without even a struggle. After a few days of argument we decided, however, that death seemed preferable to the fate we'd been promised by the "New Teknosis" (as the Colonel had stridently called it)—and so we resolved to make *some* attempt, no matter how risky, in an effort to win free.

At this point we decided to consult the divinatory powers of the Ancients. I (Wali al-Taha) turned to that venerable text of Cornelius Agrippa, the *Lunar Mansions*, and came up with the very last Mansion, number 28:

"Albotham, Alchaley, that is Pisces: increaseth harvests & merchandise, secureth travelers through dangerous places, maketh for joy of couples, but strengtheneth prisons and causes loss of treasures. For to gather fishes together they make a seal of copper, being the image of a fish (or two fish), & perfume it with the skin of a sea fish, & cast it in the water, wheresoever they would have the fish to gather together."

As the 28th and last day of the last Lunar month (Rambam) was to fall in precisely seven days, we took the dubious omen as probably positive, and decided to launch our plans on that day, which was also the announced day of the Colonel's return to our island to launch her Hearings.

Now, we calculated we could still enjoy a few days of freedom, however attenuated, before the Colonel returned to begin her Inquisition and put an end to our comfy exile. And we'd laid our new plans for that very day of her return, when the island would bustle with confusion and seethe with paranoia. So, to wrangle over a few final details, we decided to have one last pic-nic by the sea on our favorite concrete-littered beach, followed by a conversation secure from all eavesdroppers.

For the pic-nic, Count Apicio and the Twins prepared a *Fish Dinner*, viz.: a large Octopoid was slow-baked in herbs till tender. Of the variety known as "sheep's-head," the creature was then displayed on a great platter in life-like pose, sitting on a sea-bed of rice dyed black with its own ink. Each tentacle was wrapped around some kind of fishy prey: an eel, a mudgeon, a lorch, a shad (with roe), a lobster, salmon, butterfly-shark, and basket of periwinkles in garlic butter. The platter was kept warm by a little electric stove.

This culinary joke (the Twins' influence was apparent) smelled divine, and we were about to sit down around our pic-nic rug and begin cracking shells, when suddenly I seemed to myself to have gone quite mad.

A voice came from *above*! As if from heaven!

This was impossible.

Cease this disgusting cultic ritual at once! Do not move! You are all under arrest!

The voice seemed to be the voice of Lady Col. Agate herself—no doubt I was hallucinating.

We craned our necks domeward. There, hovering above us, we saw a sight never beheld before by any one of us—a *flying ship*. It seemed about the size and shape of a Police Cruiser, but it had no treads beneath it, and it had been... streamlined, I suppose you could say—and painted with reflective white chrome or perhaps actual silver—or fixed quicksilver, if such a thing exists.

Captain Svetlana breathed out in awe. "A *graviton* ship," she guessed. And so it turned out to be—just like the ones in storybooks. So... the Teknostics *had* after all rediscovered at least one secret of the Ancients—the very one we'd joked about when we liberated those antique graviton cans in Apollonius, months ago. *Flight!*

Slowly and perpendicularly the ship descended to ground and came to rest, half-floating in the shallows of the lake, half on the beach. It displayed a front window made of one large crystal, curved like a shark's smile; and within the ship we could easily make out the forms of Col. de Trouvelot and four attendant lieutenants in the white uniforms of the Fist. The ship was named "Trismegistus."

A door flipped open with a sucking wheeze, and the Colonel walked out, head upright on neck, in cool command of the situation. The soldiers followed.

Greetings, Eleuthera, she said to our amazement. Greetings to the most dangerous opponent of Teknosis in the whole of Mare Crisium—perhaps in the whole of Luna, now that you've joined with this perverted pirate, the so-called "Captain" Svetlana. I've read all your dossiers and you're all either disgusting or dangerous or both. You are monsters, at war with all the world. You are a disease. You will be neutralized—for all eternity.

Eleuthera merely glared at her—goddess of life vs. goddess of death—simply sneered at her. Svetlana hiss-whispered, For devil's sake, *say* something to her.

Er... my comrades and I (Eleuthera said), resent your every slur. We demand to be accorded...

We never learned what lost rights—or last rites—she intended to demand. Svetlana's hand crept into her open jacket and whipped out again holding a dart-gun.

It was a home-made dart gun, although since Svetlana had made it herself, it was well made—but it clearly held only one shot at a cock. Had *she* now gone insane? Well, partly. She said later she'd been *inspired*, may the saints preserve us!

The reader must imagine each of the following acts as taking one beat of quick-measured time, quick as *that*—but not quite too fast to follow:—

Col. Agate reacts to the sight of the gun pointed at her, not by raising her hands, or ducking behind her men, but by going for *her* gun, in a holster on her hip.

Reacting at once to this motion, Svetlana shoots her dart almost without aim, depending on some occult martial-arts power to direct it, presumably. It tears through the left sleeve of the Colonel's uniform blouse, leaving a burst of blood and red tattered cloth.

Everyone freezes in shock. The Tek lieutenants are too stunned to go for their little weapons, but gawk open-mouthed at the scene.

Svetlana begins fumbling another dart into her pistol. The Colonel recovers, and deliberately unholsters her pistol, a slick-looking lightweight "non" lethal multi-shot army-issue dueling handgun.

"Everyone—hands in the air!" she ordered.

Everyone raised hands to the sky.

The Colonel takes careful aim at Svetlana.

Suddenly—

a great flash and BANG splits everyone's ears and dazzles all our eyes. What was *that*?

A great cloud of smoke seems to have enveloped Chef Johnson, whom no one had been looking at. Had he somehow exploded?

Col. Lady Agate de Trouvelot falls over backwards and hits the sand with a thump, dead as dead. Her throat has been severed by some missile.

At this disgusting sight several of our party *and* several of the Tek soldiers begin either to vomit or to faint.

As the smoke clears around the Chef we see him (both hands still raised!) cool as a pear (apparently), blowing the last plume of gunpowder smoke from the barrel of…

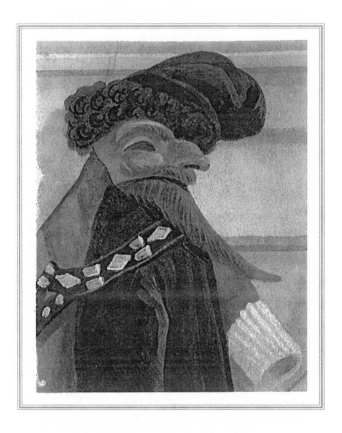

a completely illegal totally *explosive* pistol, weird as a magic wand with flints and bits of iron attached. The Chef had just committed the worst of all Lunar crimes. Not murder—although that was rare enough, and hideous enough. No—*explosion* was his real sin. The shock on the beach bloomed, palpable as sudden poison.

But then we noticed that the Chef's two hands were empty. A *third hand* had appeared from under his layered waistcoats, holding the lethal weapon. The *metatail!* Count de Johnson shot the policewoman with his *tail*.

The Chef spoke.

Captain Svetlana, he said, I am covering those four thugs with my gunpowder pistol. Do you load your own gun, and then relieve them of theirs.

Eleuthera now spoke: Distribute their weapons to our friends, please, Svetlana. Now—which of you is pilot of this craft? You? You will now fly us *out* of this Domeyne, and onto the Surface. You will tell Customs at the Lock that the Colonel has sent you to escort seven dangerous prisoners to be tried in Aristotle for high treason. We promise to release all of you at the nearest emergency entrance to the traffic tunnel (with air) as soon as we can, unhurt, if you obey our commands. If not… Well? Good, now—let's go.

We left behind the corpse untouched next to the uneaten octopus.

As he was about to walk onto the ship, the Chef looked once again at the pistol in his metatail's hand, grimaced in repugnance, and threw it out into the lake. He retracted his tail into his clothes.

It was only good for one shot, he muttered.

But we all heard him quite clearly.

Agrippa's judgment on the *xxviii*th Mansion turned out quite accurate in our case. As Eleuthera said later, once we had reached Giordano Bruno and safety, "gone to ground" like frightened pheasants:

We have indeed travelled safely through dangerous places, and as "couples" (or triads) we could now be described as joyful. Nevertheless, we have really changed nothing on any greater scale. The regime at Mare Crisium was still creaky and corrupt the day we made our escape—but by now I'm certain the late Colonel's plans have been put into effect and the Prison System there has been "strengthened" indeed. In fact, unless we can somehow turn the tide of history, I'd say the whole of our beloved Selene, or Sin, or whatever name you give our White Rabbit, the Moon will soon become all one giant prison. The Teks will spread everywhere, like germs—the Domeynes will sicken and die, converted into Undead Machines. Humans as such could very easily become outmoded—and the last of us could disappear, isolated and alone, one by one into the cold night of the Singularity.

We've lost all our treasure—we even had to sacrifice the graviton ship "Trismegistus" in order to escape our pursuers—but at least we've saved ourselves. For now we must split up into units and lie low for a time—incognito if possible—obscure as hibernating moles. In secret codes we'll communicate by post. Send your first messages to me here under the name

Lucy Freere
c/o the Rector
Giordano Bruno

Svetlana and I will stay here till we know where each of you has safely settled; thereafter we may move again—and again. We must begin to organize everywhere for a full-scale war against Teknosis. Whether it can be a war waged without murder remains to be seen. I hope so.

Speaking of murder, some of you have asked me whether I condemn or condone the killing of Col. Agate by the Count de Johnson. Certainly the act broke all taboos—and laws. But as a pirate I must confess I have not only to condone but applaud his act. The Colonel may have had an immortal soul, I don't know. All life is sacred—agreed. But on the freedom of our bodies and minds I place a value above life and death. We were and are prepared to die for it—so we must be prepared to kill as well.

Sylphie said, I alone cannot agree to this. I think we might still achieve much even by suffering martyrdom. Peace can act as strategy as well as goal. Love trumps freedom. Life above all. However, since I *do* believe in peace, I shall continue in the path of love with all of you, my comrades in the revolt against lifelessness we must undertake. I *reserve* my objections until a future that might need them.

Wali al-Taha said, As an indolent and festal poet I tend toward a career desultorily devoted to the arts of peace.

> Pleasure demands no vast ambition
> Poetry asks no martyrdom—only
> Evil takes energy, and we are
> Too lazy not to be good

as Johanna the Bardessa put it.

But I admit that *emotion* for me constitutes a kind of absolute, and that I *hated* the late Colonel, on sight, with a passion that involved no morality—nor ideology—not even my inherent sloth. I would've killed her if I could have, on instinct alone, the way some dogs are born to hate and kill rats.

The Twins as always stood and spoke together: Speaking on behalf of ourselves and our Master in gastrognosis, we believe that the self (that elusive butterfly) must exist beyond all morality and judgment, to be "really free." Ethics are suited only to servants... Is that right, Uncle?

It's odd, the Chef mused aloud, that I, who gave my whole life to the social, should add such a maxim to my little collection of ideas. I'm not denying that the Hive has its own warm reality. I'm simply pointing out that the being who *experiences* liberty of lack thereof is ultimately the self, the subject. I cannot wait till the world perfects itself to enjoy joy, what little of it there may be—and I expect to enjoy our little revolution, win or lose. But go on, Flip. What next?

If Flip it was, he resumed: We've heard a rumor that a giant bird killed the Colonel!—and that our seafood dinner was taken as evidence of an occult ritual held to summon the bird from hell. The bird then carried us all to freedom. That's our one regret, said Flip (or Flap)—that we never got to eat that masterwork, our *Fish Dinner*.

Flying is a kind of ecstasy, Eleuthera, said Captain Svetlana. We must pursue it—must search again for more graviton stashes…

Eleuthera answered: Yes—but—our flight reminded me of my childhood ecstasies, with the mysterious shelf fungus "crag" that makes "dreams come true" as we used to say. Then, because of ecstasy, I flew. But now… because of flight, I feel ecstasy. One could become used to flight, and it would then lose its magic. But one could never *get used to* ecstasy…

※ ※ ※ ※ ※ ※ ※

Svetlana said: Look, all of you, at Sylphie. He/she has gone so pale as to appear blue, his eyes have rolled up in her head, she trembles…

Wali al-Taha rushed to her side. Are you not well, beloved? he asked.

Sylphie spoke as if in trance.

On an island of jasper in a sea of emerald in a palace of jade in a garden of viridescence and vision vines, a child… no, two children are waiting to assume their empty throne. Wali—it is our old dream—of the Moon Child. But…

Sylphie, it seems, was pregnant.

From the operations of the Moon they make an image for
travelers against weariness, at the hour of the Moon, the
Moon ascending in its exaltations; the figure of which was
a man leaning on a staff, having a bird on his head, &
a flourishing tree before him. They make another image
of the Moon for the increase of fruits, & against poisons,
& infirmities of children, at the hour of the Moon, it
ascending in the first face of Cancer, the figure of which
was a woman cornuted (with horns), riding on a bull,
or a dragon with seven heads, or a crab; & she hath in
her right hand a dart, in her left a lookingglass, clothed in
white or green, & having on her head two serpents with
horns twined together, & to each arm a serpent twined
about, & to each foot one in like manner.

AGRIPPA, *On the Images of the Moon*

Next day the Seven decided to enter into a *group* marriage—each of
them to wed all the others simultaneously—to make an unbreakable
union for the sake of the Child or Children to come.

Wali al-Taha then composed a marriage hymn for them:

Epithalamium for
a Heptad

You know my flower that ancient romance
at sycamore's foot beneath white laurel
olive myrtle or trembling willow
that love-song that always starts over again?

Remember the TEMPLE's immense peristyle
& the bitter lemons you printed with your teeth
& the grotto (fatal to impudent intruders)
where the vanquished dragon's antique seed
                                        still sleeps?
They'll return—those gods for whom you're always weeping
Time will restore the order of ancient times
Luna   has shuddered with prophetic breath.

White roses—fall!—you insult our gods
fall—blank phantoms—from your sky of fire
—the saint of the Abyss is holier in my eyes

O human freespirit—do you believe in yourself
sole thinker in this world where life
                                bursts in everything?
The forces you hold are given in freedom
but from all your councils the universe
                                        is absent.
Respect in beast an agitant spirit
each flower a soul that Nature discloses
a mystery of love reposes in metals
All things feel & are potent to your being

Fear (in a blind wall) a spying gaze
Word is attached to matter—let it
not serve an impious usage

Often in obscure being lives a hidden god
& like a nascent eye covered by its lid
pure spirit ripens under the skin of stones.

NOTES

On the *Lunar Mansions* by Cornelius Agrippa. This "ancient scripture" is quite genuine, written by a sage whose name appears on the Moon. But it is cobbled together from various chapters and sections of his great *Three Books of Occult Philosophy*; the best edition being by Llewellyn Publications (2000) with extensive notes & index.

The Mansions comprise a kind of Lunar zodiac. The system is ancient, possibly Mesopotamian. Agrippa knew Arabic sources. The Mansions are rarely used in modern Western astrology, but remain very important in India and China.

On the *Epithalamium*: Wali al-Taha has clearly been helping himself to an ancient corrupt edition of *Les Chimères*, by the voyant Gérard de Nerval, esp. sonnets "Delfica," "Artemis," and "Vers Dorés." Wali says he was given permission in a dream.

The *Moon*. All place names actually exist on the moon. Readers may follow the travels of our characters by consulting the large poster-sized Moon Map by National Geographic, although its index of place-names lists only a selection of the names that actually appear.

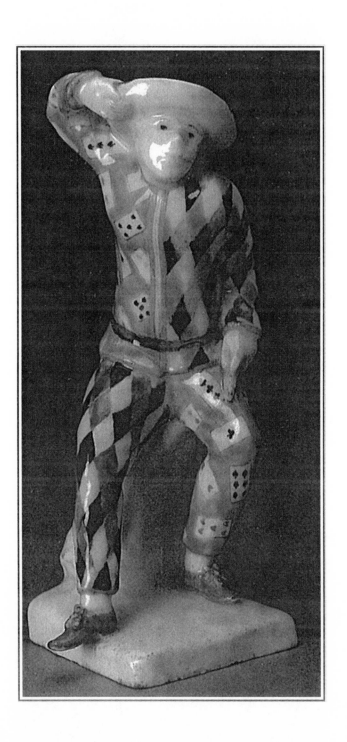

Sources of the Texts

"Visit Port Watson!" *Semiotext(e) SciFi*, ed. PLW, Rudy Rucker, Robert Anton Wilson: Brooklyn, Autonomedia, 1991.

"Incunabula." I've tried hard to find the obscure and long-vanished zine in which this first appeared, but without success. It's literally "lost in legend." Can any reader help?

"Ong's Hat." *Edge Detector,* no. 1, Summer, 1988. Note: This text and "Incunabula" both appear in the book *Ong's Hat: The Beginning*, ed. by Joseph Matheny and Peter Moon. Sky Books, 2002.

"Pastoral Letter: a fragment." *Fifth Estate*, no. 367, Winter 2004-5, Vol.39, no. 4.

"Glatisant and Grail." *At the Table of the Grail,* ed. John Matthews. London, Routledge & Kegan Paul, 1984.

"Nestor Makhno and the Elixir of Life." Unpublished.

"The Hyperborean Fragments." *New Pathways,* Nov. 1986.

"A Nietzschean Coup d' Etat." PLW, *Escape from the Nineteenth Century*, Brooklyn: Autonomedia, 1998.

"Treasure of the Pre-Adamite Sultans." Unpublished.

Lunar Mansions, or, the Whole Rabbit. Unpublished.

Sources of the Illustrations

Cover: Meredith Chilton, *Harlequin Unmasked: The Commedia dell'Arte and Porcelain Sculpture* (New Haven & London, 2001) [HU]; anon., after Jacques Callot, 17th cen. Museo Teatrale alla Scala, Milan;

Frontispiece: Franz Rottensteiner, *The Science Fiction Book: an illustrated history* (New York, 1975) [SFB]; Virgil Finlay in *Famous Fantastic Mysteries,* Apr. 1995;

Page 27: art by James Koehnline from the original publication of "Incunabula";

Page 29: SFB, from Jules Verne, *20,000 Leagues Under the Sea;*

Page 59: A. Zamperini, *Ornament and the Grotesque* (London 2008) [OG] (Man looking out of a screen);

Page 60: SFB; (Flying boat with sail and balloons), B. Zamagna, *Navis Aerea;*

Page 72: SFB; (Anonymous Soviet artist);

Page 75: A. Roob, *Alchemy & Mysticism* (Koln: 1997/2006); (Theosophical thought-form);

Page 77: ibid.; from J.V. Andrea, *Die Alchemische Hochzeit von Christian Rosenkreutz* (1616), ed. J. van Rijckenborgh, 1967;

Page 87: HU; P.P. Bacqueville, A fantasy costume from *Habits des Masques,* 17th cen. Staatliche-Kunstsammlungen Dresden, Kupferstich-Kabinett;

Page 88: OG; (Gryphon in 8-shape);

Page 119: OG; (Grotesque column with face, woman and man);

Page 238: *Callot's Etchings,* ed. Howard Daniel (New York 1974) [CE];

Page 239: Leonardo da Vinci, "Portrait of a Youth";

Page 246: HU; John Bulwer, *Chirologia* (1644);

Page 248: HU; Josef Lederer, from "Ball of Masks," 1748, Český Krumlov Castle, Czech Rep.;

Page 263: CE;

Page 282: HU; F.A. Bustelli, Nymphenberg (Ger.) porcelain, Gardiner Museum of Ceramic Art;

Page 294: CE;

Page 297: CE;

Page 318: HU; Lederer, *op. cit.;*

Page 326: HU; attributed to the "Muses Modeller," porcelain;

Back Cover: "Ombres Chinoises," 19th cen. in Emma Rutherford, *Silhouette: The Art of The Shadow* (New York 2009).

CPSIA information can be obtained
at www.ICGtesting.com
Printed in the USA
FFOW04n1753261015
17919FF